LOVE & JUSTICE

LOVE & JUSTICE

RIQUE JOHNSON

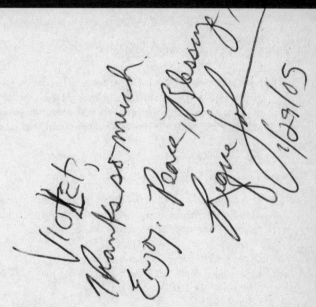

A

SBI

PUBLICATION

A STREBOR BOOKS INTERNATIONAL LLC PUBLICATION

DISTRIBUTED BY SIMON & SCHUSTER, INC.

Published by

Strebor Books International LLC
P.O. Box 1370
Bowie, MD 20718
http://www.streborbooks.com

ISBN 1-59309-002-1
LCCN 2003100092

This book is a work of fiction. Names, characters, places and incidents are products of the
author's imagination or are used fictitiously. Any resemblance to actual events or locales or
persons, living or dead, is entirely coincidental.

Distributed by Simon & Schuster, Inc.
1230 Avenue of the Americas
New York, NY 10020
1-800-223-2336

Front cover concept: Rique Johnson
Cover design: Brian Marilla

First Printing July 2003
Manufactured and Printed in the United States

10   9   8   7   6   5   4   3   2

THIS BOOK IS DEDICATED TO MY LOVELY WIFE, SHARON,
who suffered through the first words on paper to this creation.
Thanks for being there.
To Myoshi Marilla. Thanks for your support and encouragement.
But, most of all, thanks for your editing skills.
And to Ricardo Parker, my good friend.
Without you, the journey to this end would not be in progress.

CHAPTER 1

Some say finding Love in someone else takes Forever,
And believe that Forever is unreachable.
My Forever is Today,
My Forever is Now,
My Forever is, I do.
Forever is your smile,
The way it brightens my day,
Enhancing the world with brilliance.
Forever is each time I hear your voice,
The sedating calming effect consumes me.
Forever is your embrace,
Tantalizing, engulfing, warming my being.
My Forever is Today,
My Forever is Now,
My Forever is, I will.
Forever is the chance you've given me to be
all the things I see in you.
Forever is the peace instilled in me
by the presence of your Love.
Forever is our Love that looked beyond the obvious,

Strong, Relentless...Unyielding.
Forever is God's blessing of You.
My Forever is Today,
My Forever is Now,
My Forever is, the Truth in our Vows.
JASON AND JULIE
MARCH 26, 1988

Julie Roberts embraces the paper she just read against her chest hoping that the very words that enveloped her on the day she married would ease the pain of her heart. She sits in the middle of her bed rocking endlessly, squeezing herself tightly as if to force the words through her skin, to the heart, to be consumed by her soul. The crackle from her actions awakens her senses. In a panic state her arms fling open, the poem falls to her lap; both hands cover her mouth with the fear of damaging it. She lays the poem on the bed and tries to undo the wrinkles in the paper with her palm before carefully placing it back into her photo album, simultaneously recalling how sentimental Jason's voice was when he read it to her on their wedding day.

Tears swell in her eyes, and then roll deliberately down her face, induced by the haunting reality of losing her precious Jason. Her saddened expression conceals her model beauty, high cheekbones, petite lips and hazel green eyes. As if she were abruptly snatched from her position, she springs to her feet and rapidly paces the floor, allowing her near-perfect figure to be silhouetted by the sunlight entering through the bedroom window. A troubled voice buried in the deep corners of her mind taunts, "I told you so," sending a feeling of sorrow throughout her entire being. Years gone by bring on the realization of her life's greatest mistake of leaving the only man that truly loved her inner-self, not just her outer beauty.

Her body yearns for his gentle touch. One administered so softly and soothing it makes her skin melt uncontrollably. A touch that she remembers being generated by genuine love and not the heavy lustful feel that most men have served since she left Jason. The agony she feels burns deeply inside her, creating turmoil that flows through her veins like poison, making her even more determined to win back his love and affection. Experience through time has proven to her that he is the only man alive that can bring a sense of peace within her.

"I have to let him know exactly how I feel," she expresses loudly. "This time I'll get my point across because once he knows that my heart never left him, we'll be one again. The awful things I did to him won't matter. I'm sure of it. This is a new me talking. I'll be the perfect wife, his prized possession."

Across the nation for a select few, people's lives become a possession of another, controlled for the last few moments before their existence terminates. They die ungrateful for the time they did live, but only acknowledging the terror that reaped their hearts and minds during their last minutes of turmoil. Such a thing happens in Virginia City, the most promising city of Virginia. Burglaries and other mayhem run rampant; far too often a rapist that kills his victims and remains anonymous establishes himself as masterful. This one slated by the police as the Invisible Man plays a game of cat and mouse, defying the authorities as they wreck their brains seeking a clue to his identity.

Often, more in recent times, he lies on his bed and acts out his ritual before stalking his prey. He stares at the ceiling until imaginary objects dance in his deranged mind, controlling his every thought. Swiftly his head darts erratically from side to side. With his belt and pants still fastened, he lowers his zipper and works his hand through the slit in his briefs; he pulls the weapon of choice out and fondles it until an erection occurs. Squeezing tight while making up and down motions with one hand, with the other, he pushes the speaker button on the telephone sitting on a nightstand next to the bed. He pushes another button and the telephone dials automatically.

"Hi," a cheerful voice says, "I'm Candy and I've been waiting just for your call. First, I need to tell you that my job is to talk and excite you; all you have to do is enjoy, obey my commands and say nothing. If you understand this, respond with silence. So, for the next few minutes we're going to have some adult fun. I can tell that I can get nasty with you. Hum, you're already hard. Great, because I'm soaking wet just thinking about your hard dick. No need to kiss me, give it to me, slide that hard thing into my wet box now. Make me feel like the bitch I am. Oh, yes," Candy's voice pants. "I want it all. Deeper, baby, deeper! Fill me with your hard...throbbing cock. Baby, you feel so great, I know you feel my wet pussy all over your hard dick. Harder...yes...push harder. Yes!"

With each of her voice commands, he continues his hand motions while simultaneously moving his weapon forcefully up and down the height of his zipper causing several places to trickle with blood.

"It's working...I'm coming," Candy cries. "Yes, harder. I'm coming. Baby, I'm...oh...oh...umm," Candy pants as she reaches her make-believe ecstasy.

He moans once before his weapon fires, sending several long stringy shots high up over his head which he then attempts to catch with his mouth. He jumps to his feet suddenly, picks up the handset, then repeatedly slams it down, yelling, "Bitch! Bitch! Bitch!" while Candy concludes phone sex. Afterwards, he showers, puts on a change of clothes before setting out to stalk his next prey.

These women walk the red-light district streets. Self-proclaimed professionals in the art of lovemaking. They have willed themselves the masters of men. Women destined to fall short when climbing the ladder of success, yet determined to succeed in their chosen profession. Some wear very short skirts and halter tops while others wear bikini panties, a garter belt with stockings and a lace bra. They all wear high-heeled pumps, strutting to advertise, shaking their goods while propositioning men that pass by them and stopping some cars on the street. Rejections are plentiful, especially for the lone one or two freelance artists working their territory on the opposite side of the street.

He stalks these prizes, carefully selecting a woman who might resemble Candy the way he's envisioned her. Approaching one who is above-average looking, he admires her long sexy legs and large but firm breasts. After a brief conversation they begin the several-block walk toward her pleasure haven. She tries to engage in small talk but he reminds her to save it for later.

"I betcha you want me to talk dirty, don't cha?" she replies with a Southern accent. "Don't worry, baby, I'll put some cheer in that voice of yours."

His expression is empty, cold. It would send chills down the average person's spine.

"I can tell you're nervous," she says while grabbing his rear. "We'll put a smile on your face."

They turn into a semi-dark alley and approach a vehicle parked between two dumpsters. It's a pickup truck with a medium-sized camper in the cargo area. The camper's interior is basic, containing a fold-down bed, a small refrigerator, a tiny sink in one corner and a trunk with a blouse sleeve hanging out of it. She turns on the lime green-colored bulb hanging inches from the ceiling and lowers the fold-down bed. It occupies most of the camper's living area, leaving only enough room for them to stand bent over at the waist.

"Now, let's see what you have for me," she says, simultaneously grabbing his member. "You're gonna have to do better than this. We can't get our cum on without this guy's cooperation. So, just relax and let me bring him to attention."

"Talk dirty to me," he finally states.

"I knew you were that type," she lies. "The quiet ones always want the nasty talk. Lie down."

She lowers her miniskirt, leaving her bottom bare. He admires her short but well-groomed bush. Next, she pulls her teddy over her head and tosses it playfully onto his face. Her medium-sized frame boasts large breasts with oddly sized nipples. He picks up the teddy in one hand and rubs the soft silk tainted with her fragrance at his throat. Her eagerness to please him shows as she tackles his belt and unzips his pants. Lowering his garments below the knees, she straddles him just below his semi-loaded weapon. Her body moistens one of his legs.

"Do you feel that? I'm ready," she says while fondling him. "We'll fix him right up. He will be standing tall in less than a minute. You just need the touch of an expert. Have you ever had your cock sucked with ice in the woman's mouth?"

His face continues to be expressionless but his mind reaps excitement with just the thought of it.

"Did my wetness surprise you?" she boasts while rubbing her money-maker on his leg.

"Do you kiss or talk better?"

"Honey, I fuck much better than I kiss, but my kisses are known to drive men wild."

She leans forward, determined to make her strange trick's night one worth living. Instead, she finds herself gasping for breath, fighting to remove the teddy he has clutched around her neck. His powerful grip tightens. She bucks wildly, pounding his face and chest in defense. Her fair skin turns shades of red as she aimlessly tears at the garment, reminiscent of a rodent scratching through a paper cup. Her neck bleeds profusely, torn jagged by her adrenaline-aided strength. His struggle for dominance along with her fight for freedom has them tumbling across the limited space of the bed. The victim's eyes widen, on the verge of exploding from their sockets. Veins protrude from her face and neck while beads of sweat roll down her face. As life leaves her body, he flips her over, gaining the dominant position. In the process her head hits the light source causing it to swing back and forth, hypnotizing his staring eyes. His mind drifts from its conscious state to la-la land as his imaginary objects crawl inside the camper's walls. He mounts her motionless body and instantly his weapon loads.

"Bitch, bitch, bitch!" he yells as his weapon fires.

Afterwards, he wraps the teddy around his index finger and shoves it into her moneymaker and writes with her discount mart lipstick, "She wanted it," across her semi-naked body. Covering his tracks, he uses her skirt to wipe the camper clean of evidence of his existence and escapes unnoticed.

The next morning a huge pale-white trash truck with its metal praying mantis arms suspended and folded over the cabin approaches the pickup truck. While the driver empties both dumpsters he notices that the camper's door is open. Losing to his unrestrained curiosity, he investigates the camper for signs of trouble.

The police arrive on the scene. The once abandoned alley is alive with vigor. Several police cars block both ends of the alley with other officers securing the immediate area. The coroner, a forensic team and a couple of unmarked cars surround the victim's pickup truck.

The officer in charge is Captain Frank North. He's a tall silver-haired man, distinguished-looking with a reputable face. And, he just happened to be in the immediate vicinity when the dispatch for all cars in the area to report to the crime scene was announced, making him the senior officer present. The trash truck driver shares his knowledge of the incident, and then is soon released. The coroner examines the body before Captain North grants its removal. The forensic team dusts for prints but finds no signs of the killer's true identity. The only incriminating factor is the location of the woman's teddy. Captain North and police officers from the neighboring precincts recognize this as a trait of the murder-rapist deemed the Invisible Man.

"Bitch, bitch, bitch!" he cries while slamming down the phone on Candy again.

That same morning, before business hours, the killer stalks his next potential kill. His keen eyes watch from the faraway corner of a shopping mall parking lot. The lot is empty except the cars arriving minutes apart, each perceived to be owned by store managers. He spots a prime target turning into the parking lot from the main street. This car satisfies a couple of requirements to strike his next prey: one, it is large enough to hold him and his prey; and two, it contains a woman driver. He would have preferred a van to fuck and kill his victim, but the imaginary objects tell him that the station wagon with dark tinted windows in the rear will do nicely.

He walks toward the vehicle as it turns into a parking space. The woman notices his approach from across the parking lot but brushes off any thoughts of trouble based on his appearance. A clean shaven, well-dressed man in a fitting two-piece suit arrives simultaneously as the woman exits her car. She is Mrs. Juanita Smith, a very short petite woman in her mid-twenties with short dark hair, pleasant features and wears a blouse and a flowing skirt with many pleats.

He clears his voice, preparing to falsify his tone, "Excuse me, Miss, I'm Stephen Day," he lies. "I hate to trouble you but may I borrow your tire iron? I have a flat tire on the other side of the mall. Unfortunately, mine can't be located. I searched but it's nowhere to be found."

"Murphy's Law," the woman jokes attempting to ease his stress.

"That's right. Wouldn't you know it, I'm going to be late on my first day of work."

"I'm not sure I have one," she replies while heading to the rear of the vehicle. "Which store do you work in?"

"Oh, Hecht's," he responds quickly, choosing a name at random.

She raises the back glass and lowers the rear door, then folds down the seat allowing her access to the cargo area. She begins to open the trunk compartment when suddenly, he grabs her with one hand covering her mouth, and the other with a knife pointing at her throat. Immediately, fear consumes her igniting an instant tremble throughout her body.

"Listen, bitch," he directs using a new tone. "If you want to survive, don't fucking fight me. Don't yell, don't make a fucking sound. Just crawl into the back and you'll live through this."

Initially, she resists his forceful effort to guide her into the cargo area of the vehicle, but she is quickly reminded of the seriousness of her dilemma when he seizes a hand full of hair, pulls her head back and uses the pointed end of the knife to make a tiny puncture at her throat. As blood fills the cut, she surrenders to his wishes and begins to crawl into his temporary haven with him following closely behind.

The thought of her demise reaps her mind like a raging storm bringing on more frantic trembles, extreme fear and strong survival instincts. Before he gets the majority of his weight into the car, she swiftly kicks one leg backward—reminiscent of a donkey's kick—connecting the spiked end of her shoe's heel into his chest. The impact of the well-timed maneuver sends him flying to the pavement gasping for air. The bewildered woman exits the car and races frantically toward the mall's entrance. In a short moment, he gathers his breath and composure, rumbles through the contents of her purse and flees in the opposite direction holding his throbbing chest.

Inside the safety of her workplace, she telephones the police and tries to relax from her hysterical state. When the police arrive, two rookie officers question her and gather the information on the incident. Their persuasion tactics fail with Mrs. Smith refusing to come to the station to look at their photo books of known criminals. The officers leave with only her statement and a clouded description of her attacker.

CHAPTER 2

The two officers report directly to Captain North with their findings. Captain North listens carefully, trying to decide if this assault relates to the Invisible Man's attack last night. The less than perfect description they received is well short of being enough to send a sketch artist to Mrs. Smith's home to compile a rendering of her attacker. Captain North ponders his next move knowing that two attacks within his jurisdiction in less than twenty-four hours dictates assigning this case to one of his already overworked men. Adding more pressure to his departmental investigation is his superior and a call from the District Attorney's office. Both parties stress a need for immediate action; their lingering words plague his mind heavily. He rears back in his chair and taps his middle finger on his desk, thinking.

"Troubled?" one of the officers questions.

"Yeah, this person has moved into our territory, thus putting pressure on us to stop this lunatic. I need someone to investigate...no, catch this asshole."

"I will volunteer my services...I'm not working on anything too important."

"You are so young," Captain North interjects, very concerned with his officer's comment. "Heed these words: Everything you work on while you wear that uniform is important. Besides, no slam against your abilities, but I need someone with more experience to handle a case like this. The question is who? We are so understaffed."

"Give it to the Boy Wonder," he replies jokingly.

"Don't make fun of people...actually," he states as an afterthought. "That's not too bad of an idea. Your misplaced humor may be the answer I need. Go, both of you. Let me think about this."

The officers turn, snickering to themselves about the Boy Wonder nickname floating around the station, while Captain North dials one of his officer's extensions.

"Sixteenth Precinct, Austin."

"Kevin," Captain North states. "Is Jerrard in yet?"

"No, not yet."

"Send his ass to me the moment he arrives."

"Thank you," Sgt. Austin replies with gratifying enthusiasm.

"Thanks, for what?"

"Oh nothing, I'll send him to you."

Jason Jerrard drives the streets of his country surroundings on a beautiful spring day observing the relaxed atmosphere. The birds are chirping; some animals are mating; all flowers are in bloom. The southerly breeze seems to be perfect, blowing nature's way. Tall trees bowing in the wind are almost life-like with color. The acres of open fields project a perfect picture any artist would love. There are clothes hanging on the line being wind-dried. Suburban people sit on their porches engaging in afternoon chats, seemingly carefree with no worries in life. Children play in the grass; the older ones gather around a checkerboard giving one the sense of security and serenity.

A short ride later, most times too short for Jason's liking, exists another world. Side-by-side with the country but opposites in almost every way lies the contrasting city limits. Wall-to-wall cars decorate the city streets, tall buildings replace tall trees and mostly, the only birds seen are pigeons that pollute the city streets in their quest for scraps of food from the human counterparts. The few trees are landscaped by man, stuck in the middle of the sidewalk virtually unnoticeable to the passing humans.

The children play chase with policemen and make trouble with the pedestrians as their form of entertainment. The older ones, commonly referred to as the working class, are so busy making a living, they have forgotten how to have a life as they ride and walk down the busy streets oblivious to most dangers that surround them.

Jason Jerrard, known to everyone simply as Jason, except the small few who'd like to make him superhuman, is a tall handsome man, medium build, in his early forties. He is often accused by his peers of selecting the wrong profession because of his exquisite taste in clothes and a body that complements the garments he wears, making him a perfect candidate for a male model. He rides through the city streets observing, more alert than most, aware of all activities that surround him. He is trapped between both worlds. He loves the freshness and peace of the country but equally craves the thrills and danger of the city. The always-present, high-strung action motivates his character in ways he has difficulties understanding.

Jason parks his car on police grounds in a space marked DET. JERRARD. Stepping out of the car, he reflects on his earlier days on the force, thinking back to the times when he didn't have to worry about what to wear being a cop in uniform. His pride shows as he walks confidently, bordering on cockiness, up to the station. He reads, "Virginia City Police Precinct No. Sixteen," and as always acknowledges the pictures of his predecessors hanging on the wall.

"One day," Jason thinks. "I'll be up there. My picture will hang before all who enter."

A heavy voice interrupts his thoughts. "Daydreaming again, Detective?"

"Hello, Kevin. What's new?"

"Nada," he replies.

Sgt. Austin is a husky balding officer, so unlike Jason when he was at that rank. His attitude toward his work is different from Jason's. He has already given up, settled for and become complacent with his rank, letting it show in the way he speaks.

"Jason, Captain North wants to see you immediately. He asked me to have you see him the moment you arrived. I have to tell you, I didn't like the sound of it. His tone was stern and reprimanding. Frankly," he replies in a jealous tone, "it serves you right. I hope your ass hangs for using police vehicles for your personal use. Why don't you use that expensive BMW of yours? This is a police station, not a rental car place. It's about time you were caught."

"Yeah, thanks for those encouraging words," Jason says while picking up his nameplate. "You see this—it reads Detective Sergeant Jason Jerrard." He pauses for effect. "I made detective in less than half the years you have been on the force. I," Jason's voice rises as he thumps his chest twice with his palm, "accomplished this through hard work but mostly through taking chances. I do the things that most of you wouldn't dare. I'm not trying to say that I'm better than you. No man should be judged over another by the position he holds in life—but, I am saying it makes me a little smarter."

"Oh, you're a big shot now," responds Sgt. Austin as he abruptly walks away.

Jason shakes his head and commences to complete the report in front of him when the telephone rings. "Sixteenth Precinct, Detective Jerrard speaking...right away, Sir."

Jason heads toward Captain North's office with no suspicions, no inhibitions over the things that Sgt. Austin expressed but admittedly, Captain's urgency puzzles him as he knocks on the door. A deep voice from within instructs him to enter.

Inside the Captain's office is a wall filled with many plaques. Other certificates and forms of recognition hang behind him. His desk is neat and organized. The antique chair Jason sits in blends perfectly with the matching desk of deep mahogany. The only thing representing a modern era in the entire room is a folding lamp sitting oddly on the desk.

"You wanted to see me, Sir?"

"Jason, call me Frank, please. I've told you more than once to cut out the 'Sir' bullshit. We try to be on a first-name basis around here. What are you trying to do, make me feel old or something?"

"It's just my upbringing. My parents stressed respecting elders. However, I will try to remember not to call you 'Sir.'"

"Do that. Now, are you familiar with the serial rapist that's stalking the streets?"

"The Invisible Man, are you referring to him?"

"Yes. He's terrorizing this city, committing his acts in the most unlikely places. He never leaves a trace, no incriminating clues, nothing to identify him. The few surviving victims are never able to give us an accurate description of this man. We believe he's responsible for several rapes and deaths within our city limits alone. I saw his handiwork yesterday, and my instincts tell me that he had the audacity to attack someone in broad daylight at the mall this morning."

"You've had a report today, already?" Jason sounds surprised.

"Yes, that location falls under our jurisdiction and already the District Attorney is applying lots of pressure to find this person. That's why I'm turning the case over to you."

"Me, Sir, uh, Frank? You just said that there are no clues at all. How do you expect me to find him?" Jason questions, almost unable to contain his laughter.

"The word around here is that you use some rather unorthodox methods in your police work. I don't always approve of your ways, but they produce results. Take this folder. It has all the information we've gathered on this serial rapist. Study it carefully and good luck. The bottom line is, we need an arrest, something to ease the public's fear."

"I'll get right on it," Jason replies confidently, befitting of his manner.

Leaving the captain's office, Jason wonders where to start on a case that seemingly has no beginning. Back at his desk, Jason studies the files intently, nearly unaware of Sgt. Austin approaching with a cup of coffee in one hand and a doughnut in the other with a huge bite missing from it.

"Jas, I'm sorry I acted the way I did," Sgt. Austin says while attempting to swallow a dry mouthful of a doughnut. "I've watched you shoot up the ranks like a rocket. Truth is, I wasn't willing to understand how or why you progressed the way you did. It's jealousy, I imagine. While getting my coffee, I realized I didn't have the courage to be more like you."

"Like me?"

"Yes, this lack of courage made me give up the dream of ever being more than an average cop. Shit!" he says after white powdered sugar falls on his jacket with his next bite. "Through the years I've progressed average. I've produced average results, average arrests, and because of that, I've been promoted average. Unlike you, I have a fear of stretching my authority and living on the edge. After awhile, I lost sight of being more than what I am."

Sgt. Austin sits and the chair squeaks loudly.

"Listen to that, I started gaining weight because I didn't really care. That's why I look lousy from the neck down. You always take chances. You take matters into your hands. Your methods are unusual at times but effective. The rumor around here is you're some sort of boy wonder, a super cop."

"Wait a minute, super cop!" Jason says laughing. "That's a funny one. I'm no more a super cop than anyone else. Sure, I take chances. I take many, possibly stretching the line at times, but these are only human abilities. Super cop, nope, just a man who will do anything short of breaking the law to get results. My philosophy is to observe the masses and do the opposite. This way of thinking gets people talking about me. However, when they talk I know I'm doing something—enough of this, okay? No harm done?"

"Naw," Sgt. Austin replies shamefully.

"Well, put down that vending machine coffee. Let's go get a real cup of coffee."

"I'm right behind you...where are we going?"

"To a sandwich shop not far from here." Jason diverts his attention to the other officers. "Hold down the fort until we get back. If any of my stockbrokers call, take a message for me."

"Stockbrokers, huh? So that's what you call women in this day and time."

"Stockbrokers are a better name for them. We invest our time and money into them, hoping for a positive return."

"That's a chauvinistic view."

"I'm just kidding, joke, ha-ha, forget it...are you coming with me?"

CHAPTER 3

They select a table overlooking the street. Sgt. Austin 's face reveals a curiosity similar to a child puzzled by the unknown. Sitting, he waits impatiently for Jason's return.

"Two cups of coffee, one black, the other...one second," Jason yells across the room, "how do you like your coffee?"

Kevin barely turns his head to reply, "Black with sugar," immediately diverting his attention elsewhere. Jason returns with the coffee and is intrigued by Kevin's mood swing.

"Okay, I give up. What is it now?"

"Jas, do you mind if I bring up a sour subject?"

"Not about me borrowing police cars again?" Jason sighs.

"Not that. I'm curious to know what's it like to be on the edge, always making judgments on your gut feelings?"

"With that look on your face, I thought you had something real heavy. Can I be frank?"

"Please do."

"I can be honest, if you prefer," he says jokingly.

"I'm serious, Jas."

"To be honest, it's not easy. It's scary all the time, but you must not let the fear keep you from second-guessing or going with your gut feeling. The best method I've found is to do things that hopefully will make the receiving party uncertain of what to do next. Dangerous as it may be, I live for it...tell me, would you really like to know how it feels?"

Kevin nods "yes."

"Okay, I'll set up the scene...you follow with your natural instincts."

"What are you up to?"

"Just listen and keep your eyes open. We'll leave this fabulous coffee and stage a fake quarrel. Yell at me about fooling around with your wife or something."

"Huh?" he questions.

"Listen, will you? Throw me out the door, pull your gun and back me across the street. I'll follow along with the wife thing. Just get us across the street."

"But why?" he says filled with anxiety. "I can't think of anything to say."

"Don't think, react!" Jason yells.

Suddenly, Sgt. Austin cuffs Jason in his collar pulling him into his face, replying, "Enough is enough, I've followed you and my wife for months, from one hotel to another. The shit's gonna stop. It's gonna stop right fucking now! If she won't leave you alone, I'll make you leave her ass."

He opens the door and tosses Jason into the street. Jason, like any good actor, stumbles, nearly falling to the street but catches himself with a three-point stance.

"If you were taking care of home like you should, you wouldn't have to worry about me fucking her," Jason boasts. "She tells me you don't know how to fuck, says you don't have any strength in bed. You can't blame me for fulfilling a desiring woman's needs, 'cause I fuck her real good."

A crowd gathers at the sound of all the commotion. They assemble as if they were watching a circus sideshow with Sgt. Austin pulling his revolver, threatening Jason.

"You want fucking strength. This is my strength, asshole! Come on, big shot, you and your fancy clothes. Let's see you make her feel real good now. I'll blow the damn thing off before I let you fuck her again."

Jason backs across the street, disrupting traffic as they fake out the crowd. He fumbles, falls and pleads for mercy while drawing the spectators deeper into their unfolding drama.

"Easy, man, take it easy! I'll leave her alone. The whole thing was just for kicks. I don't care for her."

"That's worse!" Sgt. Austin yells forcefully. "You used her for a piece of ass while toying with her emotions all this time. I should blow a hole right through your fucking chest. Animals like you deserve to die!"

Unaware of Jason's intentions, he follows along playing with the scene they've created until he notices he has crossed the street and stepped inside the doorway of Billings Pawn Shop.

"I told you, I'll leave your wife alone," pleads Jason.

To Sgt. Austin's surprise, a heavyset man dressed in military fatigues with camouflage paint concealing most of his facial features is holding the owner of the shop at gunpoint. The proprietor is nervously emptying money from the register into a brown paper bag.

Disturbed by the excitement, the gunman yells, "What the fuck is this? This job's mine!"

"I'm not trying to take your money," replies Jason. "This maniac thinks I'm fucking his wife. I have my own life to worry about."

The gunman, nervous and fearful, points his gun back and forth between the shop owner and Sgt. Austin while Jason backs away virtually unnoticed.

"Freeze! Police. You're under arrest," Sgt. Austin instructs.

"Damn, I knew you were a bastard cop," the robber responds wryly.

The dark paint underneath and surrounding the gunman's eyes fails to conceal the anxiety that's overwhelming him caused by Sgt. Austin's threatening gun. With death hanging a mere few feet away, their faces intensify. A cold silence takes place with sweat beginning to form on their foreheads. Sgt. Austin stares directly into the robber's eyes, all along telling himself he must keep his interior calm even though his underarms and back are rapidly becoming drenched with sweat. He knows he must hold his ground until his point man reveals himself.

"Drop your gun and nobody will get hurt," instructs Sgt. Austin.

"Fuck you, man. I won't go down alone."

"But you will go down...let's die together," suggests Sgt. Austin, unsure what the robber's response might be. "Or you can drop your gun, I'll cuff you and..."

The sound of Jason's automatic pistol being cocked breaks the conversation and echoes between their ears. It symbolizes a sign of relief for Sgt. Austin but proves to be more turmoil for the robber.

"Maybe this will uneven the odds. Drop your fucking gun...NOW!" Jason instructs, emphasizing the word "now" through his diaphragm, startling both Sgt. Austin and the robber.

"This way," Jason says amusingly, "you won't leave here in a body bag."

The robber's gun falls to the floor. His hands fly up as if he's trying to rebound a basketball. Sgt. Austin handcuffs him and begins reading him his rights. Jason darts for the door. Outside he stands against the building casually waiting.

Seconds later, a late-model Chevy arrives slowly in front of the pawnshop. The driver leans from the steering wheel to look out of the passenger window, notices his partner's apprehension and proceeds to flee the scene.

"This is the police," Jason yells. "Stop the car!"

Hearing Jason's demands, the second assailant pulls off in a fury. Clouds of white smoke rise from the spinning wheels with the rear of the vehicle fanning like a fish out of water. Two gunshots are fired absently toward Jason. Only a kneel down is required to elude harm's way, which Jason does instinctively before returning two shots at the rear window of the fleeing car. The engine roars louder with a sudden burst of energy, then the vehicle travels straight, running uncontrolled into a corner drugstore. It destroys doors, windows, and takes a huge chunk of wall with it as it stalls three-quarters inside the building before bursting into flames. Jason checks the accident scene to see if the assailant survived the crash and determines it would be an impossible feat based on the amount of debris and flames entertaining the car. He returns to the pawnshop to call the fire department.

Puzzled by the turn of events, Sgt. Austin questions, "Jas, how did you know there was a robbery in progress?"

"I didn't. I assumed it was going to take place."

"But how?"

"Well, the burning torch down the street was parked in front of the building when we arrived for coffee. While ordering our coffee, it circled the block twice. Each time, the driver stopped to look inside the pawnshop's window. I guessed, took a chance if you will, and assumed something was going down. So," pauses Jason, noticing Sgt. Austin's mood change again, "when the car left to go around the block again, we put on our act and foiled the robbery attempt."

Outside, many policemen are now present. Sgt. Austin places the gunman in the custody of an officer.

"Lock him up on attempted robbery and assaulting an officer with a weapon. I'll fill out the report when I get back to the station," says Sgt. Austin.

"What about that cup of coffee?" Jason asks.

"You mean now?"

"Why not? The situation is out of our control at this point. The fire-fighters have the blaze contained. One suspect has a one-way ticket to the morgue and you arrested the gunman. We might as well get what we came down here for." Turning his attention to the pawnshop's owner, he says, "We'll need a statement from you. When can you go to the station?"

"I can leave now. I want to get this ordeal over."

"Fine, we'll see you there."

Back at the table, they sip on a fresh cup of coffee with Sgt. Austin's adrenaline running high.

"I wouldn't have believed it if I hadn't had a part in it," Sgt. Austin says amazed. "You really are aware of what's going on around you. I've heard you tell officers, myself included, to be aware of most things, if not all things around you. It's probably one of those things that makes you a better cop. I'm learning, Jas, I'm learning, but don't you think it would have been easier to tell me what was happening?"

Jason pauses, smiles and continues to drink his coffee before replying, "Aren't you going to drink your coffee?"

"Answer me," Sgt. Austin replies wryly.

"Well," Jason replies between sips, "I didn't want you to react like a cop. If I'd told you what was happening, you might have charged across the street and alarmed the gunman. There could have been a hostage situation, stand-off or more shooting."

"That's great, but I am a cop; acting like one is what I do. One of these days taking matters into your own hands will lead to serious trouble."

"My, what a different tune you have from a few sentences ago," Jason jokes.

"The proper procedure would have been to tell me and call for back-up..."

Jason interrupts, "Is this turning into a lecture on proper police procedures? I get enough of those from Captain North."

"No, I worry about you because one of these chances of yours will eventually backfire."

"At that point I'll be ready for the consequences."

"How can you be so sure? Confidence can't defer Murphy's law."

"I always ask myself, am I going to regret this action? If I even think the negative, I don't do it," Jason responds positively.

"Yeah, but you can't predict the future."

"True, I can't. I'll just do it anyway, then live with the results."

"You're one crazy cop."

"Thanks, I know."

Sgt. Austin's mood changes once more as he becomes more relaxed and content with what happened. In turn, he changes the tone of the conversation.

"Jas, let me ask you something."

"What?"

"Something personal."

"Can I be frank?"

"Fuck you. This is really serious."

"Okay, okay."

"I've been thinking about getting a hair piece. There's no hiding that I'm rapidly going bald. I thought this way I could get back some of my looks. I'd like to believe that I was a looker back in my day, but..." Sgt. Austin pauses somewhat ashamed. "I'm not sure of how people would react. You know how the guys at the station are."

"I can't make that decision for you. Surely, that's a decision that clearly falls on your shoulders only. However, may I add my own personal thoughts?" questions Jason sincerely.

"Sure, by all means."

"One, never let what people might say influence your decisions. People are going to talk about you one way or the other, good or bad. It's just human nature. Two, never let these words leave you. God made only a few good heads in this world. All the others he covered with hair."

Staring blankly for a brief moment, Sgt. Austin gains some comfort after contemplating Jason's words before they burst into ridiculous laughter.

"Let's get back," Jason says.

Back at the station, Captain North is on the rampage. Jason's constant inability to follow standard operating procedures is wearing him thin. Not following them is one thing but to back that up with gunfire is unheard of in his mind. Jason, expecting small glory, receives bitter anguish from Captain North.

"Damn it, Jason. Did you have to fire your gun in public like that?"

"I only fired my weapon after being fired upon," Jason replies in his defense. "Besides, the suspect was getting away. It was a matter of action-reaction. I yelled for him to stop. He acted by firing and trying to flee. I reacted with return gunfire. Surely, I can't run a car down."

"Action-reaction, my ass. You may have cost the city tens of thousands of dollars in damages. We'll end up paying for that corner drugstore, and let's not forget the seriousness of the person dying."

"I'm sure that their insurance will cover the damages and repair of the store," Jason interjects. "But in retrospect, the driver decided his fate when he fired his weapon."

"Should I mention the innocent bystanders that could have gotten hurt or worse, killed? You are extremely lucky that the store was closed, and let me remind you that you don't own this town, you know."

"Sir, I don't claim to. I only claim to do my work to the best of my ability. When that falls short, I'm to blame. Don't hang me on the line because I reacted the best way I saw fit. If the situation presented itself again, I would react the same."

"Yeah, I'd be on your ass again, too. Listen, it's okay police work in detecting the crime but try not to be so trigger-happy next time. The commissioner will be on my ass about this."

"There aren't any guarantees, but I'll try to evaluate the situation differently next time."

Jason, turning to leave the office, stops to hear Captain North's last comment. "Jason, correction, damn good police work in detecting the crime. If you tell anyone I said that I'll deny it wholeheartedly, because I think you're two fries short of a Happy Meal."

Jason smiles and returns to his desk. A loud voice echoing through the halls belongs to Sgt. Austin. He's boasting to his fellow officers on how he and Jason stopped the robbery.

"I didn't know what to expect when he said create a scene. I yelled, screamed, and waved my gun at him. The next thing I knew, the robber and I were at point-blank range. It was the wildest thing I've ever done."

One officer at Jason's desk says, "Detective Jerrard, that was one crazy stunt you dreamed up."

"I'm crazy. I keep trying to tell you that, but none of you realize this is why I'm so good."

"He doesn't have a modest bone in his body," says Sgt. Austin.

"Okay, enough. I have these files to study," Jason responds. "Kevin, you'll file the incident report, right?"

"My pleasure. I shall take great joy writing this one."

Jason transforms into another person, totally consumed by the information presented to him. Determined to find some clue, he sits for hours scanning the photos taken at the crime scenes with a magnifying glass. He studies hair samples retrieved by some victims, searching for anything that could lead to the identity of the unknown murderer-rapist. Filled with purpose, he reads the statements of the surviving victims, studying them so hard a pounding headache develops, then intensifies to the point where he has difficulty keeping his eyes open. He leans back in his chair, rubs his eyes and looks at the clock above him.

"I haven't eaten anything since this morning. Some runny eggs would be fine about now. Twenty minutes to get across town to Rosalina's. I'd better get a move-on."

He places the files in his drawer, grabs his jacket and almost makes it away from his desk when the telephone rings.

"Sixteenth Precinct, Detective Jerrard."

"Hello, hunk, you don't have to be formal with me. After all we once shared the same bed."

These words, spoken in a soft sultry voice, are unique and unmistakably Julie.

"Hi, Julie. What's up?"

"Do you have time to talk?"

"Well, I was on my way to get something to eat. I can call you later."

"Are you going...?" Julie pauses seeing a window of opportunity. "Yes, please call me later. Goodbye."

"Fine, I'll talk to you later. Goodbye."

CHAPTER 4

Rosalina's restaurant is no fancy place. Located in the heart of the city, the older brick building looks quite odd compared to the modern sculptures that are erected around it. Inside, the decor is basic with no gimmicks or elegant fixtures standing out as a main attraction. Booths on one side, tables on the other. Burnt-orange walls downplay the red-and-white checkered tablecloths covering the square tables. One would wonder why every evening, people wait in line sometimes hours to be seated.

The restaurant's best delicacies are authentic Italian foods that rank second to none to the hierarchy, the "who's who" in Virginia City and surrounding areas. On any given night, this plain unattractive restaurant enchants this type of clientele as well as common folk. The Italian foods attract them, but for Jason, breakfast is the main attraction.

The maitre d', Alfredo, a tall, skinny aging Italian man with deep eyes and a thin mustache, is everyone's favorite as well as Jason's close personal friend. He is always kind, polite and extremely helpful while making sure you feel special with his charismatic ways.

"Ah...Jason, nice to see you again," Alfredo greets. "Are you dining alone tonight?"

"Yes, unfortunately," replies Jason with a half-smile. "A fine evening to you."

"Same to you, Sir. I guess you'll want your usual seating?"

"Please."

"Right this way, Sir."

Several people speak to Jason as he walks to his booth; being a regular customer at Rosalina's has its benefits. Alfredo tells the cook Jason has arrived and without an order, they prepare his favorite meal of three runny scrambled eggs, hash brown potatoes, three strips of bacon, toast, orange juice, coffee and a side order of corned beef hash. He receives a coffeepot placed on his table, whereas the other customers get one cup at a time. In addition, he's the only person the establishment allows to run a tab. Furthermore, they permit him inside when the restaurant has reached its capacity or when there's a line waiting to enter.

"Your meal will be ready momentarily," states Alfredo.

"As always, thank you very much. How's the family?"

"The Madam is quite well, thank you. Even though, she and I are no longer acquainted as a couple."

"You do talk with her regularly, right?"

"Not as often as I used to, but we communicate from time to time."

"I'm sure that one day, you two lovebirds will get back together."

Alfredo's response is an acknowledging nod before he turns and walks away.

The location of Jason's booth is in the rear near a window. To him it's cozier and most romantic sitting inside. In the daytime the sunlight shines through the window, bouncing off the glass salt and pepper shakers, sending colorful beams of light throughout the restaurant. At night, the dim light hanging above creates a softness only motion pictures can duplicate. The shadows coming from the rear fall diagonally across half the booth. A person could sit back in the shadows, concealing himself or lean forward to be visible to all. He likes to sit in the shadows to observe his surroundings. Jason watches the waiters caught half in an Egyptian dance, wondering when they will get that operation to remove the round thing that lays flat on their palm. He snickers. "It can't be too bad; it's great for carrying food and drinks."

The waiters dash in and around the tables with precision—no mishaps, no collisions. It's like watching an instrument, individual yet creating total harmony with the whole. The people here gobble down their food as if it were their last meal. When food is on the table, the spoken words come few and far between. They chew, nod and smile. Soon the main course disappears from their plates. Next, they lean back in the chairs and talk, one table after another until the conversation magnifies to a point resembling a break at a convention.

This place also breeds romance. Young couples sit across from each other holding hands, exerting youthful charm, gazing eye-to-eye, making each other's heart glow. An older man on a mission to impress his female companion helps her with her coat and pulls out her chair. He presents her with a rose as she closes her eyes to receive a special gift. Opening her eyes to the sight of a diamond solitaire, she jumps with amazement to give a big hug of approval. Rosalina's proves to be a proper setting for the rituals of love to be acted out.

Alfredo walks to Jason with a smile on his face. "I have something unusual for you."

"Nothing can be unusual in this place."

"This may very well be."

"What is it?"

"This."

He hands Jason a folded note. It reads, "May I come sit with you?"

"Who gave you this?"

"The madam sitting there," Alfredo states while pointing across the room.

"May I borrow your pen?"

"Surely."

Jason writes with heavy bold strokes, "With a penmanship as lovely as yours, it would be my pleasure." Handing Alfredo his pen and the note, Jason asks, "Do you mind delivering my reply?"

"Not at all, Sir."

After reading Jason's response, the woman stands. Her cream-colored blouse matches well with her navy-blue, two-piece suit. The briefcase in her hand gives her a professional appearance. She's an average-looking woman with curves that would make any woman proud. Her styled hair adds a nice touch to her overall look.

"Hi, my name is Leah, and you are?"

"Jason Jerrard," he says, standing to show proper manners. "Please sit. Your last name is?"

"Davis, I'm Leah Davis."

"Pleased to meet you."

"Likewise."

"Tell me, Leah, do you often send strange men notes?"

Her embarrassment begins to show. "You might not believe this, but this is totally uncharacteristic of me," she states, stumbling through her reply. "Normally, I'm too shy to do something as bold as this."

"So what prompted you this time?"

"I'm intrigued."

"Intrigued...why?"

"This happens to be my third time here, and each time you've been here in the same booth, doing the same thing. Curiosity got the best of me."

"I see."

"Besides, each time you've been alone."

"Are you saying I'm alone or lonely?" Jason says, interjecting his immediate thought.

"Neither. Just thought two single individuals who are possibly in denial about their loneliness might want to engage in simple conversation."

"Interesting proposal."

"And," she adds inquisitively, "there is something more that I've watched you do that also interests me."

"Oh? What's that?"

"It's intriguing to me the way you sit here and observe people."

"How so?"

"You ask many questions, but anyway, I would like to know what you notice when you're watching people."

"Little things about them."

"What kinds of things?"

"Things like, the way you talk out of the corner of your mouth on certain words."

"I do? I never knew that. Is it really that noticeable?"

"Don't be alarmed. I'm a cop, a detective actually. It's a hard habit to break."

"A detective, interesting. I'm a writer for the Sun."

"Any further ambitions?"

"I'm hoping to become a true journalist someday."

The placing of Jason's food on the table widens his eyes with great expectation. "Forgive my manners. I'm so busy gloating over my food. Would you like coffee or something?"

"Yes, coffee, and please bring my food to this table." The waiter turns to walk away. "And bring him a straw for his eggs. How can you eat them like that? That's disgusting!"

Jason smiles. "It isn't hard. It's a matter of developing a taste for them."

"When you can arguably have the best Italian food in the city, why order breakfast?"

"I guess I'm a little strange."

"I think you're right."

"Excuse me while I dance."

"Dance...what does that mean?"

"Nothing, it's a phrase I use for many things. This time I mean eating."

"Oh, I see."

"I'd better wait for your food to arrive."

"No, go right ahead. We wouldn't want to disturb your tango, would we?"

A tall, smooth-skinned woman in her early thirties appears at the table wearing a hugging dress which complements her luscious figure. Her makeup is flawless, red lipstick brings attention to her mouth, and sculptured nails are of matching color and decorate her hands. Draped across one arm is a white full-length mink coat. She speaks directly to Jason, ignoring Leah's presence.

"Jason, can we talk?"

"Now?" he responds astoundedly. "Julie, I'm with a new friend. Leah, this is Julie. Julie, this is Leah."

"Nice to meet you," responds Leah.

Julie remains silent.

"Who is this woman?" Leah questions.

"Julie Jerrard, Jason's wife," Julie says abruptly.

Jason's mouth flaps open in amazement. He quickly corrects her. "If I recall correctly, my divorce papers read Julie Roberts."

"I think I'd better leave. It's obvious you have things to discuss," says Leah.

"I think you'd better," Julie instructs.

"Julie!" Jason recites with an ever so slight hint of anger. "Leah, don't leave. Julie, can't I talk to you later?"

"No, I think it's best. I'm not one to be in the middle of a domestic dispute. I've enjoyed our meeting. Maybe I'll see you again sometime."

As Leah leaves, Jason stares at Julie bewildered. "Julie, why did you do that? Your abruptness is very rude. Furthermore, you're no longer my wife! If I recall correctly, you divorced me. So, why be so dramatic and scare people away?"

"I leave messages on your machine but you never return my calls. Also, I've left messages at the station and you still refuse to return my calls. So, when we spoke earlier and you mentioned you were going to get something to eat, I knew you'd be here. I'm determined to talk to you."

"Did you have to be so rude? I'm sitting here having a friendly conversation with a new friend and you appear out of nowhere like you're the shit."

"I know, but it's important."

"What is?"

"Our talk."

"What talk?"

"The talk about you and me. Our togetherness."

"Again, what can we say to each other this time that will be different from all the talks we've had before?"

"I don't know. Maybe we'll gain a new confidence in what we once had. Can you truly deny our love?"

"That's not the point. I love you in many ways, but our thought patterns are too different. When we divorced, the lack of love was not an issue. I believed you loved me; you just had a weird way of showing it."

"They say love can conquer all. Don't you think we're worth another try?"

"We've tried countless times before. Why put us through the pain of separating again? Those times were hard on both of us."

"We'll make it this time. I just know it."

"Maybe so, but I'm having a hard time forgetting."

"Forgetting what?"

"The things you did. The things you wanted yesterday, things I couldn't provide. I asked you to wait, but patience wasn't your virtue. All I've ever asked of you is to believe, in me, believe in us—together we could have made the luxuries of life come our way. Instead, you left because you developed the 'I've got to have it now syndrome.'"

"I'm sorry. I'm so sorry. That was the old me. I shouldn't have left. I made a grave mistake. Can't you forgive me?"

"Julie, you're a well-spoken, headstrong person. Normally you get what you want. That mink coat there—you asked me for one several times. I was in no position to afford something like that, so you left me without a second thought to find someone who could provide those kinds of things and..."

"I know," Julie interrupts. "You don't know how sorry I am. I've been given almost all the material things I starved for, but there's one thing I overlooked. Money doesn't bring genuine love. That's what we had once and that's what I want back. After the thrill of receiving gifts died, I found I couldn't fake it. I couldn't love those wealthy men. I had this emptiness..."

"Wait a minute," Jason responds to that nerve-striking remark. "Emptiness is what I felt when you left. I could give you a six-hour lecture on that alone. I'd given so much of myself to you for years. I wrapped myself, my whole life around you. My sole reason for living at that time was one giant quest to be the kind of man you wanted me to be. When you left, you took almost all of me, leaving me with barely the will to go on. Gone was my personality, my dignity and all thoughts of ever loving again. You see, the only person I knew how to be was the person that strived to please you. I could easily say that I lost my soul. Do you remember all those pictures I took of you?"

"Yes."

"When you left, I'd light a fire, lay the pictures in a circle on the living room floor, sit in the middle and cry for hours. I used to pray you'd call or knock on the door and rescue me from my own self-pity. I was a real mess. My police work got sloppy; Captain North wanted me to take a leave of absence. The day you did call and told me you had found someone to take care of you, I lost it. Mental anguish I tried to deal with, but when it reached my physical, I couldn't take it. That day after you hung up, I collapsed. I fell to the floor. My entire body was in a tremble. No matter how hard I tried, I couldn't control it. I lay there for minutes trying to regain my composure and somehow, I could begin to see the error of my ways. When I was finally able to pull myself together, I made changes in me...my personality. I made me important to me, made me responsible for my own happiness. I swore no one would ever affect me that way again. I cared no longer what people thought of me or my actions, seemingly freeing myself of all the manmade restraints. I set out to please myself without caring what people thought of it. It took me awhile to come to grips with what was happening, but, when I did, I knew I was a changed person. I am this person now."

"Can this new person forgive and love me again?"

"You know, I ask myself daily, would I ever love the way I loved you and, to this day, I draw a blank. Parts of me still feel empty, but I've learned that its life being itself. Life will go on with me participating or not. I choose to play and not be a spectator. Not having children is the only thing I regret."

"Jason, I'll give you children, anything. Just give us another try. It hasn't been easy for me. You're just thinking of yourself. It was hard on me as well. You know I came from a wealthy family. I thought I could handle the adjustment of us making it on our own. I tried. Honestly, I tried. I've always believed in you, but the culture shock took me by complete surprise. I never had to worry about how to pay bills or would we have enough money to buy groceries. I loved you enough to give it all up when we married. I defied my parents because you weren't on their social scale. Besides, I left because of a hidden reason, one I've been carrying since I left."

"Please enlighten me."

"Jason, you were trying hard, trying to make life as close to what I'd been accustomed to. You worked long hours, shooting for promotions. At one point you took on a second job. I only left because I couldn't stand the sight of you killing yourself anymore. I figured if I left, you could get some rest and I could get what I felt I needed then."

"You left me for me, without discussing something of that magnitude with me. That's awful hard to swallow after all this time."

"I did."

"Look at me. My hands are shaking, my heart is pounding and I'm doing everything that I can to hold back tears. Let's stop this before I have tracks of tears running down my face like you. We can continue this conversation later."

"When?"

"I don't know. We both need time to clear our heads. I'll call you."

"Jason?"

"I will, I'll call you soon."

"Tomorrow?"

"Julie, I'll call you. I promise," he replies a bit more forcefully.

"Okay, but I want you to remember that I've learned something since we divorced. I realize now that love is heaven-sent. Some people say it's forever; forever means all your life. That's how long I plan to love you because over the months, I've also learned that you never fall out of love; you simply learn to live without that person in your life. But, in our case, I not only want but need you in my life. Say what you want, but our love is worth another...no," Julie states after a deep inhale and a pause. "I'm going to fix my face. Then I'm leaving. Don't misunderstand. I haven't given up. This isn't the proper place to continue. People are starting to stare. We can talk about this another time but remember I will have you again, mentally and physically. Take care."

"Goodbye."

Julie walks away as abruptly as she came. Jason pushes his food aside and falls into the shadows in dismay.

CHAPTER 5

The next morning after a night when Jason spent most of the would-be sleeping hours rehashing Julie's closing remarks, Jason wakes tired yet determined to start his day focused on his case in hand. After reviewing the files, he sets out to question someone he's nicknamed "Lucky"—she survived, she's sane and she still has her wits about her. He arrives at Mrs. Smith's home and knocks on the door. A short moment later, the door opens slowly, providing only a two-inch gap allowed by the security chain.

"Hello, Mrs. Smith?"

"Yes, who are you?"

"I'm Detective Jerrard of the Sixteenth Precinct. I've been assigned to investigate the series of rapes and murders in the area."

Mrs. Smith has always been rather timid and shy, but after her attack, she is jumpy and suspicious of everyone.

"May I see some identification?"

"Surely," Jason replies while presenting his badge.

The door opens and Jason enters.

"I'm sorry but you can't be too careful nowadays."

"It's perfectly understandable. We believe your case relates to others in the surrounding areas. If I may, there are a few questions I need to ask you about your attack."

"Sure, anything to help. I wasn't in any shape for questions the day it happened."

"That's fairly obvious. The description you provided when you were first questioned is fairly sketchy. Do you think with clearer thoughts you can come up with more details? Think hard," Jason states, careful not to push too hard. "Is there anything you can remember about this person? Any physical scars that you can recall?"

"He dressed nicely, seemed very articulate until he pulled an exorcist and tried to attack me. Then, his voice changed to something awful. There was something eerie about it...still sends chills down my spine when I think about it."

"Is there anything more you can tell me? Hair or eye color? Did he take anything? I'd appreciate anything you can give me."

"My mind scrambled that day. I'm still finding it difficult to remember exact details about the attack—seems my memory is in denial. Although I remember sitting in my office afterwards trying to regain myself, and one of my employees brought me my purse from the parking lot and told me that the contents were scattered all over the ground. My credit card is missing, but I can't be sure it was him who took it."

"That's something. It could be a lead. What card was it?"

"My Visa."

"Have you noticed anything strange on your bill?"

"Can't tell. I haven't received a statement for this month."

"If you allow me, I can run a check on it for you. May I have your account number?"

"Yes, if you think it will help."

"It could become an important factor. Oh, by the way, when was your last purchase?"

"It was about three-and-a-half weeks ago. Let me get my account number."

When Mrs. Smith returns with the information, Jason thanks her.

"If you think of anything, feel free to give me a call," he says, handing her a card. "Please accept my apologies for rehashing your unpleasant experience. I know you'd rather forget it happened."

"No, I had to come to grips with it. I'm scared at night, but I'll survive—tell me, have there been more attacks? Is this man still out there?"

"Yes and yes. There have been attacks in neighboring precincts. Your case ties in with those. The common factor between you all seems to be his voice. It is the most outstanding thing mentioned. However, it's odd that you mention his dress."

"Do you have other leads on who he is, or how you might find him?"

"My training dictates that I answer 'yes' to this question, but under the circumstances I won't lie to you. You deserve to know. The evidence we have collected so far is scarce, making him seem invisible, but I assure you, he can't remain anonymous forever. We'll get him. You will have your justice."

"I hope so. As I said, I'm scared but not as frightened since I got my little friend. If anyone looks at me like they're going to lay a finger on me, I'll fill them full of holes. I'll empty my little six-shooter in them."

"Don't be impulsive. Everyone out there isn't out to harm you."

"Impulsive? I have a right to protect myself."

"Yes, you do, but don't endanger the lives of the innocent. Listen," Jason says with great concern, "there's a class, a therapy session every Wednesday at the station for women who have suffered an attack. May I suggest you attend? It gives you the chance to vent your hurt, your anger, and slowly remove it from your mind."

"You can never forget an attack like that."

"I'm sure, but the classes might help put it behind you so you can live a normal life. I'd much rather see you do that than walk around with a pistol, loaded, cocked, ready to fire at the first man who looks at you the wrong way. Please consider my offer."

"I'll think about it. I may even attend, but I'll have my pistol with me."

"Fine, just get to the sessions. Again, if you come up with anything, call me."

"Okay and thank you for being honest with me."

"I'll let you know the status of your Visa account. Take care."

"Thanks."

"I want to see you Wednesday."

"Maybe," she says with a smile.

"Okay, I'll see you there," he responds positively.

Jason leaves Mrs. Smith's home, fearing if he doesn't catch this madman soon, he'll have a city full of women carrying loaded weapons, a disaster in the making.

Back at the station for what's sure to be a day at his desk studying the criminal pattern of the unknown rapist, he prepares for the intense work.

"Jas, the captain gave me instructions to have you meet him at Twenty-Third and Vine. There's an attempted burglary that turned into a hostage situation," says Sgt. Austin.

"Damn, I just left that area." Jason dashes out the door wondering if his case is almost solved. "Is this the man I'm looking for?"

Red and blue lights flashing with siren on, Jason races to the scene where you'd think ten of the most wanted criminals were hiding inside. Police cars surround the block, and officers have the entire house surrounded. The SWAT team is on the scene with sharpshooters covering all the windows and exits anxious for a clean shot at the burglar. The media cover the scene, doing what they do best, reporting bad news. There are people behind the police barricade waiting for the drama to unfold.

"Jason, over here!"

Responding to Captain North's voice, Jason reports for the status of the situation.

"What's happening?"

"We have a burglary attempt that tripped the silent alarm and when the first officers arrived on the scene, the burglar grabbed the resident and is holding her captive with a knife. He's demanding free passage to the airport and a flight out of the city. He says if there are any rescue attempts, tear gas or anyone nearing the house, she dies."

"Bullshit," Jason responds defiantly.

"Jason, be cool. Don't be rash."

"Rash, how long has this situation been at a standstill?"

"Too long, I'm afraid, but the hostage negotiator is en route."

"Damn it," Jason says as he backs away from Captain North. "Someone has to make the first move."

"Jason, come back here. Bring your ass back here now. Damn it, Jason," Captain North screams to no avail. "I know you hear me. That's a direct order!"

Jason continues to journey toward the house, instinctively pulling his pistol.

A voice from inside, leery of all the commotion outside, yells frantically. "I'm warning you, if anyone comes into the house, her ass dies."

Jason continues, hoping that the change in the burglar's words from "near" the house to "into" the house is all the leverage he needs.

"Please stay away. He has a knife at my throat," the woman cries.

"You tell them, bitch. Did you cops hear that? I'll slit her fucking throat. I want out of here!"

Jason kicks at the front door near the doorknob, administering each kick a little harder than the other until it surrenders to his brute force. His conduct is driven by an uncontrollable urge to end this situation, placing all involved on the edge.

"You fucking pigs don't seem to understand. I'm serious. Don't come near me."

"I'm coming in and we all are going to walk out of here."

"Fuck you!"

"No, please don't come any closer. I don't want to die," the woman pleads.

"Fucking pig, I'll kill her!"

Jason carefully follows voices until he finds the careless burglar and the woman seated on the kitchen floor. The burglar—an unshaven heavyset man with worn clothes and muddy shoes—is sweating while the woman is in tears, terrorized with the knife at her throat. She's Ms. Kathy Waters, a short large-boned woman dressed in a bathrobe with her wet hair pulled back.

"You must be out of your fucking mind. Now you get to watch the knife open her neck. Watch pig; watch her warm blood drip from the knife's tip."

"Hmm, you don't look like a killer. Burglary is one thing; murder, that's totally different, so let's end this masquerade before you get yourself in too deep. So," Jason responds evenly, "what's it going to be?"

"Fuck you. You can't sweet-talk me. Your arrogance has cost this bitch her life."

"Think it over. This is the last time before all hell breaks loose."

"Her ass dies," the burglar threatens.

"Bullshit!" Jason responds, changing gears. "Cut her throat. Go ahead."

"No, please," the terrorized woman pleads. "Please don't make him do that. I don't want to die."

"You have big balls. I want out of here..."

"Or what?" Jason questions in a commanding tone.

"I'll waste her, pig."

"Kill her," Jason says, cocking his pistol. "Then I'll have a clean shot at you."

"Fuck you, pig!" the burglar shouts.

"Fuck you, too!" Jason responds in the same courteous manner.

"You're a cop. You can't do anything to me."

"Presently, I'm the only hope your ass has of getting out of here alive. Sharpshooters are covering all the exits so take my advice and don't stand up."

Jason approaches the burglar with the pistol barrel aimed between his eyes.

"You stay back. Stay back or she'll get it! I'm warning for the last time, pig!"

"Do it! You crazy fucking maniac."

"What are you saying, this is my life...please don't encourage him," she pleads.

"That's right, pig. I don't have anything to lose."

"You're about to lose your fucking life."

"Stay back, stay back, man!"

"Do it. I really want you to. You see, the moment she dies, I'll kill your dumb ass." He smiles. "I'll tell everyone outside that you went for me—self-defense and, best of all, no witnesses. She'll be dead and you'll die, too. I'll walk away smelling like a rose. Quite simple, I think. So, kill her," he says nonchalantly.

"No, please," she begs. "Don't make him kill me," she pleads with tears falling off her chin consistent with her terrorized emotional state.

"I'm gonna do it. Watch her body become limp."

"Shut the fuck up!" Jason yells. "Make a move."

"Stay back, you crazy fucking bastard."

"Now, you understand," Jason responds evenly.

"You can't do this. You're a fucking cop. I have rights."

"Rights? You're fucking crazy. You barge into someone else's home looking to steal, get caught and threaten to kill. Why in the fuck can't I threaten yours? Make it easy for me. Do it. I beg you to. You chicken-hearted bastard," Jason teases. "Kill her!" Jason shouts.

"Stay back! Don't push me, pig!"

"Do it, you spineless jack ass."

"She's dead, cop!"

Jason pictures himself playing a movie role, in an intense scene accompanied by dramatic music in the background, bringing it to a climactic end. Strangely enough, he finds himself amused.

"No, I don't think so. If you were going to kill her, you would have by now."

Jason gets within arm's reach of the burglar and places the gun barrel on the burglar's forehead.

"Now, you fucking prick, do something. Live or die; your choice."

"Okay, I give. Don't fucking shoot," the robber replies, bewildered by Jason's unorthodox demeanor.

The burglar throws the knife to the side. The woman stands hysterically, chastising Jason.

"You're a crazy cop," the woman rages. "How could you encourage this maniac to kill me? How...could...you," she cries with her fist accompanying each word onto Jason's back.

"Miss, please go outside. We'll need a statement from you."

"Statement!" she shouts. "I'm going to report you to your superiors."

"Ma'am, do what you have to, but please leave now," Jason instructs. The woman dashes toward the front door frantically screaming, uncontrolled in her wildness.

"Get your ass up," Jason instructs, slamming the burglar face first into the wall while pulling one of his arms back to be handcuffed.

"You're not all here. You're a crazy ass cop."

"I make a living being crazy. You have the right to remain silent. Anything you say can and will be used against you in a court of law." Jason continues reading him his rights while walking out with the criminal in hand. "Take him away," Jason instructs while passing him to an officer.

The victimized woman is on the rampage. Not only does she feel threatened by the burglar, but she feels stripped of her human right to live by Jason's actions. She's raging about Jason's conduct, providing the media with all the drama of a staged play.

"There he is," she rages while pointing at Jason. "He's the one who tried to get me killed! You don't deserve to be a cop! You're crazy!"

"Are you going to file a formal complaint against Detective Jerrard?" asks Captain North.

"Yes, I most certainly am. He's a lunatic."

"Jason, you disobeyed a direct order, playing that damn super cop again. I want your ass in my office first thing in the morning with a full report. Take Ms. Waters down to the station for her statement."

"I'll make my own way, thank you," she responds while staring at Jason with piercing eyes.

"Can I go now?" Jason asks.

"Get the hell out of my sight. I want your side of this drama before first call."

The next morning Jason reports early to put the finishing touches on his report. However, he wasn't able to arrive earlier than Captain North. He's in his office, pacing the floor, anxiously awaiting Jason's arrival but uneasy about what he must do.

"Where in the fuck do you get off disobeying my direct orders and threatening the life of Ms. Waters?!" Captain North questions in such a harsh manner, it momentarily catches Jason off guard. "Don't give me any action-reaction shit. She has reported in her statement that you encouraged the burglar to kill her."

"I did."

"Damn, Jason, you can't play God and decide when someone dies. You were way out of line."

"I wasn't playing God...to deal with crazy people like him, you have to act crazier than them. I only called his bluff."

"Is that another one of your personal beliefs?"

"Yes, it is. My beliefs have helped me out of many jams before."

"Yes, but you forget your first priority is to protect the innocent."

"With all due respect, Sir, I did. I made a judgment call based on the situation when I arrived. Besides, everything turned out fine. Didn't it? No one got injured, no one got killed, so what's the big problem?"

"Damn, Jason, damn! That's not the fucking point. You're just lucky these days. The District Attorney is already on this one. The media caught everything she said when she came running out. She fed the media the impression that she was more upset with you than the burglar. Believe me, she was singing, playing it up for them. The DA wants a full investigation. It says here that you threatened to shoot him if he'd killed her. That's fucking absurd. This kind of conduct gives the department a bad name. Especially coming from someone with your credentials. Tell me something, Superman, would you have shot him?"

"It's hard to tell. As I said, I was merely calling his bluff. Besides, my gut feeling told me that he didn't fit the profile of someone who would commit murder."

"So, you based the entire escapade on idle threats. You put Ms. Waters' life in jeopardy with false pretenses. You're abusing your badge, buddy."

"Sir, I know I took a big gamble, even could have gotten someone killed, but the situation required a more aggressive action. Someone had to act. Hell."

"And that someone had to be you," Captain North interrupts.

"Again," Jason stresses, "more importantly, deep down I felt that I was making the right decision."

"I've often admired your tactics but not when you jeopardize innocent lives. This one is political; my ass is on the line. I have no choice but to suspend you."

"Suspension, isn't that a bit much?"

"It's not my idea; it's the DA's recommendation. You're suspended until we settle on Ms. Waters' complaint."

"Doesn't the DA want to hear my side of the story before he makes a decision like that?"

"Probably if the media had not covered her hysterics but at this point I don't think it would do any good. Take some time to regroup. The DA wants to handle this one without any additional media coverage. If it looks like we've taken some type of disciplinary action, it might help your case. I'll keep you informed of any changes."

"All right," Jason says reluctantly, "I guess I blew this one, huh?"

"It looks that way. This wasn't one of your better moves."

"Well, you know where to find me if you need me."

"I'll be in touch."

"Oh, give this account number to whomever is going to handle the Invisible Man's case and have it traced. It's from Mrs. Smith, the woman attacked at the mall, and if there are any recent charges on the account, it could be our rapist. Also, I promised Mrs. Smith a reply one way or the other."

"Consider it done."

Jason leaves Captain North's office disillusioned, wondering how a perfectly executed plan could be perceived so sour. He tries to figure out how to prevent sheer boredom with the extra time forced upon him.

At his home he throws his jacket across the sofa's back, flops down on it and stares into nothingness. He slowly scans the room, watching his possessions that all suddenly seem meaningless. Dismayed by the suspension, he walks over to check his messages.

"Oh, I seem popular today," he says, noticing the constant red light on his answering machine indicating at least six calls.

"Hello, Jason, Bob. Need to talk to you, important, give me a ring."

"Jason, we need to talk. Call me when you arrive, Julie. Jason, pick up if...why can't you see that we are right for each other? Jason, I just called to say I love you. I'll await your call."

"I don't need this now," Jason says while turning the machine back on. The phone rings, he ignores it and lets the machine answer the call.

"Jason...Jason?" Julie's voice comes through the speaker. "Just checking to see if you're home. Call me."

With the suspension and the added stress caused by the DA's investigation, Julie's timing is all wrong. To be involved in an emotional conversation at this time would be unbearable. Jason lets her hang up and passes out on the sofa.

CHAPTER 6

"Well, Miss Fong, you've watched these cars for many years. Now after all this time, you get to finally drive one off the showroom floor that's actually yours."

"I know. It's hard to believe. I've bugged you for years, promising you that one day I'd own one. Now I can finally say it's mine. My shiny black Carrera Cabriolet convertible, front and rear spoilers, shiny chrome rims, plush leather interior and five-speed transmission. Listen to the sound system, eight speakers and an equalizer. It's crisp, isn't it? It'll be me, the road and the wind."

"It sounds like you're trying to sell me one."

"Oh, I'm sorry. I'm just overly excited."

"You've waited a long time for this. I'd guess being promoted to vice president was the deciding factor enabling you to purchase this car now."

"Yep, it sure was, and let's not forget my savings I had especially for—my dream car—tilted the scale. You know I've been saving practically a lifetime."

"All I can say is congratulations. Working with you on this project has been a pleasure...now go, enjoy your new car."

"My pleasure."

Sasha starts her brand-new Cabriolet with all of seven miles on the odometer. The engine purrs smoothly. It falsely relaxes her mind about the purse string attached to her new possession. She enters the street carefully, looking in both directions twice before pulling into traffic. Cruising down the street, all sorts of eyes are on her as heads turn and women look with envy. The men watch and stare as if they were thinking, "And fine, too!"

Everything is perfect—a gorgeous spring day, little traffic, hair blowing in the wind as she rides with the top down. Her pride shows as she wonders whether it's the car or her drawing all the attention. Both.

She pulls into the supermarket parking lot looking for a faraway place to park and spots a place in the last row on the end.

"Perfect, I can only get a door from one side. Besides, who would park this far away from the entrance when there's closer parking available? Some nut like me with a new car trying to prevent unwanted nicks from careless drivers, that's who. I want her to look new as long as possible." She walks toward the entrance smiling to herself. "I can't believe this. I finally got it."

Inside the store, she picks up a pair of stockings, deodorant and a half-gallon of milk, and for her own celebration, she selects a thick juicy steak and wine, realizing this might be her last decent meal. She zips through the express lane with an anxious smile brought on by her temptation to settle behind the wheel, only to step outside to discover that someone is driving away in her car. The bags drop to the ground and the frantic chase begins.

"No, stop!" she shouts. "That's my car! Please stop! Don't take my car!" Her chase ends with her screaming at the top of her lungs with one final yell, "Stop!"

Sasha rises to a sitting position in her bed with her heart beating frantically. Her hair is damp, forehead wet and the bed covers lay on the floor. She shakes her head, startled. Everything is black except the light-blue glow from her alarm clock displaying three thirty-three in the morning.

"Damn, that was a dream. It felt so real. Look at me. I'm soaking wet." Falling back to her pillow, she smirks. "I must want that car awfully bad—one day. But for now, back to sleep, hopefully with no strange nightmares."

The next morning the loud buzz from her seven-thirty alarm causes Sasha to spring to the ceiling like a cartoon character. She descends from the ceiling, floating down like a feather in a gentle breeze and stumbles her naked body featuring nice curves, a five-foot-seven frame, long flowing black hair falling just below her shoulders to the bathroom.

She glances in the mirror. "I look awful! It must've taken me longer to fall back to sleep after that crazy dream than I realized. Was that wild or what? I even got a promotion out of it. Sasha, I'll tell you, girl, you're losing it." She shakes her head in disbelief to the fact that she was actually talking out loud to herself.

Sasha turns on the shower, waits a minute and disappears into the steam. After putting herself together, she walks out of her condo, briefcase in hand, in a navy blue business suit with matching pumps. Her fine black hair is styled and pinned atop her head with the front teased. A fashionable Gucci watch is the accessory to her outfit. She gets into her car and departs for Virginia City National Bank where she, Sasha Fong, holds the title of bank manager.

En route to the bank, she stops at a red light and a man in a blue sedan pulls alongside her. His passenger window comes down without Sasha noticing. He gives a slight tap on the horn, and her head turns, greeting his words.

"Nice day for a drive, isn't it?"

Sasha only smiles.

"Are you on your way to work?"

"Yes," Sasha reluctantly replies.

"Where do you work?"

After pondering the question, Sasha responds, "Down the Boulevard."

"What's your name?"

Sasha begins to get annoyed with the thousand questions, and then notices that the light is now green.

"Got to go. Goodbye."

Driving down the street, she reflects on her dream last night. Riding in her 300ZX is nice, but she knows she must find some vehicle to give her enough capital to someday afford that car. She realizes that wanting a car so bad to the point of nightmares is more than just desire; it's an obsession.

Sasha laughs to herself. "Though it was a dream, it felt good driving it."

At the bank she enters to find her assistant manager, Joseph Tucker, has opened shop. He is an older man, ten years her senior with graying temples, short and stocky. His face has few wrinkles for a man in his early forties.

"Good morning, Sasha. My, don't you look divine today."

"Morning, Joe. After the night I had, waking up every other hour—I even had the nerve to have a nightmare! I take that as a big compliment."

"Well, you do."

"Thanks, Joe. I can always look for a compliment from you. How is everything this morning?"

"It looks all right to me."

"Look here, remind me to have a talk with the boss of the cleaning crew today. They forgot again to dust the tellers' booths."

"Will do."

The tellers and other bank personnel arrive and normal operations begin. Hours pass and mounds of paperwork consume Sasha's awareness.

A woman's voice interrupts Sasha's thoughts. "I need your signature on these loan applications."

"More, this sure is the age of credit."

"You got that right. By the way, what are you doing for lunch?"

"Is it that time already?"

Sasha looks at her watch. To her amazement, it's after twelve noon. She's spent the entire morning without a break, lost in the never-ending shuffle of papers.

"I'm going to grab a light snack," Sasha states. "Then I have something I want to do."

"Care to have any stragglers?"

"Thanks, but I'll move faster alone. Maybe some other time."

"All right, just thought I'd ask."

Sasha stacks the papers in a neat pile on her desk and leaves for outside to enjoy the sunshine. The warm beaming rays soothe her face, but she is hesitant to get into the mad rush. Congestion fills both the streets and the sidewalks. Yet, people flee their workplaces for a moment of relief from their stressful jobs to enjoy a moment called lunchtime. They hurriedly walk down the street, some gobbling food in the process. She takes a deep breath and vanishes into the crowd, only stopping for a not-so-healthy lunch at a nearby hot dog stand. Afterwards, she twists and pushes through the crowd, virtually unnoticed. She passes the Ritz of Hollywood, Virginia City's fashion palace, promoting designer lines from New York and Hollywood. She stops to admire a black hip-hugging, low-cut, slit-up-the-right-side dress that appeals to her senses. She taps on the glass, getting the attention of the woman putting the final accessories on the mannequin.

"How much?" she asks, making a dollar sign on the window.

The woman signals a peace sign and says, "Two."

"Two hundred?" Sasha mimics.

Smiling while shaking her head, the woman replies, "Two thousand."

Sasha's eyes pop open as if she's just seen a ghost. Well, the price of the dress scares her just the same.

"Two thousand. I'm beginning to think something is wrong with the world. That's definitely too rich for my blood." She smiles and walks away. *I can't believe it,* she thinks to herself. *That much for the dress; they must think they're in Hollywood for sure.*

She picks up a rapid pace, dodging through the crowd to her destination. Her journey ends at Reynolds Beer & Wine, Virginia City's discount mart for alcoholic beverages.

"I'd like five random picks for the thirty-eight-million-dollar lottery and to play these Pick Three numbers straight."

Reaching in her purse—with thoughts of winning big—she pulls out her numbers and money.

"You know, you'd stand a better chance by playing these numbers boxed," states the cashier.

"That's true, but if I'm going to hit, I'm going to hit straight."

"You're a gutsy woman."

"Thank you. I like that."

"That will be fifteen dollars, please."

After paying the cashier, she checks her numbers and starts her trip back to the bank.

It's closing time at the bank and Sasha and two other management personnel are the only ones remaining. Ben is a well-groomed man in his late twenties. He is so professional and courteous during business hours but, after hours, he loosens his tie and relaxes his attitude. The other one, Carl, comes from a different school. He's the bank clown, their own funny man. He jokes with the customers, always having something cheerful to say.

"Hey, Carl, are you going to make the game tonight?" asks Ben.

"The game is tonight. I thought you told me it was on the seventeenth."

"Earth calling Carl, today is the seventeenth."

"Oh, I must be out there somewhere. What time is the game?"

"Eight-thirty sharp at Steve's place."

"What are the stakes?"

"Two and four tunk."

"No, steaks like T-bone, rib-eye or something of that nature."

"Funny, beer and chips are more like it. Are you coming or not?"

"Not at the moment," he replies jokingly. "Okay, seriously, two and four, I'll be there."

Walking over with an exaggerated pimp's strut and gestures of a streetwise person, Carl asks, "Yo, Sasha, you play cards?"

"All kinds."

"Do you gamble?"

"Yes, I like to play poker, dealer's choice."

"Ben, Sasha thinks she knows how to play cards. You do play tunk, right?"

"I was raised playing tunk."

"How about coming to play with the big boys tonight? You won't have to stay long because we'll take your money fast."

"That's not a bad idea," Ben interjects. "Hang with us tonight."

"I can't tonight, guys. I've already committed myself to another engagement. You know you guys are lucky."

"Ready Carl, together now."

"How so?"

"Simple. I'd walk away the winner."

"Are you sure?" asks Carl. "I would be cashing your next paycheck."

"Some other time, guys."

"If you change your mind, we'll be at eighteen forty-two Apple Spice Way. That's Steve Young's house," Ben says.

"Okay, let's finish up. I've been in here long enough."

CHAPTER 7

Sasha's engagement takes her to Rosalina's. She's attempting to get to know a new friend. Their initial meeting was successful. Now, she hopes this evening will be as nice as the first encounter.

"Your face is familiar. You are?" asks Alfredo while snapping his fingers as a method to make him remember. "Where have I seen you before?"

"Here maybe?"

"No, I would remember that."

"Virginia City Bank?"

"Ah, yes, the bank, that's it. You're the manager, aren't you?"

"In the flesh...by the way, I have dined here several times before."

"Have you? And I missed you. My age must be catching up with me."

"You see hundreds of people each day. It would be hard for anyone to remember them all."

"I guess you're right. Just yourself this evening?"

"Actually, I'd like a table for two. My guest should arrive shortly."

"Right this way, Ma'am. May I get you something while you wait?"

"Yes, thank you. I'll have fried cheese sticks and a glass of white wine."

"Would you like wine for your guest also?"

"Yes, I think that will be proper...oh, he will be asking for Miss Fong's table."

Alfredo walks away. Sasha, being ten minutes early for her engagement, studies herself with a mirror from one of her makeup compacts. Everything seems in order—lipstick flawless, makeup flawless, and hair, let's just say she wishes she had styled it differently—as she waits patiently for her guest. She has been long removed from the dating scene and has not accepted a date since her divorce other than associating with her girlfriends. This is the fourth attempt with the same person. Desperate, she thinks, then tries to shake that feeling away.

"This one has to go right. The other times he has canceled at the last minute due to what he calls business."

Not having received a canceling call, she is confident of his arrival.

At seven thirty-five, Sasha stares toward the entrance trying not to let the anxiety build within her but with no sign of her dinner date, it is all but too late.

"Here you are, cheese sticks and two glasses of wine. What time are you expecting your guest?"

"Anytime now. He's never prompt," Sasha recites more for her benefit than the server's.

Ten more minutes pass and she's not only aggravated with the apparent no-show of her guest; she has an attitude to boot.

"All right, mister man, you'd better show. I'll wait only fifteen more minutes. Then I'm leaving. I can't believe," she scolds herself. "I let him talk me into a fourth time. How stupid can I be? He assured me this time that nothing could go wrong and I fell for it. Sometimes, I feel so gullible."

Sasha sits for what seems like hours, finishes her glass of wine and walks to Alfredo.

"Here, this should cover my order," Sasha states while attempting to hide the frustration in her tone.

"You're leaving? But you have not eaten."

"It doesn't appear that he's going to show. Besides, it's eight-fifteen. I believe I've waited long enough."

"Very well, Madam. Have a good evening."

Sasha is steamed. This isn't what she had in mind when she agreed to a guaranteed fun-filled evening. She walks to her car with a brisk pace evident of the disappointment in herself.

Mentally she finds herself pondering Steve's address but absently recites the thoughts flowing through her mind. "I remember the street name, but the house numbers have eluded me. Sixteen, eighteen or was it the thirteen-hundred block. Well, the street is only so long. I'll look for Ben's car. He's always boasting how fast his Turbo Z28 is. Ben and Carl are going to shit when they see me. After all, I was invited. My plans didn't work out so I'll go win some money."

Upon reaching Apple Spice Way, she slows to look carefully for a recognizable car. She travels blocks before she comes across a Z28 with the license plate BEN.

"That's it, the house number eighteen...eighteen forty-two. That sounds right."

Inside the boys are in what they call a serious card game. Bluffing, selling wolf tickets for hands they know are surely losers.

"House man, someone's at the door," states Carl.

"Get that for me, Ben. I'm in the middle of the ice tray," he yells from the kitchen.

"No problem," Ben responds. He opens the door and to his surprise stands Sasha. "Well, I'll be. You showed up. What's wrong? Your plans weren't as interesting as a good card game?"

"I don't want to talk about it," Sasha relays, trying not to reveal her disgust. "Are you going to let me in or what?"

"Hey, Carl, you'll never believe who's here."

Sasha walks into the smoke-filled room. Empty beer cans overflow the wastebasket and bowls of chips are spilled on the table. Their concentration breaks from the game as all heads turn to see the unexpected guest.

"Hey, everyone, this is Sasha, our boss."

She's introduced around the table and admiration of her fills the air. Sasha is unsure if it's because of the way she looks or that she had the courage to show up.

"Are we here to play?" asks Carl.

"Yes, I could use some extra money," Sasha boasts. "No sore losers tonight, guys, all right?"

"What do you play, Miss?" Steve asks.

"Just about everything. What's the game tonight, tunk?"

"Actually we were playing dealer's choice."

"Enough talk. Give me the cards. Let's play."

Sasha shuffles the cards with a touch of an experienced player, causing the men to consider themselves carefully. She mingles well with the group of men in a game that continues well into the morning.

Saturday morning after a few hours' sleep, Sasha calls to find out the Lotto and Pick Three numbers while simultaneously counting her winnings of the previous night. She becomes pleasantly surprised with her small fortune, compliments of the guys. Immediate thoughts of a new dress dance in her mind until interrupted by the call-waiting signal. She clicks over without receiving the information she called for.

"Hello?"

"Sasha, this is me. I called you last night until two o'clock in the morning. Where were you?"

"Me?" Sasha replies, feeling her temper flare. "I'm so upset with you, I don't even want to speak your name or speak to you. If I were as rude as your actions, I'd hang up the damn phone," Sasha recites before realizing she'd cursed. "Where was I? Where were you last evening at seven-thirty? Answer that for me and I don't want to hear again, you had business to take care of."

"I...I was..."

"Listen to you," Sasha intrudes abruptly. "You can't even get your lie straight."

"I just had things to take care of, that's all."

"That's it; you had things to take care of," she says hostilely. "With an excuse like that, I wish you had lied to me."

"Something important came up."

"There's something called a telephone. I sat forty-five minutes waiting for you. People were looking at me funny while I sat there with the glass of wine I ordered for you. I don't like looking like a lush. You've stood me up for the last time!"

"Wait a minute. You can't claim the other times; I called on them."

"Nevertheless, I was left alone. It's perfectly clear to me that you don't have time for me. So let's drop this idea of getting together. It's just not meant to be."

"Sasha, trust me, when I say something came up important, it…"

"Look, I don't have time for this. I have enough pressure with every-day living and don't need the added anguish of wondering if you'll ever show up. When you grow up and can keep an engagement, maybe we can talk, but," Sasha says almost as defiant as she is feeling, "it will be on my terms."

"Sasha, think about…never mind, are you sure?"

"Yes, maybe at a later date we can get together," Sasha lies with hopes of ending the unwanted conversation.

"Okay," the disturbed caller reluctantly states. "Talk to you later."

"Goodbye."

Sasha, in disbelief, wonders what men think sometimes. She ponders, how long did he think she was going to stay interested in him when he habitually breaks dates? The whole idea amazes her. She makes journal entries of last night's events and starts recording the gist of this morning call until her hunger pains snap her concentration away. Sasha uses the Lotto tickets as a bookmark for her return to the journal.

The next Monday, business hours go as usual—nothing out of the ordinary except a phone call from Howard Normin, one of the card players from the previous Friday night. She finds it odd that would call her. During the entire evening, they spoke less than ten words to each other. His call came with a luncheon invitation from the quiet one at the card game. He was polite and courteous when he asked her for the get-together. Ever so curious, she is so puzzled by his actions, she accepts his invitation for the next day.

CHAPTER 8

Howard Normin is in his early thirties, six feet two with hints of gray at his temples. His navy blue, two-piece, double-breasted suit, paisley tie and pink shirt complement his tanned complexion. He waits impatiently for Sasha to arrive. The scheduled one-thirty afternoon luncheon with Sasha is at a café down the street from the bank where he occupies a table for two with a view of the street. His eyes are focused in the direction of the bank.

"May I get you something while you wait for your guest?" asks the waiter.

"Yes, thank you. A glass of wine, please."

"Will that be red or white wine?"

"White."

"Would you like something for your guest?"

"I don't...ask her. Here she comes now."

Sasha enters the café looking profoundly for this person she has only seen once in a semi-dark, smoke-filled room. She vaguely remembers his face but notices a hand waving at a table near the window and walks in that direction.

"I was about to order a drink. What would you like?"

"I shouldn't drink during banking hours, so I'll have a cup of hot tea."

"My drink and hot tea, please...," Howard orders before directing his attention to Sasha. "It's nice to meet you again."

"Likewise."

"I know my call came to you as a complete surprise yesterday. You're a busy woman, so I apologize for taking you away from your work, but there are some things I want to discuss with you."

"That's all right. I needed a break. It's been one of those days. Howard, is this luncheon business or pleasure?"

"Would you be disappointed if I said business?"

"Not at all."

"Should I be insulted?"

"Don't be—what can I do for you?"

"Well, to get to the point, I need a loan."

"A loan. This can be handled at the bank."

"No, not this time. There are unusual circumstances involving this one."

"What is it? You have bad credit and you want me to help you get it approved?"

"Not exactly."

"Let me guess. You need sporting equipment, a new car or a boat?"

"It is nothing like that. I need a business loan for a company I run. The problem is we're new."

"That does not sound like much of a problem. How much does this business make a month after expenses, and what is the nature of your business?"

"That's just it. I'm still operating in the red. The only thing of value is the building from which I operate, and I'm sure it can't cover the loan amount."

"How much do you need?"

"I guess somewhere in the neighborhood of a half-million dollars. Four hundred and fifty thousand, I'd guess would be more accurate."

"Four hundred and fifty thousand. What kind of business do you operate?"

"I'm in the import/export business."

"Import/export, huh. You need that kind of money to operate your business?"

"I'm afraid in this case I do. You see there is a shipment of rare artifacts coming in from the Orient. The seller has agreed on a lump sum price of four-hundred-fifty-thousand dollars for the entire seven-piece collection. The market value of just five pieces is well over the loan amount."

"I see, and you'd pay the loan off after you've sold a few pieces."

"That's right."

"Howard, how long would it take to sell such expensive pieces?"

"I can't be sure, but I suppose it will take about seventy-five days or so."

"That's approximately two-and-a-half months. So, you'd be looking for a ninety-day note on this loan?"

"Yes, if those terms are what it takes to secure the loan."

"Interesting, however, I may not be the person you need."

"What do you mean?"

"It's true I approve many loans daily but none of this magnitude."

"Sasha, please push it through for me. I really need your help. Anything you can do will be greatly appreciated. Securing the pieces of armor will most certainly put the Far East Import Company on the map. After all, it's not your money."

"That's not the right thing to say, Howard. First of all, not only my signature will go on a loan this size. After me it has to be okayed by the bank president and then a committee, so my signature could be worthless in this case. Secondly, you talk as though I've already agreed to help you. Mister, I don't know you from Adam. This is only our second time meeting; you plead a Dear John case and have already assumed I would help you. Something is amiss here."

"I'm sorry. I've been pushy, but I need a break somewhere. After meeting you, I dreamed this idea of how to make my business work with no harm to anyone."

"You forget my career is on the line. You want me to overlook the truth and approve your request on a pile of lies. I've more to lose here than a night's sleep, and how do you propose to show income for a company that has none?"

"I can bring you profit and loss statements showing an increase in business of X percent over the past few years."

"All falsified, right?"

"It's the only way I know to make my company look profitable."

"I don't think I have it in me to approve a loan based on a bunch of lies. May I add, I'm doing all the giving here. Let's say I agree to help you, what's in this for me?"

"What do you want?"

Sasha, believing she could end this unwanted conversation quickly with an outrageous answer, reflects on her dream of a few nights past. "A Porsche, a black 911 Carrera Cabriolet to be exact."

"I promise you, you will get it," Howard states willingly.

"What?" she says, astonished by his reply. "That's a seventy-one-thousand-dollar car we're talking about."

"Look, Sasha, this loan is so important to me, if that's what it takes, I'll buy it for you once a few pieces are sold."

"I have to admit, I wasn't expecting that reply."

"Does this mean you'll help me?"

"No, it doesn't."

"Will you at least think about it?"

"I'll give it some thought...oh, it's late. I'd better get back."

"All right and thanks for considering what I guess we can call a deal."

"No deal, just simple consideration."

"Fine, I'll contact you later."

"Okay, talk to you later."

As Sasha walks out of the café, an omen occurs. A 911 Carrera Cabriolet passes in front of her. The eerie feeling it brings causes her to stare until it's out of sight.

The next day, after a night of tossing and turning contemplating the offer presented to her, she can barely keep her mind on her work. She's still undecided about what to do. The temptation of getting her dream car without the hassle of large monthly payments is very appealing and whets her appetite of cruising along Virginia City streets, envied by her peers. On the other hand, the possibility of prison turns her stomach. A huge husky woman probably named Bertha would claim her off-limits, drag her into her cell, making her a sex toy.

"I wish I'd not gone to meet Howard. This is too much for me to handle. Being bribed...that's it, a bribe. It's against the law. I should turn him in...maybe not. It was I who asked what I would get out of the deal. Oh, I don't know, I could push the papers through like they're legit. If the shit hits the fan, I could always play dumb. Nope, how would I explain the car? No jury in the world would believe me, even though it's my word against his. There's no proof that we talked other than the card game. Oh shit, the waiter at the café...he blows that. Sasha Fong, listen to you, you sound schizo. I know I can't do it. I'm frightened, I have no guts, and again it's against the law. What else do I need to talk me out of it? When Howard calls, I'll simply tell him I can't help him. It's too risky and besides I'm not that type of person."

No sooner than Sasha finishes her sentence, Howard is making a beeline toward her. Astonished by his sudden appearance, she fumbles with the papers on her desk.

"What are you doing here?" she states in a low voice.

"I came by to see what you've decided."

"Don't you think a decision like this requires more time than, let's see, twenty-and-a-half hours? I told you I would think about it. I didn't mean I'd give it immediate attention."

"I know, but I must have the money in less than two weeks, and you seemed to be on the positive side when you left yesterday. Especially after knowing about your little gift involved."

"You know this could be considered a bribe."

"No bribe. Let's call it a business transaction between associates."

"Look, Howard, this is not an easy decision to make and your added pressure isn't going to make it any easier. I've been up all night with this thing."

"So you have given it some thought."

"Thought only. no decision has been made one way or the other. To be honest, I'm leaning toward not helping you."

"Why?"

"Something like this has to be done discreetly. You popping in here today surely doesn't make it that."

"I don't have to tell you how important this loan is. I gathered some things I thought you should review."

"What are they?"

"Profit and loss sheets for my business."

"Already, you had this planned all along didn't you?"

"I'm just prepared."

"It's cunning the way you have an answer for everything."

"Not really, I'm just making sure everything on my end is in proper order. If all of my information is together, it could help expedite matters."

"Howard, I'm going to need more time to think about this. In the meantime I'll look over these so-called profit and loss sheets to determine if indeed they warrant a loan the size you need."

"Good enough. I'm out of here. I'll be in touch with you later."

"Mr. Normin, I'll contact you."

"That's fair," he says, smiling as he leaves, "and have a wonderful day."

"You do the same, goodbye."

Sasha leans back in her chair and shakes her head in amazement on how pushy Howard is. However, she's intrigued by the papers given to her. After studying them, she finds that everything seems to be in order and that the Far East Import Company shows an eight-percent increase in revenue over the past three years. Its annual yield would be enough to handle the loan requested, but she is uneasy about submitting papers with false information.

Outside, Howard stops at a nearby pay phone. After dialing seven digits the ringing phone is answered by a heavy British accent.

"Hello? Far East Import."

"Boss."

"Yes, Howard. So..."

"I think we may be on our way. I presented the papers to her and according to the way I fixed them, it's almost a sure thing."

"Has she agreed to help?"

"No, she is still unsure but I'm confident the papers will turn her."

"Let's hope you're right. In any case give it a few days, and then present her with a gift."

"What kind of gift?"

"I'll discuss that when you get here."

"I'm on my way, boss, bye."

"Chow."

CHAPTER 9

The Far East Import Company is located between a fish company and a paper factory at the pier. The two-story brick warehouse has a huge sliding metal door and four pane windows that are painted black. Inside on the first floor there are all kinds of artifacts from different cultures dating back two to three centuries. However, these pieces have no significant place in history, as worthless now as they were in their time. The Far East Import Company spent countless hours buying items it'd hoped to be of value. Thus far, their efforts have been wasted. It would need somewhat of a miracle to make it a profitable company.

It's managed by Howard Normin and partially owned by Charles Livingston, a tall elderly Welshman. Howard arrives from his meeting with Sasha confident of the outcome.

"Boss, I'm back."

"How did things go?"

"Very well."

"Can you assure me we'll get the loan?"

"No, but I just know that it will go through. She was surprised to see that we had everything covered."

"Let's hope you're right. These pieces are worth a considerable amount of money...that's good, but this time they have an extra flair."

"Extra flair, what do you mean?"

"These pieces have a legend behind them. This might give them added value and more appeal. If we don't sell them, we could always rent them to museums. They are sure to sell."

"These pieces have a legend?"

"That's what I'm told. I understand a couple of centuries ago during the Yang dynasty a Yang Prince was to marry a Wu Princess to make peace between the two clans. They didn't love each other so the agreement was contingent upon the Wu Empire making seven pieces of armor from the finest metals. These pieces were a helmet, chest and back guard, shield, an arm guard, both leg guards and a sword. Meanwhile, waiting for the pieces to be made the Prince and Princess began dating to get acquainted with each other. Coming from different worlds they were in a constant conflict but through their fights they became closer, began to understand each other's ways and eventually fell in love.

On the wedding day, the pieces were presented to the Yang Prince. All the pieces were handcrafted beautifully. They fit him perfectly, polished to a high gloss—everything was perfect except the sword. Everyone knew that a sword of fine metals was to be folded at least three-hundred times. Knowledge came to the Yangs that it was only folded two-hundred times. This outraged the Yangs. The Emperor negated the wedding. Both the Prince and Princess pleaded their case for the marriage to go on but the Yang Emperor ordered the Wu's banned from the palace. The Prince grabbed the sword and beheaded the craftsman who made the pieces. He swore no one would have the Wu Princess if he couldn't. His rampage started a massive fight. Many people died that day including both Emperors, guards, laymen and his beloved Princess. The only one left standing was the Yang Prince. The armor consequently was passed from generation to generation and rumor has it that whoever puts on the entire seven-piece collection is cursed, doomed to destroy himself and all around him."

"That's a wild story. How much truth is in it?"

"I really don't know."

"Do you believe in legends?"

"No, but sometimes these legends are well-documented."

"Will the public pay money to see old armor?"

"Yes, providing we market them correctly."

"Yeah, but, would they bring in enough capital to pay back the loan we need?"

"I doubt it, that's why we'll sell them, hopefully to more than one buyer. We don't want to be responsible for causing anyone a bloody end, do we?"

"We couldn't do that," he replies, smiling while heading for the second floor.

The upper floor is a huge loft area inundated with dust and cobwebs here and there. There are many unopened crates. Customs stamps from different parts of the world decorate their frames. Most of them are covered with sheets. There are several rows of hanging lights and a patch of pane windows providing light. The others are also painted black.

"Hey boss, any of this stuff up here worth anything?"

"We won't know until we unpack them and set them out down here. I've been meaning to do that but I've spent most of my time tracking those armor pieces. That wasn't easy."

"I have an idea. Is it possible to get a store downtown somewhere? When we unpack this stuff it would be nice if the public could see it. You never know what people will buy. We could possibly recoup some of our money."

"That's true."

"As they say, one man's junk is another man's treasure."

"You know, that's not a bad idea. If we get the loan and after selling some pieces, I'll look into it."

"Oh, you mentioned on the phone to wait a few days, and then present her with a little gift. What were you referring to?"

"Well, you said she's skeptical. I propose that if we give her encouragement, she'll turn our way."

"Well, I sort of promised her a new car if she pushes the loan through."

"Really, and what kind of car might that be?"

"Ironically, one like yours...are you planning to give her yours?"

"No, in a few days I want you to take her my keys. Lead her to believe that the car is already purchased. She surely will push our loan through then."

"I see. Suppose she demands the keys that day? Surely I don't give her yours."

"Right, stall her. Let her know that when the loan is approved, the keys are hers."

"Is there any truth in that? We would have to go out and buy the car she wants."

"Not necessarily."

"Yes, knowing how important the loan is to you, I promised her."

"I'm not trying to sound like a cliché but promises are made to be broken. What can she do, tell the world she was bribed into pushing a loan through for an expensive car? She wouldn't do that; she has too much to lose—her job—as well as her reputation. She would never be able to work in finances again."

"We have to also think about our reputation. An investigation of any sort would put us down the drain. The authorities can confiscate anything we buy with illegal money. It could mean the seven pieces of armor being taken away, and then they'll be placed in the Smithsonian with us receiving no fee at all. Besides it's bad business."

"Bad business, it is our survival. You know the fate of our business relies on these pieces. The investors that have supported us through our rough times are hot on receiving these pieces. In this business you need a killer attitude to survive. I suggest you develop one if you intend to last."

"If she does push the papers through and we do get the loan, would you buy her a Cabriolet convertible?"

"Don't get me wrong, I haven't completely ruled out buying the car, but now I'm not sure it will be necessary."

"Interesting," Howard says under his voice.

"What was that?"

"I said interesting."

"What is?"

"The scheme of things."

"Don't worry about that. Give it a few days and work my plan. Everything will work out fine."

"You got it, boss."

"Now let's see what's in these crates."

They start unpacking the crates and Howard wonders what the outcome of the whole situation will be.

CHAPTER 10

Jason, with time on his hands, has the opportunity to get some neglected things done. While on suspension, he has gone to the dentist, taken care of long needed repairs on his car and fixed the leaky pipe under the bathroom sink. Although he has tried to occupy himself, his efforts are menial. Out of work he feels out of sync knowing that police work is what he does best. The other things he does in the interim give him no real satisfaction or sense of purpose.

Having done everything imaginable around the house—for the sake of sanity—he enters the city for more of a relaxing venture. One of the most enjoyable things he enjoys is shopping for clothes. However, he doesn't buy his clothes like most men; when he shops he hunts for tailors. Ninety-five percent of all garments worn by him are tailored to his exact body dimensions. He likes conservative tailors who design with a slight touch of flair. The feeling of wearing an original is something that drives him. He can walk down the street and not worry about seeing his suit on another body coming toward him. That alone, gives him a sense of freedom.

He is successful in his search, and leaving the measurements for a black double-breasted suit, he exits the shop to return at a later date to pick up the finished product. On the way to his car the sun warms his skin. Turning directly toward the sun with his eyes focused, intent on capturing all of its rays, his reward is green spots that dance in front of him. After they clear it's hard to focus, however, even with the blurry vision he can detect someone at his car with a hanger trying to unlock the passenger door. Jason, surprised, begins to run in pursuit of a boy of no more than thirteen years of age.

"Stop, you're breaking into a policeman's car!"

The youth is clever. He turns the corner, darts and weaves through the congested sidewalk. Jason has more of a difficult time—his larger frame doesn't maneuver easily through the crowd yet he continues his pursuit. Determined, he gives it his all, reflecting on his track years in high school and actually begins to make ground on the youth when in his path a woman appears. In full stride there is little he can do to avoid a collision with her. The impact is hard and real time seems to Jason like slow motion. The force takes the woman off her feet. Her bags fly yards down the sidewalk. With a last effort to avoid any serious injury to her, Jason does a one-hundred-and-eighty-degree turn with her clutched tightly in his arms. They fall to the cement with Jason as a cushion absorbing the impact as their bodies meet the ground, sliding for a small distance. Jason ignores the obvious pain of her weight crashing onto his frame but seemingly can hear the tear of his jacket from the slide.

"Are you okay, Ma'am?"

"I think so...," she says standing, inspecting herself and clothes for damage. "Why are you running down the sidewalk like a madman?"

"I'm sorry Ma'am, I was chasing after a kid who was trying to break into my car."

"It's Ms., you can cut the Ma'am business...my things, look at them. They are everywhere."

"I'll help you gather them."

"That's okay, I can manage. I think you've done enough."

"I insist, it's the least I can do. Our abrupt meeting is due to my inability to maneuver. Please accept my utmost apologies."

"They are accepted, Mr.?"

"Oh, it's Jason Jerrard. You are?"

"Sasha Fong."

"Would it be incorrect to say, nice to meet you? I mean under the circumstances."

"Not at all."

"Are you sure you're okay?"

"Really, I'm fine. How about you?"

"The only thing hurting on me is my ego."

"Your ego shouldn't be hurting. After all you did keep me from being smashed like a pancake."

"I know, but if I can say this without upsetting you, I rather enjoyed our encounter."

"You what?" she states astonished.

"I have to admit that you're a soft woman."

"I'm a soft woman," Sasha replies curiously joking. "Are you sure this wasn't planned?"

"Honestly, I was chasing someone. How would I know you would be coming out of this store?" Compelled by overpowering thoughts, he replies, "If I may be forward, how about having lunch with me?"

"Nice, real smooth. First you knock me down, and then you ask me out. Very unusual."

"Let's call it my way of apologizing to you."

"Where do you plan to go?"

"Does that mean you'll go, and what do you have a taste for?"

"My tastes vary but I don't have a need for anything particular at this moment."

"Ever heard of Rosalina's?"

"Yes, I've dined there on occasion."

"Will that be okay with you?"

"Yes, that's fine. My car is up the street. I need to put these things away. "re we taking both cars, your car or mine?"

"If you don't mind, I'd like to take my car. I need to see what kind of damage the kid inflicted on it."

"That's fine," Sasha remarks, unaware of why she accepted the invitation.

Along with the escort to her car, Jason apologizes again for their collision. Although he considers himself a gentleman, the manners are being poured on heavily but carefully, hoping to make a good lasting first impression. Not knowing this woman, he is compelled to get to know her better. Driven by his nervousness around her, he is determined to find out why.

Sasha is also amazed at their encounter-wondering why she accepted a luncheon with a strange man. Though he is seemingly harmless and polite, when asked to lunch, her immediate mental thought was a definite "no." When that thought verbalized itself to the spoken word, the reply was a direct opposite. Furthermore, to agree to go to the very place where she was stood up last added extra irony to the situation. All of this intrigued her.

On the way to Jason's car, they exchange views on the shops in that particular part of the city.

"I bet that's your car," Sasha states while pointing in the direction of Jason's car. "Is that yours?"

"Which one?"

"The black BMER, am I right?"

"You're right...how did you know?"

"I was looking for a damaged car. It is the only one I see damaged."

"Damaged? Where?"

"Looks like the kid broke your antenna."

"That's a good guess." Jason chuckles. "It's not my antenna. My antenna is electric. That's a coat hanger hanging out my window."

"It would appear that I need to have my eyes checked. My comment about the antenna sounded confidently foolish."

"Not at all, I thought it was cute."

They head for Rosalina's with an immediate task of relaxing with each other but, looming in each other's mind dance all sorts of unanswered questions, each being hesitant of being the first to acknowledge them. Being new to each other, proper timing is essential.

"Jason, look at that. There is a line outside Rosalina's."

"No problem."

"No problem. It's the middle of the lunch hour. We'll definitely have a long wait to be seated."

"Don't worry."

"What are you going to do, flash a badge using it as your authority to jump to the front of the line?"

"Interesting."

"What is?"

"Another good guess. I'm a cop—detective, but I won't use my badge to get inside."

Immediately, she feels as though her sarcastic remark causes the seat to open, dooming her to be swallowed rapidly. She imagines that her hands and feet are waving wildly out of the closing hole, desperate to grab onto anything that will save her from her ill fate. Her feet disappear, then one hand. The other is clawing at the leather seat, crying out for Jason's help.

"I didn't mean to imply," Sasha apologizes.

"No harm taken, I took it as a joke."

"Really, Jason, I was joking."

"I'm not touchy like that so please stop apologizing."

"Okay, but I do feel bad."

"You shouldn't."

Arriving at Rosalina's, Sasha's glimpse is correct. There is a line of people stretching fifteen feet out of the entrance waiting eagerly for their turn to enter. Extreme hunger shows on most of their faces— some of being sized up, visually placed between two slices of bread with a touch of mustard as they stand behind each other smacking their jaws.

"I don't see how we'll get in here anytime soon," replies Sasha.

"Are you ready?"

"Uh...yeah?"

"Be prepared for anything."

"What do you mean?"

Without an answer Jason grabs her by the hand. "Come with me."

Jason passes the outside line. The people look puzzled—some make comments about their jumping ahead of them. Through the first set of double doors there is a crowd of people waiting in the foyer. He pauses for a second.

"Here we go," turning to Sasha, "this is where the fun begins. Excuse me...please excuse me, the lady is pregnant. The lady is pregnant...excuse me...pardon me, Sir."

Sasha's head falls with embarrassment as Jason pushes their way through the crowd. After entering the second set of doors, he finds Alfredo standing at the podium. He walks up to him and whispers into his ear.

"Right this way, Sir," replies Alfredo.

He directs them to Jason's booth as Sasha looks back to see the people waiting are in awe. Seated, Jason begins to smile. Sasha is amazed, amused and embarrassed.

"Nice to see you again, Madam."

"Likewise, I guess after Jason's stunt, I'll be remembered for a long time."

Alfredo smiles. "Mr. Jerrard isn't the character from your last visit here?"

"No, actually we've just met only moments ago."

"That's splendid," Alfredo replies. "Would you like a cocktail, Madam?"

"Wine, white wine."

"Very well, Madam." Alfredo turns to walk away.

"You didn't get his order."

"This is no need, Madam," Alfredo comments while continuing his stride.

"Relax, everything is fine. Tell me, do you drink often?"

"Not really, I'm a social drinker. Let's say I drink on occasion and after being embarrassed like that I think this is a good occasion. What did you say to him?"

"I asked him for this booth."

"But people were waiting."

"Don't worry, I do this all the time. I know the manager."

"Oh, you're a VIP around here."

"Well, somewhat."

"How dare you embarrass me like that?"

"You were embarrassed? Come on, tell me, wasn't that a little exciting?"

"Well...it was different, that's for sure. Do you normally make spectacles of new friends?"

"No, I'm just a kid at heart."

"A menu and wine for the Madam, and here's your coffee, Sir."

"I think I'll have the shrimp salad with extra French dressing."

"Will that be all?"

"Yes, at this moment."

"Very well."

"Jason, why is it that you haven't ordered anything, yet you are being served?"

"I'm a regular here. Ninety-eight percent of the time I order the same thing so they've developed a habit of ordering for me unless I say otherwise."

"I see. Is that why you receive priority seating?"

"Yep. Okay now," Jason states while raising a brow, "let's talk about you."

"Me, I believe detective work is more interesting. A conversation about me can't possibly compare."

"Don't say that...what do you do?"

"I'm a bank manager."

"See, that's interesting, I bet you get all kinds of people, each with different requests."

"You got that right," she replies, thinking of Howard.

"Sasha, I think you're interesting and I hope you feel the same about me, but let's take a different approach to getting to know each other."

"Meaning?"

"Instead of us going through a series of questions in an attempt to prompt answers we hope are pleasing to each other, let's find out those things naturally."

"How exactly do we do that?"

"Just through everyday contact. It'll be more interesting living through you than verbally walking me through how you are or what you like to do."

"I've never done such a thing, but it should prove to be very intriguing."

Their first encounter lasts for hours. Lunchtime turns into early evening and the dinner crowd invades Rosalina's. The table setting changes around them as new faces appear.

"I hate to tell you this but, do you know that it's after five. We have talked for hours," Jason says.

"I thought you didn't want to do that."

"It wasn't my intent. However, I'm not one to run away from a captivating conversation. Also, I'm sure there are many things that I can live through with you. I hope I haven't ruined your day."

"Not really, I didn't have anything planned."

"Tell me the 'not really' part, that's the part I feel guilty about."

"Okay, I didn't have anything planned...so why do you feel guilty?"

"Because of my selfishness. I noticed that the hours were passing, but I let our conversation continue because I enjoyed it so. That falls under the category of selfish."

"You fail to realize that I kept tabs on the time, too. I watched it slip away but things were going so well I didn't say anything."

"Listen, would you like to do something dumb?"

"Like what?"

"Let's go out tonight and cut-a-rug or two."

"Dancing? I haven't danced in eons."

"All the more reason to agree. It will be fun."

"I don't know about that."

"I only ask because I know you don't have any plans tonight."

"I said that, didn't I?"

"Well?"

"Aren't you tired of me by now?"

"Actually, it's refreshing to meet someone like you. Someone I can freely express myself with."

"Don't you think you're rushing things a bit?"

"Am I? I guess I shouldn't be so selfish."

"I'm not saying you are but we just met hours ago. It's not normal for things to happen the way they have."

"Am I allowed to say something corny?"

"Corny? Like what?"

"Normally I don't do things like this but since I met you, I haven't been normal."

"That would be sweet if it weren't a line."

"Don't disregard that statement totally. It holds some truth."

"So, truthfully, tell me what you mean."

"Dancing would be a terrific ending to a great beginning."

I agree with you as well, but, actually I was referring to the 'it holds some truth' comment."

A half-smile forms in one corner of Jason's mouth. He knew that his diversion tactic would not keep his honest feelings from collecting in her ears.

"I've never," Jason states bashfully, "in my life, met someone, asked her to lunch and didn't want the conversation to end. I fear losing everything magical that our meeting has invoked in me."

Sasha stares through Jason for a brief moment, attempting to understand the warm feeling Jason's last sentence brought to her being.

"Where do you have in mind?"

"You pick the place. Wherever we go, I'm sure it will be fun."

"I know of a place on the West Side called Mystiques. They play decent music. You could meet me there at nine-thirty."

"Is that what you prefer?"

"What?"

"Me meeting you there?"

"Yes, I have to get myself together. You know what they say about women getting dressed."

"You just don't know."

"What does that mean?"

"Never mind, let's get out of here."

"Okay."

Jason takes a huge gulp of his coffee, drops a tip on the table and heads for the door. After paying the bill, he thanks Alfredo for his excellent service and they leave. On the ride back to her car, they discuss the last-minute details of their upcoming evening. He walks her to her car, opens the door and watches as she drives out of sight. He drives home with great expectations, knowing that if the evening hours come close to the afternoon ones, it will be a memorable one indeed.

On his race home to prepare for his upcoming date, his mind wanders back to their meeting, one that appears to him as a meeting of happenstance. He smiles as he rethinks their collision, wondering why Sasha has been placed into his life at a point when he entertained no thoughts of meeting anyone. However, their vibes seem to blend well. He has never felt so comfortable with a new person on the first meeting in his entire life.

CHAPTER 11

After Jason showers and puts on a fresh set of clothes, he prepares himself carefully, making sure his nails are clean, his hair is groomed and his beard is shaped nicely. He wears a black double-breasted tuxedo made of worsted wool, black tie and copper cummerbund with matching handkerchief. His patent-leather shoes are highly glossed. After countless trips to the mirror making sure everything is intact, he leaves for Mystiques. Arriving several minutes early for their date, he walks into the lobby only to find that Sasha has already arrived. Spotting her, he makes his way over to greet her.

She's wearing a red sequin dress that sculptures her figure. The dress has more than a moderate cut in the front and a long slit up the side. Walking toward her he views her entire body and his heart begins to race. His eyes take one complete picture of her. He smiles pleasantly but in his mind the picture is being scanned up and down, admiring her almost flawless body. He tries hard to keep his eyes on her lovely made up face but the efforts fail him. His eyes pop out of his head powered by their own will. They dance up, down and around her body in admiration, studying every inch of her frame as he stands there dumbfounded with a silly grin on his face.

"You look absolutely lovely."

"You're quite handsome in your tux also."

"Thank you...you know I figured you'd dress formal."

"You did. Are you trying to figure me out all in one day?"

"No, I guessed after calling here first to see what kind of attire most people wore."

"Can't you stop being a detective for a small while?"

"Sorry, it's a habit...I guess I miss it."

"What do you mean?"

"I'll tell you later, let's enjoy our evening."

They enter the club and all eyes focus on them. It appears on this particular evening they both overdressed. Looking at each other they laugh and take a booth away from the dance floor. The waitress comes over for their order.

"What would you two like to drink?"

Jason motions for Sasha to respond. "I'd like a strawberry daiquiri, please."

"And you, Sir?"

"Strawberry daiquiri...that sounds good. Bring me one also and make mine with no alcohol."

"You want a virgin daiquiri then?"

"No, please, no gin, everything except the alcohol."

Sasha, on the verge of laughing, interrupts, "Jason, most drinks like that, which contain no alcohol are usually called virgins."

"Hmm...virgin daiquiri then. I knew that," Jason replies.

"Sure, you did."

"Really, I've been suffering from a case of CRS."

"CRS?"

"Yes, can't remember shit."

"Fool, I thought something was really wrong with you."

"You'll learn that my sense of humor is strange, very strange."

"I suppose that I will. But you did make a spectacle of yourself."

The waitress turns to leave and Jason's blood rushes to his head.

"Is my face red? I must look like a real one."

"If I had doubts about you drinking before, they've all been erased now. That was cute though. How did you mistake gin for virgin?"

"I don't know...well, you know what they say, the first thing to go are the ears."

"You're a character."

The waitress comes back with the drinks. "Let me guess, you two are newlyweds, right?"

They look at each other in amazement.

"What makes you say that?" replies Sasha.

"Well, first of all you two look so good together and secondly you both have that gleam in your eyes that most newlyweds have."

"Boy, we are married already," says Jason. "Would you believe we just met hours ago."

"Really? You two will have a long life together. It's written all over your faces."

They are unable to speak. Jason pays her for the drinks and gives her a decent tip.

"Do you think she said that because she wanted us to leave a good tip?" asks Sasha.

"It's hard to tell."

They look at each other and smile. Conversing most of the evening, they take time to dance here and there. The disc jockey calls out "last call" as they sit and wonder where the evening has gone.

"Jason, let me ask you something?"

"Yes, anything."

"Why haven't you asked me to dance slow?"

"The right time hasn't arrived."

"The right time, what does that mean?"

"I've been waiting for my nervousness to dwindle some."

"You're nervous? Surely not because of me?"

"I can't say it's because of you but I'm certainly nervous around you."

"That's unbelievable, after talking with you most of the day I've come to believe that you're a strong person. A person like me can't possibly make you nervous."

"I'm not talking about your physical being. I think it has something to do with the aura between us. It comes from somewhere. I don't understand it but I've been this way since our abrupt meeting. Look at me. I look calm on the outside but on the inside I'm a nervous wreck. My stomach is turning flips."

"Okay, get up."

"Why?"

"This is a nice slow song. Let's dance."

"Now? You're kidding me, right?"

"No, you can handle it."

"You know, I've felt less nervous in the line of gunfire. My legs won't move."

"Just stand up, I'll help you. Convert some of that energy you use on fast songs. You're a wizard on those, doing moves I've never seen before. It seems like every eye in the place was on you, both men and women. The more they watched the more you showed yourself and I couldn't help but notice some of your seductive moves."

"That's different. I didn't have to hold you to do that. Besides, it was an individual effort; dancing slow will require us working together. I'm not too good at that."

"As I said, think fast when you dance slow and everything will work out fine."

They stand awkwardly on the dance floor before Jason slowly pulls her into his embrace. He immediately realizes that she's much softer holding her with his free will than forced by their earlier collision. As he smells the fragrance of her perfume, they hold each other not like it was their first real embrace but like it's been rehearsed a thousand times to sheer perfection.

"See, I told you it would be fine."

"Don't talk."

"Should I ask why?"

"It will break my concentration."

"Con-cen-tra-tion, Jason?"

"Yes, I'm concentrating."

"Do I need to know why?"

It happens. His thoughts are interrupted by all the conversation, causing his right leg to shake uncontrollably to its own beat.

"What's that?"

"My leg."

"Why is it trembling?"

"I don't know...it's nervous."

"Would you like to sit?"

"No, I can make it until the song ends."

"You're not putting on an act, are you?"

"At this point I wish I were."

"This is so unusual...come let's sit. I don't think you can handle two slow songs in a row."

"I'm so embarrassed."

"You know, Jason, it's refreshing to have this in reverse."

"Reverse? Are you normally the nervous one?"

"No, most men try to be macho, acting as though nothing in the world bothers them. You have a sensitive side that's cute. To me, macho-ism is a big turnoff. I'm allowed to create my own 'ism,' aren't I?"

"Sure, but I'd like to be able to keep my leg from shaking."

"Don't worry, it's our little secret but do you have any idea why it happened?"

"I think it has something to do with holding you in my arms."

"Surely you've slow-danced before?"

"Yes, but I've never had that reaction so severe before. It makes me think of what I told you earlier about being normal."

Sasha sips her drink with a smile, awed by this strange man. Seeing that he's strong and sensitive is a definite plus.

"Are you ready to leave?" asks Sasha.

"Yes, but may I ask you to tell me something first?"

"What is it?"

"Tell me a secret, something at this point in time that you really think I should know."

"Let's see...the first thing that pops in my mind is my streak."

"You have a lucky streak? Gambling streak...what kind of streak are you referring to?"

"No gambling streak, however I do gamble. Anyway, sometimes I have this uncontrollable jealous streak. I'm not what you call a jealous person but when it hits me, I go into a rage."

"Interesting, you don't seem to have a jealous bone in your body."

"Like I said, it's only on rare occasions. Does that bother you?"

"It can be a factor. I don't think jealousy fits my personality too well."

"How so?"

"I'm more or less a carefree individual. I like to joke and have fun with everybody. Sometimes jealousy takes that the wrong way."

"I don't think harmless fun will make it act up."

"Let's hope not."

"Okay, now, tell me something you think I should know."

"The biggest thing you should know is...my job keeps me very busy. My time gets very limited. That's of course, when I'm working."

"I understand being a detective can be very time-consuming. You probably don't have time for yourself."

"Many times that's so true."

"You are still on the force aren't you? I only ask because you said 'when' you're working."

"Yes, I'll explain that later."

"I like this, getting things in the open. This is very different for me."

"Can I assume you'd like to continue past this evening?"

"That's a safe assumption."

"I like that. You know I've had a wonderful time but this place is closing and we have to get out of here. My question to you is, must this evening end now?"

"I don't know, do you know of any other place that's still open?"

"Are you hungry?"

"I could eat something, I suppose."

"There's a breakfast joint across town. Care to ride with me?"

"Since it's across town, let's go to my place. It's closer. If you want more runny eggs I'll fix them for you."

"You know, I once said that the woman who could fix my eggs exactly the way I liked them would eventually become my bride."

Sasha gives a bashful smile. "Follow me."

"No problem."

They leave. Jason follows her, bewildered over how great this day has been since their meeting.

asha has a third-floor condo, two bedrooms, two baths with a combined living and dining area. Her furnishings are all very modern and stylish.

"This is nice."

"Thank you, it'll do for now. Do you want your eggs like you had them at Rosalina's?"

"One minute on those, let's talk some more."

"Okay, what do you want to talk about this time?"

"Let's talk more about you."

"Me, enough of me for now...answer a question for me. How come you have lots of free time on your hands? Also, what did you mean earlier when you said, 'when' you're working? That was two questions, wasn't it?"

"Yes, two, but no matter how many questions you ask me, I'll answer them. Well, you might say I'm a suspended detective."

"You've been suspended from your job?" Sasha remarks surprisingly. "May I ask why?"

"I was suspended for being a good cop, for doing my job the best I know how."

"That doesn't make sense, explain?"

"I'm good at what I do. I take matters into my own hands so I don't stand for much nonsense."

"Yeah, go on."

"I barged in on a hostage situation. Minutes later, I walked out with the criminal. No one got hurt."

"So, why were you suspended?"

"Because of what the woman said when she ran out."

"Wait a minute, this story was on the news, right? The woman was raged at a detective who told the burglar to kill her. Something of that nature...that was you?"

"In the flesh. I thought I'd done a great job of rectifying the situation but the media, my boss and the victimized woman didn't see it that way. She filed a formal complaint. I've been suspended until the DA does a complete investigation. This is why I have lots of time."

"Tell me, do you think your actions were in line?"

"Yes, I do, I took control of a stalemate situation. If it presented itself to me the same, I'd react the same."

"Even knowing from experience that you'd get suspended?"

"Yes."

"You feel strongly about your actions don't you?"

"It's the only way I know how to be and remain honest with myself. Okay," Jason replies switching places, "it's my turn."

"What is it this time?"

"It's sort of personal."

Sasha takes a deep breath. "Shoot."

"You mentioned in one of our earlier conversations that you were married. What happened?"

"You hit a sore spot this time."

"I understand. You don't have to talk about it if you'd rather not."

"No, I can talk about it. It's a form of therapy. Actually it's not too bad. I met Bill, William when I was a freshman in college. We dated all four years and married after graduation. It was much like a storybook romance. He set out to be a financial analyst and I went into banking. Everything was perfect. Many of our friends were envious. We bought a house and had no problems at all until D-Day."

"First mortgage payments, right?"

"I wish it was that simple...picture this. I leave my doctor's office bubbling, full of joy. I plan the mother of all evenings. A soft romantic candlelight setting, wood burning in the fireplace and I put on the sexiest dress I owned. I prepared all of his favorite foods and purchased his favorite wine. Everything I'd planned had come together. He came home on time as usual and he was impressed by the atmosphere. We ate dinner and talked about our days. After dessert I sprung the most exciting news I'd ever had to tell in my life. With overwhelming happiness in my voice and on my face I told him that I was proud to be having his baby. His head fell between his hands. He sat there silently staring through me."

Sasha pauses to muster enough strength to continue. After an obvious sigh, she recites, "I thought his silence was his means of gathering himself. Soon I discovered that the news wasn't pleasing to him at all. My smile slowly diminished when I noticed the troubled look on his face as he stood up and began yelling at me. He asked me over and over if I were crazy, had I lost my mind. Children weren't part of his plans and he surely didn't want any by me. He didn't want any part of it. The baby we created was hated by him. He demanded that I dispose of it, like it was trash. My heart fell to my feet over him not being excited about our baby, but when he wanted me to kill an innocent life, I became outraged. The evening turned into a shouting match. I saw a part of him I never knew existed. The night ended with him storming out of the house screaming he didn't want any part of a baby."

"You can stop now," Jason says after noticing her emotions drop. "There's no need for you to continue."

"No, I'm okay. The next few weeks or so we didn't have much to say to each other. We existed in the same house as if we lived alone. His only conversation to me was for me to go rectify the situation. I told him that I would do no such thing, so he left me high and dry. Three months pregnant, without a hope or prayer."

"That must've been a horrifying experience."

"Wait, it gets better. On the day he left, I was standing by the front door. For reasons that still boggle my mind I was pleading, begging him to stay. With suitcase in hand, he pushed me aside calling me trash and other horrible names, then he stormed out. The impact of his shove bounced me off the wall. I started hemorrhaging. After the pain stopped I rushed myself to the Emergency Room. The doctor took one look at me, performed a sonogram, then ordered a D&C. I lost it all, my baby, good-for-nothing husband and my faith in the way life is supposed to be."

"That's too much for any woman to handle. I wish that there was something I could do to take away the pain."

Sasha sits with pools of tears in her eyes waiting to drop. Her expression is sad with no indication that happiness ever existed on her face as it had only minutes before. She stares through Jason with her eyes wide, silent in a daze.

"Come back, Sasha. I'm sorry, I should've stopped you. I didn't mean to bring back any pain. Come to me."

Jason takes her from behind into his arms, leans back on the sofa with her resting comfortably embraced. Moments later, her breathing slows and gets heavier as she drifts into a sound slumber. Jason sits there afraid to move, not willing to disturb her peace.

The next morning the phone rings and Sasha's eyes pop open. Half in a daze, she excuses herself from his arms.

"Hello? Yes, I was." Looking back at Jason to review what she'd done, she gives him a puzzled expression. "Let me call you later, goodbye. You're still here?" Sasha questions Jason.

"Good morning."

"Good...morning," a bewildered Sasha responds back. "You're still here? I don't remember what went on after I told you about my ex-husband."

"Well, when you finished telling me about your ex, you weren't emotionally here. I lost you somewhere out there. I grabbed you into my arms and held you as you slept."

"I'm sorry about that, really I am."

"Believe me, no apology needed."

"Did you sleep?"

"No, I tried but I wasn't comfortable enough."

"You poor man."

"I'm fine, just a little stiff and hungry."

"I was supposed to fix you breakfast, wasn't I?"

"That was one of my intentions for coming here last night."

"I'll fix it now, if you like."

"No, I think I'll be going, it's after nine o'clock. Where's your bathroom?"

"Around the corner on the left. You know, you don't have to leave, I don't mind making breakfast for you."

"That's a nice gesture but I'm about to drop. I can honestly say, I'm too tired to eat."

"That's more of a reason to stay. If you're too tired to eat, how can you possibly drive to the country?"

"I'll manage somehow."

"Jason, thank you?"

"Thank me," Jason replies picking up her sincerity. "For what?"

"Respecting me. I was emotionally unstable last night. Thanks for not taking advantage of me when I was at my weakest."

"That's not my style. Besides, we're off to a terrific start; why ruin it with a cheap attempt?"

"I appreciate that."

"No thanks necessary."

After freshening up Jason comes out of the bathroom to begin his goodbyes. Sasha appears sexier than ever. She has changed clothes; the red sequin dress doesn't drape her body any longer. Instead, she wears a huge men's shirt covering her lace panties and bra. It falls midway between her thighs, buttoned high to reveal the beginning of her cleavage.

"My, you've changed," Jason says playfully.

"After sleeping all night in that dress, I couldn't stand it any longer. I grabbed the first thing I could find."

"No explanation needed, this is your home. Are you okay now?"

"I'm much better, thank you."

"Good, I'll be leaving now...I'll give you a call later."

"No, that won't be possible."

"Oh, I thought things went well. Am I the only one assuming this?"

"We did and again your assumption is correct."

"What is it then?"

"You must be tired. You're not thinking like a detective now. Do you realize that we've spent almost twenty-four hours together and we haven't exchanged numbers?"

"You're right! Let's correct that now before I make a drastic mistake by walking out of here without any way to contact you. I wouldn't come here without you knowing of my arrival in advance."

They exchange telephone numbers, and then Jason gives her a polite kiss on the cheek. Surprisingly, Sasha expected a more passionate kiss but didn't question his action. Assuring her that he'll be in touch, he walks down the stairs to his car and suddenly stops. A wide grin appears on his face as he turns around headed back to Sasha's place only to find her standing in the threshold with the door wide open. The light shining from inside peers through her thin top and creates a silhouette of her body that suddenly awakens his adrenaline. Jason blushes internally while wondering if she can see externally.

"Yeeesss," she says teasingly.

"Why were you watching me?"

"I wasn't watching you. I happened to glance out the window and I saw you turn around. Did you come back for the breakfast?"

"No, I came back to ask you something."

"Yes, I will."

"Boy, that was easy."

"Okay, what's up?"

"How would you like to take a trip with me?"

"Where?"

"To the beach...actually via my mom's place."

"You want me to meet your mother?"

"Actually, you'll meet both of my parents."

"Already? I haven't known you a complete day yet. Don't you think it's a bit premature?"

"If it will make you feel better, we will say it's an unofficial visit. I'd like to take you to the beach and I might as well say hello to Mom while I'm there."

"When are you leaving?"

"This afternoon—that'll give us Saturday evening and most of the day Sunday."

"Where would we be staying? Not at your mother's, I hope."

"At a hotel on the beach. I'll get a room facing the ocean."

"Might I ask, where I'd be sleeping?"

"Don't worry, you won't have to sleep with me. I just want to get away for a while. Please come."

"I just think it's a bit soon to be staying in a hotel with you. We're moving too fast."

"Is that so bad? This is life. Things of this nature happen only once in a lifetime. Two people meeting under bizarre circumstances and instantly feeling drawn to each other."

"Is that the way you feel?"

"Yes, I don't know why. Even though my entire being is willing to go with the flow."

"I'll go, a small trip would be nice. I trust that you will be also."

"You're safe." Jason's hand rises. "Scout's honor."

"That's not how the Boy Scouts do it," she says after a quick glimpse of his hand. "That's a...a 'Star Trek' thing. You should say something like, 'Live long and prosper'."

"I'm caught, also happy that you can find some humor in it, but, I promise you'll be safe."

"Pick me up...shall we say about four-thirty.

"Fine, I'll see you then. Goodbye."

"Goodbye."

CHAPTER 13

They arrive at Jason's parents' home after somewhat of an exhausting drive, but one that proved to be enchanting. Throughout the three-hour trip Sasha endeavored to keep him alive and alert with knock-knock jokes and constant horseplay. Jason is relieved to find someone like her, someone not stuffy, and someone who isn't afraid to have a good time. The drive opened his eyes to a refreshing side of her. This side matches his composition best.

"Sasha, do me a favor. On the way back, don't tell knock-knock jokes."

"Come on, they weren't all bad. I received good laughs from you several times—maybe you're right, you have a very unusual laugh."

"I only laugh like that when someone is striking."

"Listen to what you're saying. What's that about my knock-knock jokes?"

"I'll give you credit for a few. Are you ready for this?"

"Wait a minute, the last time you said something this general, I all of a sudden became pregnant. Are you about to pull a prank?"

"No, I mean meeting my parents."

"I'm as ready as I'll get."

Jason enters the house calling out, "Hello, guess who the wind blew in?"

A voice coming from the kitchen cries, "Is that my baby I hear?"

"No, it's your youngest son," he states while turning to Sasha. "She has a habit of not letting me grow up."

"All mothers are like that. Mine does the same thing."

"You know you'll always be my baby...either you've developed an alter ego or you have someone with you."

"Part two is the correct answer. Mom, this is Sasha. Sasha, meet my mom."

"I'm pleased to meet you, Mrs. Jerrard."

"Very nice to meet you."

Mrs. Jerrard is in her early seventies with few wrinkles and a frame appearing younger than her years of age. Tiny black moles on her neck seem to be her only sign of aging.

"And to what do I owe the pleasure of this visit?"

"We're on our way to the beach so I thought we'd drop by to say hello to two of my favorite people. Where's Pop?"

"Doing his usual."

"He's lying down on the den sofa with the TV on. I'll bet the TV is watching him."

"You're right. He is sleeping."

"He hasn't changed."

"I'm up! I'm up! What's all the fuss in here?" Mr. Jerrard says. He's a man in his late sixties with salt-and-pepper hair. He's a quiet person with a Southern accent and country ways.

"Pop-a-san," Jason greets while hugging his father.

"Howdy, howdy, howdy."

"Pop, Sasha; Sasha, my pop."

"Hey, hey, hey."

"Hello, Mr. Jerrard."

"You'll have to excuse my pop. He talks in threes."

"I've been killing your father with the bones."

"Sasha, do you know what she's talking about?" Jason asks.

"Can't say I do. What are bones?"

"They're dominoes. There's a battle between the three of us to see who the best is," Jason explains.

"Oh, I see."

"It looks like my pop is losing his touch."

"I let her win a few to keep her happy," Mr. Jerrard says.

"You both need a lesson from me."

"Well, let's play," Mr. Jerrard suggests.

"I don't have time today. We are on our way to the beach. The next time I'm down I'll show you how the younger-generation Jerrards play."

"Jason, I see where part of your personality is derived," Sasha says.

"Grab a chair, big mouth...get the bones, let's play."

"I can't stay. I came down to entertain Sasha."

"Jason, you can play if you'd like."

"No, you don't understand, it's an all night affair when the three of us play. Besides, I have to find someplace to stay at the beach."

"Son, at least stay for dinner," Mom suggests. "It's almost finished."

"Is that okay with you, Sasha?"

"That's fine."

They enjoy a wonderfully cooked dinner and engage in small conversation after dessert. Late evening has arrived.

"Mom, Pop, we have to be going now."

"Okay, I'm glad you stopped by, even if it was for a short while. Now I can get down to business and put a whipping on Ladye J."

"Don't be too hard on her, okay, Pop."

"It has been a pleasure meeting both of you."

"It's been very nice to meet you," replies Mrs. Jerrard. "Jason, let me have a word with you before you go."

"Excuse me, Sasha."

They leave the kitchen for a private talk in the living room.

"Now son, is there any seriousness with this one?"

"I can't tell at this point but things have been terrific since we met."

"How long have you two been dating?"

"I wouldn't say we're dating because I've known her all of a day and a half."

"A day and a half," she whispers, "and you bring her here."

"That's just how well things are going. I can't explain it but since our meeting I've been compelled to have her near me."

"It must be something because the other two ladies you've brought here had a time span of four and five months before I met them."

"My mental state was different with them."

"Seriously, are you sure she's not just another attempt to help you get over your past?"

"I'm sure, those days are over."

"And she isn't just another pretty face."

"No, Mother," Jason responds to the drilling.

"Good, she seems very nice. Try to hold on to this one."

"That's my intention at this point."

"What is she?"

"She's a bank manager."

"That's not what I mean."

"Mom, you know, race, creed or color doesn't matter to me, so the correct answer would be, she's someone that I'm attracted to."

Jason's father comes out of the kitchen to interrupt. "All right, boy, this girl is waiting for you."

"Mom, I have to get going."

"Okay, I'm glad you dropped by, I'll see you later. Sasha, please come back again and son, you remember what I said."

They leave with Jason feeling that the dinner was a success.

"It's a twenty-five-minute drive to the beach. I know a hotel that I'm sure you'll enjoy."

"You're the host, you choose."

"If you don't like it we can see what else is available on the strip."

"Okay." Sasha sighs, showing a bit of impatience. "How long are you going to make me wait?"

"You're waiting for?"

"Tell me what the little conference with your mom was about."

"Oh, that...," he says, smiling to himself. "She asked me about our meeting. That kind of stuff."

"I knew that the conversation was about me."

"Did it make you feel uneasy?"

"Slightly, when things of that nature happen, it makes you wonder about the tone of the conversation."

"Nothing bad was said about you."

"Well?"

"She did say that you appeared to be sweet and that I should hold on to you."

"She's a charming woman and what a great taste in character she has."

"Patting your own back these days?"

"Just kidding. Tell me, how old is your mother?"

"I don't know exactly. I think that she is in her seventies. "Jason, you're lying. Your mother is not that old."

"Would I lie about something like that? What purpose would it serve?"

"Your mother is seventy, I can't believe it. She looks good. I hope when I'm her age I look as good and healthy as she does. She still has her figure."

"I'm sure you will. You don't look a day over twenty-nine," Jason responds playfully.

"Like most women," Sasha jokes, "I'm twenty-nine and holding."

They check into the Grand Finale Hotel, Virginia Beach's finest, most luxurious hotel on the strip. The lobby has long crystal chandeliers hanging from its ceiling. Huge oil paintings—copies of Van Gogh and Picasso—decorate its walls. The furnishings are from the French Revolution era. The only room available to his liking is on the eighth floor with a balcony facing the beach.

"Jason, how can you afford this?"

"The room doesn't cost too much."

"Yeah, but you're suspended."

"That's with pay," Jason adds in his defense.

"Still, the room is quite a bit. Detectives make a good living?"

"We do okay. I sometimes do things I can't afford."

"Why do you do them?"

"It's a bad habit I guess. Something I learned from my mom."

"Are you trying to impress me?"

"Don't take this the wrong way but I'll never try to do that. I probably will say and do things that will lead you to believe that but they were done because I felt a desire to express myself in the manner, not just to impress you."

"You mean, like bringing me here."

"Exactly, I figure if you're impressed and or flattered in the process then it falls in my favor."

"I'll say it again, you're an unusual man."

"Okay, what would you like to do now?"

"I want ice cream."

"Ice cream? That's an odd request. What flavor do you want?"

"Actually, I'd like a banana split. Would you like to share one with me?"

"Oh, no. I once shared a banana split with a woman and I would swear to you that she had three spoonfuls to my one. It was gone before I finished my second swallow."

"Come on, Jason. You're stretching that a bit."

"Maybe a little but she had the majority of it...I have an idea."

"What might that be?"

"Let's go down to the lobby. There's an alley called Walking Through the Past. It has some gorgeous duplicates of the most cherished paintings throughout the past centuries—some dating back eight centuries, or we can go walk on the beach."

"At this hour?"

"Yes, it's the best time to go. It's roman...ah, the most relaxing."

"No, no, you know I'll not let you get away with that. Finish it."

"I wasn't saying anything."

Sasha gives him one of those looks. A look of "whom are you kidding" as her hands rest on her hips.

"Okay, walking on the beach at night is romantic."

"Under all that strong will and silliness there is a romantic side. That's sweet."

"I'd like to think so."

"Can we get a bottle of champagne?"

"And who's to drink it?"

"We are. It's part of the romance."

"I'm afraid."

"Nothing scares you, Jason."

"I'm afraid of the effect that it will have on me."

"What do you mean? Getting drunk?"

"No, surprisingly, I have a high tolerance for alcohol."

"What then?"

"Picture this scenario. There was a woman whom I was dating. One night we went out and she had three or four mixed drinks. Then she asked for a bottle of champagne. I shouldn't have but I bought it. She drank most of it; she only shared it with a friend who dropped by the table. She poured the last glass and I asked her if we could leave. She insisted on finishing that glass before we departed, then proceeded to sit there for minutes running her finger around the rim of the glass, all along staring at me. I asked her again to leave. She just continued stroking the glass. I politely removed her hand, took the drink, then let my head fall back and drank it straight down. Fast, too," Jason boasts. "I got our coats and took her home but when I got back to my place it hit me. I got in bed and my eyes popped open and this strange sensation hit me hard."

"You threw up?"

"No, I lay there in a mood for a two- or three-day love-making session. Excuse my language, but to put it more properly, it would have been a serious fuck. No matter how hard I tried to sleep I couldn't."

"You went through all of that to tell me that champagne makes you horny."

"I believe that's what I intended," Jason replies somewhat bashfully.

Sasha chooses the beach. They walk up and down the beach holding hands with their shoes in the other. His playfulness begins to shine by chasing her down the beach while threatening to throw her into the water. They run on the sand in a childlike way, forgetting the world around them. After catching her, he picks her up into his arms and walks to the water's edge.

"This is my favorite spot," he says. "Right here where the water breaks, just missing my feet." He sets her down, takes her hand and they take their place on the sand. "This is where everything comes true...listen...one could lose themselves here."

"What am I listening for?"

"The breaking waves. If you listen long enough, it automatically cleanses your mind of all thought. It's nature's way of hypnotism. When that happens, anything is possible. All your dreams, your fantasies materialize and play as if they were on a silent screen. You know that it's only playing in your mind but as you listen and fall deeper to its powers, you'll profess you're living it on the horizon."

"You sound passionate about this experience," Sasha relays with a hint of skepticism.

"Of course, the down side is if you're suppressing unwanted thoughts, it has a way of bringing them forward."

They sit welcoming the silence between them and become disillusioned by the long quiet moments before their conscious thoughts are consumed by the soothing tranquil sound of the crashing waves. Over and over the waves ride in, creating an endless whisper, each timed to perfection, each breaking precisely as the other is on its way out sending a cool mist across their faces. For the moment, all other sounds are nonexistent, filtered out by nature's charisma. They are frozen in time, locked in by their self-contained solitude with the only escape being a place known by all men as reality. Jason drifts back to the real world and glances at Sasha.

"Sasha...Sasha, you can come back now."

"Huh? Did you say something?"

"I've been calling you for two minutes."

Her mood has changed from playful to melancholy. Her voice reflects a tone of a person who is feeling the effects of a glass of wine.

"Wow, I was out there, I don't believe it. It's like nothing I've experienced. It's like..."

"No need to explain," he interrupts, "I felt the same when I first experienced it."

"How long have you been doing this?"

"Quite awhile. I practically lived here when I resided in the area."

"I don't think I'll ever forget this."

"I'm sure you won't. I've come down in the past and used it to help me with difficult cases."

Jason places his arm around her, holding her near. Staring at her under the full moon which reflects brightly in her eyes, he kisses her softly on the lips attempting to disguise the yearning for more, a more passionate kiss, one filled with the exuberance his heart feels. Conceding to the fire burning within him, Jason administers a forceful, aggressive, heated kiss. Sasha responds positively. Her kiss is returned with acceptance as her mouth opens seemingly devouring Jason's manly ways. Falling back into the sand in a tight embrace, their feet become drenched by the incoming waves that once soothed their minds.

Jason comes to his knees and looks at her with overwhelming lust, only to discover that same desirous expression occupying Sasha's face. She pulls him closer, pecks him tenderly on the lips, then suddenly pushes him back into the breaking waves. Immediately his clothes absorb the water and she runs off down the beach. The pursuit begins again, this time on the water's edge. With revenge in mind, Jason scoops her into his arms and walks waist high into the ocean.

"Don't put me down," Sasha pleads. "I don't want to get wet."

"It's too late for begging. You got me wet and now I'll return the favor."

"No, please! You walked out here on your own. What about our clothes?"

He disregards her rebuttal and takes a leap into the air, throwing his legs in front of him. The water swallows them instantly. They are unseen for a small moment.

Sasha plunges from the depths first, pleasingly bewildered, stating, "Jason, I don't believe you, look at me. My hair!"

He rises from the water. "Are we a pair or what?"

"I can't believe you did that."

"Wasn't that fun?"

"Yeah, very different but we're going to be the spectacle of everyone's eyes when we return to the hotel."

"If they look, I'm sure they'll be jealous."

"Of what?"

"Us, because we had a good time. When was the last time you acted like this?"

"Probably never."

"I say, enjoy the moment and let the childlike heart burst through all that adulthood."

"Everything about you is unreal."

"I'm an illusion—everything about me is."

"No, this moment we've created is real. Very real."

They stand together in the water. Jason places her arms around his waist, pushes her long wet hair out of her eyes and kisses her fiery lips. Embraced, their wet cool clothes are becoming increasingly warmed by their ever-rising body temperature.

"You are incredibly beautiful," he says, looking at her from arm's length. "Seeing you under the moonlight creates shadows Picasso would love."

"That's sweet."

"The moon also provides enough light to enable me to see your high beams."

"My what?"

He looks directly at her nipples standing tall and erect. She quickly covers them.

"You're embarrassing me."

"I'm not trying to, it's admiration."

They lie down on the shore kissing, rolling on the beach, undisturbed by the sand or the breaking waves that continue to wet their bodies.

"This has been a terrific day," Sasha says.

"It's been the most enjoyable two days I've had in years. Thank you for helping take away a few sour feelings."

"Something has been bothering you. What is it?"

"Let's not ruin this evening with that. However," Jason pauses, "Let's get back before we both come down with pneumonia."

Once settled in the room an eerie feeling looms in the air like a morning fog. They both have ignored the fact that the room has just one king-sized bed and now they are suddenly faced with the reality of the sleeping arrangements. While drying their bodies and hair, Sasha is the first to speak of their predicament.

"Jason, there's a problem."

"No problem, you can have the bed," Jason replies, as if he had the same thought.

"You're a doll, but that's not what I'm talking about. I only brought enough clothes for tomorrow. I wasted an outfit on the beach. If we go out again, I'll be putting on my outfit meant for tomorrow. Are we going out again?"

"Not unless you want to do something, I've had an exhausting day."

"Would you object to me walking around in a towel?"

"If yes 'flows' out of my mouth, I give you permission to admit me to a mental institution. Better yet, I'll admit myself. Seriously, I've no objections if you don't mind my drooling."

"I figure it can't be any worse than that shirt I wore this morning. Now, if you give me the bed, where would you sleep? There's no sofa."

"Give me a pillow and the comforter and I'll be fine."

"You don't have to do that, you can sleep in the bed. I trust you. Scout's honor," Sasha recites while delivering a symbolic Vulcan hand gesture.

Jason chuckles. "I appreciate that but I prefer to take the floor."

"Why? I should be safe. You didn't have any champagne."

"True, however, I'm a cuddle person when I sleep with someone. In the middle of the night I probably would grab you and form the fetal position."

"That's my favorite position. I enjoy the secure feeling it gives me."

"More of a reason not to sleep with you. Number two, I sleep naked."

"Nude? Why?"

"It has something to do with freedom."

"Oh...are you afraid of me?"

"It's more of I'm afraid of me. Let's say it has to do with timing. I'll explain later but for now let's get some sleep. The sandman is calling me something awful. Be advised that part two comes tomorrow."

The room darkens and Jason avails himself to the floor, getting as comfortable as possible while she crawls between the sheets.

"Sasha, I forgot something," as he gets up and avails himself bedside and gives her a very passionate kiss—an overwhelming breathtaking kiss that turns her breathing heavier. The next kiss is less passionate but a well timed one, placed softly on the forehead, creating an equal effect on her just the same. "Goodnight."

"Goodnight, Jason."

Jason settles back on his pallet. Sasha's eyes gaze him intensely, watching his journey into slumber.

"You can stop staring now."

"How could you tell without opening your eyes?"

"Lucky guess."

"No, really, tell me."

"I just sensed that you were."

"Goodnight again."

"Nite."

Early the next morning Jason awakes with only brief moments of darkness remaining. Excited and hurried, he wakes Sasha.

"Get up gorgeous, we don't have much time."

"Its morning already," Sasha replies without opening her eyes.

"Not quite, but move fast, we can't miss this."

Her eyes open slowly, "It's barely dawn. What could we possibly miss at this hour?"

"The sunrise," Jason confesses enthusiastically. "You've probably seen it rise in Virginia City but it can't compare to watching it rise over the ocean."

"You're serious?"

"Yes, very. Hurry!"

"I need time to get myself together. My hair, my makeup."

"Trust me, you'll be fine."

She runs to the bathroom and throws a little water on the face. After a quick brush of her teeth she puts on clothes and they again head for the beach.

"It's chillier now than last night," Sasha says, rubbing her forearms for warmth.

"Even with dry clothes on?"

"It was a romantic moment. I suppose that's what warmed me. This time it will be the sun."

"Don't you find watching the sunrise romantic?"

"Yes."

"I believe we're watching God at his best. The colors are magnificent."

"Brilliant is a better word."

"We are watching an awakening, when all things created come to life."

They stand looking over the horizon as night magically turns into day. Gray tones transform into shades of orange and red, illuminating the clouds.

"Do moments like this last forever?" she asks.

"In your mind they can last a lifetime."

"Yes, but will you change?"

"Change is the only thing certain in this world but these kinds of things make up my character...my being. They belong to my soul and that can't be sold short."

"These past few days have been extremely enjoyable ones. I haven't had this much happiness in a long time. I hadn't allowed myself to feel but you make me see that feeling doesn't have to be done with caution. I thank you for that. I hope these words aren't ones to make you fear me but I feel something for you. I don't know what or how much but feelings are there. It's hard for me to believe I'm saying this because I've never been one to believe in whirlwind romances. Therefore, my actions since we met have been a total shock to me."

"Much of what you've just shared we have in common. For me it was instant; the moment I helped you up I knew that the collision triggered something. Instantly I felt I could care for you. I do now, and like you—the degree is unknown. Let's hope we can grow into a bountiful long-lasting relationship."

"I'll kiss to that."

They kiss under the now-risen sun, more passionately than before, with more emotion and greed than the previous night. The seemingly never-ending kiss is disturbed by simultaneous actions. Sasha's stomach roars as Jason's leg begins to shake.

"What was that?" They both ask.

"Your stomach!" "Your leg!" both respond together.

"My leg will stop when I let you go."

"No, hold me. I don't mind it. I never knew I could feel this way again."

"Your stomach will quiet when it's fed," Jason replies as he kisses her on the forehead. "How about some breakfast?"

"It's early; would the kitchen be open now? Before we eat I must get myself together."

"In that case we'll have breakfast delivered to the room. We can eat it on the balcony."

"I'd like to take a shower first. I need to rinse the salt water out of my hair and off my body. It's beginning to make me itch."

"Me, too. I guess we should have showered last night."

"Yes, apparently we were both too exhausted for that and settled for just drying ourselves off."

Back in the room Jason places the call for breakfast as Sasha grabs a few things and heads for the bathroom. Afterwards he sits on the bed, content with the sunrise venture and listens to her movements in the bathroom.

A few minutes pass before he hears, "Jason, look into my bag and bring me the comb, please."

After locating the comb, he walks into the steam-filled room. Behind the shower curtain is the woman he has undressed with his eyes many times and fantasized about while sitting on the beach and all his manners will allow him to do is reach between the wall and the shower curtain to pass her the comb.

"Here."

She grabs his wrist, holding him captive and tenderly bites his fingers.

"Thanks, without it I'll never get the tangles out of my hair. Are you going to take a shower, too?"

"Yes, a hot shower would be nice."

"I'll save you some hot water—or would a cold one suit you better now?"

"As big as this hotel is, I doubt that the water will run cold and I don't believe in cold showers. They make matters worse."

"May I ask you something?"

"Yes, go right ahead."

"Personal?"

"Anything."

"Do you like making love?"

The unexpected question stuns Jason greatly. His mouth opens to reply but nothing is echoed except the hard swallow that sounds as he attempts to regain himself.

"Jason, are you still in here?"

"Yes."

"Why didn't you answer?"

"I was thinking."

"That's something you have to think about?"

"No, you caught me off guard with that one...Yes, I do."

"I thought I'd have to wonder about you," she replies while turning off the water. Jason's eyes widen with anticipation. "Since you're in here, pass me a towel."

He hangs the towel across the shower rod and hurries out of the room. Minutes later Sasha exits the bathroom.

"It's all yours now."

Jason begins his soothing hot shower with his mind paralyzed by a picture of Sasha standing in the very same place with lather trailing down her body, between her legs, finally falling from the hairs of...but his joy is disturbed by Sasha.

"Do you mind if I show you what it's like?"

"What are you talking about?"

"And you won't get mad, right?"

"Mad about what? What are you up to?"

"It's time to initiate you to the cold shower club."

"The what? Sa...sha?"

"It only hurts for a second."

In a quick motion, Sasha places one leg on the outside of the bathtub, pulls herself up with the assistance of the shower curtain and dumps a glass of cold water on top of his head. The chill is instant, leaving trails of goose bumps as the water drains through his hair, down his chest and back. He quickly ducks under the shower's stream while she laughs endlessly to the sound of the screams and quivers of his dilemma.

"That was cruel. That's right, laugh now. When I get out you'll get yours. It's definitely on now."

"That is payback for dumping me in the ocean last night. Admit it, that was a real head rush. I now make you an honorary member of the cold shower club."

"And what are the benefits of such a club?"

"That's my secret."

"Give me a hint."

"Oops," Sasha says upon hearing a knock on the door. "Got to go, that must be our breakfast."

The delivery man wheels in the breakfast cart and Sasha directs him to place the food on the balcony's table. Jason enters the room dressed and tips the delivery man.

"Shirt and tie for breakfast?"

"Well...," Sasha states with a devilish grin, "Let's eat."

"I thought you'd see it my way...I'm glad this is here, I'm starving this morning. The shower has made me hungrier."

"Let's eat. The food can't stay warm too long out here on the balcony."

"It smells good."

"A hotel this elegant should have great food."

"Unless they spend their money on decor instead of quality chefs."

"There isn't much wrong one can do to breakfast food."

"You'd be surprised."

During breakfast, Jason drifts into a stare while intently glimpsing at her dreamy-eyed. With a pleasant expression on his face he searches to reach her soul, wondering whether deep down she's as perfect as the past few days would indicate. Staring continually as if it were a form of hypnotism, Sasha slides into a trance of her own. They gaze with no spoken words; periodically a smile appears on their faces. This lasts for moments, only to be broken by the faint sound of a blowing horn coming around the building's corner.

"I'm sorry for staring at you. Maybe it's the aura of the moment but I saw something I'd overlooked."

"What can you possibly find by staring at me?"

"You're beautiful. Your natural beauty is fresh," Jason confides. "Looking at you without any makeup, I see warmth. However, I didn't find exactly what I was looking for but that will surely suffice."

"What was your original intent?"

"I wanted to find your soul to determine if you're real."

"I'm real. All of my actions since our meeting have been sincere. There's no searching required when the answer is sitting directly across from you. Was your search clouded by doubts infiltrating your mind?"

"No, the deeper I got, I saw our events being played in reverse order. You dumping cold water on me, our escapade on the beach last night, even back to our collision. These visions brought joy and happiness. I smile just thinking about it. I quit searching because the journey back was enjoyable."

"You're a psychic now?"

"Just weird at times."

"May I ask you a heavy question?"

"Will it break my back?"

"Yours, I doubt it. I gather from your conversation that you think I'm attractive. My mental being as well as my physical, right?"

"That's correct."

"Do I turn you on or even excite you in some way?

Jason fills his lungs with air, sits straight in his chair and locks his eyes with hers and delivers a seductive, "Unbelievably so."

A warm smile spreads across Sasha's face. "Are you intimidated by me?"

"Not at all."

"If that's true then why haven't you tried to do more than kiss me? You haven't even attempted to fondle my body. Would you like to make love to me or do you feel it's too soon?"

"Wow, that was a question, a statement and two questions in one sentence. I'll answer in reverse." Jason pauses, and after a careful thought, evenly delivers, "I don't feel it's too soon because everything about us has been abnormal. It's been one continuous high. I care for you enough and feel comfortable enough to be intimate with you at this early stage. I've seen indications that you feel the same."

"I do."

"Obviously, next would be 'yes,' and...the timing hasn't been right. This may sound strange but my body has to wait for the proper time."

"Who or what tells your body when it's the proper time?"

"My mind."

"And who tells it?"

"No one, I just know."

"You're strange in a cute kind of way."

"One would think that...so let me tell you what the plans are before we return to Virginia City."

"Jason, if you don't mind, I'd like to leave soon."

"How soon?"

"As soon as we finish this meal."

"That soon, huh? Mine is cold now. I'm through, but, why the sudden rush?"

"I want to take some time to stand back, observe and figure out our true direction. It's true, while we're riding this roller coaster, things are fantastic and I want more, more, more but I need to figure out what happens when the ride ends. How would I feel then? We can't possibly keep this pace up forever."

"True, however, things don't have to change and our feelings should grow providing we never stop courting. Courtships can be as it has been for us or they can be simple. The act of courtship makes a new relationship grow. If two people carry courtship through the years, how can they fail?"

"I understand that, I just want to stand beside myself and ask me if all of this is actually a dream. I never cared to this degree so rapidly in my life."

"I believe I understand what you're saying. Realistically our relationship is hard to conceive...we can leave as soon as we pack."

The packing is fast and they vanish from the luxurious surroundings into the already hot and humid morning. The return trip back to Virginia City is quite different from the drive down. Instead of knock-knock jokes and humor, Sasha is silent, melancholy, totally opposite from before.

"Sasha, are you okay?"

"I'm fine, just thinking."

"Tell me, have I offended you?"

"Really, you've been great, a perfect gentleman. It's hard to believe anyone better could exist."

"You're so quiet; it makes me wonder if something is bothering you."

"No, I'm just in limbo. I'm standing on a mighty high pedestal, dreaming how wonderful my life has been since meeting you. Things couldn't be better."

"What are your dreams?"

"I'm dreaming of a continuous life of this—I feel like crying."

"Please tell me what's bothering you," Jason states firmly but filled with concern.

"Nothing."

"Why would you cry?"

"Sometimes when I'm extremely happy I cry tears of joy. Every now and then in the midst of lovemaking I cry."

"How does your partner react? I'd panic thinking that I'd hurt you."

"I suppose it could catch someone off guard. In fact, it does. I've only done it twice, both times with my ex. The first time he made all sorts of apologies to me. For what, I don't know."

"He was probably frightened by it."

CHAPTER 14

Arriving at her condo, Jason leaves the car running and opens her door.

"Aren't you coming up?"

"I thought I'd drop you off so you could be alone to continue your thoughts."

"True, but, I'd like you to come up first and take a rest before driving out to the country."

"Coffee?"

"Yes, I'll fix coffee."

"Sold, let me park the car."

Inside she relaxes. Her shoes come off as she enters the door and she throws her bag on the sofa.

"Boy, I'm sticky," she says. "Fresh air is great but it makes your skin feel awful."

"I feel okay."

"I'm sure you do. The only things exposed on you are your hands and face."

"I do have that outdoor smell in my clothes so my shirt and tie aren't a direct benefit."

"Would you like your coffee now?"

"When you're ready, it's no rush. Well, we made it to and from our first adventure in one piece."

"How about that? If you don't mind," Sasha states, changing the thought, "I think I'll take a shower while the coffee brews."

"I'm patient. Make yourself comfortable; after all, this is your home."

"I'll be right back then."

Sasha enters the bathroom and leaves a three-inch crack in the door allowing Jason to hear the water running and its interruption as she enters the shower's stream. He toys with the idea of returning the cold shower initiation but only stands at the door for a few moments before deciding to speak.

"Sasha, a question for you."

"Did you say something, Jason," Sasha asks loudly, attempting to compensate for the shower. "Are you in here?"

"I'm standing at the door."

"Come closer, I can barely hear you," Sasha instructs.

"I came to ask you," Jason says nearing the tub. "Do you like making love?" Sasha remains silent. "Did you hear me?"

"Yes."

"Why didn't you answer? Since you asked first I wouldn't dream that you'd be stuck for an answer."

"I was smiling to myself," Sasha confesses. "What makes you ask?"

He responds to her question by sliding the shower curtain at the rear of the tub and pops his head in out of the water's reach. Her eyes widen-several shades of red take over her pigment. Not only does a radiant glow illuminate from her face but from all parts of her body as she stands there dumbfounded, reaching for some sort of reply.

"See...something you like?" Sasha questions while stumbling over her words.

Again, Jason is silent as he steps into the tub, fully clothed, shoes and all. He embraces her tenderly as if he is starving, as if her lips are the only source of food and gives her a long hard kiss.

"You're crazy, you'll ruin your clothes."

"Tap water has to be better than the saltwater of last night."

"But why shower with your clothes on?"

"It's safer this way."

"Safer for whom?" He kisses her on the neck behind the ear. "Not for me, that's for sure."

Jason runs his hand slowly down the crevice in her back, caressing it gently, proving that the warm water isn't enough to keep the chills from running down her spine. His falling hand passes her round firm buttocks to the rear of her thigh. Lifting that leg he places the foot on the top of the tub, follows with the other leg, placing it on the tiny edge of the tub that connects with the wall while lifting her to a new height. She braces herself with the wall and the curtain rod. Running his tongue around her erect nipple while slightly pinching the other he notices an instant response. Sasha enjoys the warmth of his mouth with mixed emotions. She's somewhat uneasy by her nakedness and the vulnerability of her position but eagerly waits for what that position could possibly bring. He makes a trail with his tongue between her breasts, down below her belly button and nibbles on the inside of her thigh.

"Oh God," she says with a shortness of breath.

Jason moves slowly to her womanhood, finding a wetness created by her body that the flowing water can't duplicate. He concentrates hard not to choke on the rushing water filling his mouth; nevertheless, he continues aspiring to please her. She grabs a fist full of hair as her body breaks out with tiny chill bumps while her knees weaken.

"I can't take this," she states while stepping down into the tub. "What are you trying to do to me?"

"What I do best."

"I was under the impression that detective work is what you do best."

"I lied," Jason boasts.

"Is this one of your favorite shirts?"

"No."

Sasha removes his tie eager to meet him flesh-to-flesh, releases the top two buttons, cuffs his shirt with both hands and swiftly snatches it open. Buttons fly, sounding like tiny pellets as they bounce off the tile wall and into the tub. Jason steps out of his shoes as she attacks his pants with the vengeance of a rabid animal. She loosens his snap, lowers his zipper and the heavily drenched pants fall to his ankles. Astounded by his lack of underwear she finds herself aroused greater.

"I've never known a man that didn't wear undergarments," she says while grabbing his pulsating penis.

They hug and kiss, lusting for each other with a desire stronger than the world's most muscular man. Their bodies half-covered with lather slide as they embrace.

"Hold me," she replies.

"I don't intend to let you go."

"I've dreamed of this happening. Not in the shower, of course."

"Have you? When did this dream occur?"

"Last night. It was hard for me to sleep after our adventure on the beach and your bedside kisses."

"I, too, entertained naughty thoughts."

"Why didn't you try something this morning?"

"You hadn't given the okay."

"Huh?" Sasha questions dumbfounded.

"After our talk at breakfast I was sure it was time but I didn't know if an action of this nature would've been premature. I didn't want to offend you in any way."

"I'm sure you could tell I wanted you. That's why I invited you to sleep with me. All you needed to do was read between the lines."

"True, but I also assured you that you'd be safe."

"I gather you do things in your own time."

"Something like that."

"Turn and put your back against the wall."

Responding to her command, she leaps on him, places her arms around his neck and locks her legs around his waist.

"That's better," she replies.

"Playful thing, aren't you?"

"I have my moments...you can take it, right?"

"The question is can you take it?"

"I can hold on forever."

"Riding?"

Sasha, feeling timid about her sexual promiscuity, states, "I've had a few lovers in my life, my husband and a couple of others but I don't consider myself very experienced so, how do you plan to do that?"

"Grasshopper," Jason replies while smiling to himself. "Don't worry, you'll be fine."

Jason clinches her behind the knees and unlocks her legs spreading them wide. He slowly lowers her onto him, invading her, filling her, tantalizing her desires. Sasha's body tenses to his timed round motions yet she flows smoothly to the rhythm as one does on a galloping horse. She holds him loosely, leaning back with her head penetrating the shower curtain, making it resemble something from a freak-show. Her arms are stretched full length with her fingers clasped tightly behind his neck. The timed round motions are suddenly replaced by hard sporadic up and down thrusts as he practically bounces her off him.

"Oh, no!" Jason cries.

"What's wrong?" she says short of breath.

"The water is turning cold."

"I hadn't noticed. Get me closer and I'll turn it off."

"Shall we continue in the bedroom?"

"By all means...put me down."

"That's not necessary. Hold on." He slides the shower curtain back, without thinking about the gripping of his wet feet against the ceramic bathroom floor and steps out of the tub, squeezes through the door and descends slowly to the bed with no mishaps. "I was worried there."

"So, you do admit that you may have dropped me."

"Me? Impossible."

"What then?"

"I was frightened that my curve would put me off target."

"What curve?"

"Well...my friend has a noticeable curve. I call it my experiential curve."

"Oh?"

"Sometimes manual maneuvering is required."

"I can't believe...are you one of those men who give their penis a name?"

"I've never given it any thought."

"Yeah, right."

"Have you ever been turboized?" questions Jason.

"What's turboized?"

"Poor child, you haven't."

"Maybe."

"Believe me, if you've experienced it, you'd never forget. Oh, I forgot, no one knows this maneuver but me."

"I assume it's about to happen."

"Brilliant deduction."

"I see...and what's my part in this?"

"Simple, just enjoy."

They indulge for countless hours, until the early hours in the morning with only a few interruptions in between. The first break came after the initial session ended. Sasha got up to wash and Jason quickly reminded her that he wasn't finished with her. Aside from the few interruptions, he pulled all stops and performed every imaginable position physically possible. Sasha responded favorably to all except the one that rendered her upside-down. They covered every inch of her queen-sized bed, initiated each piece of furniture in the bedroom and explored the living area for added measure to finally conclude with one last session in bed before passing out exhausted with Sasha's head resting on his hairy chest.

Seven-thirty the next morning their sleep is disturbed by the buzzing alarm.

"I think that's your queue."

"It's morning already? I'm too tired. I can't possibly function with all of two-and-a-half hour's sleep."

"Come on, you're a big girl."

"But you wore me out last night and I can tell by your actions that it was a mistake to ask you if you liked to make love. It shows, very much so...your turbo, the very fast, I mean extremely fast short strokes drove me crazy. Damn," she shouts, "that felt good. See what you did, I can't even get up...my eyes won't stay open. It feels like I have weights clamped to them keeping my lids shut."

"You should do something. Maybe a fresh cup of coffee will open your eyes. Or maybe..." He looks down at his now-erect penis.

"I don't believe you. He can still stand?"

"Like a natural man. I believe he has a mind of his own."

"I'll call in, I'm sick today."

"Oh?"

"It requires some preparation first."

Sasha removes her naked body from the bed to the bathroom for her robe and necessary materials. She hurries by Jason's watchful curious eyes attempting to hide her face. Moments later he hears what appears to be a chopping sound radiating from the kitchen and gives into his catlike instincts, slips on his pants to investigate.

"Why, all the preparation to make a phone call? You pick up the phone; dial the number, 'boss I'm sick today.' He says 'okay' and you're out of work...what in the world have you done to your face?" Jason responds after taking a double-take at her.

"Well, I have to make it sound convincing."

Sasha has stuffed cotton between her teeth and inner jaw to make them seem swollen. Looking like she has had an awful day at the dentist, Sasha stands there chopping onions to make her eyes tear.

"What are the tears for?"

"The same as the cotton, to change my voice. It'll distort my voice, giving me a deeper tone."

"Sounds like you're talking from experience."

"I use this method about twice a year."

"If you want a deep tone, set your alarm for a time a few minutes after you're due to work and then call in. With the frog in your throat you'll have the tone you wish naturally without all the hassle involved."

"That's true but I don't want to sound sleepy. I have to appear sick. You don't know the man I'm dealing with."

"Is he that much of a stickler to put you through all of this?"

"Very much so."

"Do what you have to. I'll see you back in bed. I've never seen anyone go through so much trouble to make a sick call. It's funny."

"I have this call to make. Then, I'll answer this guy's tempting plea," she states while seizing his penis. "I have more work for him."

"So you do...isn't it a bit early to call in sick?"

"I'm calling him at his home."

"I see, like I said I'll wait for you in bed."

After completing her call she returns to the bedroom, ready for much of the same sweet harmony experienced last night. With an entire day free her anticipation increases as she plunges into the bed with him.

"Well, how did it go?"

"Great."

"You were convincing?"

"I was more than that, I should be an actress."

"Maybe you should but learn to do that without all of the preparation."

"You know what?"

"No...what?"

"You talk too much."

She kisses him sliding her tongue deep into his mouth.

"Do you know what?" Jason replies.

"What?"

"This is crazy."

"What is?"

"You calling in sick."

"What's crazy about it? It's life."

"You're jeopardizing your job on a new relationship."

"We have a relationship?" she asks smiling.

"What else would you call it?"

"We've spent a lot of time together...point made."

"Come closer," he says, raising his eyebrows.

"Anytime."

They indulge in hot and steamy lovemaking sessions throughout the morning and much of the afternoon. After an exhausting finale to end lunch, they nap and wake to extreme hunger. They shower, dress and seek food. Ending their journey with Chinese, they devour several delectable hot and spicy dishes. Afterwards they return for more repeated sessions, which last again until the early morning hours. The next morning Sasha repeats her award-winning performance with another sick call to her boss. After a complete breakfast they engage in minor conversation. Being overwhelmed by the past two days they find it difficult to do more than repeat how wonderful they each are. Jason gathers his things and heads toward the door while promising to call her later. That afternoon Jason lives up to his promise; he invites her to lunch at Rosalina's and she eagerly accepts.

CHAPTER 15

Ms. Waters sits in her lawyer's office undaunted. She's about to receive a favorable word concerning her complaint against Detective Jerrard. The DA found Jason guilty of misconduct, accumulated misuse of the badge and jeopardizing the lives of the innocent. She'll be granted a trial and a judgment against the city is almost certain. However, she's uneasy; nervousness shows as her body trembles slightly as she stares through the wall into nothingness. Her attorney enters the office. Mr. Ronald Ourisman is a man in his late forties who's aged well. On the other hand, his practice since bar approval has been unstable, traveled on rocky roads. The ups and downs of his chosen profession have been mostly down. It took him quite some time to develop a knack for selecting quality cases but today should prove to be a turning point in his career. He's smiling, anxious and joyful. The preliminary battle with Ms. Waters's case has been won. Eagerly he waits for his moment to advise her of the outstanding news.

"Ms. Waters, I've received the latest word on the DA's investigation. It seems that Detective Jerrard has been quite a character, not only with your case but with others. They let your encounter be the straw that broke the camel's back. Reviewing his file they overturned other questionable decisions involving his work ethics and claim them to be misuse of the badge. He's been found guilty of endangering your life. This means to us that we can file a lawsuit immediately against the city for your emotional damages. It's guaranteed with the DA's report in our corner. I propose that we seek a thirty-million-dollar suit against Detective Jerrard and the city. We will not receive that much but you should clear enough money to live the rest of your life very, very comfortably. My argument will be, who can put a price on human life. I called you down here because I felt a need to advise you in person. I couldn't resist the temptation of seeing your reaction to the news. Ms. Waters, didn't you hear me? You're going to win your case; you're going to be wealthy."

No positive emotion shows on her face. He lost her somewhere at the beginning of his conversation, losing her self-contained solitude. His words seemed to have passed her ears as she continually stares through him until he walks to her and shakes her shoulder.

"Ms. Waters, are you okay?"

"Huh, I'm sorry."

"Didn't you hear anything I said?"

"I heard everything."

"Pardon me for expecting more of a favorable response."

"I'm sorry but the possibilities of that incident keep haunting my mind."

"I'm sure it does and I'll do everything to prove your emotional distress in court. Having your life put on the line like that must be a horrible thing to live with."

"True, you know before the police arrived I was terrified. I'd just finished a shower when I thought I heard some movement downstairs. I slipped my robe on and proceeded to investigate, only to greet the maniac with a knife. He dragged me from room to room taking things at random and stuffing them into a laundry bag of some sort. We ended up in the kitchen because he said he was thirsty. He said he had a thirst for ice-cold water and me. After drinking the water he began looking at me with those piercing deep-set eyes of his, sending chills throughout my body. He lusted after me with a desire of a man recently released from a twenty-year prison sentence. Well, that was the impression he gave...yes, he was hungry but not for food. He tore at my robe, threw me on the floor and began to undo his pants. That's when the police arrived. He jumped up, clinched me with the knife at my throat and became scared, angry, more like raged, thinking I'd tipped the police. He said that he might as well get something out of the ordeal since he was caught and going to jail anyway. So, he tore open my robe with his free hand and began to fondle my breasts like they were bean bags. Squeezing, pulling them at will. He ran his rough hand down between my legs, trying to force them open but I refused. His grip tightened around my neck as he said I'd die here and now if I didn't cooperate. Then he slid one of his fingers into me. I cringed when he then smelled it stating "perfect." He forced me on my back and pulled his thing through his zipper and was lying on top of me...about to...well, that's when Detective Jerrard entered the house. He quickly stuffed his thing back into his pants and grabbed me with the knife at my throat again. When Detective Jerrard located us, we were on the floor. I was leaning on him as he rested against the cabinets. That's about when Detective Jerrard started encouraging him to kill me."

"Horrifying, simply horrifying. His actions are inexcusable."

"Yes, but you and I realize that I would have been raped if Detective Jerrard hadn't broken direct orders to come to my rescue. What the burglar did, I can live with but I seriously doubt I could lead a normal life if I'd been raped."

"What are you trying to say, Ms. Waters?

"Reluctantly, I want you to drop all charges against Detective Jerrard."

"You what!" Mr. Ourisman states appalled.

"Drop all charges against Detective Jerrard."

"Is this some sort of joke? If it is, it surely lacks humor."

"No, I'm serious."

"Why would you want to do that?"

"I've had several nightmares about the attack. In my dreams everything happens as it did, from the breaking in, to our ending up on the kitchen floor but this time there was no Detective Jerrard to foil his rape. In my dreams the police used their bullhorn to negotiate with him. He simply ignored their communication efforts and raped me as they talked. The thought of that possibility haunts me just about every night, making me ill inside."

"You can't live your life based on what could've happened. If the thought of being raped bothers you and you must dream about what could've happened, think about this. You could be dead!"

"True, however, I'm alive. I wasn't raped, for this I should be grateful to this man Detective...Detective Jones."

"Detective Jerrard."

"Jerrard, not Jones, my mind is tired of the pressure from trying to figure out what to do. Nevertheless, I thank him, for it was certain that I would've been raped if he hadn't reacted the way he did. I can't ruin his life like that."

"Do you realize what you're saying?"

"Yes."

"And you also realize how much money you're throwing away?"

"Yes I do. No amount of money in the world could buy back the mental stability I would have lost if I'd been raped. I would have been stripped of human dignity and money cannot buy that back, no matter how much it is."

"You've seriously thought this over?"

"I assure you this isn't a rash decision. It has taken several days to come to this conclusion. I wasn't completely sure until moments ago when I informed you of my intentions to drop the charges against Detective Jerrard. A great burden lifted off my shoulders. You see when I began to feel grateful to Detective Jerrard for preventing my rape a little voice in the back of my head kept asking me if I really wanted to ruin this man's life. I ignored the question until now because consciously I pictured dollar signs."

"Big dollar signs. You have a chance to reap more money than you can imagine."

"I never knew I could turn down a great deal of money but I don't feel it's important enough to destroy his career, much less his life considering what he prevented."

"Don't you think you should be concerned with you and your life?"

"I am."

"Are you?"

"Money can't buy happiness."

"Yeah, but it can buy the kind of misery you could thoroughly enjoy."

"I pass, Mr. Ourisman. Enough has been said. My decision is final. Would you please notify the proper people to have my complaint against Detective Jerrard dropped?"

"There's just one other matter."

"What's that?"

"My fees. Originally we agreed to have them be one fourth of the settlement. Since there will be no settlement I have to charge you my regular fees."

"Understood. Bill me, please."

Ms. Waters thanks him for accepting her case and assures him if ever she were in need of a lawyer that she'd consider him. They exchange farewells as she prepares to depart.

"Ms. Waters."

"Yes," she says, turning as she is about to exit. "Yes, I'm absolutely sure."

"How did you know I was going to ask that?"

"What more could you ask? Goodbye."

"Take care."

As the door closes his head falls between his hands. He ponders over another case turned sour and questions his motives for becoming a lawyer.

CHAPTER 16

Jason and Sasha arrive simultaneously outside Rosalina's. They greet with an affectionate hug while commenting on each other's new attire.

"Master," Sasha says playfully.

Jason's face brightens to a huge smile.

"Yes, I understood perfectly what you meant when you called me 'Grasshopper' the other day. Master and Grasshopper—loosely translated, Teacher and Student."

"I didn't mean to imply," Jason apologizes.

"Oh, I'm not upset. I think it's cute. Besides, after what we did, I feel as though I'm learning. Just promise me one thing."

"What's that?

"No pregnant gestures today."

"Relax, there isn't a line."

They proceed up the steps only to be stopped in their tracks by the door being forcefully opened. Three women exit, two of them more than average looking and shapely. The third has an attractive face but is much huskier than the other two who argue. The other follows shamelessly behind with Alfredo on her heels and a few spectators looking on to see the excitement.

"Madams, I have to ask you to carry your disagreement off these premises. This is a respectable establishment," Alfredo states.

"Please excuse them. It's all a big misunderstanding. I apologize for the three of us," the third woman says.

"Misunderstanding, my ass, you cheap little whore. I gave you everything only to find you here with this bitch, Miss Prissy here," Jackie angrily rebuts.

"Who are you calling a bitch, bitch! I'm more of a woman than you'll ever be, slut," argues Sarah.

"Please stop, both of you. Jackie, Sarah, let's not lower ourselves more."

"Why are you protecting this bitch? After all we've shared...you slept with her didn't you?" Jackie asks.

Lauren says nothing.

"Didn't you? Didn't you!?" she demands.

"You don't have to tell her anything. Let the thought kill the bitch."

Jackie slaps Lauren's face, leaving a glowing red hand print traced on her face.

"Yes," Lauren replies in a low voice.

"What's that? Louder!"

"I said yes!" she rages. "Yes, I did. Are you happier now?"

Sasha stands there astounded. Her mouth drops as she finds the entire escapade bewildering. Jason observes.

"You cheap little whore, how could you do this to me? I thought we loved each other. You..."

Jackie plunges toward Lauren while Sarah grabs her from behind.

"You want to know," Sarah replies, "I'll tell you. She's a delicate woman who should be handled with tenderness. Not like a rough piece of meat you try to beat tender."

"You don't know anything about her. We've been together for years."

"It's true, Jackie," Lauren intrudes. "You stopped treating me like a woman sometime ago. I don't care to be treated like a possession. I have feelings and these very same feelings are what you've trampled over. I tried telling you how I felt, but you ignored my efforts."

"Why didn't you make me listen? I thought that was what you liked.

No, it's this bitch's fault," Jackie replies with redirected anger. "She's to blame. Everything was fine until she influenced you."

Jackie breaks Sarah's grasp. She and Sarah stare angrily before they pounce toward each other. Jason jumps between them.

"Enough, calm down everyone," Jason directs. "Pull yourselves together. You're becoming spectacles and are on the verge of disturbing the peace."

"Mind your own damn business and keep your chauvinistic views to yourself," Jackie states.

"I'm only trying to help."

"We don't need your help. We can settle this ourselves."

"Fine, just do it elsewhere."

"Don't tell me what to do...get the fuck out of my way!"

Jackie tries pushing him away but the push turns into a shove and the shove turns into two windmills of circling fists.

"Miss, stop, I've had enough of this. You're assaulting a cop."

"I'm really scared. I don't care what you are," Jackie replies with continuous wild punches.

Jason does everything short of returning fists to protect himself. "This is the last time I'm warning you. Please stop."

She ignores his plea.

"Okay, you like women like men, I'll start treating you like a man." Jason rushes her. In one quick movement, he has her hands behind her back ready to be handcuffed. "It didn't have to come to this."

The other two women start moving toward Jason to answer Jackie's cries.

"I advise you to stay back unless you'd like to be her personal escort downtown."

"Lauren, don't let him take me away. Please, Sarah help me."

A police car arrives answering a disturbing the peace call placed by Alfredo. The two officers approach Jason.

"I'm Detective Jerrard, Sixteenth Precinct. Take her to the station and lock her up. I'll place a formal charge when I get there. Alfredo, do you wish to add any further charges?"

"No, Sir, I think not. She's in deep enough."

"Very well then."

"What charges shall I use to hold her?" questions an officer.

"Charge her with disturbing the peace, assaulting an officer and ruining my lunch."

"Right away, Sir."

"Oh, read her rights to her. Well, do you two women want to go also or are you willing to leave quietly?"

They turn and walk away without any further incident.

"Alfredo," Jason replies. "I'm sorry for adding more to the scene."

"You did what you had to do. I truly understand."

"Sasha, I give you my utmost apologies. I've got to go to the station. You can ride with me or I'll call you later at home."

"I think I'll go home. I'm not in the mood for a police station and suddenly, I'm not hungry. Call me later."

"Okay."

Jason escorts Sasha to her car, kisses her on the cheek and they leave in separate directions. As soon as Jason arrives at the station, he is given instructions to report directly to the captain's office.

"How have you been?"

"I'm maintaining. With all the solitude I've managed to keep my sanity. How's the case coming?"

"Never mind that. What have you been doing to occupy yourself?"

"I've had female companionship."

"Anyone I know? Julie?"

"No, you don't know her. Sasha is her name. She was with me when we walked up on this incident."

"That's too bad. Where is she?"

"She went home in lieu of this charming place."

Captain North leans against the wall and scratches his head. "You have a unique knack for putting me in uncomfortable positions."

"What do you mean?"

"What's your status now?"

"I'm still under suspension."

"Exactly, didn't you realize because of that you couldn't make an arrest? You can't place charges against her. Again you fail to follow proper procedures. It would have been proper to have someone from the restaurant come down and charge her formally. I would have thought your little rest had taught you something."

"Well, everything you said I'm already aware of."

"Yet, you still made the arrest."

"Yes, I had no intentions of placing charges against that woman but I thought a night behind bars would help calm her vengeance. Her hurt and anger caused her to attack me. In some ways I can understand her position."

"And you want us to hold her overnight?"

"That would be enough to help her understand that she can't put on a display in public."

"On what grounds? You're suspended!"

"She doesn't know that. Hell, call it a citizen's arrest."

"Jason, you can't keep making up rules as you go. If it's the last thing I do, I'm going to teach you that. You're going to have to stop playing by your rules or else your police career will end abruptly. Didn't you realize that it could be over for you already? The DA found you guilty of all charges placed against you and they seem to have fabricated some new ones based on past cases."

"When did you get this information?"

"A day or so ago."

"Interesting, however, I'm aware of the consequences of all of my actions."

"I truly don't understand you. You..."

Captain North stops to answer the telephone that is interrupting his reprimand. His conversation is brief and his replies are "yes," "oh really" and "understood." He hangs up the phone and shakes his head while taking a deep breath.

"You know Jason, when I received the DA's word I pictured you on a rope, dangling by your neck, gasping for air. Hung by your peers, your face turns blue as your last breath seeps from your body, but, as fate would have it, the rope breaks and you escape unharmed. That was the DA's office again. It seems that Ms. Waters has changed her mind. She's now grateful to you. They didn't give a long explanation but the woman dropped all charges against you. Something about you being an unsung hero, saving her sanity, therefore, as the DA put it, without a formal complaint, the other findings are meaningless. You're to be reinstated at once. You're one lucky son-of-a-bitch. I grant you that. Be careful though, one day your luck will run out."

Jason sits physically unmoved as if Captain North said nothing. Mentally his conscious is reassuring his beliefs in his actions. After asking to be excused, Jason walks toward the door with Captain North's blessing.

"Oh, Jason, we can detain that woman now."

He smiles. "Hell, let her go."

"I thought you'd say that."

Jason closes the door behind him and walks down the hall with his shoe's metal-heel plates sounding proudly against the tile floor while Captain North sits at his desk wondering if Jason possesses some kind of gift.

He stops at his desk and picks up the telephone.

"Hello?"

"You sound lovelier each time I talk to you."

"Jason?" Sasha questions.

"Yes, I'll have to spend less time with you and call you more often so you can recognize my voice over the phone."

"Don't do that. Besides, I only had little doubt...is everything okay?"

"Things are perfect."

"Good, I suppose that woman calmed down."

"I'd think so since I let her go."

"You did...Why?"

"I'll tell you Friday. My original thought was to have you celebrate with me tonight but I figured if I did you'd miss work again tomorrow."

"Come on, tell me."

"No, I'll wait for Friday night. That's if you're free."

"Friday seems so far away, tell me."

"It's only three days. Surely you can wait that long."

"Must I?"

"You must."

"Okay...what's up for Friday?"

"Oh, that's a surprise, too."

"What?"

"I'll just tell you that it starts with dinner."

"Rosalina's?"

"It doesn't have to be. You pick the place."

"I'll choose someplace good but not too expensive."

"It doesn't matter."

"You're suspended, remember?"

"I forgot. Listen, I have a few things to take care of. I'll call you tomorrow."

"Please do."

"Stay sweet."

"I like that, take care."

"Goodbye."

"Bye."

After his call to Sasha he returns to the captain's office for an update on the case given to him before his suspension. He finds it surprising that there's no favorable news to report. The department has received no new leads in solving the murder-rape cases. However, there have been three additional murders. Each victim sexually-assaulted before killed, each with the same MO as the previous cases. A fourth victim survived her attack but proved to be no help to the police. Her attack rendered her mentally unstable, placing her in a void, allowing things to flow through her mind that only she can understand. She currently resides in the state's mental institution where she only rocks back and forth. She doesn't eat or respond to her doctor, family or friends. Her mind has lost its touch with reality as it floats somewhere away from the reality of what happened to her.

At his desk he reviews the older cases, then the new. A determined Jason studies the files for just one clue to set him on the right path. An eerie feeling consumes him, realizing that the maniac is lurking the city streets. His thoughts correspond with the everlasting changes that exist constantly on the streets. As he studies the files, mayhem is a present treat on the streets.

In any major city, on any given day, there are all kinds of watching. There's bird watching, girl watching but most of all the uncanny watchful eyes of people watching people. After his call to Candy, he stalks his next prey. He finds a group of women leaving a health spa. Stopping for their last-minute goodbyes, three women leave to the right; two depart in the other direction; a lone one crosses the street unaware of any deliberate attention drawn to her. She walks two blocks to the nearest subway station and vanishes underground. She boards the semi-crowded last car and occupies a seat on the far end before retrieving a novel to make her long trip across town seem shorter. He sits watching her several rows back on the opposite side. Minutes pass and slowly the train empties. The book falls to her lap as she closes her eyes and her head starts to bounce to the rhythm of the speeding train. Moments pass. She suddenly opens her eyes to an empty train, except for a strange man with his eyes peered on her from across the train. With an effort to disregard his stare she pretends to read but the tension and anguish gets the best of her, unnerving her.

"Why are you staring at me?"

He only smiles. The train stops at the next scheduled point on the line to let on another passenger. Her tension eases for the moment, a very short moment because at the next stop the passenger exits the train, leaving her with a twenty-two-minute ride remaining to her destination with no stops in-between.

"What do you want?" she cries.

He ignores the question while scanning her hungrily, causing her to plead mercifully for him to stay away. Again, he ignores her cries. Her arms fly and legs kick wildly in defense.

"Don't fight me. I won't hurt you," he states coldly.

He forces her body down on the bench seat and climbs on top of her using one hand to hold her down by the neck. Slowly, the other hand moves up her thigh, pushing her dress with the upward motion, then pulls her panties down below her knees. She fights frantically, biting and scratching, rewarding herself with three scrapes embedded in his face. The exposed white skin slowly turns red as the scratches fill with blood that race down his face, dripping off his chin onto her face while she fights aimlessly to free herself. He shifts his weight to his arms, tightens his grip around her neck, choking her. He lifts her head by the neck and repeatedly slams it against the hard seat. Still her will holds, refusing to submit to his wishes. Forcefully he punches her twice in the face, causing her right eye to quickly blacken followed by a swollen mouth. His power destroys her strength and her will vanishes, killing her once-fighting spirit. Tears run down each side of her face as he climbs off her and removes her panties. His pants fall below his knees before he remounts his prize, once again placing his grip around her neck. With the forced penetration, her heart pumps blood but all other body functions are lifeless.

Giving her a quick thrust, he says, "Move bitch, move!" with coordinated slaps to her. "What happened to all your spunk? Move!"

For the battered woman the next few moments seem to last forever. The train enters a tunnel and the lights flicker on and off giving the effect of a strobe light. The sporadic lighting effects excite his thrusting abilities to the point where it seems that he is trying to penetrate the other end.

"Move, yes, move," he states while pounding her with a galloping motion.

In her mind she captures snapshots created by the flashing lights. Each picture reveals an expression of his, one closer to an orgasm than the other. The train exits the tunnel and the lights return to normal. He lies atop her breathing heavily, not realizing that his grip is still perched tightly around her neck. He dismounts her body and wipes his penis off with her dress, pulls up his pants, picks up her panties, wraps them around his index finger and forces them up her womanhood. He then pulls her dress down neatly.

"Bitch, put your panties on. I told you you'd be all right. Hey, I'm talking to you."

He shakes her body. It moves like spaghetti, flowing between the seats to the floor, lifeless. Strangulation is apparent, suggested by the bruise marks on her neck. Another death—again he watches her with no indication of sorrow, no remorse. The thought that runs through his mind is that she should have cooperated from the beginning. The train stops at its final destination, the doors open and he exits rapidly. Invisible again, he quickly steps to the street and walks away carefree. His crime is perfect but not flawless.

CHAPTER 17

S asha reports to work promptly the next morning, showing no indication of sickness. She's joyful, full of vigor and cheer.

"Good morning, guys."

"Boy, you look lovely," Ben flatters. "I wish I could be sick for two days and come back looking as lovely as you do today."

"Well, you know how those forty-eight-hour bugs are."

"Okay, fess up," Carl states.

"What on earth are you talking about?"

"The man's name. I haven't seen that look on your face for some time now, but I can still recognize it."

"Oh, you can? What makes you so sure?"

"Look me in the eye and tell me I'm wrong."

Carl's immediate accusation stuns her as she attempts to gather her composure. She looks him directly into the eyes.

"You're wro...his name is Jason," Sasha confesses.

"I knew it. A woman gets a certain air about her when she meets someone interesting."

"Men, too!" Sasha recites defensively.

"You know you'll have to bring him by. He has to have our stamp of approval before you can date him further."

"Who claimed you as my father on their deathbed?"

"That's right, Sasha," Ben states. "It's our unspoken duty to look out for you. You're like a sister to us."

"Will the two of you relax? So far I couldn't dream of a better man."

"It always starts that way, then the next thing you know he's slapping you around."

"I don't think he has the capacity to do that. Besides, it wouldn't be in his best interest."

"What do you mean?"

"He's a detective."

"A detective?" Ben and Carl both announce together.

"What's his name?" Ben questions.

"Jason Jerrard."

"Jason Jerrard...Jason Jerrard. Detective Jerrard, that sounds so familiar."

"Detective Jason Jerrard," Carl interjects. "I know him. He's that person on the news a while back. Right?"

"Yep."

"And you call yourself safe. What he did makes me wonder about your safety."

"I've spent much time with him lately and I feel quite safe. Thank you."

"Regardless, you bring him by so we can formulate our own opinion," Ben states, too protective for Sasha's liking. "You're like family...right, Carl?"

"Definitely."

"I appreciate your concern and I'm sure you'll meet him in time but I'll be fine. Now let's get things together. We only have a short while before we open."

She walks to her desk more cheerful than before because she finally got an opportunity to tell someone about her newfound happiness.

The bank opens at nine o'clock. One minute later, Howard Normin stands at her desk smiling. Moments pass before she feels his presence.

"Howard?"

"I didn't mean to startle you."

"You didn't. I'm just surprised to see you."

"Oh? I told you that I'd be back in a few days. I came by yesterday and the day before but you were out. Hopefully you've decided in our favor. You know my shipment arrives Saturday and I trust that you've studied our papers."

"Yes."

"Was everything in order?"

"Perfect."

"And we look like a profitable company?"

"Yes."

"Why are you giving such abrupt answers? Is something wrong?"

"Look, Howard, I've made no decision to help you. Actually, the more I think about it, the more I..."

"Wait, don't finish," he interrupts. "Before you complete that sentence, feast your eyes on this."

He pulls a white envelope out of his sport jacket pocket and passes it to her. She opens it slowly under her desk, hiding it from unsuspecting eyes.

"I told you this had to be discreet...what is this?"

"It's the keys to the car you want."

"The Porsche?" she says with more excitement.

"Precisely."

"Is it parked outside?"

"No, but with the correct answer I can leave you the keys and tell you where to pick up the car."

"You've bought the car?"

"Obviously."

Sasha sits with her heart pounding and wonders if Howard can hear the echo as she begins to fantasize.

"This is totally unexpected. When I asked you for the car, it was an attempt to deter you from continuing your conversation. I never thought you'd follow up on it."

"Now that we have, what are you going to do? The ball is in your court."

"Wow, this is a lot to digest. My heart and mind are struggling. It's tempting, extremely tempting but I have to do what's right. I reluctantly decline the car and all thoughts of helping you."

"The car can be yours...it is black, also."

"You drive a hard bargain, but I can't do anything illegal."

"You can be driving it tomorrow."

"Yeah and how do I explain it?"

"I don't have all the answers. All I know is I followed up on my end of the deal."

"Deal? What deal? Deal as in agreement?"

"Yes."

"Wait a minute. I never agreed to anything. All I said to you was that I'd think about it."

"I assumed when you mentioned the car that those were the conditions upon your agreement."

"Mr. Normin," Sasha states firmly, "you assumed wrong."

"Is there anything more you want that could help persuade you?"

"Nothing."

"Look at it this way. It's illegal but we're going to pay the money back. I'll agree to a ninety-day note. Since our last conversation, I've come across some potential buyers, which means the money could possibly be repaid even earlier," he lies. "Besides, who has to know?"

"My conscience, that's enough."

"Please help me," Howard begs less spirited than before.

"I just can't. I thank you for entertaining one of my greatest fantasies. Just holding the keys gave me thrills beyond your imagination."

"Just imagine what driving it can do for you."

"Again, I decline. Now, if you'd be so kind, I have work to do."

"This is your final decision?"

"Correct."

"My boss isn't going to be pleased with this. I practically assured him that you'd agree."

"Sorry to disappoint you but you should not do things like that without being absolutely sure."

"I'll take my leave now. Have a nice day. Goodbye."

"So long."

As he leaves, Sasha sits in her chair relieved. She's glad that the ordeal is over. No more stressful decisions to sway her mind from her work.

"Sasha, Sasha," Carl repeats. "Yo, Sasha?"

"Huh? Yes?"

"Five-six is for you."

"Thanks...Miss Fong, how may I help you?"

"Miss Fong, this is Charles Livingston and I'm calling to ask you to reconsider your decision."

"Livingston, Livingston, I can't recall our conversation. What is this concerning?"

"I'm Mr. Normin's boss."

"Howard Normin, Far East Import. He just left here, not more than ten minutes ago."

"He phoned me with your decision."

"Boy, you guys work fast. How many people am I going to have to tell 'no' before my message gets across?"

"I thought I'd take the liberty of asking you to reconsider. There's much at stake here."

"I understand that but I'm standing firm."

"Can't you help a struggling company?"

"I have the power to, but not the will to do it."

"Listen, the Porsche can be delivered to you immediately. They're nice cars. I drive one myself."

"Still 'no.'"

"Please listen to reason..."

"I've listened to all I care to on this subject," she intrudes forcefully.

"Howard tells me you're quite an attractive woman. One such as yourself should learn to be flexible."

"Flexible, I'm flexible enough to know when I'm being harassed but I haven't called the police."

"There's no need for police. I'd hate to see you in some sort of accident."

"Threatening me, you don't know me. I don't scare easily. I don't know you from Adam."

"That's right. You don't know who you're dealing with. I'm no ordinary man."

"Mr. Livingston, you are wasting my time and yours. I surely won't help you after your so-called threats."

"My dear, I'm far from threatening you but heed these words. I'd hate it if something happened to your pretty face."

"Are you through?"

"Just one other thing: be careful who you double-cross."

"Let me say this one last time. No one is being double-crossed because, despite what you heard, there was never an agreement for anything. That's my final word!"

"Whatever you say. Just know that all people can't be pushed around by people in high places."

"Goodbye, Mr. Livingston." She hangs up the phone without his reply. "The nerve of some people."

She leaves her desk for a short walk to calm her emotions. Mr. Livingston's conversation has been taxing. That evening she returns to her home from a busier day than usual. Sasha heats water in the kettle for a cup of hot tea while she listens to her calls. There's one from her mother and three consecutive messages from someone unknown, each muffled to disguise the identity of the voice.

"You should have tried to work out something with me. You don't know who you are dealing with" is the first. "Things could have worked out but you had to blow it" followed. "You haven't heard the last of it. I'll be watching you" is the third.

After listening to her messages, a stronger uneasy feeling overwhelms her. Her mind wonders if these are idle threats or if there is true meaning behind them. She sits staring at her answering machine trying to temporarily put the calls out of her mind. The effort fails, overwhelmed by her desire to give a careful ear to learn the caller's identity. The messages replay, but just as before, she is still unsure who placed the calls. She finds it difficult to believe that Mr. Livingston would carry his antics this far over a misunderstanding, knowing that the only enemies she possibly has are those involved with the Far East Import Company. She contemplates whether the muffled voices are Howard or Mr. Livingston? Or, is it someone they are using to put a scare in her? Moments later the telephone rings and she ponders whether to answer it. Her immediate thought is to pick up the receiver yelling, cursing out the originator of the call, however, she gives in to her fear of whom it might be and allows the machine to take the call. Her greeting is followed by Jason's voice coming through the speaker.

"Hello, Sasha, Jason here. Just thought I could..."

Quickly, Sasha retrieves the telephone.

"Jason," she speaks with anxiety, "I'm glad it's you."

"I'm glad it's me, too. How are you?"

"I could be better. It has been a crazy day."

"What's wrong? I detect worry in your voice."

"I have a situation that I need to straighten out, but it's nothing I can't handle. Don't be alarmed."

"Can I help in any way?"

"No...I guess you could but I need to do some detective work, rather confront some people before I start pointing the finger."

"Okay, I give, tell me."

"If I need you, I promise to consult you. I'm not too shy to ask."

"You're sure you're okay? You definitely don't sound like your old chipper self. Whatever the situation is, it is disturbing to some degree."

"Like you told me the other morning, I'm a big girl. I can handle it."

"If you're sure, I'll say okay. But, if you need me you know where to turn. Say, are we still on for Friday?"

"Tomorrow is Friday?"

"No, Thursday...but I called to ask you what time I should pick you up?"

"Is seven o'clock agreeable with you?"

"Perfect. Where did you decide to eat?"

"I have several places in mind, but I'll know for sure Friday."

"Okay, I'll see you promptly at seven o'clock, Friday."

"Great. Goodbye."

"Goodbye."

CHAPTER 18

Friday morning Jason's day drags in anticipation of the planned evening with Sasha. His trips to the crime scenes of three murder victims for evidence are wasted efforts because his thoughts are more focused on the upcoming evening with Sasha. He acknowledges that there has only been one other occasion in his entire career when he couldn't keep his mind focused on the investigation. This being the second, he quickly scanned over each location paying less to detail than usual.

After a restless night, Sasha finds herself exhausted from hearing every noise her troubled mind acknowledged throughout the night, leery of the possible threats on her life. Somehow her workday flew by quickly. She hardly had time to focus on concealing her anxiety to Jason. Driving home she played mind games with herself, eager to change her mood to a more pleasant one for her upcoming engagement.

Jason rings the doorbell ten minutes early for their date. Sasha answers his call with unbrushed curls still in her head. Otherwise, she's sporting a lovely evening dress, matching pumps and evenly administered makeup.

"Good evening," Jason greets following a strong hug and polite kiss.

"Good evening, you're early. Obviously, I'm not exactly ready."

"No worry. I grew tired of circling your block."

"You've been riding in circles? Why so early?"

"I'm anxious to get our evening started."

"Well, I'll be just a few more minutes."

"Take your time. I have glimpsed you; I have more patience now."

Minutes later, she returns to the living room with purse in hand. "Tada! Ready. Did you miss me?"

"It was well worth the wait. You are simply stunning."

"Flattery gets you everywhere."

"I'll take you up on that offer later."

"If you forget, I'll remind you but thank Anne Klein, Maybelline and others."

"They are thanked...we can't leave yet."

"What's wrong?"

"You haven't given me our destination."

"I know this quaint little French restaurant off the boulevard. I forget its exact location but you make a right turn by the fire station downtown."

"Do you normally travel by landmarks?"

"It's just a habit I need to break."

"So I get on the boulevard and follow it until you advise me to turn."

"Something like that."

Riding to the restaurant, she succeeds in disguising her inner turmoil with heavy joking and sexual innuendos for later that evening.

"Oh no!" Jason cries. "Help me hold the wheel. This is going to be tough."

"What is?"

"Grab the wheel quick!" Jason panics. "We must prevent the wheel from turning. Hurry, we're almost there." Sasha seizes the wheel while being puzzled by his sudden burst of tension. A quick moment passes and he sighs heavily. "Whew, that was close. I thought we'd surely lose that battle."

"What on earth are you talking about?"

"We just passed Rosalina's. I have to hold the wheel tight, with all my strength to prevent my car from automatically turning into the parking lot. It's programmed to park there."

"You fool," Sasha says with a quick punch to Jason's shoulder. "You scared me."

"It's just another part of my deranged humor."

"You really enjoy that place, don't you?"

"One could say I live there."

"Turn around. Let's go back. We can eat there."

"That's not necessary. I promised you an elegant evening."

"I know but your face lights up with just mentioning the name."

"You'd feel comfortable dressed as you are?"

"I'm fine. I'm with you, remember. Truly, I don't mind. This can make up for our spoiled evening the other night."

"I owe you one but the next part of the evening is my treat."

"There's one small stipulation."

"Okay."

"No runny eggs tonight."

"Agreed."

Alfredo greets them pleasantly. "Welcome again. I apologize for the mishap the other day. Those women ruined everyone's meal."

"No apology required. You couldn't have anticipated the scene," Jason says.

"I'm sure you'll find this evening much more enjoyable and I might add, you two look splendid, like you stepped out of a magazine. What's the occasion?"

"We're celebrating!" Jason boasts.

"What event?"

"Yes, I'd like to know also," Sasha says, turning to Jason. "He has kept me in the dark about this celebration."

"I guess now is as good a time as any. I've been reinstated. All charges against me have been dropped."

"Congratulations, Sir."

"Yes, kudos. When did this happen?"

"Believe it or not, it was the same day I took that woman to the station."

"You should not have kept such wonderful news from me," Sasha complains.

"I know but that's only the first part of it. The second part comes after dinner."

"I believe that," Alfredo states after picking up Jason's leading remark. "That doesn't concern me—your usual booth, Sir?"

"Please."

"Jason, that's great. No wonder you've been so bubbly. You're complete again."

"That has more to do with your presence," Jason expresses with a tender gaze.

Sasha smiles, hoping that she did not reveal the way the comment really felt to her insides.

"Would you like a cocktail, Madam?"

"White Zinfandel, please."

"Very well, Madam. Your usual drink will be here momentarily, Sir."

"Thank you."

Alfredo returns with Jason's coffee and Sasha's wine.

"Chicken Florentine and a small house salad suits my fancy tonight," Sasha states.

"Very well, Madam," Alfredo states while turning to walk away.

"Alfredo," Jason delivers, "I'll have lasagna with garlic bread instead of my usual tonight."

"You're ordering a different meal, Sir?" he states, stopping in his tracks. "Are you feeling well? Maybe the effect of being reinstated has altered your memory."

"I'm fine. I promised her no runny eggs tonight and if I have to go to the detox center, I'm going to make it through this."

"I must admit I never thought I'd see the day. There's hope for you after all. The cooks will be surprised."

"There's a first time for everything."

"I see that now."

They devour their food over a stimulating conversation of leading sexual remarks. Sasha becomes playful by removing one of her shoes and rubbing her foot up and down his lower leg while making suggestive manners with her mouth. He responds by taking his thumb and wiping the corner of his mouth.

"What's that supposed to mean?" she questions.

Jason holds up his middle and index fingers, then asks, "What's this?"

"A peace sign."

He holds the fingers horizontally at his mouth and sticks his tongue between them. "Get the message now?"

"You nasty man...and your thumb is to wipe your mouth afterwards, right?"

"You got it."

"That made parts of me throb."

"Where?"

"Where do you think?" Looking at him strangely, she says, "Dumb looks are free." She softly runs her foot up his inner thigh toward his penis, lowers her foot and wiggles her toes on his semi-hard member. "Ooh, I see this conversation has touched you."

"What do you expect? You've been playing with me since we sat. When I get matters under control I'll fix you. The second part of our evening is about to begin."

"And what's that?"

"I thought a stroll around the park would be a perfect topper for our evening."

"We're going to drive around the park in your car?"

"No, much better than that."

"We're going to ride around in a horse and carriage?"

"Yes."

"That will be romantic under the full moon. I've fantasized about riding in one with someone I cared for, but so far it's only been a dream."

"Tonight one of your dreams becomes reality."

After thanking Alfredo for more great food and excellent service, he pays the bill and they head for the park.

Grand Park is located in the middle of the city. It's huge, measuring six city blocks by six city blocks. In the summertime during the day, different cultural activities are held. At night it's filled mostly with couples holding hands as they walk together sharing love or riding in open carriages snuggling as they stroll.

They arrive at the rental booth but have to wait patiently for the next available carriage. A few moments pass and a carriage arrives. The couple leaves. Sasha starts toward it.

"Wait, this isn't the one," Jason states.

He informs the people behind him that they can proceed ahead of them. Minutes later, another one arrives carrying an older woman and her dog.

"I suppose this isn't the right one either?"

"Nope, this isn't the one. The one we're waiting for is special."

"What's special about it? They're all the same."

"I beg to differ. There's only one like this in the city and I intend to ride in it."

"So, what's special about it?"

"See for yourself. It's coming now."

The next carriage that arrives is quite different, something reminiscent from years past. It's a closed carriage sitting on two oval springs to smooth the ride. It has an arched roof and a door. Old-style lanterns are mounted on each side of the entranceway. Each of its two windows—one on the door and the other in the rear—are covered with a semi-sheer curtain. Inside there are a couple of plush leather seats facing each other that comfortably seat four. The interior walls and roof are covered with velour padding for added flavor. The only modern feature is the hand crank that operates a version of a sunroof. The inside compartment is illuminated by four small battery-operated lanterns in each corner that possess a knob at the base to control the brightness.

"This is the one."

"You're right. This one is definitely different from the others."

Jason helps her into the carriage and passes the driver a couple of crisp folded bills.

"More of these will follow if you just ride until I tell you to stop."

"Yes, Sir," he says with excitement.

"Now isn't this cozy?" Jason says.

"It's quite nice. It has its own romantic air about it, and it looks like someone spent a small fortune on these seats."

"Then you're pleased."

"Very much so."

"Then I'm happy. Shall we crank the roof back to enjoy the view of the full moon?"

"Not yet. I want to enjoy this as it is."

"Fine...now, where were we?"

"When?"

"Before we left Rosalina's."

"You were being naughty."

"Me! We both were. You were playing with hidden toys with your foot."

"And you gestured about eating things."

"Mind if I pick up where I left off?"

"Press on."

Jason dims the lanterns' illumination before engaging in a deep passionate kiss followed by one on the cheek and one softly on her ear, melting Sasha with his gentle touch. He runs his hand down between her breasts, to her side, all the way to her hemline at her knees and reverses direction, caressing her inner thigh with his fingertips before she clamps her legs shut, leaving his fingers just short of her womanhood.

"What are you doing? You can't do that here."

"Why not?"

"We'll be stopping soon."

"Who says? I paid him well to keep riding until he hears otherwise, so relax."

"What if someone hears us? It could be very embarrassing."

"What if? Hewlett Packard would love you. Everything's taken care of."

"Are you sure?"

"No, but what the hell. I've never let you down before. What are they going to do, arrest us if we're caught?"

"Jason..."

He bites her on the neck, then lets his head fall to her cleavage and licks her between the breasts. Her breathing instantly changes and the pressure on his hand subsides, allowing him to reach his destination. He's stunned to find her wetness has already soaked through her pantyhose.

"It's hot down there," he says.

"Wet, too!" Sasha boasts sinfully.

"I noticed. I like it that way."

She repositions herself, and then uses one of her hands to fondle his throbbing member. Slowly to a timed rhythm she caresses her toy, loosens his tie, unbuttons the top four buttons and bites him greedily on his nipples. After pulling his shirttail out she finishes the remaining buttons while her tongue flows down his chest to the waist.

"Now who's getting carried away?"

"You started it but I'll finish it." After opening his fly, his member stands at full attention. She skillfully strokes her joystick softly, paying much attention to its tip, in turn making him squirm. "All he needs is someone to talk to," she says while lowering her head.

His legs straighten and his thigh muscles tighten as he enjoys her continuous rhythmic motions. Each stroke is masterfully executed as she goes as deep as possible, swallowing to add more pleasure. His legs begin to shake to her quickening movements. Jason bursts into an explosive climax with her continuing to drain her makeshift candy of all of its juices. Nothing is wasted.

Sasha sits up pleased with Jason's response to her and uses her thumb to wipe the corner of her mouth before saying, "Now, he's all better."

"I'm lost for words...kiss me." He sits her on the adjacent seat. "You're wonderful."

"I try to be. I just can't believe we're doing this."

"Don't get settled; the fun has just begun."

Jason reaches under her dress and pulls her pantyhose down with one smooth motion. Sasha's hips cooperate willingly to his skillful moves. She melts to his tantalizing hands as he removes the hose from her legs one at a time. Her dress is pushed above her hips and Jason maneuvers himself on the floor between her legs.

"You don't have to do me just because I did you."

"That's not what this is all about. You treated me freely and I'll do the same. Mainly, because this is something I enjoy doing."

Sasha's feet are placed on the opposite seat. A sudden nervousness overwhelms her caused by the vulnerability her position provides. As quickly as it developed, her nervousness dissipates when Jason begins to nibble on her inner thigh, biting one side, then the other while brushing his tongue against her womanhood when changing sides. Jason attacks her eagerly, hungrily tasting her only to find the extreme wetness is a trap. His tasty delight pulls on his face with the gravitational force of a spatial black hole. His nose, ears, his entire head vanish into her hotbox, closing around his neck, making him resemble an animal with its head buried in the ground. Still he continues his plight to unleash her juices. The closer she gets to her peak, the more his head is forced out. Just before her ecstasy, his head pops out and he quickly tackles the man-in-the-boat to ignite the explosion. After a short moment, she wiggles in the seat, releasing the floodgates into Jason's mouth. Not willing to lose the momentum, he quickly sits on the opposite seat while dropping his pants and pulls her into his grasp. After positioning her feet, he lowers her onto him and thrusts himself hard into her with a broken, uncontrolled rhythm until they both begin to pant. Her moans grow louder as she again peaks with Jason continuing his movements to drive her wild.

"Stop," she says. "Stop, I'm too sensitive."

Ignoring her cry, Jason continues.

"Stop!" she screams uncontrollably.

"Whoa!" the driver says.

"Not you!" Jason yells. "Keep driving!"

"Jason, you're driving me crazy. I need a moment to rest."

He stops his movements while she rides him to the rhythm of the bouncing carriage.

"You're trying to kill me," Sasha states.

"Can you think of a better way to die?"

"Do you think people heard us?"

"It doesn't matter. They can only assume."

"The bouncing carriage tickles me. I have to move." She slowly lifts herself and sits next to Jason, still experiencing quivers from her back-to-back orgasms. "I'm sensitive all over. You touch me anywhere and I'll get chills."

"As they say, I done good."

"You done did excellent...How about a nightcap at my place?"

"Sure, can we enjoy the full moon first?"

"That's it! The full moon. It's responsible for me behaving this way. Making love riding around the city isn't me."

"They say strange things happen when the moon is full."

"I'm inclined to agree."

"You have regrets?"

"Not at all."

"We can do this again someday."

"Anytime, lover."

They get their clothes back on straight and proper. Jason cranks the sunroof back and they sit embraced, gazing into the stars for minutes without speaking. After awhile he makes his wishes known to the driver.

"When you get back to our starting point, you can stop."

Moments later, the carriage stops and the door opens. Jason exits with no remorse while Sasha peeks her head out to see who's watching before allowing him to help her down. He gives the driver another folded bill and thanks him for his cooperation before leaving. On the way back to Sasha's home, she sits silent with a pleasant smile glowing on her face. She thinks about how different and wonderful the surprise has been while trying to conjure up something equally special for him.

"Talk to me. I still respect you," he says jokingly.

"Cute. My thoughts are nothing but pleasant."

"Care to share them with me?"

"No, I prefer to show you."

"Oh?"

She embraces him with a tight squeeze, followed by a soft kiss on his cheek. She caresses his pants at the crotch until they bulge, then pulls his erect member through the zipper opening for her enjoyment.

"I see he wants to play."

"Would you do something with him? I can't control him," Jason jokes.

"As you wish."

"Wait a minute. What did I get myself into?"

The car carrying two passengers suddenly gives the appearance of only one passenger. Her actions are successful as she notices his speech becoming very broken. Too successful, accompanying her timed mouth motions, she becomes aware of the car's series of sways. Each descending motion brings a sway to the left and an opposite sway as her head rises. The car quickly projects two passengers again.

"I'd better stop before I get us killed. You were swaying something awful."

"I was? I hadn't noticed."

"I'm sure. There's no telling what would have happened if you'd climaxed. You probably would've put us in a compromising position."

"I suppose you are right."

They picture themselves trying to explain the cause of the accident and burst into laughter.

Sasha enters her condo, kicks off her shoes, drops her purse on the sofa and gives Jason an unexpected passionate kiss.

"You can get yourself in trouble like that," Jason suggests.

"I enjoy your kind of trouble...Coffee?"

"Please."

Jason approaches from behind, gives her a strong hug and a quick nibble on the ear before whispering, "No instant coffee today?"

"You've earned a reward, so I'm grinding beans. Actually, it became a waste to make a full pot with me only drinking it."

"Let's start a fire."

"More body heat, sounds lovely. I love it. We should shower first, then you can be the doctor and..."

"No dear, sorry to disappoint you. I mean in the fireplace."

"Spoiled sport."

"You have wood and fire logs."

"True but the weather is delightful outside."

"It doesn't have to be cold to enjoy the crackling and brilliant colors of the flames. We can dim the lights and sit close to the fire."

"I've never known any man as romantic as you."

"Do I take that as 'yes?'"

"My pleasure," she replies while turning to kiss him.

Jason prepares the fire while the coffee brews, dims the lights and invites Sasha to join him on the floor in front of the growing fire. All is dark except the magnificent glow from the fire and a blinking green light in the distance.

"Is that your answering machine?"

"Yes," she states after a brief pause.

"Why don't you see who's called? It might be something important. I count five messages."

"Let's not spoil this mood. There's no rush," Sasha states upon feeling an anxiety attack coming on. "I can listen to them later."

"Pardon me, but is it me, or did your mood change slightly with the mention of it?"

"No, it didn't. I'm just not interested in who's called," she replies more defensively than she would have liked.

"Excuse me for being persistent, but, I get paid to detect these kinds of things. So tell me, is there someone you're afraid to hear from?"

Sasha stares into the fire with no reply.

"I am correct and I'd venture to say that the same thing upset you yesterday. Correct? I only ask because I'm concerned."

"Jason, I can handle it."

"Okay, handle it but at least tell me what you're attempting to handle."

"Jason, please."

"It isn't that simple. Something has you frightened and I believe I deserve to know what that something is. I have all night."

"All right, maybe my fear will lessen once I tell you. I received a threatening call at work yesterday and when I got home there were more on my machine."

"Someone threatening you is my business. Do you know who it is?"

"The one at work came from a Mr. Livingston. Well, he didn't threaten me directly, but he did make strong accusations that if you read between the lines there could be threatening overtures. The ones on the machine could have been him or someone else. They weren't clear; whoever it was muffled their voice."

"May I listen to them?"

"You can't. I erased them yesterday because I kept playing them over and over again."

"Why would Mr. Livingston make threats...better yet, what is your association with him?"

"It's a long story."

"I have nothing but time."

19

Walking into Jason's home, there is a long entrance foyer covered with Oriental characters and paintings. To the right is the living area. The couch is low; it has small wooden legs with an Oriental design etched in the fabric.

"Thanks for letting me stay here. I'm frightened with everything going on," says Sasha.

"No problem...actually I prefer you staying here while I conduct my investigation."

"That's just another great part of your character. Like your exquisite taste in furnishings. I know few men whose decor is Oriental."

"Actually, I like contrast. Each room tells a different story expressing the different chapters in my life."

"Oh?"

"Okay, expressing my many moods."

"I do feel terrible. You've been recently reinstated and now you're going to work on my problem. How can you possibly have time for your case? I hope your Captain doesn't find out."

"Don't worry. I can handle him. Besides, it shouldn't take long."

"Are you sure? I wouldn't want to cause you any undo hardship."

"Piece of cake."

The next morning Jason is awakened by the smell of freshly brewed coffee. Sasha is preparing a nutritious breakfast. The only things missing are the runny eggs and Jason. Following his brief moment in the bathroom, he stumbles into the kitchen and is surprised at his findings.

"Good morning, sleepyhead."

"Morning...what's this?"

"Wake up and smell the coffee. It's breakfast."

"I see that...you're full of surprises."

"I knew you'd have a full day, so I prepared a little something to get your engines started. I would have prepared a complete breakfast but your cabinets are bare. I assume most bachelors live like you."

"Probably not, the others can cook."

"Regardless, a good breakfast will help you think clearly."

"I suppose you're right. However, most of my work will be done by others."

"No riddles this early in the morning, okay?"

"Let's say I have a few chips to cash in."

"People around town owe you favors."

"Kinda."

"Where do you intend to start?"

"I think I'll drop by the Far East Import Company. I want to see what this Mr. Livingston has to say. Then I'll go to City Hall and pull a few strings to discover their history."

"I think you're forgetting something vital. Today is Saturday. Those people should not be working."

"Where's my head? You did say that today their shipment arrives."

"That's what Howard told me. They could be hanging around the docks. Maybe not, because they didn't get the money."

"It can't hurt to check. I wish you hadn't erased those messages. I would have liked to make voice comparisons of my own."

"They were muffled but believe me, you'd recognize Mr. Livingston's voice. He has a heavy English accent."

"That's helpful."

"Just promise me something...please be careful. This man could be potentially dangerous."

"I'm attracted to danger. It ought to be fun."

"Promise me...promise me!"

"I promise. Make yourself at home. My home is your home."

"Okay, get out."

"Oh, I'm the guest now."

"Not funny, huh?"

"Close, it kinda tickles my throat."

After completing his meal, he charges forward anxious to free the burden from Sasha's shoulders. The first part of that task begins at the station. He asks Barbara—a young desk clerk who has been striving for his attention—to get any information on arriving vessels. His next step is to get information on the Far East Import Company, starting with the new police computer. First he must get through Bob, an officer who plays by the rules. One would do better to ask him for his right hand than to break the rules.

"Hey, Bob, what brings you here Saturday?"

"I'm trying to familiarize myself with this new computer. I'm giving training classes on it starting Monday."

"How's it coming?"

"Okay, I guess...there's so much to remember. The bottom line is to enter commands, push a button or two and 'presto.' Your information appears. It's a little complicated but I'll get it."

"Tell me, is this linked with the other precincts?"

"Once I finish setting it up, it could access any precinct in the state. Actually, all of our files are stored in a common database. The trick is getting the network connection to work properly. Then we can access DEA, FBI, CIA or any other government agency as well, with a few additional commands."

"What about the local government?"

"It should access state agencies as well."

"City Hall?"

"All right, why the twenty questions? Where are you going with this?"

"No place special, just trying to give you some practical experience."

"Oh, no," Bob states with his head shaking from side-to-side. "Captain's orders. I'm not to go on line until Monday. He's budget-conscious lately and each precinct is to pay for its individual usage."

"Come on, some quick information from City Hall. I'll owe you one."

"No way, you know how Captain North is. I'd hang."

"What would I do if you were asking me?"

"You'd probably heed to my request and face the consequences later."

"Right, so what's wrong?"

"I'm not you. It would require my head being put on Captain North's chopping block and unlike you, I don't like being in that position."

Jason cleverly changes his tactics and creates a new rumor of his own. "I think Barbara has the hots for you. When I walked in, she was looking this way very curiously."

"Think so?"

"I know so," Jason lies. "I might be able to arrange something between you two."

Bob straightens his tie and glances across the room at her just in time to receive a pleasant smile intended for Jason.

"See," Jason states. "What did I tell you? She's yearning for you."

His deceived ego begins to shine. "I kinda thought that all along. She's been giving me the eyes for a while now."

Got you, Jason thinks. "I'll go over and put in a good word if you do me this favor."

"You honestly think she would go out with me?"

"Absolutely. It is in the bag."

"Hell, what do you need information on?"

"Get me anything on the Far East Import Company at the docks, and I'll go over and charm Barbara for you."

"Great...by the way, how soon do you need this information?"

"Yesterday."

"On it."

"Any news yet, Barbara?"

"This matter is going to take a while."

"Fine, I have to make a run. I'll be back later and you might want to concentrate your efforts on ships arriving from the Orient. These are the ones I'm mostly concerned with. Also, Bob wants a date with you," Jason states casually.

"Our Bob?"

"Yep."

"Isn't he gay?" Barbara whispers.

"That's news to me. He is shy when it comes to approaching women."

"That's it, huh."

"Really, he likes you."

"I'll feel him out, but what about you?"

"What about me?"

"Do you like me?"

"You're a charming woman."

"Jason, that is very sweet. Now, answer my question. Do you like me?"

"If I allowed myself, I guess I could."

"You guess...this could be a ten-minute lecture, but your urgency shows so we can stop this for now. But, rest assured, this conversation is far from being over."

"Okay, I must get a move-on."

The second part of the quest ends at the Far East Import Company where Jason finds Howard inspecting a few items. After a brief introduction, he begins his questioning. Howard is professional and courteous while answering Jason's questions to the best of his knowledge and promises to get answers to all of the unanswered ones. He's relieved that no charges of perjury and attempted bribery will be filed if all contact with Sasha ends. And, he quickly jumps at the chance to eliminate any criminal charges. Moreover, the questions relating to threatening calls to Sasha stun him. However, he sincerely relays no knowledge of them.

"Oh, I'm sure my boss isn't behind such actions. That's not his style."

"Will he be available for questioning later?"

"I couldn't tell you. I only manage the place. He's more of the owner, so he pops in whenever."

"I hope you're right about him. If I have to come back, it surely will not be a social call."

"I'm sure I am."

"So, to recap, without the required loan, you have no further need to contact Ms. Fong?"

"This is correct. Her services are no longer needed."

"I'll hold you to your word."

Unaware to them, their entire conversation has been overheard by Mr. Livingston. After Jason leaves, Mr. Livingston appears out of nowhere, angry.

"Howard!" Mr. Livingston yells.

"Huh? What?" he utters startled.

"What the hell do you think you're doing?"

"Boss? Where did you go?"

"That's no concern of yours," Mr. Livingston rages. "I come in the back way only to find you spilling all of our business."

"I didn't tell him anything. Hell, I didn't have anything to spill. He seemed insistent about threats to the woman at the bank. I denied it, of course. I know I didn't make any...did you?"

"I made a few hard statements out of anger."

"You what? Threats?"

"So what, threats. I thought I could force her into helping us get the loan."

"That's not good business."

"You want good business, sell hamburgers. There's so much you don't know about this operation. Why did you tell him about our bribe to that woman? You talked to him like you wanted us to get busted."

"Busted? Please enlighten me because I'm in the dark. Not knowing we have something to hide, I may have told him something you didn't want revealed."

"You never guessed something was fishy? You never noticed most things we bought were hollow? Howard, my naïve compadre, the major support for this operation is drugs."

"Drugs!"

"How else do you think we survived all this time?"

"I thought the few sales we had kept us floating above water."

"Right," he says sarcastically. "If it weren't for the drugs, you would've been out of a job a long time ago."

"This loan from the bank. It is for drugs?"

"Yes, the shipment arrives tonight."

"So, the story about the seven armor pieces was fictitious?"

"Now you're getting the picture."

"I wish you'd told me. I wouldn't have peddled drugs, and you threatening an innocent woman is far beyond my comprehension. I can't believe this is all true. I'm glad she decided against the loan. Drugs are out of my league."

"You've heard me talk to the investors that keep this place operational. I buy the drugs and they sell them. Our profit margin increases daily. Also..."

"Wait! I don't care about that. The threatening calls to Ms. Fong bother me the most."

"Only to scare her."

"That's it," Howard testifies. "I'm out of here. I want no part of this. Please accept the door closing behind my back as my official resignation."

"What do you plan to do?"

"I'll find employment elsewhere."

"I don't care where the fuck you work...I'm talking about your new-found information."

"What you do is none of my business, but I'll apologize to Ms. Fong for your unethical behavior."

"She mustn't know the true nature of our business."

"You don't care but I do. Sell your drugs and leave me and the woman out of this."

Howard grabs his jacket, briskly fleeing toward the door while Mr.

Livingston watches him with fire in his eyes. He had given a nobody without experience a manager's position. Feeling as though some gratuity should be returned, he can't understand how Howard could leave without trying to see his point of view. Howard storms off with Mr. Livingston continuing to plead his case. Anger flows through his trembling body, forcing rage to seize a nearby crowbar. Two thuds are heard. The first one occurs when Howard is hit in the back of the head, and the other sounds as his limp body collapses to the floor.

"I'm sorry, Howard. You've been a trusted employee, but I can't risk you revealing my operation. You could've had it good."

Mr. Livingston musters enough strength to drag Howard's deadweight body to the rear and out the door. After searching for unsuspecting eyes, he hauls the body to the seawall and pushes it helplessly into the water where it is instantly swallowed, seemingly without a chew. He waits for the water to calm itself, watching closely, making sure the body doesn't resurface. Afterwards he kicks around loose dirt to cover the tracks created by Howard's dragging feet. Knowing that much is at stake—including his life—he returns to the shop to prepare for the incoming shipment.

CHAPTER 20

Returning to the station, Bob greets Jason with a report on the Far East Import Company. The computer provides Jason with one new piece of information, verifying Sasha's initial statements of Howard's and Mr. Livingston's existence plus its owners. A company called Worldwide Investments owns it.

"Thanks a bunch, Bob," Jason states. "You work fast. It appears that the Far East Import has a clean record—nothing unusual about this report. Good buddy, you know what this means?"

"Let me guess. You need a background report on Worldwide Investments."

"Just as a precautionary measure. I'd like to know who I'm dealing with."

"I thought you would. It's already in the making. It should be completed in a few minutes."

"Great, I owe you one."

"You owe me a date with Barbara."

"You bet."

He picks up the telephone and dials the number listed for the Far East Import Company. After a few rings, Mr. Livingston answers the call.

"Far East Import. If we can't get it, it doesn't exist. This is Mr. Livingston. How may I help you?"

"Catchy slogan. Hello, this is Detective Jerrard, Sixteenth Precinct. I'm investigating a complaint against your company, so I wonder if I could come down and ask you a few questions. I dropped by earlier but I missed you."

"You were here?" Mr. Livingston pretends.

"Yes, didn't your manager, Howard Normin, tell you?"

"I'm sorry but when I arrived, he wasn't here. I assume he'll be returning shortly."

"Since I've already questioned him, would you mind my asking you a few questions?"

"Surely," he replies cooperatively. "Questions concerning what?"

"Your dealings with one Ms. Sasha Fong."

"The woman at the bank?"

"Precisely."

"Charming woman, though I've never met her personally. What about her?"

"It's my understanding that the Far East Import has requested a loan from her place of employment."

"True, is that illegal?"

"It's the ethics surrounding your request that raises suspicions. To be more precise, I believe falsifying your profit and loss sheets is a huge red flag."

"I can't deny that our information was altered a little but not to the point where it would be illegal. Let's face it, this is big business and in corporate America, lying is a standard survival practice. With all the massive takeovers nowadays, it's the only way a small company like mine can stay afloat."

"I've empathy for you, but surely you didn't expect her to push your loan through based on a bunch of lies?"

"Certainly I did. Everything was in order. She would've been compensated for her efforts."

"You mean your attempted bribe. I'm aware of your measure to persuade her to participate in your illegal dealings."

"I'm not sure I know what you are referring to."

"Allow me to use your words: Call it a little business proposition involving a Porsche."

"That was merely kindness, my gratitude for her cooperation."

"Sending a card and/or flowers is the politically correct way to show your appreciation, but in police terminology, what you did is called a bribe."

"Call it what you like but no harm or illegalities were intended."

"So far you could be charged on two criminal offenses, but Ms. Fong asked me to bargain with you first. She only wishes that you stop harassing her. If you agree to stop, she agrees not to press charges."

"I never meant her troubles."

"I was told that you called her at work and were more than irate."

"I was troubled by the news that she rejected my kindness. As I explained to her, my company's survival depended on that loan. I may have said some things out of disappointment and anger."

"And you're fine now?"

"I assure you, Sir, my emotions are now intact."

"Well, Mr. Livingston, it appears our little chat has proved to be helpful. I'll advise Ms. Fong that you apologized for your actions, and your threatening calls to her home and office will cease from this point."

"You can't prove that I called her," he defends aggressively.

"Whoa, Mr. Livingston, if I had a previous doubt about you placing calls to her home, they've just been justified by such a defensive tone."

"Prove it!"

"I don't need to. I know you wouldn't be smart enough to call from your office or home. I could get a listing from the phone company on the origin of all Ms. Fong's incoming calls for the past few days, but you know as I know, it would be a waste of time."

"I believe so."

"Your arrogance is amazing—anyway the number 946-6321 is unknown to you?"

"For the last time, I've never dialed 946-6231 in my life and I don't intend to!"

"Interesting...very well. Since we understand each other, things should be fine. I'll contact Ms. Fong and you'll receive her reply later."

"Good enough. Goodbye."

"Chow."

After the call, Jason is amazed how little humans can control a conscious thought under duress. He deliberately had superimposed the suffix of Sasha's home telephone number, and Mr. Livingston unknowingly recited the correct suffix back to him, verifying his original thoughts.

"What's that all about?" Bob questions.

"That conversation ties in with the information you're getting me."

"I see...the captain has you really humping. Two cases at once."

"This one is sort of personal. I'm trying to stop the harassment of a friend."

The report on Worldwide Investments shows it is owned by a group of five men. One has a prior drug arrest but no conviction, and the remaining four are under surveillance by the Federal Drug Enforcement Agency for suspected drug trafficking. Each co-owner has several aliases. Most damaging to Worldwide Investments are its businesses located in Miami, China, Panama and Cuba.

"Now isn't that special," Jason states.

"The report?"

"Yes, it appears that I've stumbled onto something. Worldwide Investments owns businesses in the major drug capitals of the world. If my hunch is correct, she was misled from the beginning. Barbara's information should tie nicely with this."

"What's going on? Who's she?"

"I'll explain later. You may even get rewarded for using the computer early."

"Everyone could use a little recognition but you may be reprimanded. You're stepping out of your boundaries."

"Why would you say that?"

"This is the kind of thing the narcotics department should know about."

"We're all officers of the law."

"Detective McAllister is floating around here somewhere. He should be notified of your findings."

"Chris? He wouldn't listen to me. He still carries thick air between us. It goes back to..."

"Jason," Barbara interrupts, "got some news fresh from the press."

"Be right there...I'll get back with you, Bob."

Jason reviews the information presented and discovers three possible arrivals at the dock later that evening. He's mostly interested in a ship named the Vessel. All information available suggests that the ship is headed there from Shanghai, expected to be dock sometime near midnight.

"This one called the Vessel. Is it the only one arriving from the Orient?"

"It's the only one. The Coast Guard reports that it radioed in claiming minor engine trouble."

"Shot any dirt lately?" a voice intrudes sarcastically.

Detective Christopher McAllister heads the Narcotics Division. Equal to Jason in age, he often competes with him in dress, grooming attitude and career moves. Although they're matched in rank, he has kept some resentment toward Jason since he edged him out of the top of the class years ago in the academy.

"Come on, Chris, drop it. That was years ago."

"Some things haunt you for life. Anyway, what do you know about this ship the Vessel?"

"I know enough to suspect it for drug trafficking. We homicide detectives have our methods of obtaining information."

"Yeah, I know. I've heard about your methods."

"What can you tell me about this ship?"

"Our local snitch tipped me off about it weeks ago, but it wasn't until today that I decided to pay attention to his information."

"Is this snitch reliable?"

"He was caught stealing and sang like a bird when he realized he would be sent to the slammer. At times I've found his information to be more reliable than the computers, but it was an anonymous caller that sparked more interest. An unknown caller said that a vessel...the Vessel could've been what he said...would be arriving today. He was pretty insistent about this ship's cargo, well, some of it containing drugs. I checked with my people. None of them has received any information, but after overhearing you, there must be something concrete to his call."

"Why didn't you act upon the caller's tip?"

"I thought it was some sort of coincidence at first, but after putting one plus one together and your investigation making three, the situation deserves my attention. Additionally, there has been an ongoing investigation of the overflow of drugs into the city for months. All we've been able to discover is that their mode of transportation has switched from the airways to the waterways. Thus far, their operation seems to have their gears well-oiled."

"Not that well-oiled. I know of one mistake that was made."

"What do you know, Detective?"

"I know for some reason they ran short of money. If you could put aside that chip you carry, we could grab a cup of coffee and compare notes."

"I guess."

"You guess. Don't do me any favors."

"It's possible. The ship isn't expected until midnight."

"So, you do know something."

"All right, let's get this talk over so I can get on with my case. There's much preparation involved."

"Your case...you don't even know where the drugs are stored once they enter the city."

"Nevertheless, I'll know soon enough because you are going to tell me. You're not going to steal this bust from me. To infiltrate this drug ring would mean lieutenant bars for me."

"Would you stop trying to race me and act like a narcotics detective? Do you want to talk or what?"

"Let's get on with it."

They discuss all available information on the arriving ship, finally concluding that a shipment of drugs will indeed be arriving later. With strong intentions on foiling the delivery, they carefully plan a stakeout and discuss each other's roles in the upcoming assignment.

CHAPTER 21

The dock is semi-lighted, making for poor visibility. Tall lampposts helplessly shine over the fog creating more of a haze than light, and the beam from the lighthouse plays more like a dim flashlight as it attempts to pierce haze. Silhouettes of ships of all sizes sit in the night. Abandoned forklifts along with other types of machinery rest from their twelve-hour day. A gull sings in the dark while tiny waves crash against the sea wall.

Appearing into the most lighted spot on the pier is a street person—commonly referred to as homeless by sophisticates—being observed through infrared binoculars. His worldly possessions are kept inside a laundry cart lined with a torn trash bag. Outdated clothes, a bicycle seat and a naked doll with one leg protrude from its top. Desperately, he searches the trash receptacle for food. Moments later, his reward is a partially eaten candy bar. He moves closer to the water and takes a seat leaning against a ship's tie pole, then enjoys his delicacy before he drifts into slumber. All else is quiet.

Detective McAllister and a small arsenal of other officers wait impatiently for the ship to arrive. They set their ambush adjacent to the docks in an abandoned warehouse. Several rows of windows provide an adequate view of any movement on the dock. Each man is armed with a military issue C16 rifle loaded with tracer bullets. Several other magazines of ammunition hang at their waists. Only two differ; these men carry submachine guns. The men study the dock quietly and carefully. Moments pass and a late-model car with only its parking lights on slowly inches its way closer in the distance. The car stops and the lights disappear. Concealed by natural elements the car is virtually invisible.

"I'll bet Detective Jerrard arrives simultaneously with the ship, pulls a John Wayne and charges it," Detective McAllister says to himself disturbed. "I knew I couldn't count on a homicide cop in the dangerous world of narcotics."

The midnight hour passes and with forty-five minutes remaining in the hour, the ship arrives. A faint foghorn is heard. Moments later, a huge cargo ship maneuvers its way alongside the dock. The engines die and a small motor boat makes its way to the seawall, followed by four thick ropes that are flung over the ship's side. Two men emerge from the boat and quickly tie the ropes around the poles. Wakened out of his slumber, the bum moves just long enough to have the rope tied, then falls back into his position trying to regain his comfort zone. The roar of other straining engines sends clouds of smoke into the air. Its struggle overtakes the silence as the ship hoists itself closer to the seawall, revealing large capital letters painted in fluorescent orange, displaying the vessel's name along the width of the ship.

"There's no mistaking," Detective McAllister says. "We have the right ship. The name is visible from here at this hour. Okay, men," he whispers, "we wait for anything unusual. Normally the men would exit and the ship would be unloaded at dawn. Something out of the ordinary is bound to happen."

The trigger-happy young recruits wait anxiously for their shot at stardom while the ship sits oddly in the dark against the pier. A ramp slowly descends from its side and many men depart, looking relieved to be on land. Several chatter their way out of sight while the bum begs for loose change from the few men who cross his path.

"Nothing strange about that," an officer states.

"Just hold your horses," Detective McAllister responds. "This is a good tip. I know it."

A lone man appears on the ramp wearing a suit and tie complemented by spit-shined shoes. He slowly walks to the dock to wait for his counterpart. He stops to light a cigarette. After a few pulls of the cigarette, it falls to the ground with the burning glow reflecting off the highly glossed shoe before it is crushed under his feet. He walks over to the bum and shoves him away. In a hurry to gather his belongings, the doll falls from the cart. He retrieves what he's able and reluctantly walks away making obscene gestures at the man as he vanishes into the darkness. Another cigarette is lit; he stands there enjoying its aroma. A dim glow appears, followed by the thud of a closed car door. Heavy footsteps at a distance grow louder. Soon Mr. Livingston greets the man. Following some small talk, Mr. Livingston points toward his car and the man points up to the ship's deck. Like the few times before, they return to their respected vehicles and Mr. Livingston presents a medium-sized suitcase. The man struggles down the ramp with an oversized box marked "Oriental Antiques."

"Stand by, men," Detective McAllister orders. "We must wait for their exchange."

They place their items at their feet and exchange sides. Mr. Livingston tears open the top. Inside there's a sword among many other items. He screws off the knob at the end of the handle. Concealed inside the hollow handle is a white powder. After wetting his pinky fingertip with his mouth, he tastes the merchandise.

"Good shit."

"The finest quality as always. Now, let's see what kind of goodies you have for me."

He struggles with the straps of the old-fashioned suitcase and releases the final buckle when an unsuspecting body emerges from the lower platform where small boats let passengers on and off. He wears a long drab green poncho, a rain cap of the same color and fisherman's boots that cover his entire thigh. His face is wet, but the fury he has burns the wetness like butter in a hot pan. Even with a noticeable shiver, he quickly descends upon them, pointing a cocked pistol at Mr. Livingston.

"Livingston! You bastard!" Howard cries. "I've been waiting hours for this. This deal is over now and so is your life."

"Howard?" Mr. Livingston utters in shock.

"Who's this man?" the third man asks.

"But you're..."

"Dead," Howard interrupts. "You should make sure when you kill someone that their living ghosts don't come back to haunt you."

"Now, don't be hasty," Mr. Livingston recites, short of a plea for his life. "I can explain."

"No need. You simply wanted to kill me; I simply want to kill you."

"Livingston, what's this all about?" the third man interrupts.

"He's a former colleague who became a threat to my operation, so I tried to dispose of him." He turns to Howard. "Surely you can understand my position."

"Dispose of? I'm reduced to garbage now? I'll never understand when someone tries to kill me. You wanted me dead!"

"Surely we can come to an agreement. Just relax."

"Excuse me," the third man intrudes. "This doesn't concern me so, Livingston, when you get yourself organized, maybe we can bargain."

"You stay where you are. You're no better than him."

"But I'm not involved in your dispute."

"You stand still or you'll die, too."

"Howard," Mr. Livingston says. "Let's bargain."

"Right," the third man says suggestively. "What do you want? Anything...money?"

"No!" Howard snaps. "The bastard tried to kill me because of something I didn't know. So, it is going to be an eye for an eye, dead for dead."

The third man slowly bends. He turns the suitcase facing Howard and lifts the lid revealing the contents.

"Here, there's close to half a million dollars here. Take it and let's forget we ever met."

One quick glance and Howard discovers more mayhem.

"I didn't want your drug money in the first place and I surely don't want a suitcase full of newspapers."

"Newspapers! Livingston, you double-crossing son-of-a-bitch. You tried to rip me off."

"We didn't get the money, so I figured if you tried to kill me, you would try to deceive whoever was delivering the drugs. What were you going to do now, kill him, too?" Howard asks.

"Both of you try to understand. My life is on the line," Mr. Livingston pleads.

As a distraction, the third man throws a small fit by jumping up and down with his arms waving wildly. "You bastard!" he yells.

He reaches to his back underneath his jacket and produces his revolver, pointing it at Mr. Livingston. With quick actions for a person of his age, Mr. Livingston magically produces a weapon of his own. As in an equally matched chess game, Howard points his gun at Mr. Livingston, Mr. Livingston points his gun at Howard while the third man fans his gun between the two producing somewhat of a stalemate. The fury that once consumed Howard's eyes has transformed itself to rage, tainting and feeding the third man's rage while fearful tension reaps Mr. Livingston's face. In the heat of the moment their eye contact gets interrupted by the bum entering the scene, pushing his cart to retrieve his doll.

"Get out of here, you homeless freak," the third man states. "I've already told you to go away once."

"Me just want doll," the bum responds with all eyes peered on him. He picks up the doll by its one leg and shoves it head-first into the cart. His hand disappears for a quick second. The other hand flips off the three out of disgust. With an unexpected motion, he unleashes an automatic pistol. "Freeze!" he yells.

Instantly, the trio becomes a quartet and the scenario becomes more of a chaotic foray of nerves. The third man's and Mr. Livingston's guns point back and forth between Howard and the bum. Howard's weapon remains on Mr. Livingston, and the bum's lone pistol flags the three down.

"Okay, men, party time," Detective McAllister instructs. "It's gotten out of hand. Let's get them!"

The huge sliding door flies open and the small renegade of men charge forward like a calvary coming to the rescue of a fallen fort. The police scatter attempting to surround the criminals, only to be deterred by a wave of automatic fire shot from atop the vessel deck. Relentlessly they return their own firepower. Tracer bullets dance through the night like speeding miniature flares. Some officers drop for safety; others fall either injured or dead. The assault disintegrates quickly into only Detective McAllister and two other officers shooting blindly at the arsenal of fire coming from the ship. Mr. Livingston darts for safety while Howard maneuvers his way behind him, yelling for the police to hear.

"Don't shoot! I'm the anonymous caller!"

The third man runs to escape in the other direction. The bum executes enough vertical rolls on the ground to reach the dock's edge. He rapidly depletes the rounds in his pistol blindly at a shadow atop the ship's deck. Seconds later, a human silhouette tumbles over the side into the water. Detective McAllister quickly covers the bum.

"Police! Freeze, scum. Don't even blink," Detective McAllister demands.

"Easy, Chris. It's me, Jason."

"Jason! You fouled the entire operation. We each had our roles but you...what the hell was that? This was a well-executed..."

"Save it, Chris. Be a good cop and let's help capture the fleeing men. I'll help your men chase the man off the ship and you go after the other two."

"I can't believe you," Chris responds, starting his pursuit. "I'll help my own men. You haven't heard the last of this."

"Yeah, yeah, be quick and careful."

Their chase begins as they vanish into the darkness. Detective McAllister's journey ends prematurely when two officers escort the third man back to their staging area before he could get more than a few strides under his belt. Jason instinctively follows the sound of gunfire at a near distance to discover shadows of Howard and Mr. Livingston playing a childish game of hide and seek while on a desperate mission to destroy each other. Knowing that the many machines furnish adequate concealment from a deadly bullet, Jason eases into the game reflecting on his childhood years when he had to hide from the older teens to prevent bodily injury to himself. He maneuvers soundlessly on and around the machines, using the darker shadows to his advantage.

"Howard," Mr. Livingston cries, "must it come to this? Let's get away while we both can."

"It's too late to be reasonable. One of us isn't walking away."

"Howard, this is Detective Jerrard. There's no need for more killing. You can practically walk away from this with a smack on the back of your hand but not if you commit murder."

"Sorry, Detective, he tried to kill me."

"That's just another charge we can place against him. He'll be behind bars forever."

"Howard, don't listen to him. If I go to jail you go, too!"

"I don't care. Revenge flows through my veins. I'm going to kill your ass."

"Calm yourself, Howard. You have nothing to worry about. Mr. Livingston is the one we want."

The talk suddenly ends and the game resumes. Jason realizes that sometimes it's better to be pursued than in pursuit and hides in the darkness waiting for them to reveal their whereabouts. The long wait is taxing. However, he is rewarded in the end when Mr. Livingston turns the corner where he hides. Content that he's found a safe haven to screen himself, he backs toward Jason.

"The boogieman has you now," Jason says. "Slow and easy, pass me your gun."

Mr. Livingston raises his hands above his head with the cocked revolver dangling on his index finger. As Jason reaches for the gun, Mr. Livingston lets it fall to the ground. The impact jars the hammer loose and the gun fires. Jason's natural instincts cause him to duck, while Mr. Livingston picks up a running stride away from Jason. He collides with Howard, they fall to the ground and Howard's gun is lost in the darkness.

Once on their feet, the prizefight begins with them making an imaginary ring only a foot from the dock's edge. As in modern times a strong young contender fights his way through the ranks competing for the fight of his life. His flashy style, arrogant words and media hype play an important role in his quest. The champion's greatest bout continues to be Father Time's struggle against his poise and stamina. The legs that once floated him through the bout tires in the beginning rounds, and the confidence in his experience lacks conviction to intimidate his younger opponent.

Howard moves around lightly, threatening bodily injury while Mr. Livingston pivots to his every move, pleading with him to understand. Howard moves in throwing punches wildly. Mr. Livingston's slower arms counter most of Howard's efforts. Jason approaches intending on making an arrest when a slight glare from a switchblade that Mr. Livingston suddenly produces waves in the night.

"Enough of this shit," Mr. Livingston states. "I'll show you, youngster, how the game was played in my time."

He charges Howard knife-first. Howard grabs his hand and the struggle for the knife's control sends their hands flying upward. The momentum of Mr. Livingston's charge sends them tumbling over the side into the water. They disappear underneath the water for a brief moment, delaying the bout's outcome. A lone body surfaces from the depths gasping for air. Jason follows the shadow making its way to the lower platform.

The drenched body struggles to pull himself onto the cement platform. "He's dead," Howard says. "It was an accident. Somehow he tried to brace himself for the water's impact and I didn't. The knife is lodged in his stomach."

"I'm sure we won't prosecute if we have your cooperation from this point."

Entourages of back-up men arrive, twice as many as the original assault team. The man from the boat is arrested, the ship is seized and boarded, the remaining crew is apprehended, and armed guards are posted until morning when the ship can be dry-docked and thoroughly searched.

Jason leaves the final clean-up to Detective McAllister and retires home for fresh clothes, a shower and a decent meal. When he enters his home, Sasha is sleep on the sofa with some folded paper laying across her chest. He attempts to sneak past her without disturbing her, but Sasha suddenly sits upright, eyes wide open to a racing heart.

"Whoa, Sasha it's me," Jason quickly states. "I'm disguised."

"Disguised, you're dressed like a bum. Being suddenly awakened like that I couldn't tell who you were trying to tiptoe past me."

"This is my disguise for the stakeout we had tonight."

"You staked out the Far East Import?"

"No, we staked out the dock."

"Oh, I thought you'd found out something about them. Wait a minute. Their shipment was to arrive today."

"Right, it came in shortly after midnight. I'll give you all the details when I get cleaned up."

"Please do. You don't resemble the Jason I know in that costume of yours."

After his shower, Sasha is writing again on the folded paper. He watches her writing intensely, with depth and in heavy thought. Her involvement is so great that she doesn't feel his presence.

"Anything in that about me?" Jason interrupts.

"Just a second," she says without looking at him. "I don't want to lose my train of thought." After a brief moment, she replies, "I hope you don't mind. I looked everywhere for paper and found some on the top shelf in your bedroom closet. I also borrowed one of your shirts."

"I have no problem with any of that. What's this heavy writing about?"

"Nothing really...I just had a good series of sentences that I didn't want disturbed."

"Exactly, what are you writing?"

"Entries for my journal. I keep a record of all of my daily events. Someday I'll put them together and write a book."

"You write about everything?"

"Everything."

"Everything," he says, raising his eyebrows.

"Yep, that, too."

"That's in there," Jason says while sitting next to her. "Let me read my part."

"No, Jason, it's not for public eyes."

"Just let me read part of it."

"Definitely not. These are private thoughts, mind you."

"Okay, but if you don't, I'm going to do something I know you can't handle."

"You'd better not."

"I'm serious. I'll trickle you to a slow agonizing death," teases Jason.

"Please don't, that's not fair."

His fingers begin their work; he tickles her at her most vulnerable spot, her waist. She falls back on the sofa, trying to control her laughter and the papers. Her attempt fails, revealed by a burst of uncontrollable laughter. Using what strength she can muster, she tries to muscle her way from underneath his wrath by wiggling her way to the edge of the sofa, causing them to tumble onto the floor, providing Sasha with the dominant position. Confident that Jason will concede to her, Sasha becomes interestingly aroused by the change in his physical structure created by the mock wrestling match.

"What's that?" she questions.

"What does it feel like?"

"Mr. Goodbar," Sasha utters sultrily. "You're so bad."

Jason fights to gain the dominant position. Seconds later, he sits atop her waist with her arms pinned down at the wrists.

"Now you're in trouble...punishment time," Jason says.

He bends to give her a deep passionate kiss, one that generates a willful response from Sasha.

"Torture me...I'm your prisoner," Sasha volunteers.

He runs his tongue along the curve of her neck, causing her body to chill. Rapidly her nipples harden as she smiles with approval to his form of punishment. Jason descends below her waist while pushing her shirt above her vulnerable spot. Moments later Sasha's hips begin to jerk as sweat forms on her forehead. He tries to control her bucking hips by clutching her legs under the knees. During the first part of her orgasm, she wiggles wildly as she grinds her now-flaming womanhood. The second one is more intense as Jason quickly enters her, thrusts himself deep and hard, causing a frenzied state throughout her being. She shakes uncontrollably to her quick multi-orgasm.

CHAPTER 22

Morning arrives as several Coast Guard ships along with Detective McAllister and more officers from the Sixteenth Precinct replace the armed guards. A complete search of the ship reveals many freight boxes. Most contain no addictive substances and are legit cargo—the exception is a few crates decorated with customs stamps from various locations in the Orient, destined for Panama. These three crates contain a total of seven pieces of ancient armor collectively as well as cocaine-filled padding for protection of the pieces. The crates are discovered to be the property of Worldwide Investments and are seized. Detective McAllister escorts many crewmembers downtown for questioning.

The next day when Jason arrives at the station, he finds Detective McAllister reporting to Captain North the events that took place two nights earlier.

"Captain, we planned everything out to the last detail. All we had to do was wait for the exchange and apprehend just one of them but..."

"Knock, knock," Jason says. "Am I interrupting something?"

"Jason, have a seat," Captain North instructs. "It seems you've been up to your antics again. I've just been told that you didn't follow plans Saturday, costing the lives of many men."

"What? Me!" Jason sounds surprised.

"Yes, you, but I'll give you the pleasure of listening to your side of the story before I tear you a new asshole."

"There's nothing much to tell. When we discussed the stakeout we failed to consider back-up that they might have. Surely, when drugs with the street value of millions exchange hands, someone is secretly watching to make sure everything goes smoothly. When I realized this, I changed my role."

"Why didn't you notify Detective McAllister of your intentions? He's the narcotics cop."

"Captain, I tried. We were to leave for the dock at ten o'clock but Detective McAllister and his troops left early. On the way there, I phoned here at nine twenty-five, trying to reach him but they had already gone. I was informed that they left minutes before my call. I asked to be patched through but my request was denied because Chris had ordered radio silence with strict orders for it not to be broken."

"Is this true, Chris?"

"Well, yes but..."

"No 'buts'...Captain, you can check with the dispatch officer. As you know, all calls are logged."

"That still doesn't excuse him. If he hadn't pulled his gun, we could've made an arrest possibly without any fire."

"Look Chris, you're so concerned about my presence, you forget the man in the poncho, Howard. He pulled a gun first, disrupting the entire stakeout."

"He could've been arrested, too."

"How? The way I see it, my role saved your life."

"You saved my life, ha!"

"Jason, get to the point," states Captain North.

"Gunfire from the ship took down many of Chris' men. My disguise allowed me to get close enough to take him down before he killed all of us."

"Okay, okay, stop both of you. Finish your reports. I want them immediately and, somehow, put a lid on this battle between you two.

It's time to end it and I mean now. Neither of you can be effective cops when you're always at each other's throats."

"Captain, Jason always tries to steal the show. He embarrasses the station constantly with his antics."

"You mean I embarrass *you*. If you remove that chip off your shoulder..."

"I don't have a chip," Chris interrupts.

"Yes, you do, the same one you had back in the academy. The first thing you said to me Saturday was, 'shot any dirt lately?' Remember that? If you let that rest, we could work better together."

"But you cheated."

"I improvised. I did what I had to do to win," Jason urges.

"Captain, you judge."

"I'm not the referee for your dispute."

"Hear me out. I just want your opinion. In the academy Jason and I were equally matched throughout. Top of the class came down to marksmanship at the range. I skillfully shot ninety-eight of one-hundred targets ranging from a distance of one-hundred-fifty to two-hundred-fifty meters. With five shots remaining, Jason's ninety-fifth shot went wide. He fired his next four shots into the dirt in front of the targets. The loose gravel caused by the bullet was enough to trigger the sensitive targets. With his cheating he beat me out by one shot and stole top of the class with his deliberate action."

"Jason, you made those shots purposely?" asks Captain North.

"Yes, at the halfway mark just milliseconds before I pulled the trigger, I sneezed and the round went short into the gravel. I was surprised when the target fell, but I knew I had an ace in the hole."

"You cheated," Detective McAllister demands.

"As I have said, I did what I had to do to win; now live with it," Jason recites with his frustration apparent.

"Quite ingenious I think," Captain North says.

"You're condoning his actions?"

"I see that he was much the same years ago. No wonder you have difficulties following orders."

"No, I just believe in my abilities."

"I knew I shouldn't have allowed you to participate in my case. Captain, doesn't he have a case of his own? From now on, leave the narcotic affairs alone."

"In fact he does...how's it going?"

"Today is my first day back with the investigation. I have to get the follow-up from..."

"Saturday should have been your first day," Detective McAllister rebuts.

"Save it, Chris. Let me handle this. Jason, where do you intend to start?"

"Where I left off."

"Which is?"

"I don't know. You tell me."

"I'm not investigating the case. You are."

"Same old Jason," Detective McAllister says. "Passing the buck as usual."

"Chris, you're excused. I'll handle him." Once the door closes behind the departing Detective McAllister, Captain North continues. "Now, what are you talking about?"

"I recall giving you an account number of a victim to have a check run on it. How did that turn out?"

"Account number...Mrs. Smith, right?"

"Exactly."

"I gave it to Sgt. Austin. He should have some information for you."

"Then he is where I start."

"Listen, I'll handle Chris. Don't worry about your involvement Saturday. Just find this rapist."

"You'll get my best as always."

"That's what I'm afraid of. No super stunts, okay?"

"Don't worry," he says with a huge grin.

Jason leaves Captain North's office with one thought in mind: to locate Sgt. Austin and gather the much-needed information.

"Yo, Kevin, que tal?" Jason asks.

"Que tal? You've said that to me before...how's it going? Fine, everything is great. Welcome back and all that stuff."

"Thanks."

"How are you doing?"

"Terrific, no complaints. Listen, while on suspension Captain North gave you a Visa account to run a check on. How did that turn out?"

"Hey, take a break...relax, we have some catching up to do."

Jason gives him a hard look.

"All right, if I remember correctly, the trace on her card didn't pan out. No new purchases."

"Then what did you do?"

"Nothing."

"No follow-up check?"

"Sorry. I didn't think a second time was necessary."

"Where's the number now?"

"I placed it under the lamp on your desk."

"Thanks, I'll take over from here."

"Jas, do you really think a person who has eluded our efforts would be dumb enough to use someone else's account?"

"I look at it this way. The most perfect crimes have invisible flaws. If I were to use someone else's account, I would wait until the heat is off. I'll run another check to satisfy my curiosity."

"I guess that's not a bad idea."

Jason's second effort proves to be rewarding. A few days earlier, Mrs. Smith's card was used to the amount of six hundred ninety-five dollars. He checks with Mrs. Smith. She denies purchasing any items. A check with the bank card company reveals that the purchase was a telephone order placed to Videotronics Wholesalers, located three counties away. Videotronics records show that a Gregory Smith phoned in an order for a discounted hi-tech camcorder using Mrs. Smith's card. It was sent via registered mail to a P.O. box across the state in Johnson County. Further detail inquiries suggest that the package should arrive today with the afternoon mail delivery at the Johnson City Post Office.

"If I hurry, I can get there before he picks it up," Jason says.

"You got something hot?"

"The fish are biting."

Jason reports to Captain North, advising him of his fiery lead.

"Do you have the registration number of the package?" asks Captain North.

"In my pocket."

"We can notify the post office and ask them to retain the package until the Johnson County Police arrive."

"You mean, until I arrive. I'm dying to end this case. Besides, it was my efforts that possibly revealed him."

"But, Johnson City Police can react faster than you."

"The shipment isn't scheduled to arrive until this afternoon...with all due respect, Sir, you dumped this case on me. I've wrecked my brain from the beginning to find a start on this one and I might add, during my suspension it was a constant thought."

"Okay, I'm convinced. We'll do it your way. Just don't screw this up. I will clear everything with the Johnson County Commissioner."

Jason jumps into action with the new approval. He almost makes it out of the door.

"Don't use sirens."

"No kidding," Jason states sarcastically, a little too arrogant for Captain North's liking.

He races across the state and arrives several minutes before the afternoon truck is due. He jumps out of the car with the intent of making a calm entry. Simultaneously, as he reaches the door, it flies open. Jason and the exiting man collide. His small mailing bag and stamps fall to the ground. Jason bends to help retrieve the man's belongings.

"I'm sorry," Jason says. "Everyone's in a rush nowadays."

"Excuse me, I should've opened the door slowly."

"Call it a draw."

"Agreed."

The six-foot-three man has deep-set dark eyes and boasts a large powerful frame. He excuses himself politely and drives off. Jason finds himself reflecting on the man's Pierre Cardin suit—identical to the one he has hanging in his closet—and the light coat of makeup he wears, attempting to mask his blemished skin.

"Wouldn't you know it? I spend hundreds of dollars on expensive clothes and literally bump into someone wearing an exact duplicate of mine. He had to get it from the Ritz. It's the only place you can get that particular cut around here. Maybe I'm not so unique after all."

Confident that he's arrived before the afternoon shipment, Jason stands in the long line that wraps around the inside of the post office's walls. After a few minutes, the anxiety of the wait coupled with tension he placed on himself to catch the criminal urges him to break the line and approach the counter. A few comments are made concerning his cutting ahead of the line, especially the irritated remarks coming from an overweight construction worker with a few days' beard growth and mustard splattered all over his coveralls.

"Hey man, you have to stand in line just like the rest of us."

Jason ignores his words and continues to wait for the clerk to return.

"Hey man, get back in line...I've been standing here too long for you to just walk in front of me."

Several other people join the bandwagon, making comments supporting the construction worker's argument. The construction worker grabs Jason's jacket from behind.

"Okay, everyone, listen up," Jason says while flashing his badge. "I'm a cop."

"That does not make the world yours. You have to wait just like the rest of us."

"This is official business."

"Yeah, I bet."

Several clerks rush from the back, leery of all the commotion.

"Sir, you'll have to wait," a clerk says.

"I'm Detective Jerrard. I can end this with one simple question."

"Anything to quiet the crowd," the clerk states. "What is it?"

"Has the afternoon shipment arrived?"

"No, Sir, we're expecting it any minute now."

"Fine, I'll wait. I just needed to know."

Jason settles in an empty spot along the wall and the crowd calms down. He waits for what seems like hours before finally observing out the window the mail truck turning into the parking lot. After allowing more time for it to be unloaded, he asks for the station manager.

"Good afternoon, Sir. I'm Detective Jerrard. I'm investigating a case of great importance. All indications suggest that a package containing a camcorder has just arrived with the afternoon mail delivery."

"What package, Sir?"

"I need to know if this registered package has just come in," Jason says while handing him the number. "Most importantly, I need to know who the person is that comes to retrieve this item. I'll need to ask him a few questions."

"One moment. I'll check."

Briefly, the manager returns.

"No, Detective, your package didn't arrive on this truck."

"Damn...more than likely it should be on the evening truck."

"No, Sir, not that either."

"What then?"

"It has already been picked up. Seems it came on the morning truck."

"Fuck," Jason cries, letting a bit of his frustration show. "Picked up, when?"

"Oh, let's see...less than forty minutes ago."

"Who signed for it?"

"The signature here seems to be a Gregory Smith and it was initialed by Lester over there."

"Get him for me, please. I need to ask him some questions."

"Hey, Les, when you finish with that customer, I need to see you."

Seconds later, Lester reports and is introduced to Jason.

"Les, this is Detective Jerrard. He needs to ask you a few questions. I'll handle your station while you talk with him."

"Okay...what can I do for you, Detective?"

"I need to know if you can remember anything about the person who picked up this package."

"Hmm...that wasn't long ago. He was a well-dressed man, quite polite actually, but he did seem awful hurried."

"I can't believe I missed him."

"You didn't."

"Please, explain what you mean," Jason says puzzled.

"He was the person you bumped into when you first got here."

"Him!" Jason sounds astonished. "The man with the nice suit?"

"That's him. I'm sure of it."

"I helped him gather his things, but he wasn't carrying a box big enough to be a camcorder."

"His hurriedness caused the small mailing bag and stamps to fall off the box. So, he put the package in his car. I'd assume he came back for the small items."

"I'll be damned...anything more you can remember about him?"

"He wore a noticeable amount of makeup."

"Thanks, that's helpful. I noticed that, too."

Jason rushes back to the station even more determined to track down this unknown assailant. In his mind, he repeats the description of the suspect, trying not to forget it while it's fresh in his memory. At the station he gives the police artist a complete description, and he's immediately summoned by Captain North.

"Well, how did it go?"

"The package I was looking for came in early. It was on the morning run instead of the afternoon run and..."

"And he had already picked it up."

"That's correct, Sir."

"Was anyone able to help you with a description?"

"Somewhat."

"At least you have something to build on."

"I have more than that. I saw him."

"What?"

"I went racing into the doors and we collided. I helped him pick up his things and he left. When I went inside, the afternoon shipment hadn't arrived so I didn't think anything of it."

"Wait a minute. Your intent was to look for anyone carrying a huge box, correct?"

"Right."

"You run into someone like that and think nothing of it. What's wrong with your detective work?"

"Nothing, Sir...Frank. This person wasn't carrying a large box. He only had a small mailing bag...I'd better explain what happened."

Captain North is satisfied with his explanation and urges him to continue his efforts in finding this suspect. Sgt. Austin knocks on the door. He has new information regarding the case.

"Frank, Jas, there's been another attack."

"Did this one survive?" Jason asks.

"Nope. She was raped and strangled on the train."

"Subway?"

"Right."

"Anything more?"

"Nothing other than traces of human skin under her nails and blood on her face. This time he was marked," Sgt. Austin says as if the information will prove to be the turning point in the case.

"If he's scratched, he'll have to use bandages to cover them up," Captain North responds.

"How about makeup?" Jason remarks in an afterthought.

"Why makeup?"

"The man at the post office wore a good amount of makeup. I have a gut feeling that this is the person we are looking for. Did you get his blood type?"

"The lab hasn't sent it over yet."

"Get it quickly. It could prove to be an important factor."

"I'll push them."

"Okay, Jason, we finally have something concrete to go on. Stay on top of this. This bastard has to be caught soon."

"I have a couple of leads I'd like to follow. Do I have your permission to do things my way?"

"You've never asked before. I'll live to regret this but, whatever it takes, get the job done."

"Now you're talking."

CHAPTER 23

Jason returns to his desk determined to cover all possible leads on the discovery of the man he knows he must find. He calls the Ritz of Hollywood to inquire about the Pierre Cardin suit the man wore. The manager at the Ritz informs Jason that he would have to check his files and call him back.

"Sixteenth Precinct, Jerrard."

"Jason, Julie."

"How are you doing?"

"Missing you...I miss the way you used to hold me at night."

"I can't talk now. I'm expecting a call back involving a case I'm working on."

"Are you still upset with me for the way I acted at Rosalina's?"

"That crosses my mind but lately, for some odd reason, I keep thinking of that day you begged for your car keys and what followed."

"Please try to forgive me for that. That was the old me," she pleads.

"I wish it were that simple. Lately, I've been getting heavy flashbacks of not-so pleasant memories."

"Jason, let's think ahead..."

Julie continues with a long conversation on why they should reunite and try once more. Jason pushes two things aside—the files and her conversation—allowing his mind to drift to a place where he fights constantly to keep out of his past. He hears Julie's words, but his mind converts them into a past conversation.

"Where have you hidden my keys, Jason?"

"I haven't moved your keys. Hiding your keys serves no purpose. I can't control you. If doing the right thing can't keep you straight, hiding your keys surely won't."

"Save the lecture. I'm going. This is important to me."

"He's more important than me, us, or what we have?"

"Obviously, we don't have anything or I'd stay home."

These words tear through him now almost as dreadful as they did in the reality in which they occurred.

"We have a marriage to try to save. Can you honestly say that there's no magic left?"

"I lost it. I can't live this way. You know my background."

"I know it well. I also know while we were dating I gave you my own short stories on starting at the top. I only talked logic and we agreed to do things without your parents' help..."

"Your stories about starting from below and working together as a team kept me motivated when I was younger, but now, in this more mature state I know what I need. I know what I want. Your process is just too slow. So, where are my keys?"

"I didn't hide your keys but I know where they are. Before I tell you, I just want you to know that someday, somehow, and somewhere you'll regret what you're doing."

"Save it, Jason," Julie replies firmly.

"Is there anything more I can say to keep you from throwing all we dreamed of away?"

"You've said enough. Let's just exist in this house until we can separate. I know you can't afford the house payment by yourself."

"I can manage."

"You should stop thinking that you can do everything, stop thinking of us and stop trying to control every situation that you're a part of...where are my keys?"

He pictures himself telling Julie the location of her keys, again feeling the exact bitterness he experienced when it actually happened. The scene replays through his mind like reruns of an old western. The door slams. Julie is beyond reasoning. She hurries to meet her date, her new key to personal happiness. Jason stands motionless for a moment, and then suddenly grabs his keys in pursuit of her. When he enters the street, Julie is turning the corner a few blocks down. Jason tails her cautiously, eager to spoil her evening. He's led across town to a secluded motel off the main highway. Julie exits the car and knocks on a door. It opens and she disappears behind the confinement of the tiny room.

Jason remembers how a void overwhelmed him as his chest opened, letting his heart fall onto his lap only to jump out of the window and run aimlessly in circles on the ground like a chicken with its head wrung off. He chases it with his remaining will, trying to regain his soul, trying to regain any dignity his turbulent emotions might have.

He remembers exiting his car after contemplating disturbing their solitude and walks slowly toward their room with a stride filled with determination and purpose. Doubt shortens his stride as he nears the door, almost hesitant to continue. "Return to the car" flashes through his mind, but his feet are controlled by the increasing moans of his wife. His feet march closer, finally resting him on the outside wall next to the door. His insides decompose with the intimate sounds of the woman he would do anything to please, being pleased by another lover. Listening until the moans intensify, his heart pounds—seemingly loud enough to be mistaken for a knock on the door—as he forms a fist to bang on the door. A power unknown to him wills his hand away and forces him to walk quickly to his car. He sits staring hard as if he could force his vision through the door while pools of tears form in the wells of his eyes, then consequently drop. The door finally opens after he has waited impatiently for hours. His heart sighs. Julie and her lover engage in small talk in the doorway before embracing and kissing one last time. Her lover standing in the doorway is confident that he was on his best behavior while gazing up at the stars, seemingly thanking the heavens for his blessing.

Jason remembers how it felt as he reached into the glove box for a pair of binoculars and finds himself peering through the lenses, finding a tall man in a Pierre Cardin suit with makeup-covered scratches on his face but expecting to see a freckled-faced man whom he believes is his wife's lover. The touch of reality in his daydreaming brings him quickly back to his conscious mind where he picks up Julie's conversation with her calling his name.

"Jason, Jason."

"Yes," he replies in a sadder tone.

"Do you remember that time you followed me to the motel?"

"I'm trying to forget it. I don't know why these things are suddenly bouncing back from my memory but I can't talk about it now. We can talk about this later."

"Only if you promise to call me."

"I will."

"Yeah, like you called me the day after I saw you last at Rosalina's."

"Give me time to get into this case but, most importantly, I have some cobwebs to clear in my mind."

"It's about me, right?"

"No comment."

"That alone says 'yes.' You still can't hide your feelings from me."

"I just can't talk about it now. I'll call you later."

"Please don't make me wait too long."

"I won't...goodbye."

"Goodbye and I love you."

Jason gathers his files, places them in the drawer and excuses himself from the station without notifying anyone. He leaves his car and takes a police cruiser on an unexpected trip. With the lights flashing, he arrives early evening at the beach. These are unusual moments for him. After his divorce, he conditioned himself against any anguish or emotional stress. For some peculiar reason he finds certain emotional events of his life nagging in his subconscious. On the beach he sits on the sand, removes his shoes, followed by his socks, and pushes his heels as far as the sand will allow. Then he covers the remaining portion of his feet with sand by hand.

As before, he watches the crashing waves and concentrates on the soothing sound of the water flowing over the sand as it attempts to drift back to sea. Slowly and unknowingly, Jason falls into a self-contained solitude with the events of his life—one at a time—being lifted from his mind; all it seems but one. This particular event plays on the screens of his eyes, projected from his heart to his subconscious—created by the pain he wishes were over. After forcing himself back to reality, he tries again to clear his mind of all thought but gets trapped by that unhappy event again, skipping like a scratched record needing a little push of the needle to continue playing. Jason reluctantly pushes the needle, jump-starting his memory to somewhere after a steamy lovemaking session with Julie. As a romantic gesture, Jason suggests a walk on the beach but Julie declines the drive to the ocean and snuggles comfortably under the sheets to recuperate from their physical activity. Jason remembers driving home with mixed emotions—joy and happiness—gleaming inside, realizing that after two years of marriage the magic still exists. Greater joy is felt when he thinks of the possibility that their lovemaking session might have created a new life.

Arriving home, he finds Julie in the shower and decides to do something special before she reenters the bedroom. From her bottom dresser drawer he seizes a white legal pad and scissors. Tearing off the top sheet, Jason folds it in half and proceeds to cut out a giant heart. The hurried effort unfolded reveals a large heart approximately the size he wants but his paper cutting has seen better days. This one being lop-sided, he crushes it between his hands and tears off another sheet. He remembers how carefully the second one was cut, this time unfolding a perfectly shaped one. He colors it with a red marker and writes with a black marker, "Jason and Julie, For Now, Forever and For Always."

Jason places the heart on her pillow and proceeds to put his tools away. He slides the legal pad in the drawer, closing it slowly to make little sound while watching it disappear. In a glance, he notices writing under the top sheet of paper and pulls the pad back out to peek at her lovely penmanship. He remembers smiling to himself after reading the first few lines.

Hi, Lover, I just thought you should know that making love to you is the most satisfying experience I've ever lived through. My constant thoughts are filled with anticipation as I wait for your next embrace.

Unwilling to spoil the surprise she's prepared for him, Jason decides not to finish reading the letter. He lowers the top sheet, smoothing it out with the palm of his hand, following the motion with his eyes to the end of the pad. He raises an eyebrow upon sighting two unsuspecting words submerged in the text—Jason and divorce. He sees himself reading the letter thoroughly with rushed anxiety. Shortly after the opening sentences, his sudden joy is ripped out of him with the latter text:

I enjoy each moment we steal; I never thought something so wrong could feel so right. Lover, I don't want to alarm you but I've decided to ask Jason for a divorce. We deserve to spend our time together, free of going to faraway places. This I'll do for you, for us. I love Jason but I'm no longer in love with him; I'm in love with you. I can no longer play the role of his wife because of my guilt. Oddly, I feel guilty when I'm with him. I feel that I'm doing you wrong...doing you a grave injustice, much, much more than in reverse.

Jason rips the letter from the pad and places it next to the heart. With his heart pounding—driving him to find more evidence—he digs further into the drawer only to find birth control pills. His earlier thoughts of a new creation crushed, despair rides his emotions. He places the items on the opposite side of the pillow, and then rips the heart into pieces, letting the pieces fall freely onto the bed. He leaves the bedroom for the living room. Moments later, rapid heavy footsteps come racing downstairs.

Julie, with her hair wet and her body wrapped in a towel, pleads, "I'm sorry, Jason. I didn't want you to find out this way."

He remembers himself sitting motionless, questioning, "Why?"

Again he breaks his solitude, bounces back to reality, puzzled. He wonders why—after years of using the waves to cleanse his mind—did all efforts fail today? He concedes to the notion that because he's attempting to trust his emotions with another, all the fears he has kept suppressed have surfaced to keep him in check. He decides to put the sour thoughts and feelings behind him and let the old Jason be a prisoner—locking him away in his mind forever, leaving the new stronger Jason.

"Sounds good in theory," Jason chuckles with a shrug of the shoulders.

Arriving home well after midnight with his mental capacity nowhere near a hundred percent, Jason is pleased with the sight of Sasha's car in his driveway and wonders why she is out at this hour. He attempts to mask any signs of his inner turmoil as Sasha jumps from her car.

"Sasha," Jason says intrigued. "I'm surprised. What are you doing here?"

"I'm worried about you."

"Me? Why?"

"I called the station today and they said that you just disappeared. No one knew where you were...are you okay?"

He doesn't answer verbally. His reply is in the form of an embrace. Sasha tries to move away but he holds her tighter and closer, not wanting to let go.

"Are you okay...Jason?"

"I'm fine...I've just had a day you wouldn't believe. Thoughts about things I didn't know still bothered me have haunted me today."

"This is me. Talk to me," Sasha pleads.

"Let's go inside. I can use some coffee."

Entering the house, Sasha is more persistent about finding out the cause of his strange mood.

"Okay, what is it? You once told me that you had no secrets."

"I don't. I just have a few skeletons in my closet."

"Your humor isn't going to help you escape this time."

"It was worth a try."

"Stop beating around the bush. I know you're troubled because you didn't call me at all yesterday...you didn't notice I had dusted the furniture and finished the dishes?"

"I noticed, trust me. I mentally thanked you."

"That's not important now. What's bugging you is, so tell me...is it something I've done?"

"No, you're wonderful. I've had experiences from my past on my mind most of the day."

"Your past...involving?"

"Julie. Something surrounding our break-up surfaced today, and it threw me for a loop mentally."

"So, you did a disappearing act. Why didn't you call me? I'd like to think that I'm more to you than just your lover."

"You are. I have a bad habit of driving when I have a lot on my mind."

"Where did you drive in the police car?"

"To the beach."

"You drove to the beach and back. Surely you're tired. Why didn't you take your car?"

"I can get there faster in the cruiser. Turn on the lights and in no time you're there."

"Help me understand. You know about my downfall with my marriage; tell me about yours."

"Gosh, yesterday I would've been able to answer that question but today I can't."

"What's wrong with the question? It fits the mood of this conversation."

"On the way home, I mentally forced things back into perspective to enable me to be me. If I tell you, I might disturb that placement. But, I will tell you this," Jason pauses to collect his thoughts, and then continues evenly, emotionless, as if what he's ashamed of are his next words. "To be totally honest, I'm a changed person. I was a weak person during my marriage to Julie. Weak might be an understatement because I allowed things to happen that I wouldn't dare allow now. My love for Julie was very strong. That strength enabled me to overlook many of her wrongdoings because I believed that my love for her would be the captain of a tiny ship navigating its way through the turbulent seas to calmer waters. I truly believed that she would eventually straighten up her act and love me like I knew she was capable of doing."

"Her actions were devastating to you?"

"Everyone likes to believe that their troubles are worse than others...I didn't realize it at the time but I was destroying myself."

"At least you bounced back."

"After several years of trying to suppress fears, I'd like to think I've bounced back."

"Okay, let's change the subject...what were you like when you were younger?"

"How much younger?"

"Let's say, ah...when you were in high school."

"Back then everyone thought I was very shy." Jason gazes somberly into her eyes. "Let me rephrase that. I was shy but what they didn't know was I had secrets that would blow their minds."

"Watch out for the quiet ones."

"I wasn't dangerous; I just did things that no one would ever think I'd do."

"Like what?"

"It's a shocker."

"Let me be the judge of that."

"I had an affair with my art teacher."

"You what?"

"It's true."

"This I've got to hear."

"It was an accident. I was the yearbook photographer during the last three years in high school, and this teacher was in charge of the year-book staff. Often I'd stay after school developing pictures and she would wait for the prints that were to be used for the layout in the yearbook. One day she was standing over my shoulder in the dark watching me work. I took a print out of the developer and placed it in the stop bath. In the process my elbow slightly grazed her breast. Surprisingly, she let out a soft moan. That shocked me, so that next time I did it intentionally. The response was the same. I continued with my developing—not with the prints but with her. We worked, on each other that is. We continued for several months, having our secret sessions in the darkroom and at her place at the beach."

"The beach. Is that the reason you said you practically lived at the beach?"

"Part of it."

"How old were you?"

"Seventeen. She was in her early thirties."

"Is she responsible for some moves you do now?"

"No, that's a natural ability," Jason replies with a grin. "But, she did educate me on the true meaning behind all sexual encounters."

"Care to explain that?"

"Later...we both have early days tomorrow and it's late. You are staying?" Jason suggests.

"Have toothbrush will travel, but I do need to get my things out of the car. Then I'll see if I can help you remember some of those moves you were taught."

"Give me your keys. I'll get them for you."

"Always the gentleman."

"I've a little chivalry left in me."

"Just don't be a gentleman when we get upstairs."

"I'm allowed to change my ways upstairs?"

"Yep, I don't ask for much respect behind closed doors."

"You freakish devil, you. I'll definitely heed to your wishes."

"I'm sure you will."

"Oh?"

"You always do."

"I know no other way."

CHAPTER 24

Jason arrives the next day at the station with the case on his mind. The heavy thought and determination on his face suggests that he has pulled his mental thoughts together. Before he's summoned, he reports to Captain North on his actions of the previous day. Captain North gives him something one might consider a verbal reprimand and instructs him to get to work. Jason sits at his desk thinking hard about what he saw yesterday.

"Joy riding again, Jas?"

"Bob, you aren't going to start with me again, are you?"

"Just kidding."

"Oh...tell me something."

"What?"

"If you had a car like mine, would you put many miles on it?"

"I get your message."

"Speaking of messages, any for me?"

"You didn't get any except two."

"Cute. Is that anything like the couple that had six children, all boys except for four girls?"

"That's kinda catchy."

"What are my messages, turkey?"

"After you disappeared, you got a call from a Sasha. Someone new, huh?"

"There's always that possibility."

"She must be something. I hear your ex-wife is on your heels again. To pass her up for someone new tells me a lot about Sasha because Julie is F-I-N-E and I mean with all capital letters. I'd say she's top..."

"Top shelf, I've heard this all before. My second message, please."

"Please, are my ears deceiving me? You said 'please.'" Bob chuckles delightfully.

"Bob," Jason replies wryly.

"It came from the Ritz. The man you talked to yesterday said that there are no records of a Gregory Smith purchasing any suits."

"I figured that. I'll have to get him to compile a list of names of all the sales of that particular suit. It could turn out to be our first real lead."

Jason now sits with his feet propped on his desk, rearing back in his chair with his hands clamped behind his head, thinking aloud.

"What are you doing?"

"Thinking. I'm trying to remember something I may have seen but can't consciously remember."

"That doesn't make sense."

"Give me a minute...I remember commenting on his suit. What did I see? Obviously, it was something that I refuse to acknowledge. His car, he drove a white Cel...no, Camry. A white Toyota Camry with four doors. Now you're thinking. The license plate read...R...come on, picture it in your head. It read R ...damn, it ends with a six. What's between? Fuck, that's all I can remember. This isn't enough to put a track on the car. What were the other letters and numbers? Just relax and it'll come to you. Fuck...think, boy."

Before he finishes, the entire office has stopped what they were doing to watch the crazed man talk to himself. He drops his feet and leans forward.

"Haven't you people seen a person work before?"

"Jas, you're on to something," Sgt. Austin replies.

"No, I'm drawing a blank. I can't remember all that I know I saw."

"The license plate."

"What about it? Shit, yeah, correct me if I'm wrong but this state's rental car tags all begin with an R."

"Right."

"Fucking A, help me check with all the rental car places in the surrounding areas."

"It'll take awhile."

"I know, so let's get to it."

After dozens of calls, they discover that their suspect rented a Toyota Camry from Easy Ride Rentals, again using Mrs. Smith's credit card. The rental agent gives them a motel address located across town.

"I don't know how he was able to use her card before it was canceled but somehow he did," Jason states bewildered.

"Do you think we have the right one?" questions Sgt. Austin.

"No doubt about it. Kevin, Bob, gather two more squad cars. We're going after this fucker now."

Moments later, Jason, along with several police cars race silently to a place known as Little Vietnam. In this area, on any given night, numerous shots are fired injuring or killing many people. Most of the deaths are drug-related. Therefore, the police don't venture into the confines of the war zone without plenty of backup.

The motel is a two-story building. Soda machines stand at the bottom of the stairs and on the second level near the top of the stairs. The upper rooms are accessed from the outside by a cement walkway that wraps around the building. The officers quickly surround the motel while Jason summons the resident manager. The manager, Melvin Lowe, is a tall heavyset man wearing a bandanna around his head and bell bottom jeans that project a laid-back sixties image. The peace sign on his jacket justifies his three-decades-old style of speech. Jason explains the situation to Mr. Lowe, despite having a search warrant in his possession, and the overly excited manager agrees to open their suspect's room.

"Far out, man," the manager boasts. "Lots of hap'nens go on in this area, but this is the first time I get to be part of it."

"When we get to the room, stay back," Jason cautions. "This person is potentially dangerous."

"With the army you brought with you, why should I worry?"

Jason, the manager and four other officers report to the second-floor room. As far as they can tell the room is dark, and the curtain is pulled closed with the window shade down. Rock music is heard from within, being played at a low volume. An officer bangs on the door while Jason talks with the manager.

"What can you tell me about this man?" Jason asks.

"Nothing much. He's the clean-cut, well-mannered type. Very odd for this area. He paid his rent for a whole month in cash. We don't get many of those. When I get cash upfront, I don't look too hard or ask questions. You know what I mean."

"Did he drive a car?"

"When I saw him, he was walking."

"Hey, enough of that," Jason instructs to the officer banging on the door yelling, "Open up! Police! If he's in there, he has no intentions of opening the door."

"I'll open it," the manager states. "It's strange. A man dressed in nice rags is wanted by the fuzz."

"Curious," Jason ponders. "His attire comes up again."

"What does that mean?"

"Nothing, just something I'm trying to use to link him with other crimes."

The manager unlocks the door, opens it to a barely visible crack and pauses. "I really don't think he's in here," the manager says before ignoring Jason's advice with his next actions.

He kicks the door open and jumps into the doorway using his finger as an imaginary gun. Instantly, two shots are heard, one doubled over the other. Jason braces himself against the patch of wall just before the door. The manager and a young recruit, seeing his first action, fall the slowest. Buckshots from a double-barreled shotgun enter their bodies, tearing through their clothes, ripping their tender skin and leaving hundreds of tiny jagged holes that immediately bleed profusely. A fatal wound, the size of a large man's fist, is blown through their bodies.

Fragments of their internal organs are forced out by the multitude of grouped buck shots as well as splattering blood on Jason and another officer.

A return wave of gunfire from the surviving officers lying on the walkway flies through the open door killing a mirror, glass, the cheap furniture and puncturing the wall. Jason calls for a cease-fire.

"Come out with your hands up!" Jason instructs. "There is no escape. You're surrounded."

All is silent.

Jason points his finger toward the officers in the parking lot. Instantly, a canister of tear gas explodes in the room. Moments later, after the vapors diminish, he quickly ducks his head inside the door hoping to find the killer dead or injured, lying on the floor crying for help. What he finds is a table placed inches beyond the door's swing and some sort of mount which holds the still-smoking shotgun. A wire on both triggers runs backward through a loop that is screwed into the table. The wire makes a turn upward through another loop that's screwed into the ceiling directly above the one on the table. It flows forward through another loop and finally down where it's tied to the doorknob.

Jason ducks his head into the doorway again—this time slowly scanning the room before entering it. The other officers follow. After a careful check of the bathroom, closet, and under the bed, they put their weapons away. The astonishing part of the ordeal is the written message surely derived especially for the police on the walls. In sloppy letters written in red paint are the words, "You don't think I used that card 'cause I'm fucking stupid, do you?"

"Fuck," Jason rages. "I knew something about this felt wrong. It was too simple…I should have realized this sooner."

Captain North arrives, looking for answers and the ambulance to take the dead bodies away.

"Jason, what happened here?" Captain North questions.

"Sir, the room was booby trapped. That message shows that he premeditated all of this knowing that we would trace that credit card again. He set the bait and we attacked like hungry fish."

"Any visible clue as to his identity?"

"Nothing jumps out at me but the manager commented on his attire earlier. Boy, this fucker is smart, but I promise I'll get the son-of-a-bitch."

"He's moved into another league."

"I know, a murderer-rapist turned cop killer. It seems he does this for fun. Somehow, I know it's that man at the post office. I can feel his presence in this room."

The forensic team turns the room inside out. After the members have completely dusted for prints, the room gives an appearance of being ransacked by burglars. However, the hour-long search is unsuccessful. No additional clues are found. The inscription on the wall serves no purpose other than a form of harassment. Jason and Captain North discuss the events that occurred and plan how they intend to handle the media who has already arrived.

A small crowd gathers to observe the scene while across the street in a condemned building, the murderer views the entire episode through a pair of binoculars. Content, he smiles to himself while studying the police as they work, intent on learning the identity of the person making the decisions.

"It has to be him, the one in the suit," he swears. "He looks familiar...he has to be the one I bumped into at the post office. I'm sure it's him. Now, I have an edge."

Jason races back to the station to write his report on this bizarre incident while it's fresh in his mind. After completing his report, he prepares himself for the journey to the other crime locations when the telephone rings.

"If that's a personal call for me, take a message," Jason instructs.

"Sixteenth Precinct, Austin."

"Officer, I'm a concerned citizen. I was walking by earlier when I saw the incident at the motel. I might have some additional information concerning the case," the citizen states. "Are you the person in charge of this case?"

"No, but, thanks for calling. It's about time someone spoke up. Hold on," he suggests before covering the mouthpiece. "Jas, this one's for you. Someone has something to say about what happened at the motel."

"Thanks," Jason says while picking up the telephone. "Detective Jerrard...how may I help you?"

"Hi, my name is Steven Glebe. That was an awful killing at the motel."

"It was a pretty bad scene," agrees Jason. "A senseless killing."

"I know and how he did it amazes me. You'd think he knew the police were on his trail. The crime..."

"Sir," Jason interrupts. "Do you have anything new, something useful? Did you see anything that might help us identify the killer?"

"Yes, yes, I saw a lot. You were the man in the suit, right?"

"That's correct."

"Yeah, I saw a lot. Right before..."

"Can you identify the killer?" Jason impatiently questions.

"I'm trying to tell you. If you stop interrupting me, I can tell you."

"I apologize. Please continue."

"I can identify the killer. I saw him, in the mirror, right before I climbed out of the window."

"What!"

"There you go again. Don't stop me," he says more forcefully. "I saw it all. I saw it happen before it happened. I visualized the door opening and the shotgun firing before I set it up."

"This better not be a prank."

Jason motions to get Sgt. Austin's attention. Covering the mouthpiece, he whispers to have his call traced.

"This is not a prank. Can't you tell a confession when you hear one? Or is your judgment clouded because of the blood on your suit? I never counted on getting two. Killing two for one—I had a great day. Stop it," he says in a different tone. "You must stop me. I can't stop myself."

"Turn yourself in and I'll do everything I can," Jason encourages cautiously.

"I can't do that. You won't understand."

"Why did you kill men instead of the women you've been raping and killing?"

"You sound confident when you say that. Anyway, my friends and I needed a new challenge. Hopefully now, you can catch me faster."

"What friends?"

"You wouldn't understand."

"How many women have you raped?"

"Many, quite a few in this town."

"Have any of your victims survived?"

"I think a couple were lucky enough. Surely, not the one on the train. They wanted it though. You'd think after being force fucked, their bodies would rebel and they would become dry but no—their pussies were wet, all of them. They wanted me to fuck them and I know they loved my dick."

"Let's arrange to meet," Jason interrupts.

"I can't do that. My imaginary friends won't let me."

"How can I help you if I can't meet you?"

"Meet me in the park. My friends tell me the next victim will get her pleasure in the park. Please help me," he begs.

"Which park?"

"They haven't told me. When you find the body, you'll know. Stop me, please," he cries, sounding more off balance than earlier in the conversation.

The caller hangs up without further comments, and Jason is convinced that the caller is the true killer.

"Kevin, did we get it?"

"Yep, he talked long enough. The trace went through."

"From where did he call?"

"The telephone company is checking the number's location now."

"I've a hunch that it was a public place...maybe a mall. There was plenty of background conversation."

"Yeah, I noticed that, too."

"I'm going to get the bitch. He's trying to fuck with me. Little does he know, when he chose me, he fucked up. Royally!"

Seconds later, the telephone company calls with the trace information. Sgt. Austin takes the call.

"Jas, that number, it's here!" Sgt. Austin cries, sounding astonished. "He's in the building. The bastard called from inside this police station."

"What! Where?"

"The phone company said it came from a phone in our lobby downstairs."

They race to the lobby, looking for any suspicious characters. After a guard is placed by the telephone and the entrance sealed, Jason gathers a few men and searches the building. Again they draw a blank. The telephone has no prints. No one at the front desk remembers seeing anyone using the telephone. The search is canceled and the uneasy Jason settles back at his desk.

"He's a cunning bastard. Whatever it takes, I'll get him," Jason says angrily. "Watch me while I dance, you crazed..."

Jason's sentence is disturbed by the telephone.

"Look, you son-of-a-bitch!" Jason yells. "I don't know what games..."

"I'm nobody's bitch, though I am a son," Captain North interrupts. "Calm yourself and tell me what the fuck's going on."

"I'm sorry, Sir. That deranged maniac we are looking for just called me. I thought it was him harassing me again."

"Get your ass down here and fill me in."

"On my way, Sir."

Jason finishes his talk with Captain North and leaves his office with authorization to put several men on overtime around the clock to stake out the parks in the area.

CHAPTER 25

The next few weeks Jason becomes obsessed with finding the murderer-rapist. The communications between him and Sasha slowly diminish to a frustrating level for them both. Jason tries hard to talk to her and spend the much-needed time required to make the relationship flourish, but, with him investigating each murder or rape case—not only in Virginia City but also in the surrounding cities—he has little time for himself, rest and much less, Sasha.

Sasha is patient. She tries to understand Jason's obsession and drive to capture his greatest opponent. However, her need for companionship and the neglected feeling she gets when she goes days without talking to him and sometimes a week at a time without seeing him, disturbs her greatly.

Jason gets relieved off duty after the midnight hour. He's exhausted after a fifteen-hour stakeout and toys with the thought of visiting Sasha. But because of his physical state, he elects to have a hot relaxing shower at his home instead of an intelligent conversation and who knows what else, elsewhere. Knowing that the ride to the country is longer than the drive to Sasha's, he prepares himself mentally for the tiring journey.

At home he removes all the clothing necessary to render him bare-chested and turns on the hot water for instant coffee. Minutes later, the kettle whistles loud, almost drowning out the unexpected knock at the door.

He thinks of Sasha and smiles to himself. "You must've known that I almost dropped by your place," he says as he opens the door.

To his surprise, Julie makes an unexpected house call. She's well-dressed, as usual. With her hair pinned atop her head and her makeup flawless, she boldly steps in wearing her full-length mink coat with matching pumps.

"I would love for you to visit me," Julie says, more like an invitation.

"To what do I owe the pleasure of this visit?"

"You were heavily on my mind, so I thought I'd drop by."

"Is that so?"

"I know you've been running yourself ragged. I haven't been able to catch you at the station."

"Between following up on every murder-rape case and the stakeout I'm conducting, I haven't spent much time there."

"Believe me, I know."

"You look nice."

"Nice...you used to tell me I looked lovely."

"Just a figure of speech. I've always admired you with your hair up."

"I did it especially for you."

He only smiles.

"Excuse my manners. Let me take your coat and have a seat."

Jason helps the coat off her shoulders while Julie's shoulders draw back. The coat slowly lowers and he notices her bare back. He immediately thinks of an expensive dress she's bought to tempt him. She quickly removes her arms and he drapes it across one arm. Jason gets a quick rush as he notices her almost-naked body. After many years, Julie's still as shapely as the day he met her. The only stitch of clothing she wears is a pair of sheer black pantyhose with French-cut lace panties woven seamless to the sheer legs and her pumps. Jason takes a deep breath and stares at her for a moment.

"I remember the first time I saw you like this." Jason's mental thoughts are unintentionally addressed aloud.

"What about it?"

"Oh, nothing." He ponders looking for an easy way out, but the truth prevails. "Since then it's been my favorite look on all women."

"Does that include now?"

"You play dirty, but I'll admit that you look great."

"Why?"

"Why what?"

"Why do you like this look?"

"I don't know. I'd prefer this rather than to see a woman naked. I like having something left to the imagination."

"What's your imagination doing now?"

"Running wild."

"You're serious?"

"I've always said, facts are facts."

"So, my girlish figure still turns you on?"

"No comment," Jason unfittingly states.

"What happened to facts are facts?"

"No comment. Why are you out like this?"

"I thought I'd treat you to two things."

"Two things. Which are?"

"This look, I know you love and," Julie motions her arms as to indicate why look anyplace else, "me!"

"Interesting."

"How about it, big boy, wanna play house?"

"Julie, why are you doing this to me?"

"I'm not doing anything but expressing my desire for you."

"You're trying to tantalize me and mess with my head."

"Which one?"

"The one I think with."

"Which one is your imagination thinking with after seeing me like this?"

"Funny."

"Seriously, I just want you...us again. My feelings are sincere.

Therefore, I'm not messing with your head. Unless, it's the one below your belt."

"As I've asked you before, why now?"

"As I've told you before, I've learned what love is. We had that and I want it back."

"We had. You've just hit the nail on the head. It takes two. You don't want to duplicate my failed efforts at that. You gain wisdom from experience, so believe me, it doesn't work."

"You're saying that you don't love me?"

"In some strange...perverted kind of way, yes. I do love the way in which you'll always be a part of me but not in the way you're referring to."

"Okay, don't love me," insists Julie. "Fuck me! Some of our best sessions came after we had a dispute."

"I can't."

"Yes, you can but you're afraid. You're afraid that you'll realize that you do have true feelings for me. Plus you know how good it would be."

"I could easily reminisce on how great it felt making love to you, especially seeing you like this, but I won't allow myself to."

"Why did you stare with hunger?"

"Was I not supposed to stare?" Jason responds in disbelief. "I don't live with blinders on."

"Okay, let me hold you. I remember two things that are important to you. A wonderful smile and a strong hug. You've always said that you can tell a lot from a hug. I've adopted that theory, so hug me."

Julie walks over to him and gives him a tight squeeze. She presses her breasts against him firmly. His arms are around her but nonchalantly, more loosely than he can ever remember holding her.

"Well, what did you discover with that embrace?" questions Jason.

"You're good at acting but not good enough to fool me. You're suppressing your true feelings. I'd venture to say that you've never hugged like that before...now, care to try it again?"

She reaches around his waist with one hand and grabs his penis with the other.

"You're fighting me. Let's see you fight him getting hard."

Jason removes her lower hand and backs away.

"Listen, Julie, I'm tired..."

"That's even better," Julie interrupts. "I remember you doing some of your best work when you were tired."

"That's not what I mean. It's late, I'm not in the mood, and if you can't control yourself, I'll be forced to ask you to leave. I wouldn't feel right asking you to drive back to the city at this hour, but I will."

"Okay, let's talk."

"No emotional conversations tonight, tomorrow or the next day," Jason persists.

"All right. May I borrow a shirt to sleep in?" a frustrated Julie states.

"That's better...and when did this change take place?"

"What change?"

"You used to sleep naked."

"I still do, but not alone. Any offers?"

"No, you can take my bed. I'll sleep on the sofa."

"Fine, but remember this, you can't reject me forever. It's just a matter of time before you see things my way."

Jason leaves to get one of his shirts and Julie yells upstairs with a brilliant thought.

"I know why you're acting this way. I know you well. It's another woman, isn't it?"

"And if it is?" Jason responds.

"That's confession enough. Why else would you turn down my offer?"

"I could think of many reasons, but they probably would turn into a long discussion."

She corners him in the walk-in closet. His clothes are neatly organized. Shirts and ties are on one side; pants are on the other, and his tailored suits are on the back wall. Jason hands her a shirt. She buttons it from the bottom, leaving the top three unfastened showing most of her breasts. The length of the shirt hangs barely an inch below her womanhood. She kicks off her pumps and reaches under the shirttail slowly and removes her pantyhose.

"Easier access now," Julie seductively states.

"No thanks."

"Are you seeing somebody?"

"Yes."

"Really?" Julie says surprised. "How long have you two been dating?"

"A few weeks now, though I haven't had much time for her lately."

"I remember that well. Is she special?"

"She is."

"What's her name?"

"Sasha."

"Sasha, that's different. You won't hear that one too often."

"I think it's cute. I like its oddness."

"I can tell you really like her. You'd probably defend her against anything I say. Has she taken my place in your heart?"

"Trust me, your place is sacred. No one will ever replace you there. Unfortunately, that's not where my feelings are."

"That was cruel."

"It wasn't meant to be. Facts are facts, although I only store fond memories of you."

"I'm glad you finally found someone. After our divorce, you still chased me. I begged you to find someone. Now that you have it feels funny."

"I know that feeling well."

"I would like to meet her."

"Why?"

"I like to know my competition."

"This isn't about competition. This is about where my heart is. I'm not a prize to be won."

"My beloved Jason, you were a prize when we met. I lost sight of that years ago, but now that I have my twenty-twenty back, I not only want you—I need you back."

"God has everything predestined. Maybe one day I can trust myself, trust you enough to give us another try. Right now, both my heart and mind say 'no.' Therefore, your pressure isn't helping matters any."

"I don't try to be a pain in your rear, but my feelings for you make me react this way. I love you more now than I ever did."

"Listen, I didn't want a long drawn-out conversation. I'm too tired for it. I'll bid you goodnight."

"Can I have a kiss before you go?"

"I'm afraid not," Jason says while stepping around her, destined for the sofa.

She watches him leave. He closes the door behind him and she hears his soft footsteps descend the stairs. Crawling between the sheets, immediately her thoughts drift to the days when they had all of their ups and downs between these very sheets.

Jason falls into his slumber quickly. The exhaustion has worn him thin to where he practically falls asleep before his head hits the pillow while Julie falls asleep listening for his return steps to the bedroom. They both sleep comfortably for minutes before the telephone rings. Jason, making sure he's not dreaming, listens for more rings while Julie's half-sleep state makes her think she's answering her own and picks up the telephone.

"Hello?"

"Ja...hello? I'm sorry. I think I have the wrong number," the caller states.

Seconds later the telephone rings, and the caller is greeted again with a woman's voice.

"Is this the Jerrard residence?"

"Jerrard...yes, this is Jason's place."

"Is he in?"

"One moment...are you his, never mind. Hold on?"

Julie walks to the bedroom entrance and calls out for Jason. He barely understands her but makes his way to the kitchen.

"Hello?"

"Jason, what are you doing?"

"Leaning against the refrigerator with my eyes closed."

"No, who was that woman?"

"Julie."

"What's she doing there?"

"Sleeping...Sasha?"

"Yes, it's me."

"What are you doing up?"

"I just had a dream about you so I thought I'd call. What does she want?"

"She came by to talk."

"How convenient, you're home. I'm supposed to be your woman and you can't take time to call to see how I'm doing. I understand you're busy but a call only takes a second. You've been troubled by thoughts of Julie. I find her there so I must wonder."

"Sasha, I didn't plan this. Trust me on this."

"Where's she sleeping?"

"She's in my bed. I'm on the sofa. There is nothing going on."

"I miss you so much. You can't imagine the shock I had when she answered your phone."

"Relax, everything's fine. You woke us with your call. I guess she was half-dazed when she answered it."

"I'm trying to control it...my streak. I just needed your explanation. I believe you. When will I see you again?"

"It's hard to tell."

"I miss you something awful."

"I miss you, too."

"Can I come over tonight?"

"Now?"

"No, after you get off."

"It'll be late."

"I know, but I've done it before."

"Okay, meet me here. Better yet, I can come to your place. I'll already be in the city."

"That's fine with me. I'll fix you something to eat."

"Eggs?"

"No, I'm fixing you a well-balanced meal."

"Splendid."

"I hoped you'd see it my way. Get some sleep. You have a long day coming and I want you well-rested when you get here. Hint, hint."

"Frisky, even in the wee hours of the morning. That's a good trait to have."

"You brought out the worst...or should I say the best in me. Goodnight."

"Goodnight, love."

Silence greets Jason's ears.

"That's the first time you've called me anything," Sasha finally responds, trying not to let Jason hear her blushing through the telephone.

"I didn't mean to startle you."

"Only slightly...Jason..."

"I know already."

"You know what?"

"What you're about to say."

"Okay, smart one, tell me."

"I stopped you in the middle of saying that you loved me. Am I right?"

"How did you know?"

"Years of practice."

"Meaning?"

"I get paid to read people."

"Not ones you're involved with—especially emotional issues."

"I just knew. That's all."

"That's bold."

"Yeah, but true."

"Well?"

"Well, what?"

"Aren't you going to reciprocate?"

"Wouldn't it be better if I told you without you asking me? You know I never say anything I don't feel."

"Yes, but I need to know."

"Formulate your own opinion."

"Why should I?"

"It's better if you do."

"Why?"

"Because you'll tell yourself what you want to hear."

"True, so do you agree with what I'd tell myself?"

"In your mind, you never miss."

"I know my mind. I'm wondering about yours."

"To some degree, yes."

"Finally, that's a start."

"That answer will suffice?"

"For now. I know you do and say things in your own time."

"Now, who's reading who?"

"Goodnight, Jason."

"Goodnight."

"I'll see you tomorrow."

"Okay, bye."

"Bye."

Jason again curls up on the sofa and quickly drifts into slumber with his last conscious thought being a picture of Sasha on his eyelids.

CHAPTER 26

While Jason sleeps, the killer stalks the streets determined to carry out his last threat by venturing into the park.

Even the late hours bring out many couples who enjoy leisurely romantic walks through Grand Park. The majority, however, choose a carriage ride. Most carriages take a course around the huge park, while others deviate so riders can observe the many statues. A carriage stops to pick up a disillusioned couple. The man, hoping that the ride will set her in the proper mood for what he wants to come later, deceivingly helps his date into Jason's favorite carriage. The woman driver and the man's date make heavy but curious eye contact, both smiling pleasantly at each other. The door closes and the carriage starts its journey. After many circles the man instructs the driver to complete their run by riding through the park. His intention is to impress her with his knowledge of the statues.

The man sits with his arm around her shoulders and the hand dangles downward near her breasts. One of his fingers begins to stroke the upper part of her breast, another finger follows. The walking fingers quickly turn into a grasping hand, seizing an entire breast while making round motions. She politely places his hand back onto her shoulder. Seconds later, a lone finger makes its way to her nipple, softly stroking it like a guitar string.

"Stop it, Harold," the woman cries. "I told you not to expect anything just because you spent a few bucks on me."

"Listen to me, baby, I'm from the old school. I've spent hard-earned money on you tonight. It's time for you to produce."

He seizes her into his arms and forces her back, desperately trying to kiss her while his free hand tugs at her breasts once more. Suddenly the driver hears a loud smack as Harold's face sounds off from a well-executed slap.

"Look, I don't operate like this. It takes more than wining and dining to get me to sleep with you. Furthermore," the distraught woman states, "your forcefulness is a major turnoff."

"You look, sweetheart, you better be sure. You don't know who you're turning down."

Their conversation becomes louder to the point where it penetrates the carriage walls.

"You're becoming some sort of pervert."

"Pervert, I'll show you pervert."

He tries to slide his hand up between her legs. Defensively, her legs clamp tightly shut. "Do you mind? I want to go home. If you're any kind of man, you'll grant my wishes."

"I'll grant your wishes, all right. You make it home the best way you can."

Harold opens the door and jumps out of the moving carriage. He runs through the bushes, and a couple of officers follow him out of the park and apprehend him as he crosses the street. The driver, overhearing the conversation, stops the carriage to console the woman. She enters the carriage and closes the door behind her.

"I'm sorry. It may not be my place but men can be such assholes at times."

The woman, almost in tears, nods her head with agreement.

"I haven't known him long but I didn't think he was a creep."

"All men are creeps," the driver states. "We women understand each other. We know how to go about getting what we want."

"He surely went about it the wrong way with me."

"I'm not deliberately changing the subject, but that was some deep eye contact we had before you entered the carriage."

"Your look is striking. I tried..."

"I read more into it than you think," the driver boasts by cutting her off. "Ever had a woman before?"

"No, you aren't propositioning me! My so-called date was bad enough. I don't need a woman on my case making matters worse. All I need is to soothe my nerves. I'm a little shaken, that's all."

"I apologize. I just thought our eye contact was a revealing one. Your stunning beauty made me lose my head. So, in good faith, I have something," the driver says, reaching into the pouch that hangs off her shoulder. "This will calm you."

"What is it?"

"A mild sedative," the drive ensures. "Something similar to Tylenol."

"I don't take things like that from strangers."

"I understand."

The woman drops her head into her hands in shame, overwhelmed by Harold and then this bold woman. Her head rests in her hands for a few moments until the silence becomes uncomfortable for her. She raises her head just as the driver covers her mouth and nose with a cloth soaked in chloroform. The woman's muffled sound isn't loud enough to seep through the carriage walls. Nor is the protest of her vividly swinging hands and feet, which aimlessly battle the air. Her raging aids the chloroform to take effect much faster, sedating her just a slight moment before a sudden knock on the door identifies itself as a police officer. The driver quickly wraps her arm around the woman and buries the woman's head into her shoulder before the door opens.

"Excuse me, ladies, but we have a man in custody who says he was running away from this area trying to ditch his date."

"Officer," the driver states, "I heard their conversation through the carriage walls. He was a real asshole. After he jumped out of the moving carriage, I stopped to see if she was okay."

"Are you all right, Miss?"

The driver uses the concealed hand on the woman's neck to move her head up and down.

"Do you want to place any charges?"

Her head shakes "no."

"She's just terribly upset. Give us a moment. I'm sure she'll be fine."

"All right, she looks to be in capable hands. If you need any help, just yell. Someone should hear you."

"Thanks for your concern."

The driver listens for the officer's footsteps to fade, lays the limp body down in the seat and reaches under the woman's skirt. The driver tears off her pantyhose before moving between the woman's legs, then lowers to lick the woman's livelihood.

"I bet you're a tasty bitch," the driver states for the benefit of imaginary friends.

The Invisible Man disguised as a woman lowers his pants and underwear. He snatches off the wig he wears and wipes the heavy makeup and lipstick off his face with the woman's skirt. Soon after penetration he pounds her hard like a pile driver. Each forceful thrust seems to feed his unstable thoughts dancing within his mind. Somehow, while keeping his hips pumping, he manages to remove the woman's blouse and padded bra.

The woman slowly regains consciousness. Even in her drugged state, she realizes what's happening to her and goes into a frenzy. The rapist quickly wraps the bra around her neck, pulling tightly with his strong arms, leaving her gasping for air. He feels her strength dwindle. Thus, his thrust quickens into her once again. He gets close to an orgasm but suddenly snatches his penis out of her and brings on his climatic state by hand. The first squirt falls to her breast. The second hits her in the face. The others shoot wildly all over the walls and floor as he pumps himself like a shotgun. He pulls his underwear and pants up. After fastening the clasp, he leans forward to lick the semen that descends slowly down her face. He removes the bra from her neck, wraps a cup around his index finger and shoves it up into her womanhood. As before, he pulls her skirt down neatly. Her lifeless body falls between the seats. He locates her purse and grabs a tube of lipstick. Through tactful maneuvering, he somehow escapes unnoticed but not before cleaning up his prints with the woman's dress and leaving another inscription for the police on the inside walls. This one is purposely addressed to Jason.

Jason gets the wakening call after less than two hours of solid sleep. He quickly jumps to answer it thinking it might be Sasha again.

"Jas, Kevin, you've got to get down here. The son-of-a-bitch did it again. He raped and killed a woman right under our noses."

"What? Where did it happen?"

"Grand Park."

"Where were the men?"

"They were apprehending a suspicious character. There are unusual circumstances with this one. That's why I'm calling you."

"Shit, I'll be there soon. You did say Grand Park?"

"Yes."

"I'm on my way there."

Jason hurries to the bedroom and grabs pants and a pullover sweater. He splashes water on his face and underarms and attempts to dress without disturbing Julie.

"What is it, Jason?"

"Duty calls."

"Just like old times, huh?"

"Not quite...lock up when you leave."

Jason rushes to the crime scene and is greeted by Sgt. Austin. After his briefing he investigates the carriage only to discover the disturbing image of the slain woman—especially disturbing since his fond memories of the very same carriage are still fresh in his mind. He steps into the carriage and takes the rear seat to view the killer's latest handiwork. He reaches to close the woman's eyes and a rage runs through his blood, sparked by the killer's underlined message that reads: "This bod's for you, Jerrard."

The forensic team dusts for prints and finds a few clean ones. Many smudged fingerprints are recovered as well before Jason grants approval to have the body removed.

"Run a match on those prints as soon as you get back to the station," Jason instructs one of the forensic team members. Then he directs his attention to Sgt. Austin. "Did anyone see anything?"

"Officer Bennett saw him."

"Get him over here."

"Bennett, you're wanted over here!" yells Sgt. Austin. "Tell Detective Jerrard what you told me."

"I saw her...him. He was dressed convincingly as a woman."

"I noticed the heavy makeup on the victim's skirt," Jason states. "What else?"

"I talked with him. He gave a very good impression of a woman's voice, too. He was consoling her. She had just fought with her date."

"That's the suspect I told you about on the phone," interjects Sgt. Austin.

"Things looked normal to me."

"Kevin, what other evidence do you have?"

"Just what you saw in the carriage. The wig, blouse and samples of his semen."

"Can someone tell me," Jason questions in disgust, "how in God's name did this woman/man become a driver?"

"Actually, Sir," Officer Bennett interjects, "the company that owns the carriages states that the driver of this carriage was found unconscious in the back of another carriage being repaired and rushed to the hospital. Unfortunately for us, he was found after the attack. There is no word on his condition at this time."

"Okay, thank you, Bennett. Kevin, finish here. I'm going to follow the prints back to the lab."

The usable prints are photocopied into the computer. The computer crosschecks the print patterns with others of previous murders and rape cases. The process is slow. The check covers the local precincts and surrounding counties. None lifted from the carriage match any in the computer's database. Jason orders the prints to be run against the FBI's computer, which takes another several hours to complete, but in the end, no matches are found.

A frustrated Jason stops by the duty desk and states, "Here, if anything new develops, I can be reached at this number."

CHAPTER 27

Sasha, expecting Jason well after midnight, is surprised and elated at his call stating he'll be there soon. Impatiently, she begins to peek out of the windows in search of him. Finally, her wishes are answered as she watches Jason's car turn into the parking lot. She hurries out the door with extreme joy, down the stairs and greets him as he closes the car door.

"Well, hello," Jason says.

She says nothing. Instead, in her excited state, she grabs him and squeezes him tight while repeatedly kissing him all over his face.

"I'm glad to see you, too," Jason responds.

"Honey, you don't know how miserable I've been without you."

"It's been hard on both of us."

"Let's," she gives him a hard wet lasting kiss before finishing her statement, "go inside. You look tired."

"Exhausted may be a better word."

She gets to the door, turns the knob and nothing. With all the excitement, she failed to unlock the condo's door.

"I feel like a heel," Sasha says with somewhat of a damper on her aroused state. "A complete idiot."

"You shouldn't. Everyone has done this very same thing at least once."

"Have you?"

"A couple of times."

"Oh, my God, you aren't infallible."

"You know us aliens. We're destined to make mistakes eventually."

"Now, I have to pay the building management to unlock the door."

"Not necessarily. Stand behind me." He pulls out a credit card and in a matter of seconds the door pops open. "This goes to show you that locks nowadays are worthless. From now on, when you're home or away, lock the deadbolt also."

"Yes, captain. Normally I sleep with only the bottom lock."

"Get out of that bad habit."

"I will...I assume you're staying?"

"Yep, my clothes are in the car."

"Dinner is going to be awhile. You're here early and I haven't even started."

"No problem. I have plenty of work to do in the meantime."

"You brought work with you?" Sasha responds, noticeably displeased.

"In my briefcase. Somewhere in all these files, the killer's identity is hidden. I've studied them hundreds of times and I'll continue studying them until I find something that will break this case wide open."

"You sound as though you have a personal vendetta against this killer."

"I do, just as he has one for me."

"Why do you say that?"

"He's on to me. The fucker...excuse me, the fool actually harassed me today."

"I bet that gives you an eerie feeling."

"Right. Somehow I'll catch him though."

"You get to work and I'll start dinner."

"Do you mind if I clutter your bedroom? I need room to spread these files. Your bed would be perfect."

"What do you want to do all over my bed?"

"You understood me clearly, now didn't you?"

"You can't blame a horny girl for checking. Seriously, make yourself at home."

"Okay, get out."

"Wait, ah...oh, kinda tickles my throat."

"You win. Babe, I forgot to ask you. Have the threatening calls stopped since the downfall of the Far East Import Company?"

"I haven't turned on my answering machine since you were last here. However, I have had a few hang-ups when I answered the phone."

"Have you upset anyone lately?"

"No one that I can think of...I just tell myself that it is some kids playing."

"Maybe it's best that you do that."

She starts dinner and he begins his task. During dinner preparation and the studying, they engage in not-so-frequent conversation.

"You know, it's almost like you're not here with you being so quiet, but I'm content just because you're reachable...Jason, honey?"

She walks into the bedroom. Jason is lying on the bed asleep with the files gathered around him. She shakes her head, thinking, *Poor thing, your body finally told you enough.*

Sasha removes his shoes. She somehow manages to get him to take off his clothes and gains great amusement watching him stumble through the process before putting dinner away. Sasha returns to the bedroom to make herself a sleeping space in the bed. Accomplishing this meant picking up his folders intended for his briefcase. It didn't mean paying attention to the dates of the crimes written on the tabs of each folder. Nor should it have jarred her memory with the recognition of several dates.

Sasha is a stickler for details. She records just about every event of her life. If she hadn't seemed so desperate, she would not have a record of every broken date in her journal, brought forth to her frontal lob. She would not have suspicions of her own to investigate. Be that as it may, she considers it more than a mere coincidence that several attacks occurred the same day she logged disturbing thoughts in her journal. Also, the comment Jason has on the killer's attire is enough to persuade her to do her own snooping. She contemplates telling Jason of her suspicions but decides against condemning someone without further proof. She wakes him long enough to get him under the covers and undresses and snuggles comfortably with him, wondering if her suspicions are true.

In the morning, Jason prepares for work quietly, trying not to disturb Sasha's slumber. However, Sasha is already awake.

"Honey, are you coming back this evening?"

"It depends on how late I get off."

"I might have a surprise for you."

"Oh, what kind of surprise?"

"All I'll tell you is that it's one that would help you greatly."

"You definitely peaked my curiosity. Will you give me a hint?"

"Nope, but you'll be amazed on how small the world is."

"I'm confused."

"Don't worry about it. Have a nice day."

"Thank you. You, too."

They hug and kiss, then depart in their respective directions. Once Sasha arrives at work, the first thing she does is make the telephone call that played on her mind constantly before she fell asleep the previous night.

"Hello?"

"I'm surprised you're home."

"Sasha? How have you been?"

"Fine."

"To what do I owe the pleasure of this call?"

"I'm just trying to clear something up."

"What?"

"The true meaning behind why we had trouble getting together."

"I've explained that already."

"Did you lie?"

"Wait a minute. You call me after weeks and accuse me of being a liar. What nerve you have."

"If my suspicions are correct, you're much more than that."

"What a greeting," he responds in disgust. "Let's start over. Anything you have to ask or tell me, you can do in person. This way you can see the sincerity on my face when I say that I honestly don't know what you're talking about."

"I don't think that's a good idea."

"What am I, a criminal now?"

"You tell me."

"I'm no more of a criminal than you are. Let's have dinner."

"Again, we've been through this many times before."

"I know but this time, hell or high water, I'll be there," he pleads.

"I'll only meet you someplace public."

"What could be more public than a restaurant?"

"I just want to sit across from you, see your face and make my own decision."

"Decision about what?"

"You'll know soon enough."

Their talk quickly ends after they decide when and where they'll be dining.

★★★★★

Jason is summoned from his rounds by Captain North and reports eagerly to discover the captain's urgency.

"Jas, how's it going?"

"Well, Sir, damn...Frank, he escaped the other night but the bastard will be found."

"When will you come up with something productive, especially since this man played Houdini and vanished without a trace after his last deed?"

"At this time, that escapes me. I can't get anything concrete on him."

"This case is troubling you, isn't it?"

"Well, sometimes...why do you ask?"

"In all of your years on the force, I've never heard you say I can't."

"I can get him," Jason recites. "I just need to stay focused on the task at hand. He's bound to slip soon."

"I wonder how many others will die before he does."

"Hopefully, none, before we can stop him."

"I'm about to make it more difficult for you."

"It can't get any worse than it already is."

"You have to stop the round-the-clock surveillance of the parks."

"It's more difficult," Jason concurs.

"I think we can catch him this way but the mayor doesn't. He took one glimpse at the money it's cost the city so far and demanded it be stopped immediately. The coffin was nailed shut when the criminal killed right under our noses."

"What do we do? Wait for him to strike again?"

"We have no choice. The mayor says there's no need to watch the parks and I'll have to agree...unless he phoned you stating that there will be more mayhem in the parks."

"I haven't heard from him. If there's no need for watching the parks, let my men patrol the streets."

"It's not my decision to make. You're to end the overtime immediately."

Jason contemplates what to say. After moments of silence he expresses his idea. "Frank, play with me a minute. What if we put out a false report stating that the killer has been caught?"

"For what purpose?"

"Two things could possibly happen. He will either stop his actions, content that he's a free man, or..."

"From what you've told me about your conversation with him, he's not balanced. He is an emotionally sick man."

"True," Jason intrudes, "but it's worth a try. Secondly, the report could flush him out. He is a sick man—the frustration of knowing that he isn't caught may help him make a mistake."

"Interesting, but it might make him kill again."

"He'll kill again anyway," assures Jason.

"Let me think about it."

"Good enough."

"Now, get your people on overtime off the clock."

"Right away, Sir...Frank."

At his desk Jason places the call to dispatch to have everyone not scheduled for day hours to be released. As he sits thinking of his next move, Sgt. Austin interrupts.

"Jas, you had a call earlier."

"From who?"

"I don't know but it wasn't Julie."

"Could you detect an accent?"

"Nothing noticeable."

"What did you tell her?"

"I told her that you'd be here soon. She called right after the captain summoned you."

"Did you ask to take a message?"

"Yes, but she said she'd call back."

"He shouldn't have," intrudes Detective McAllister. "This isn't your answering service."

"I have no control over who calls me or when for that matter," Jason states defensively.

"You shouldn't try to be such a playboy."

"I'm guilty if loving to have women in my entourage qualifies me as one."

"So you do admit it?"

"I admit to nothing. Knowing lots of women isn't a crime."

"Yeah, I bet you seduce them all."

"That's the difference between you and me. I don't have to seduce all the women I know or meet to make me feel like a man. Each person I associate with has certain qualities I like, so depending on the mood I'm in, that determines who I talk to. Together, they make up one complete package."

"Sounds like a head trip to me."

"Not when you have things in the proper perspective."

"Perspective? You can't even date one woman."

"Tell me something, Chris. Have you ever experienced going out with six women surrounding you? Not only that but having all their attention directed to you?"

"I suppose you have?"

"Many times. It takes finesse to..."

"Excuse me, Frick and Frack," Sgt. Austin says. "Jas, you have a call."

"Another member of your entourage, I bet."

"No, Chris, Jason calls them stockbrokers."

"Envy is in the air...Sixteenth Precinct, Jerrard."

"Jason Jerrard?"

"Speaking."

"From Capital High?"

"Who is this?"

"You have forgotten my voice. I'm so hurt."

"Someone from high school, that long ago. It's nearly impossible for anyone to have that great of a recall."

"This is your first love."

"My first love was Maria from New York on summer vacation when I was fourteen but you don't sound Hispanic."

"No, think a little older."

"Monique...Monique Clemens?"

"Yes, I guess I should have said, 'your first *true* love.' How have you been?"

"Fine. It's been a long time."

"Over fifteen years."

"How did you find me?"

"Simple mathematics. I knew you went to the police academy."

"Well, I'll be. You're in town?"

"Only for a few days on business. My schedule is tight, but is it possible to meet with you tonight if your schedule permits?"

"Tonight. That may be hard for me but, for kicks, what time are you talking about?"

"Somewhere around dinnertime."

"Done," Jason says too fast.

"I'll treat you at the very first place we ate."

"Rosalina's?"

"It's still open, isn't it?"

"Sure is. I eat there several times a week."

"Do you? I see something good came out of knowing me. How does seven-thirty sound to you?"

"Great."

"How will I find you?"

"Have the maitre d' named Alfredo seat you at my booth."

"You have your own booth? You're moving up in the world."

"It's a long story. Oh, one more small detail."

"What's that?"

"I'd prefer if you let me pay."

"If it's that important to you."

"It is. I'm no longer the guy you used to hand twenties to when you got paid."

"You win."

"Thanks."

"Okay, got to run. See you later."

"Goodbye."

Jason finishes his work day mentally exhausted from trying to reveal a pattern to the attacks, hoping to estimate where the next one might occur. The mystery has him baffled, but he finds some relief in having an engagement to break away from the heavy thought and concentration.

He arrives at Rosalina's five minutes late for his engagement and Alfredo advises him that his guest is already seated. Jason walks toward the booth looking hard trying to find some resemblance between the woman that's bestowing his eyes now and the girl he knew as a teenager. She has developed into a tall Amazon woman who has filled out nicely, transformed from the short, slim, no-shape girl with braces. The most recognizable trait is her one dimple that shines as she smiles. She stands and they embrace for a moment before they sit.

"You're a different girl...woman, a definite change since high school."

"I've changed a little."

"You've changed a lot. Look at you. Everything about you has matured."

"What, I look old or something now?"

"No, don't get me wrong. Your face is as young as ever but the rest of you. My word."

"Thank you. I did spring up, didn't I? You look as good as the day I last saw you, and the thin beard is an added plus."

"Thank you. So, what are you doing in town?"

"I'm on assignment. I'm a photographer in town covering this year's mayors conference."

"You couldn't stand a camera years ago."

"I couldn't stand to be in front of one. I guess seeing yours glued to you got the best of me."

"Maybe so. I never pictured you as a photographer. Pardon the pun."

"Yep...how's your family? Julie, I'm sure you have kids."

"Julie is fine and no kids."

"You must be losing your touch."

"I'm divorced."

"Sorry to hear that," she says with a gaze intent on capturing his full attention.

"It's life."

"See I told you about..."

"You told me what?" Jason interrupts, already knowing what Monique is preparing to say.

"About Julie...I told you what kind of person she was. Hell, everyone knew. I could've been good to you," Monique reflects somberly.

"How could you?" he says rearing back in the booth. "You were engaged."

"I told you that I wouldn't marry and I didn't."

"But you ran away."

"I had to," she says more emotionally.

"There's nothing I couldn't have understood."

"Jason, I was pregnant," Monique admits shamefully.

The words leave Monique's mouth with her being very uncertain on how they would make Jason feel or react. To her surprise, Jason only half-smiles.

"Finally," he says after a sigh. "I've known for years. I just needed to hear you say it."

"I didn't want to hurt you."

"You hurt me more by running."

"You were going to help me raise someone else's child?"

"I loved you enough to."

"Jason, I was two months from giving myself to you. Do you remember?"

"Yeah, my sixteenth birthday we were to make love for the first time."

"I couldn't stand the peer pressure. My family, friends were on my back because you were younger. They didn't approve of our secret relationship."

"You were old enough to make decisions of your own."

"I know," she says pleading. "I folded under their pressure. I got engaged to make them happy and it started destroying you. When I saw what it was doing to you, I made the promise to you that I wouldn't marry. I walked out on my wedding day, leaving everyone in awe because of the promise that I made to you."

"Your brother told me."

"Days later I found out that I was pregnant, so I left ashamed to let you see me."

"I still carried hopes of us. I kept tabs on you. Your family kept me informed of your whereabouts. I even wrote you a few times, but after I received no return response, I started giving up. Wait," Jason conjures, "exactly what are we doing? It has been years and we can't find anything better to talk about."

"I guess it had to be said or it wouldn't have been our major topic."

"Maybe you're right."

"Before we drop this, please answer one question for me."

"Which is?"

"Are you still angry with me?"

"I was never angry. I loved you too much for anger. Actually, now that I think about it, I understood your actions. Now, I'm rather glad you looked me up. Tell me, what did you have?"

"A boy." She pauses. Looking him squarely and proudly into his eyes, she recites, "I named him after you."

"You're kidding," he says with amazement. "Give me the punch line."

"No, it's true. Jason is fifteen now. He's a big boy and when he was younger, I told him about how you were instead of his natural father."

"Why did you do that?"

"His father is a jerk. I want him to be like someone I've always admired."

"I'm truly flattered. I don't know what to say."

"Say nothing. It's done already. Now, you tell me, are you involved with someone?"

"Yes, with someone very sweet."

"Tell me all about her...where did you meet her? Here in the city?"

"You might say I bumped into her in the city. It was a chance meeting, and it's been like the Fourth of July ever since. That is," he says with some degree of disappointment, "until lately."

"What happened?"

"My work. This case I'm trying to solve occupies ninety-five percent of my time. It's really straining our relationship."

"Does she understand what you do?"

"For the most part, yes, but her irritation is beginning to show."

"You have to keep it together. Talk to her and explain that it will not always be like this."

"Why do you say this?"

"As you speak of her, there's compassion in your voice."

"Come on. She is special to me, but I don't feel that it's reflected in my voice."

"Really. Have I ever lied to you?"

"Well...no."

"Trust me on this."

They engage in more conversation about people they knew from high school, and laugh and joke as if the years hadn't passed. Meanwhile, Sasha arrives outside Rosalina's looking for someplace to park and seeking someone from her own recent past. The closest park available during the restaurant's busiest time is down the street and around the corner. Sasha's punctuality has her arriving several minutes early for her engagement. She decides to wait in her car until the last minute before she seeks her party. Minutes later, she ventures through the restaurant to make sure her party hasn't arrived before her. What she finds to her dismay is Jason and Monique laughing endlessly. A red flag, a jealous streak all overwhelm her instantly, causing her to make a beeline to Jason's booth—their booth—determined to get answers.

"Sasha!" Jason says surprised. "We just finished talking about you. What are you..."

"Never mind me," Sasha interrupts boldly. "What are you doing, here, with her?"

"I was invited to dinner by an old acquaintance of mine, Monique. Monique, this is Sasha. Sasha, meet Monique."

"Nice to meet..."

"Yeah, nice to meet you," Sasha says rudely. "How can she easily get time with you and I have to be so patient?"

"Calm down a minute and let me explain."

"There's nothing to explain. First, it's your ex-wife sleeping in your bed and now her."

"You and Julie are still an item?" Monique questions, intrigued by Sasha's statement.

"No, we aren't," Jason defends. "And I'm not guilty of anything," he says, standing up with his cup of coffee in his hands. "Please sit down and calm yourself. Listen to my explanation."

"I've seen enough. I don't need to make any more of a spectacle of myself. That's your job. Just think," Sasha comments as an afterthought. "I'm trying to help you out."

Sasha's jealous streak consumes her, leading her into an uncontrollable rage. As Jason moves aside with hopes of making room for her to sit, she suddenly knocks his hand with the coffee, splashing it on his shirt and pants, staining them badly. Sasha storms away toward the ladies room while Jason tries to shake the excess wetness from his clothes, desperately trying not to show that the heated liquid is uncomfortable to his skin. He sits in shame.

"This is the sweet one? Either my senses fail me or your taste in women has changed drastically," Monique says.

"She is a very sweet woman."

"I'm sorry. That wasn't nice."

"But it was appropriate. I just don't fully understand why she's so hostile tonight. Take this money and pay the bill. I have to get out of these clothes. I'll drop by her place after I change. Maybe she will listen to reason then."

"This was my treat, remember, and good luck with her."

"Next time...I'll talk to you later. Goodbye."

"Goodbye."

CHAPTER 28

Jason walks out of Rosalina's troubled by Sasha's actions, confused knowing that the entire scene was unnecessary. He thinks, *I just can't figure women out. Just when you think you know them, BAM, you find another side of them. Maybe that's my problem. I shouldn't try to figure them out.*

Sasha bursts out of Rosalina's in a fury. Even with the fire in her eyes, tears form a puddle in them. Jason runs over to her with his plea.

"You told me about your jealous streak, but I never imagined it would upset you so. We are just friends."

With a penetrating hard look, she states, "Not the way you two were gazing at each other."

"Listen, please, Sasha, why condemn me before you know the facts? You've already knocked a cup of coffee in my lap, embarrassed me in front of Monique and created a scene on pure speculation. I believe I'm the one who should be upset. Let's talk sensibly before the incident turns into total chaos. It was just a meeting between old friends."

"Oh, then why haven't I heard of her before? I don't want to hear it," she states while storming angrily away.

"Stop and listen to me, will you? Monique is a friend from high school who's in town on business. She gave me a call at the station and I accepted her invitation to dinner. We were talking about old times, people that we grew up with, when you walked in with a chip on your shoulder."

"Yeah, I bet your next stop was her hotel."

"That's not fair. Besides, I don't know where she's staying."

"After all this time, Monica, Monique or whatever the witch's name is, knows your whereabouts. Give me a break!"

"Your arm or your leg," Jason jokes desperately.

"Don't try to be humorous. You can't laugh your way out of this."

"Look, when I last saw her, she knew I was going to the police academy. I've been in this city all my life. It could be just simple logic. Besides, you could've sat with us and learned all of this, so please try to calm down."

"Jason Jerrard, you try to understand. You are always too busy, never having any time for me, for our relationship or us. Your police work keeps you gone ten, twelve, sometimes fourteen hours a day. Then, I find you in our favorite restaurant with some strange woman whom I've never heard of, and you want me to be calm."

"Yes!"

The tears fall from Sasha's eyes, bestowed by Jason's belief that she is overreacting.

"Yes, you're impossible!"

She suddenly storms off down the street and around the corner in search of her car.

"Come back! Our relationship is worth more than this!" begs Jason.

Jason is puzzled by the whole ordeal, wondering how their storybook romance has turned sour due to a simple dinner. He knew all along that it was not just a simple dinner or a gathering with another woman or the lack of time spent with her. But it was the accumulation of all three that has caused his newfound grief. He backs against the building behind him. Suddenly the pay telephone rings.

"What!" Jason yells into the receiver before slamming it down.

He stands staring into space, pondering the events that led to his dismay—wondering why Sasha would show up out of nowhere when Monique approaches him.

"My deepest condolences," Monique says concerned. "Are you okay? I'm sorry for the troubles I've caused."

"It's not your fault—where are you staying? I need some time to think."

"I understand. I'm at the Renaissance, room five seventy-six. I'll be in town a few more days. Call me."

"Okay, I'll catch up with you later."

"I really do hope that things will be all right between you two."

"Thanks."

"Goodbye."

"Goodbye."

Sasha pulls her car keys out of her purse, unlocks the door and out of the shadows a tall man with a strong build and dirty brown hair seems to materialize out of thin air. His clothes are old and worn reaping a strong odor—an unwashed odor of the streets.

"Sasha," the man states coldly.

"Huh? Ryan...you frightened me. I didn't think you'd show up again."

"I told you I'd come and I'm here."

"You're late. I'll have to talk with you later. I'm having a very bad evening...why in the hell are you dressed in those funky clothes? You look awful and no offense, you need a bath."

"Just in case I'm seen," Ryan states with an inflection unfamiliar to Sasha's ears. "You'd be amazed what rolling around in a trash pile will do for your body odor."

Instantly, Sasha becomes queasy with the strange manner her associate has presented.

"You calling me like that upset my balance," Ryan utters, even more unsettled. "My friends didn't like that so I came to set the record straight."

"What record?"

"I think you already know."

"How do you plan to get this record corrected?" Sasha airs, attempting to distract him while she opens the driver's door.

Without answering, he grabs her from behind, placing a knife at her throat. Death. That feeling overwhelms her, placing her in a state of shock, causing her chest to tighten as she struggles to breathe.

"The car is mine, but first I have business with you. You finally get to see," he states in a humorous tone, "what I do when I'm breaking our date. Tonight, my friends get satisfied."

Sasha's frightened being is too terrified to cry for help. Her racing heart is her only indication that she is still alive.

"One word from you," he continues, "and you'll be a dead pretty," he adds for assurance. "Then I'll still have my way with you while you're still warm."

His grip is strong, bearing hairy hands with long and dirty nails. He begins to tear at her clothes and fondle her breasts while running the other hand down between her legs.

"Oh...yeah, I'm going to enjoy this ride—you and your car. I love the way you feel."

Terror and tears take over Sasha as she squirms to his touch, not believing this is happening to her. He uses his superior strength to forcefully drag her into the alley from where he came.

Take her from the back, flashes through his mind, causing a pause as if he did not understand.

"Please, I haven't told anyone about you...don't do this. I can help you."

A flash of sanity. "So, you do know, but my friends tell me it's our destiny that I have you this way."

"Take my car, my money, my credit cards, anything but please don't hurt me," she pleads.

"Hurt you. I'm gonna please you," he says short of laughing.

The alley is filled with darkness. Visibility is poor. The only light source comes from a dim street lamp, which projects more shadows than light as it hangs from above concealing the rough pavement as loose stones lay torn out of place from the cobblestone street. There are trash-cans against the walls, each owned by the local establishments. Sasha loses one shoe, and somehow manages to feel the dampness of the cold cobblestones.

As if it were a miracle from above, his balance eludes him and they fall backwards to the damp cold street. He grunts to the impact of Sasha's weight, jarring—what feels like to him—every cubic inch of air from his body. He drops the knife as he doubles over gasping for air. Sasha scrambles to free herself by throwing his now-empty hand aside and runs toward the lighted street screaming frantically to where she had last seen Jason. Jason hears screaming.

"Sasha!" he panics.

Instinctively, his pursuit starts in the direction of her piercing cry. Just as he's about to make the turn around the corner, he and Sasha collide for the second time. The impact is forceful, but he manages to keep them both on their feet. She wears one shoe. Her clothes are torn and disarrayed. She's almost too nervous to speak yet she utters, "It's him, your killer. He tried to rape me!"

"Are you all right?" questions a concerned Jason.

"I think so."

"Go inside the restaurant where it's safe and wait for me."

"Be careful. He has a knife," Sasha screams to the fleeing Jason.

Jason reaches inside his sport jacket, pulls out his pistol and proceeds down the street to the alley with his gun pointed down as he was taught to walk while pursuing a suspect. Upon reaching the alley, Jason strains his ears for any sound that might be the rapist. Noticing what appears to be a moving shadow, Jason disappears into the alley's blackness in pursuit. His eyes are overtaken by the sudden darkness, but they desperately endeavor to focus on anything that could be the size of a human body. Slowly and carefully he steps, noting the uneasiness of the cobblestone street.

Out of the shadows, the rapist hits Jason like a linebacker creaming a quarterback on his blind side. Jason bounces off the wall into trashcans, losing his pistol as he hits the damp street while the suspected rapist runs toward the light.

"Pig, pig, catch me if you can," he says while laughing uncontrollably.

Jason fumbles at his ankle, pulls his pant leg up and produces his back-up revolver.

"Halt!" Jason yells as he fires three consecutive rounds after the fleeing rapist.

The shots are wide to the right, hitting the corner of the alley's wall, allowing the rapist to escape around the corner. Before the pursuit resumes, Jason searches for his lost pistol while simultaneously trying to regain all of his senses. Upon turning the corner, screeching tire sounds envelope his ears as the suspect flees with Sasha's car. Jason fires two more rounds at the car passing right in front of him.

"Jason!" Sasha shouts when the shots echo in her ears.

She darts helplessly down the troubled street to where Jason is and then notices her car's destructive course turning toward her, riding on the sidewalk, knocking down meters and anything that stands within its path. The horn is being constantly hammered while the suspect rocks in the seat to a never-ending laugh. Sasha turns and runs wildly in the other direction.

"No!" she cries.

Sasha's panic-stricken thoughts direct her to conceal herself behind the largest object she can find—a huge metal dumpster. Ducking out of view of the car's sight, her body shivers uncontrollably as the horn gets louder and louder, drawing nearer.

"Someone help me!" she yells.

The suspect thrusts the car into the dumpster like fighting ships of pirate days. The crash is loud. Sounds of breaking headlights, a hissing of a broken hose and a fender dragging on the ground echo through the streets. He reverses the car and continues his plight entering the main street, causing accidents as other motorists try to avoid hitting him. He drives away wildly and once again free.

The impact of the collision hurls Sasha in the air, bouncing her off the wall into the doorway of a closed camera shop. Her unconscious body lies still as blood gushes out of her mouth. Jason runs down the street to where he heard the crash and finds a dumpster out of its original position. An eerie feeling rushes through his entire being when he notices in the blackness of a doorway a human body silhouette.

"Sasha!" his heart responds. Stunned at what he's envisioning, Jason's pace slows to almost a crawl. "Sasha, please move," his heart cries out.

Jason reaches her, falls to his knees, grabs her into his arms and rocks slowly with her embraced as tears form in his eyes. He carefully lays Sasha's motionless body back to the ground, fearing his need to comfort her may be causing more damage. He finds minimal relief in her faint pulse being a sign of life. Jason weeps.

CHAPTER 29

Jason is at the hospital bed holding one of Sasha's soft hands between his. His head lays on the bed adjacent to her hip, waiting for any sign of life from her. The door opens and the doctor enters.

"Mr. Jerrard, twenty hours is long enough. She's in a coma and it could be days before she comes out of it. You must go home and get some rest before you are hospitalized for exhaustion. If her condition changes, I'll get in touch with you right away."

The doctor's advice is interrupted by the door opening again as Julie walks in dressed to please as always. Both the doctor's and Jason's eyes focus on her as she steps in.

"Doctor Bodou, this is Julie," Jason states, mentally noting that with this introduction he did not mention ex-wife.

"Pleased to meet you."

"Nice to meet you," Julie greets while sizing up the woman that has taken her place in Jason's heart. "Jason, I tried to reach you at the station today and they told me what happened. How is she, doctor?"

"I was just telling Mr. Jerrard that her vital signs are stable, but at this time she's comatose. There is nothing we can do but wait. I would prefer to have him wait at home—maybe you can help me convince him into going home to get some rest."

"I agree," Julie responds, seizing the moment. "There's nothing more you can do here. You've probably not eaten for hours."

"I know, but I have to be here when she comes out of it."

"If she comes out of it," Dr. Bodou interjects, trying not to sound too pessimistic. "The internal bleeding has stopped. Her condition has stabilized, but, I must caution you, there's a chance that she may never recover," the doctor states, driving the stake farther into Jason's heart.

"I know," Jason concurs in sorrow. "But, she is strong. She will recover."

"Jason, let me take you home," Julie suggests. "You can shower. I'll fix you something to eat. You can get some much-needed rest. Besides, you can wait at home. There really isn't anything more you can do here. It's in God's hands now."

"Okay," he agrees reluctantly. "Any changes, call me."

"I'll phone you right away, Sir."

As they leave the room, Jason turns and finds it hard to believe that only hours earlier, that motionless body lying there was full of life and vigor. What he wouldn't give to have her upset with him. The door closes and the doctor checks her pulse before he leaves.

They arrive at Jason's home with him unusually quiet. His good willful demeanor has conceded to the sorrow his inner being feels. Julie had to drag what little conversation she could out of him on the way over.

"You've made some changes since I was last here," Julie says as she takes a seat in the living room.

"Just a few...would you like a drink?"

"Yes, that would be nice. I think it could help relax me."

"Seven and seven?"

"You remember. I bet you still don't drink and only keep alcohol here for guests."

"I haven't changed much."

"What happened to the divider that was providing closure to the living room?"

"I thought it would match the bedroom furnishings better so I moved it up there."

"Look, Jason," Julie says, feeling a need to comfort him. "I know you're very upset about what has happened to Sasha. You're so tense and tight. What you need is one of my famous massages. Do you remember those?"

"Yes, I do."

"Come," Julie instructs. "Sit here."

Jason takes his place between her legs on the floor. Julie administers a squeeze on his tense shoulders. The soft but firm grip sets his mind back to the hours past.

"Maybe if we didn't have that fight," he grieves. "She'd be well now."

"Try not to think about that now and don't go blaming yourself. I'm not trying to sound unconcerned but couples fight every day. We certainly had our share. What makes your fight different from others?"

"There was an attack that followed this one, that's what."

"Yes, if I may steal some of your words, you didn't have control over the attack. You couldn't have possibly known about it. Tell me, why were you two bickering?"

"Do you remember Monique?"

"Oh yes, her," Julie states in a noticeably flatter tone. "She was the one that didn't want you to marry me. I believe she was your first love..."

"Yeah, yeah, yeah, we were only having a simple dinner when Sasha stormed in and..."

"Haven't you learned," Julie says, interrupting Jason. "We women have a hard time dealing with past associates, friends or otherwise?"

"Can we not talk about this now?"

"Okay, I'm not trying to upset you further. Just sit back, relax and try to clear your mind. This massage should help."

Julie proceeds with the massage, using her fingers on his tense and tight shoulder blades. Jason pushes against her fingers to feel more pressure but Julie's force subsides, bringing his back to the sofa and his head resting on her firm breasts. Julie wraps her arms around his chest giving him a confiding hug.

"Try to relax," Julie suggests. "Worrying will not help anything. God will take care of her."

"You seem to always have the right words at the right time."

She places her hands over each of his ears, tilts his head back and gives him a polite kiss on his forehead. Their eyes lock in a stare—an uncomfortable, passionate stare preventing spoken words. Their minds block out the sounds of the ticking clock on the fireplace mantle and the soothing humming sound of the refrigerator coming from the kitchen, locking them in an unexpected solitude. She kisses him on the tip of his nose, followed by one on the lips. Their eyes lock once more. Slowly, her head falls and their lips meet again, softly. Jason feels his heart pounding, echoing tremors that seem to vibrate through his body. Remembering how soft her lips are, his eyes close, his lips part and they kiss passionately as though they are newfound lovers. The kiss lasts for minutes, only to be broken as Jason turns on his knees. He stands and places her hands into his while dually pulling Julie to her feet. Julie melts to the tender hug that follows.

"You know this shouldn't happen," states Jason, trying to make sense of the situation.

"I know, but why fight the chemistry? A divorce hasn't ended the chemistry—better yet, the passion we've always had between us."

"But?"

"No 'buts.' Look down at your pants. That's real. This passion is real, so why fight it?"

"Julie, Sasha is hospitalized. It just isn't right nor is it the right time. You shouldn't try to use my weakened state to your advantage."

"Lust comes from a weak person. Passion derives from feelings. If she were well and out shopping somewhere, it wouldn't be right when you or I have other people in our lives that we should be committed to. According to some man's rules, you and I making love isn't right. I find that hard to swallow. We have a past. I'm confident that we share feelings for each other to base all of this on, even though you hide yours well. We'll have a future, if you let it be. Besides, we make our own rules in life. You of all people should know that. Hell, you taught me this. It's inevitable."

Jason bows his head in shallow shame. The overwhelming desire to have her again fuels suppressed emotions of his once powerful love for her, igniting a passion that has long passed. *This can't be*, faintly splashes through Jason's mind.

"Look at me and tell me this isn't what you want." Jason is unable to utter a single word as she fondles his erect penis. "Furthermore," Julie boasts. "All of this conversation hasn't dampened this guy's spirits."

Jason is first surprised by her actions but recalls that she has always been an aggressive person when it came down to intimacy. Julie tears off the top of his head, breaking the containment of his will. It flows freely to the ceiling, looking down wryly at him giving control to his thought process to his now pulsating penis. She embraces him tenderly, appreciating the comfort of Jason's strong arms around her again. Passion conquers tenderness, transforming it into a hard kiss. With no thought of his own, he responds by unbuttoning her silk blouse behind the neck. Halfway through the kiss Julie smiles to herself, realizing that she will finally be enveloped by her beloved Jason. He tackles another button as she releases the button to his pants. Hungrily she takes the zipper down and strokes his warm penis. They kiss as if there were no tomorrow, as if they never divorced, as if they were one again. Jason's pants fall to the floor.

"I'm glad to see that you still don't wear underwear."

Her kiss drops. First, she kisses his neck and lowers to nibble on his erect nipples through his shirt. She lowers more and bites him at the waist. Falling to her knees, she disappears below his waist and his head falls back anticipating the coming pleasure. He closes his eyes and feels his knees weaken to Julie's actions. The sensation has him on the verge of collapsing. He tilts her head back to stop her while he's able to stand.

"Let's continue upstairs," Jason states.

Julie reaches back and throws off her left shoe, then follows with the right.

"Follow me," she says.

Julie starts her stride toward the stairs while simultaneously reaching to the zipper on her skirt, lowering it very slowly while putting an enticing twitch in her walk. In her stride, she pushes her skirt below her hips. It falls to her ankles with her managing to step out of it without losing her pace or Jason's attentiveness to her appeal.

Jason is amazed at how seductive Julie continues to be. He steps one foot out of his pants and stumbles as the other is caught in the jumbled mess at his ankle while Julie stops at the staircase motioning him to finish the remaining buttons on her blouse. After releasing the third button she playfully switches from side to side in place.

"Ooh," Julie moans as she ascends the stairs.

Following with anticipation, Jason releases the final buttons with Julie acknowledging the action by drawing her shoulders back, letting the blouse fall to her hands. It is playfully tossed back, landing on his head. As if he needed more seducing, the blouse reaps the scent of his favorite woman's fragrance. Jason fills his lungs, capturing its aroma before knocking it from his shoulders to the stairs. Reaching the top of the stairs, Julie turns right, heading for the all-too-familiar bedroom. Following closely behind, Jason turns at the top of the stairs awed by the trail of clothes they've created.

"Jason, Jason," softly and seductively Julie summons.

He follows the voice into the bedroom and closes the door behind him.

The next morning Jason lies motionless on his bed. The comforter and top sheet hang off the bed flowing like a waterfall emptying into a pond. His pistol hangs on the bedpost. Julie is absent. No signs of her presence exists except the stains she helped create on the sheets and a note she left for his enjoyment next to him. The telephone rings and Jason answers it in a daze.

"Hello?"

"Yo, Jas," Sgt. Austin says. "There's been another attack."

"When...where, wait a minute. What time is it?"

"About nine-forty in the morning."

"Fuck."

"The captain wants you right away."

"I'll be in as soon as I can."

"I'll tell him."

Jason jumps from the bed and showers quickly. In the midst of getting dressed, he notices Julie's note that reads:

My beloved Jason, how can I tell you what last night meant to me, to us?

We've crossed over the line and stepped into new boundaries. Boundaries that I know will surely unite our hearts. I know in my heart that you share these same feelings, ones that say we can be together as one again. Let's take this as our new beginning and strive forward for a wonderful life together. Love, Julie.

"Oh, boy." Jason sighs. "What have I done? I must get this situation straight right away. Especially since I hardly remember much about it. Looking at these sheets, there's no question that something intimate happened between us last night."

★★★★★

He reports to Captain North with an unfinished report on Sasha's attack.

"Are you okay?" Captain North asks.

"I'm better," Jason replies somberly.

"Can you handle questions about Sasha's attack?"

"Yes, they shouldn't be a problem."

"My major question is: do you think this is the serial rapist we're searching for?"

"It's hard to tell. None of the MO is the same."

"Did you get a clear look at him?"

"No, it was too dark. Although, he's as tall as the man at the post office."

Sgt. Austin bursts in the office abruptly. "Jas, there's a call for you."

"Take a message."

"I asked to but he insisted on talking to you."

"Excuse me, Captain, I'll be right..."

"No," Captain North interrupts. "Transfer his call in here."

"Right away, Frank."

"Did you hear that? Do you see how easy it is to use first names?"

"I do better than I used to," Jason replies. Seconds later, the telephone rings and Jason responds. "Jerrard."

"Jerrard," the caller pauses, "what happened to the Sixteenth Precinct?"

"The first person you spoke to should've said that. How may I help you?"

"It's me again," states the caller. "You know, this bod's for you."

"I'm not too surprised," Jason assures, having a gut feeling that the caller is smiling while he teases Jason and the police. "Why call?"

"No, no, I won't allow you to trace this call. I just thought I'd let you know where the car is."

"What car?" Jason questions before reality strikes him like a boxer's left hook. "Bastard! It's you," Jason rages.

"Now you sound surprised and you call yourself a detective. Tsk, tsk."

"You attacked Sasha, you son-of-a-bitch!"

"Oh, my, you called her by a first name. Is this one personal to you?"

"That's not your fucking concern."

"Temper, temper. Since I failed with Sasha, I got one last night...and what were you doing?"

"Son-of-a-bitch, I'm going to get your ass!" Jason yells uncontrollably. "Count on it!"

"Don't blame me. I asked you to stop me but you didn't, so you forced me. The car is at the pier," he says quickly.

"Wait a minute...hold on. Meet with me."

The rapist-killer hangs up with no further words exchanged. As Jason slams the receiver down, the frustration shows on his face greatly.

"That was the serial rapist?" questions Captain North.

"Yes. The bastard. He is the one who hurt Sasha." Jason feels his blood boiling as he pounds his fist down against the desk's surface. "That mother-fucker is mine, you hear me."

"Jason, he hurt someone close to you and I feel for you. I can't imagine what you're going through, but don't let your vengeance make you do something drastic."

"Revenge? You mean, this is far beyond that. The son-of-a-bitch has to pay."

"Remember, justice first."

"Justice! What justice?" Jason rages. "Will Sasha or his other dead victims have their justice?" he asks emotionally. "The only true justice in the world is revenge."

"We must let the courts decide."

"When he's caught—he will get caught," Jason recites with a conviction that is somewhat uneasy to Captain North. "Do you think a prison sentence will bring back their lives or give Sasha back her mental stability?"

"Jason, you're not thinking straight. I know you're angry but you're a law officer first."

"I know that and I'm going to remember that when I finally confront him."

"Jason," Captain North states as a precautionary measure, "I'm afraid that I'm going to have to take you off the case. It is too personal for you. This can't be your personal vendetta."

"With all due respect, Sir, when someone hurts anyone I'm close to, naturally it's personal."

"I understand that, but you can't be effective when you're out for revenge."

"I'll still be able to do my job as effectively as ever."

"My better judgment says take you off the case, so you're off and that's final."

"Captain," Jason pleads.

"First instincts are usually the correct ones. Therefore, no further discussion is needed. If I see or hear of you anywhere near this case, I'll personally have your head."

"I can..."

"You can and are dismissed," Captain North interrupts.

"What am I to do?"

"Take some time off and pull your thoughts together."

"What I don't need is another forced absence."

"Trust me, you'll thank me later."

Jason reluctantly returns to his desk. Simultaneously as he reaches his desk, Julie arrives.

"Hello, Jason," she says with a pleasant smile plastered on her face.

"Hi," Jason expresses emotionless.

"What a pleasant welcome," she says sarcastically. "Is Sasha still on your mind?"

"Not only that. Her attacker called and confessed to her attack. That magnified everything. I was doing pretty good until that point. And to top it off, I've just been pulled from the case."

"Listen, honey, I know what can help."

"Please, not your massage again. That's a part of my troubles also."

"You call what happened last night trouble?"

"Yes, I do. It only added to my emotional duress."

"Didn't it mean anything to you?"

"Sure," he says as he motions toward the door. "Let me walk you to your car. I've been taken off the case, so I'm going to the hospital."

"Okay, but finish what you were saying."

"As I said, sure," he says, starting his walk. "It meant two adults doing what's natural when they share a physical attraction or it could mean that you took advantage of me when I was in heavy grief."

"Is that what you really think? Didn't you read my note?" Julie questions, not understanding the emotions that are now flowing through her being.

"I don't know what to think about last night, and I read your note. All I know is that it shouldn't have happened."

"Come on, Jason," she says more concerned. "The way you performed, you have to have feelings for me."

"I won't deny that, but they aren't the kind that you'd like them to be."

"Because of what we did, that should be enough to make you want to see if we could rekindle the flame."

He sighs. "As I look at it in retrospect, I realize what I did."

"What did you do, use me?"

"To put it bluntly, yes," Jason replies before actually considering what he is saying.

Julie stares blankly in a state of shock.

"Untrue." Jason pauses. "In retrospect, I thought that I used you to take my mind off my troubles, but if I'm honest with myself and you, I simply made a mistake."

"A mistake or using me. Didn't you realize that either one would create more troubles?"

"I guess not. Last night in my emotional state, I can't explain why I acted the way I did. Hell, I don't even remember last night."

Those words strike Julie like an eagle snatching its prey from the water. They are quick, forceful, deliberate, crushing her mental stability in the process.

"You can't get away with this," she rages. "You can't. Damn it, you won't."

"I'm not trying to get away with anything. Can't you see that we went too far? I apologize if I misled you in any way."

"You used me, Jason. I never thought you'd do that to me. Out of all the men I've known, I've always trusted that your actions were genuine. Anyone," Julie responds with her eyes welled with water, "but you. I can accept false hopes."

"I'm sorry for causing you troubles."

Jason opens her car door and time seemingly slows to a crawl with Julie lowering slowly to the seat. Huge tears fall to the pavement and Jason swears he can hear their impact. He closes the door and she drives off squealing the wheels, leaving Jason with an uncomfortable feeling, realizing this is his first time seeing her cry.

Moments later, Jason stands by Sasha's bed staring into her face while rubbing her forehead. The expression revealed on her face is peaceful but her motionless body, the IV and monitors connected to her indicate serious trouble. Jason starts to the door to question her new location when the door opens and Dr. Bodou enters.

"Good afternoon, Doctor."

"Afternoon, Mr. Jerrard."

"May I ask a couple of questions?"

"Feel free to ask anything."

"Why are these things hooked on her?" he questions, holding tubing from the IV. "And, why is she now in intensive care?"

"She took a turn for the worse. A nurse was changing the bedding when we noticed blood on the sheets. After further examination, we had to perform an emergency D&C."

"'D&C?'" Jason says puzzled, trying to reflect on a previous conversation with Sasha.

"We use a machine to clean out a woman's insides."

"Why did you have to do that?" Jason questions, still lost.

"Oh, Lord," he says surprised. "You didn't know."

"I didn't know what?" he questions quickly with his heart racing uncontrollably.

"She was pregnant."

"What!" Jason's body weakens. "Are you sure?"

"Yes." He pauses. "I'm truly sorry you had to find out this way. She was about five weeks."

"Couldn't you save it?"

"No. A fetus that small can't be saved once it's dislodged from the woman's uterus. After it dislocates, the hemorrhaging starts. We put the IV in to help give her some of her strength, and the monitor is to see if the procedure is working."

"Thank you. I'm sure you did the best you could." Jason's tone sorrows, revealing the pain his heart feels. "Please, Doc, let me be alone with her."

"Sure, I understand."

Jason pulls a chair close and sits with his head laying next to her hand while holding it firmly. Tears form a small wet spot on the sheet directly below his eyes. He finds himself questioning why this has happened to her. As he slowly calms himself, simultaneously rethinking their relationship from their unusual meeting to Sasha's present condition, he constantly asks himself two questions that plague his mind.

"How could you help me out, dear?" he unknowingly verbalizes. "And why were you at Rosalina's? There has to be a hidden connection somewhere. You couldn't have known I would be there."

CHAPTER 30

Jason drives down the street searching for answers that will give him inner peace and lessen the gnawing guilt for his actions with Julie. That guilt, along with the unanswered questions, directs him to Sasha's apartment with the notion that the next best thing to being by her side is to be near her belongings. He arrives at Sasha's unsure of what to look for. Maybe a note, someone's name, anything that would define to him her presence at Rosalina's. He opens Sasha's condo door so fast that any unsuspecting eyes would never guess that he was using a credit card. Fortunately for him, Sasha hadn't heeded to his small lecture about the dead-bolt lock. As an afterthought, he remembers that he could have gotten the key out of her purse.

Jason enters and glances over her things. He prepares water for instant coffee and takes a seat on the floor in front of the fireplace. He reminisces on their many nights engaged in lovemaking with the fire blazing. He sits on the sofa in awe, wishing she were near. After making his coffee, he checks her answering machine for anything unusual, but the two calls received reveal nothing strange. He checks her mail and wastebaskets for oddness but again discovers nothing that would connect her to Rosalina's that night. Jason's frustrating search ends with him taking a Nestea plunge on her bed, gazing at the ceiling unsure where to turn next. His heart pumps sorrow through his being, hindering his thoughts, slowing down the analytical processing of their last conversation. Jason glances at one of her most-prized possessions laying on the night table—her journal. After moments of soul searching, he forces himself to intrude on her private thoughts in search of some clue to the burning questions flickering in his mind. As luck would have it, the journal happens to begin with them returning from the beach weeks ago. He discovers that Sasha is very detailed when explaining their childlike play that night on the beach followed by her sensual feelings about the night in the hotel.

I lay there drifting to sleep, watching this strange wonderful man who's entered my life. He has brought me a much-needed joy. I watched him as he slept and comfort took over me. Since our meeting, I've asked myself if he's heaven sent? He has been so refreshing and enlightening, I find myself looking for wings. He lay there still, yet I felt his warmth both mentally and physically. As I watched him, physically is what I yearned for. It is what I needed. I wished he would climb into the bed and attack me. I would have submitted easily to any of his wishes. My pussy grew wet just thinking about him near as it does as I write down these thoughts. Hopefully, I won't have to play with myself now as I did that night when my desire grew out of control. I only wonder if he heard me when I came.

Jason smiles. "No, I didn't hear you, love."

He flips through more pages and sees how explicit she was when describing their first lovemaking session but as fate would have it, he is forced to close it after feeling himself get aroused by reading her words. Jason wonders what she was like before his existence in her life. Thus, the search of her earlier journals begins. He finds several journals in the bottom drawer of the nightstand in reverse order. He reads the first one that begins with her blind-date meeting a man named Ryan Kass. She describes him as tall, six feet two to six feet four with a strong build. He has dark eyes for a person with dirty brown hair. She explains how polite he was that evening until it ended abruptly when the waiter spilled clam chowder on his pants. She explains his raving about how much a Pierre Cardin suit with this particular cut cost, claiming that the restaurant would be responsible if his suit was ruined.

A man after my own heart, Jason thinks to himself.

He flips through more pages and discovers four different dates about two weeks apart circled in red marker. The most intriguing thought on each day is that a person named Ryan stood her up on each occasion. On the tab of each failed date, she has written "see entry in next journal." The oddness of these side notes is so out of sync with the other entries in her journals. They alert Jason's instincts, telling him that they were added as an afterthought. But more alarming to him is that they point to exactly one day before her attack. Jason's adrenaline flows rapidly now. He picks up the first journal, thumbs to the end and starts reading from when he saw her last.

My beloved Jason came over extremely tired. His devotion to duty showed by the tons of files he'd brought here to study, but his body quit on him before he was able to eat dinner. I found him asleep surrounded by his work. Oddly enough, I discovered something interesting while helping him to bed. The files I stacked neatly aroused my suspicions. Four of the attacks happened on the same night I was to have a date with Ryan. Is this mere chance? Or has uncanny fate led me to discover the man my loved one searches for dearly? I can't let Jason know until I'm absolutely sure. I will try to arrange a meeting with Ryan tomorrow and assess the situation before telling Jason of my findings.

"Sasha," Jason cries. "This can't be. You should've let me know. If this is the man that I'm looking for, with all I've told you about him, you should have known that he was dangerous. Why, baby, why? All you had to do was wake me."

Like a madman, he tears through her things looking for some sort of personal telephone directory. Soon the rampage ends with the discovery of her directory in the kitchen drawer opposite the wall-mounted telephone. He looks under the Ks and finds no record of a Kass. Under the Rs he finds Ryan K's telephone number underlined. He rips the page from the book, crosschecks his number with the public telephone directory but finds no such name and hurries out of the door. Jason's new destination places him back at the station hiding from Captain North's watchful eyes.

"Bob," Jason says, "I need a huge favor."

"Again, you still owe me for the last time. Barbara hasn't looked this way since that day."

"I'll fix things with her...trust me. This is very important."

"Well, it depends on what you need. Everyone knows you're again on a forced leave of absence."

"All I need is for you to get me the address of this phone number."

"That's all. Hell, Barbara can do that for you."

"Thanks for your direction," he says as he walks away abruptly.

Quickly he persuades Barbara to act on his request and directs her to relay the information in his car. Minutes later his car phone rings and Barbara's voice blasts clearly.

"Jason?"

"Yes, what do you have?"

"You're on your car phone?"

"Yes."

"It sounds like you're using a regular phone."

"The wonders of modern technology...well, what did you come up with?"

"This man named Ryan Kass lives at 779 East Side Highway. It says here, suite number eleven eleven."

"I know exactly where that is. Thanks."

"You can thank me later."

"How, may I ask?"

"Physically."

"You never give up, do you?"

"I don't plan to."

"Thank you again. Got to go. Bye."

"Goodbye...future lover."

The address is one located in the upper-middle class part of the city. It is a multi-story condo building well known for its tasteful decor. He wonders how a person living in luxury is capable of committing such violent acts, but he decides to follow-up on his burning instincts regardless. The next day, Jason waits outside the Ritz of Hollywood before its opening hour, anxiously waiting for his favorite salesperson to arrive before entering the store. He searches for the one named Mark, a slim, no-chested man who makes no qualms about his homosexuality.

"Yes, Detective," Mark says. "Need a new suit or are you here to use your handcuffs, big boy?"

"I don't need a suit, but I do need your help."

"You need my help, my Lord. I must be really doing something right."

"Get serious for a moment. This is official police business."

"Okay, sorry. What can I do for you?"

"Earlier, I requested your records to be searched for a man named Gregory Smith and..."

"That was your doing?" Mark interjects. "My boss made me look through all those..."

"It was the wrong name," Jason intrudes in fair play. "I believe I have the correct name this time. Would you research it for me?"

"What's the name this time?"

"Ryan Kass."

"Any idea of when he might have bought his suit?"

"Can't help you there. All I know is it's identical to the one you sold me last."

"Who says you can't be helpful? We keep the record of each style listed separately...the Pierre Cardin suit, right?"

"Exactly."

"One moment, please." After several minutes he returns with a card. "Here it is. Ryan Kass, oh, he lives at the Regency," he says with excitement.

"Okay."

"You don't seem surprised."

"I'm not. Your information verifies what I already have. You have him listed at 779 East Side..."

"Sorry to interrupt, but all he has for an address is the Regency, East Side. What do you want him for?"

"Never mind that, thanks. I owe you one...you can go to Rosalina's and tell Alfredo to let you order anything you like on me. The code word he is going to ask you for is 'dance.'"

"Food, a man after my heart."

"Not hardly. Thanks, see you."

"See you again."

Jason rushes to the station and bursts into Captain North's office intruding on his telephone conversation.

"Uh, let me call you back," Captain North abruptly says. "As for you, Jason, this had better be good."

"I have news on the serial rapist."

"You're off the case, remember."

"Just listen to me," Jason demands more forcefully than he should to his superior officer. "I now know who he is."

Jason explains Ryan's existence in Sasha's journals and his owning an identical suit as the one worn by the man at the post office.

"How can you be so sure he's the same man?"

"I crosschecked his name with the Ritz and they show him purchasing a suit like the one I saw. He has the same address. I'm convinced that this is our rapist."

"It's too risky. The DA won't buy it."

"Why? We have everything we need."

"What we have is a bunch of coincidences that the DA will surely rule circumstantial. None of your evidence is strong enough to hold up in court."

"Sir, this is the guy. I can feel it. Put me back on the case and I'll prove it."

"I still think it's too soon for you. Your emotions aren't completely intact. Look at you. I've never seen you so antsy."

"Trust me. I'm okay."

"No, look at you. You're so eager to find Sasha's attacker, anything will make sense to you, and what I don't want is you harassing an innocent person."

"He's not innocent," Jason demands. "Damn it, I'll prove it!"

"Jason, you listen to me," Captain North says more directly. "Leave this case alone. Turn your evidence over to Kevin and take a trip. Go to a warmer climate and pull yourself back together."

"Kevin? He can't capture this guy."

"Why? He carries a gun, too."

"Yeah, but this man is cunning. You have to beat him at his own game and I will."

"There you are with your personal beliefs again. Interfering with...Jason, you listen to me. Leave this case alone."

Jason brushes Captain North's comments aside and storms out of the office determined to unravel concrete evidence to place the madman behind bars. Before he leaves the station, he checks out a high-powered pair of binoculars and starts his own stakeout opposite the Regency high-rise condos.

CHAPTER 31

Jason places a call to Ryan's number from a nearby telephone but receives no answer. Late that evening, after hours of watching every male who enters or exits the Regency, he recognizes a seemingly familiar face, based on the darkness, which inflicts some doubt in making a positive identification. To check voice comparisons, he places another call after waiting an undetermined amount of time to allow Ryan to get into his condo. This one is meant to be harassing and is disguised with a heavy Spanish accent.

"Hello?"

"Ello, Me-ster Kass. Jew don know me, pero I know jew."

"Who is this?"

"I know what jew do—I'll be quatching jew."

"No Mr. Kass lives here."

Ryan hangs up the telephone without saying another word. Jason is convinced that he is indeed the same man who called the station and waits patiently for Ryan's next move. He spends countless hours outside Ryan's building disregarding his hunger and needed physical relief. The night passes and daybreak appears. Breakfast hours pass. Soon lunchtime comes and goes. It isn't until early evening when Jason receives his next glimpse of Ryan. By this time Ryan's face has almost healed yet he still wears a light coat of makeup. Ryan stands on the corner and waves down a taxi. Jason carefully follows the taxi, staying two to three car lengths behind. His tail ends at Rosalina's. Ryan pays his fare and disappears inside the restaurant.

"Good evening, Sir," Alfredo says.

"Hello."

"Will you be dining alone?"

"Yes."

"Right this way, Sir." Alfredo seats him with a limited view of the restaurant. "Your menu, Sir."

"Thank you."

"I'll return momentarily."

Ryan slowly scans the clientele for his next victim—any woman that he could prey on to relieve the tension from his telephone calls but more importantly, to satisfy the craving his dark twisted mental friends demand. He sees only a few women who aren't coupled off and quickly decides who his next victim will be as Alfredo returns for his order.

"What will you have tonight?"

"I'll have the spaghetti with spicy meatballs and her."

"Excuse me, Sir?"

"I'll have her," he says as he points across the restaurant. "The one in the red blouse."

"Sorry, I can't help you there. What will you have to drink?"

"Milk...chocolate. No make that a chocolate milkshake."

"That's an odd drink to have with spicy food."

"I use it to prepare my stomach for the spicy food."

"As you wish, Sir. Oh, would you like that now or with your meal?"

"With my meal will be fine."

Jason enters the restaurant slowly while peeking through the glass of the double doors and waves until he attracts Alfredo's attention. A curious Alfredo answers Jason's plea.

"Good eve...my Lord," Alfredo says with concern. "It looks like you haven't slept for days."

"I haven't. I've been watching a suspect, can't afford to sleep."

"Don't neglect your body, Sir. It's the only temple you'll ever have."

"I know," Jason agrees respectively with his old friend. "My body...my temple."

"Precisely," Alfredo concurs before getting directly to the point. "Why are you snooping around here?"

"The man I'm investigating is inside."

"Here?" Alfredo sounds astonished. "Who?"

"The man that walked in before me."

"Him? The man I just sat at table thirteen? Criminals dress nicely these days."

"Trust me. It's him."

"You're the expert...why don't you go inside and watch?"

"I can't. He knows my face."

"Anything I can do?"

"Maybe." Jason ponders Alfredo's question for a small moment. He soon questions. "What did he order?"

"Would you believe he ordered your exact meal?"

"You're kidding," Jason states in disbelief.

"After all this time, I finally pulled one over on you."

"I'm sorry, my friend. I've no time for jokes."

"He ordered spaghetti with spicy meatballs and a chocolate milkshake. A real stomach-pleaser, I might add."

"Strange," Jason states, raising his right brow. "Delay his food until I get back."

"I'll do my best, Sir."

Jason hurries out the door and takes off down the street while Ryan walks over to his next victim's table.

"Excuse me," he says. "I don't mean to intrude, but I noticed you from over there and thought I might have a word with you."

"Go on."

"My name is Ryan Kass. May I join you?"

"Well...sure. Have a seat. I'm Leah Davis."

"Nice to meet you."

"Pleased to meet you. So, Rosalina's is turning into a pickup joint?"

"I admit. I'm trying to pick you up but not in the sense you're thinking."

"And what sense is that?"

"Meaning, I hope that I'm presenting a good first impression so we could possibly meet again sometime. Not to pick you up like you were in a club."

"Either way, it's a pickup."

"No, most club pickups end with a one-night stand. This is different."

"You got that right," Leah sternly states.

"What do you do?"

"I'm a writer for the local newspaper. Since it's nearing election time, I'm doing lots of overtime."

"So, you're on dinner break tonight?"

"Right. What's your occupation?"

"I'm a teacher."

"Math, English, what?"

"No, I teach at the Repertory Theater. I give instruction on all aspects of theater and everything surrounding that. I specialize in disguises, voice, costume and of course, acting skills."

"That should be very interesting."

"It has its benefits."

Jason returns after a few short minutes and again takes his spot at the double doors. Alfredo greets him.

"I have an unofficial police request to ask of you."

"Unofficial police work."

"Yes. I need the cooks to make him a special milkshake," Jason suggests.

"Tell you what, you go to the rear and I'll let you in the back. You can ask the cooks yourself. It's about time they met the person who orders the disgusting eggs."

"Fine. I'll meet you in back."

Jason quickly rushes to the rear of the building, and Alfredo already has the door open. After brief introductions, Jason makes his request.

"Listen, Tony," Jason says to the head chef. "This is crazy, but I need you to prepare table thirteen's milkshake with this." Jason reaches into a small bag and pulls out a box of extra-strength laxative. "Melt half the box into his shake."

"You're kidding," Tony replies in amazement.

"No. I'm very serious. I need to get him to the hospital. It could be the breaking point to a case I'm working on."

"You want him to get the shits?" he states, chuckling at the thought of it all.

"More than that—I want him to appear sick."

"And Rosalina's won't be implicated at all?"

"I personally guarantee it."

"Okay. It'll be fun watching him run back and forth to the bathroom."

Ryan's milkshake and food are delivered but instead, he gestures Alfredo to bring his food to Leah's table. Before Jason returns to the front, he peeks through the crack between the swinging double doors to watch Ryan work. After a careful eye he proceeds to the front and calls Rosalina's using the pay phone in the foyer behind the front set of double doors. Alfredo answers at the podium.

"Alfredo, it's me, Jason."

"Why the phone, Sir?"

"I need to talk to the woman he's talking to. Her name is Leah Davis. Will you get her for me?"

"I'll see what I can do."

"Thank you."

Alfredo walks over disturbing their meal. She's enjoying her lasagna and wine while Ryan tackles his meal with an extra node for the milkshake.

"Excuse me, Madam," Alfredo interrupts. "There's a call for you."

"Me...are you sure?" she responds surprised.

"Yes, Leah Davis, right?"

"That's me. How did you know it was me?"

"From your reservation, Madam."

"Oh...excuse me, Ryan. It must be the office."

Leah responds to the request but is leery of the call based on Alfredo's statement about her reservation, knowing full well that she had not made one.

"Hello?"

"Leah, this is Jason Jerrard. We met here sometime ago with the note you wrote me."

"Ah, the detective, right?"

"Correct."

"I remember. How did you know I was here?"

"Look toward the front door," Jason instructs. "But do it casually."

"Why are you using the pay phone?" she asks with curiosity.

"Please don't get excited. Act normal. I need information on the man you're talking to."

"What about him?"

"What name did he give you?"

"Ryan Kass. What's this about?"

"It's important that you tell me anything you've discovered about him."

"I already know something. He teaches acting and other things at the Repertory Theater."

"Wonderful...that explains a lot."

"Am I in danger or something?"

"No, he won't be in shape to do anything tonight."

"Tonight. What about other nights?"

"I'll be following him. Don't worry. Go back to your table, be pleasant and act normal."

"That will be hard to do, not knowing what kind of person I'm dealing with."

"Trust me. He'll leave you soon," Jason assures. "Thanks for your help. Hopefully, we can talk sometime later."

"Okay, I'm counting on you," Leah states with more than a slight worry in her tone.

Leah returns to her table leery of Ryan, but forces herself to act and perform the same as she did previously. So well in fact, her performance makes her think of giving herself her own Academy Award.

"You have to leave now?" Ryan asks.

"No, they just had a few questions," she lies. "So, what are your other interests?"

"None really. Most days I work late. I'm too tired to do much of anything when I get off."

"Surely you have hobbies that keep you busy around the house?"

"Just my lessons for the next day. I—excuse me," he says in desperation. "The men's room is calling."

"By all means, go ahead. I sense your urgency."

The magical shake takes its toll. With his buttocks being held tightly, Ryan takes quick tiny strides resembling one called Morticia from an old black and white television show. He concentrates hard to contain the sudden urge. Alfredo notices his state and is fascinated that Jason's plan has come into fruition. He makes it to the toilet and lowers his pants. A gush of watery waste shoots from his rear with little time to spare.

Maybe I should have listened to that waiter, Ryan thinks to himself.

"Are you all right, Sir?" Alfredo asks, hiding his snicker.

"I believe so," he grunts.

"Yell if you need any help."

"Thanks, I will."

He sits for minutes being unsure that the urge has passed. As if the stomach cramping wasn't bad enough, his legs begin to tingle and soon fall asleep. More time passes and thoughts of his victim leaving enter his mind. He wills himself to stand, rewarding himself with thousands of tiny needles puncturing his feet. He pulls his pants up and literally has to drag his feet to the door. Upon opening the men's room door, a quick glance toward his table reveals Leah walking away. His first thought is to call out to her, but the toilet recalls his name, this time with more vengeance. Before he reaches the toilet, greater pressure builds causing stronger stomach cramps, doubling him over in pain. He lowers himself onto the porcelain throne and barely gets his pants and underwear lowered before the more pressurized waste exits his rear. His hemorrhoids seemingly tear from his insides and bleed tiny drops into the water. The burning sensation causes him to glance down into the toilet. The sight of blood, coupled with severe cramps knotting his stomach, help him determine that something is seriously wrong with him. After he has emptied everything short of his vital organs into the toilet, he gathers himself to some degree and satisfies his food bill. As he leaves, the cooks and Alfredo laugh ecstatically in the kitchen.

Ryan waves down another taxi and directs the driver to take him to Virginia City Memorial Hospital. His imaginary friends dance in the dark corners of his subconscious, trying to conquer his mind. But his concern over his health overpowers their will this time. Mostly, because his remaining mental strength is being used to keep from making a mess in the taxi. Again, Jason follows with care.

As Ryan's taxi pulls up in front of the emergency room, Jason smiles as another plan falls into place. Ryan exits the taxi doubled over again, leaving his imaginary friends crawling around inside the taxi.

It's a fairly slow night for emergency care indicated by the emergency room being nearly empty. The only hospital personnel Ryan sees is a nurse who has her back turned to him as he enters the waiting area. He walks directly to the restroom and disappears behind the stall's door. After a minute he starts yelling for a doctor. His cry echoes to the waiting room and a nurse cracks the door, answering his plea.

"Excuse me, Sir," she says. "Are you all right?"

"If I were, would I be yelling for a doctor like a madman?"

"What's the matter?"

"My stomach. I've severe cramps with the shits."

"Are you insured, Sir?"

"Insurance?" he says angrily. "My fucking insides are coming out and you worry me about health insurance."

"I don't make the rules here. It's hospital policy."

"Blue Cross Blue Shield. Is that good enough?"

"That's fine. The doctor will be with you soon."

Jason sneaks into the waiting area looking suspicious, more like a criminal than Ryan. He listens to the nurse page the doctor on duty and approaches her quickly, flashing his badge while pulling her down the hall away from the restroom door.

"Listen," Jason says. "I can help you with what's bothering the man in the restroom."

"You can? What do the police have to do with this?"

"Nothing. His condition is all my doing."

"What exactly is his condition?"

"Nurse," the doctor interrupts. "What's the emergency?"

"Doctor Bodou," Jason comments.

"Mr. Jerrard. You're ill?"

"No, I'm fine."

"Nurse, what's this all about?"

"I was just about to find out when you arrived."

"Mr. Jerrard, you're not here about Sasha?"

"Indirectly," Jason replies. "How is she?"

"Nothing has changed. I was checking on her when I was paged."

"Excuse me, Doctor," the nurse intrudes, "but I have a man yelling for you from the men's bathroom."

"Okay." Dr. Bodou sighs. "Find out what Mr. Jerrard needs and I'll be right back."

"Jason, call me Jason."

Dr. Bodou enters the restroom simultaneously as Ryan starts his cry again.

"I'm here," Dr. Bodou replies. "What seems to be the problem?"

"I don't know. Suddenly my stomach started cramping real bad and this is the second time I've had blood in my stool."

"Did you eat anything strange or change your diet in any way?"

"Nothing that I don't normally eat."

"Well, Sir, when you can leave the stall, I'll run some tests. Do you feel like you can get up?"

"Almost, I'll be out soon...hopefully," Ryan dreadfully states.

"I'll wait for you outside. In the meantime, I will have the nurse bring you something that will soothe your stomach."

"I'd appreciate that."

Dr. Bodou returns to the nurse talking to Jason. She has a smile semi-plastered on her face.

"Doctor," she says. "Don't be too alarmed with that man sitting on the toilet. He's suffering from a condition called laxative-à-la-milkshake."

"What!"

"It's true," Jason confesses. "I arranged his predicament. He has an extra-strength laxative cleansing his system."

"Why would you do that?" Dr. Bodou asks.

"I needed to know his blood type. He's suspected of several violent crimes and his blood type could be his convicting factor."

"Why don't you arrest him?"

"I'm acting on my own. My superiors don't believe it's him, but my gut tells me he's the one. If they find out about my actions, my career is finished, but I know he is responsible for Sasha being in intensive care."

"I see your concern. I can understand why you want him so badly."

"I do. I'm willing to jeopardize everything I believe in to take him down. Please act as though he's suspected of food poisoning. Anything to draw his blood," Jason insists.

"I can arrange that. I've already told him that I'd run some tests. Nurse, please give him something to ease his stomach."

"Thank you," Jason responds sincerely. "Your help is greatly appreciated.

The restroom door opens and Jason backs down the adjacent corridor as Ryan steps out into the waiting area.

"I can't let him see me," Jason says. "He knows who I am."

"I'll handle him. Just be patient," Dr. Bodou instructs.

"I'll wait upstairs. Call me in Sasha's room."

"Okay, first let the nurse get him in the back."

Ryan is escorted to the examination room. Jason takes the elevator to ICU and waits by Sasha's side. His emotions are mixed. The sorrow and pain he feels watching her in this lifeless state adds fuel to the rage and revenge he possesses for Ryan. But somewhere entangled with his wave of emotions are thoughts of the limitations of being an officer of the law.

Downstairs the doctor advises Ryan that urine and blood tests are required for proper diagnosis of his condition. After he receives both samples, he disappears behind a door marked LAB, secures the top on the urine sample with tape and drops it into the wastebasket. The blood sample is processed. After a short while, the lab technician discovers Ryan's blood type and provides the information to the doctor. Dr. Bodou telephones Sasha's room. After the call Jason kisses Sasha softly on the lips and hurries to the emergency room. Dr. Bodou hands Jason a folded piece of paper with Ryan's blood type written on it.

"I hope this proves to be helpful," Dr. Bodou sincerely states.

"I'm sure it will. What are you going to do with him now?"

"I'll make up something."

"Tell him that he needs rest. I want him off the streets until I can verify this," Jason says while holding up the folded paper.

"I could tell him that he needs to be hospitalized for further tests," suggests Dr. Bodou.

"That won't be necessary. I'll know as soon as I get back to the station."

"Fine. I know what to do."

"Thanks for your help." Jason changes thoughts. "Some movie, huh?"

"What movie?"

"The one we're living in."

"Sometimes, it seems that way," he says, shaking his head while wondering how that thought originated.

"Thanks again for your help. Goodbye."

"Goodbye."

Dr. Bodou greets Ryan with a halfhearted smile. "Well, Mr. Kass," he says. "I have good and bad news. Which one would you..."

"Nothing terrible?" Ryan interrupts.

"Right. The good news is your urine and blood cultures are both negative. There's nothing abnormal about them."

"How do you explain my current condition?"

"You've developed a mild stomach virus. Sometimes our bodies have adverse reactions to things we eat."

"Stomach virus?"

"Yeah. It should subdue after awhile. I'll bet you feel better now than when you arrived."

"The severe stomach cramps are gone, but I'm sure my trips to the toilet aren't."

"That's just your body's protection mechanism working."

"Is there anything you can recommend?"

"I'll write a prescription for something similar to Maalox, only stronger. It is the exact stuff the nurse gave you."

"What about the blood in my stool?"

Dr. Bodou assures Ryan that he will soon return to normal and suggests he take some immediate rest. Ryan finishes the necessary paperwork before he flags a taxi. Jason follows the vehicle back to Ryan's apartment. Ryan jumps out of the taxi and rushes into his building, again unaware that Jason follows behind. Jason rings the bell to have the desk clerk let him enter the secured building. Once inside, he explains because of a police matter, he'd require him to call his pager number if Ryan left the building before he returned. Jason swiftly travels to the station with all intentions of searching the case files for Ryan's blood type. Fortunately for him, Sgt. Austin is working late.

"Kevin," Jason says. "Why are you here so late?"

"I'm following your lead."

"My lead?"

"Yeah, you put in a lot of late hours to get where you are now. I, me, Kevin the slob, have decided that it's not too late for me."

"I'm glad to hear that, but there's no need to come down on yourself."

"It is part of my motivation...what are you doing here?"

"I guess I miss this place," he lies.

"Luckily, the captain has gone for the night or you'd be in hot water."

"I know. What are you working on?"

"You have to ask? The serial rapist case. If a miracle happens and I break this case, I'm sure to be promoted. The only problem is I've studied these things time and time again and I can't find any leads."

"Believe me, I know that feeling well. Is all the information there?"

"I guess so."

"Are you sure?"

"Well..."

"Did the lab complete its work?"

"Yep."

"It reported back with his blood type?"

"Yes, it's," flipping through the pages in one of the folders, "O positive."

"If I remember straight, that was the only time we were able to get a blood sample, correct?"

"Yep."

"Anything I can do to help?"

"Help? I want to break this one but with all the headaches I've had with it, part of me wishes I could turn it back over to you. However, you know the captain."

"I know if he knew we were talking now, he'd have a hissy. He doesn't want me anywhere near this case."

"Don't worry. You'll be back on the case soon."

"Thanks. I'm off. I guess I needed to smell this place."

"See ya."

Jason heads for the door. When no one is looking, he dashes through the door of the stairway. He reaches into his pocket and pulls out the folded paper the doctor gave him. As he reads it, his mind reflects back to Sgt. Austin saying, "O positive" at the exact moment he reads the identical words written on the paper.

"Now," Jason says angrily, "your ass is grass and I'm the lawnmower."

Jason's thoughts become controlled by a rage he has never known, a rage so severe it has altered his beliefs about being a cop, his beliefs in the justice system and most importantly, his inner sense of what's right. He uses the stairs as his means to travel to the Evidence Room located in the building's basement. It's a storage facility where possible evidence for unsolved and closed cases is kept. Jason easily avails himself access to the room by skillfully picking the door's lock with no remorse. Inside there is a walkway down the middle dividing the room into equal halves, which contain a cage on each side. The walkway terminates at a back cage that is built into the rear wall. The three cages are similar in design, all constructed with wood two-by-fours, sealed with a wire reminiscent of the type used to house chickens. Each cage is secured—as pointless as it seems—by a padlock that protects the lost items of time. Once a year, every item that is five years or older is incinerated, melted down to nothing.

Jason disregards a small voice of self-worth insisting that he handle Ryan in the legal fashion. The tainted picture of Sasha that plagues the inside of his eyelids constantly lures him from reality. He views each cage thoroughly until he finds exactly what his wrongful plan is in need of. He uses the tip of a flat screwdriver to break into the cage by prying loose the heavy-duty staples from the bottom of the cage that are attached to a wood base. Next he folds back just enough chicken wire for his body to shimmy through the opening. Jason retrieves a small-caliber revolver tagged "suicide weapon" with a destroy date that has already passed. The irony of the tag briefly helps him sense that his quest for revenge is suicide for his police career. After a pause, Jason exits the cage in the same manner in which he entered. He bends the wire back to its proper position, inserts the staples into their original holes and uses the back end of the screwdriver to secure staples in place, ultimately hiding any signs of tampering. He cracks open the Evidence Room door, peeping to see if anyone's near and quietly sneaks up the stairs and again exits without anyone seeing him leave.

CHAPTER 32

L ater that evening, Jason waits outside the Regency just moments
away from making a move that will ultimately change his life.
Combating within him is the struggle for dominance of his self-worth.
Rage and revenge submerge victorious, resulting in another harassing
call to Ryan.

"Hello?" Ryan says.

"Ello, Mester Kass. Es me," Jason says enthusiastically.

"Who in the hell are you?"

"Don jew worry, Mester Kass. I know who jew are. Mester Kass, I
know what jew do."

"You know what I do. So why call me? Why not call the police?"

"I wan to see jew wif mi own eyes, Mester Kass."

"Meet with me then. Let's talk. You might profit from it."

"No tanks, Mester Kass. Money no is what I'm after."

"What do you want? There must be some reason why you're harassing
me."

"No, Mester Kass. I don wan anything, just to finish making thes movie."

"What movie?"

"As I tell peoples, the one we live en, Mester Kass. Guess what,
Mester Kass?"

"Should I ask?"

"Jew have the starring role, Mester Kass."

"I'll tell you what, Jose, or whatever the fuck your name is, until you can tell me what you want or agree to meet with me, this conversation is over."

"But Mester Kass, jew..."

"No, you listen to me," Ryan boasts angrily. "Since you like my last name so well, drop the K, add an ISS and kiss my ass!"

"Mester Kass, jew are losing jew cool. Prepare to fall."

"I'll wait on it," Ryan says before he hangs up the telephone.

Ryan becomes increasingly nervous and spooked by his anonymous caller, unsure of what to expect next from his antagonist. He begins pacing his living room floor. Every once in awhile, he stops to glance through the living room window that overlooks the front of the building. Jason watches the front door with great intensity, hoping that his latest call will flush him out.

Minutes later, two full-sized vans pull in front of the building. A group of yuppies, mostly men, exits the van carrying all the necessary ingredients for a party. Jason focuses his attention on one of them who is carrying a keg of beer on one shoulder and a six-pack in the other hand. As anticipated, the keg begins to wobble on his unsteady shoulder. Jason seizes the window of opportunity and runs across the street, lending a helping hand to stabilize the falling keg.

"I'll carry this for you," he says after picking up the six-pack of beer.

"Thanks. I don't see why we need extra beer anyway," says the yuppie that's a few years Jason's junior.

"Looks like it's going to be some party tonight, huh?"

"It'll be a bash. Why don't you join us?"

"Well..."

"There's plenty of women," he says suggestively. "And, as you can see, plenty of booze."

"Tonight's a bad night. I'm..."

They introduce themselves and engage in minor conversation as they follow the crowd in the building. Jason enters unnoticed by the guard at the front desk. He and most of the crowd pack themselves into one elevator.

"You're sure you don't want to come?" asks Jason's new associate.

"Thanks again, but I decline. Push ten for me."

"If you change your mind, we're on nine. Just follow the noise."

When the elevator doors close at the ninth floor, Jason's the only person preventing the elevator from being empty. He exits on the tenth floor and takes the stairs to the eleventh. He glances through the tiny window on the stairway door and discovers the direction of Ryan's place. He walks down the hallway to the connecting corridor that forms an "L" and peeps around the corner in the direction of Ryan's condo. He starts his turn around the corner when the spooked Ryan is seen leaving his residence. Jason backs away, hides in the stairwell from which he came and listens for Ryan's footsteps to draw near before pulling the stolen revolver. He watches Ryan pass the stairway door and ignite the "down" elevator button.

Rage. Is this the driving factor that makes his heart pound so angrily? It beats so rapidly, he could almost swear it can be heard echoing throughout the stairwell. Jason stands with his back against the wall. Both hands clutch the gun. The gun's barrel rests under his nose and is supported by his top lip. He slowly lowers one hand to the beckoning call of the doorknob as perspiration forms on his forehead. The unclear vengeance that drives him flows through his body like a turbulent storm forcing his next move. He takes a deep breath. Ready. Seconds before he opens the stairway door, the dinging sound of the elevator's arrival taints his ear. The elevator doors open and an elderly couple exits the elevator holding hands. Ryan freely enters the elevator and the doors close behind him. Jason puts the gun back in the holster at his ankle—the place where he'd normally carry his backup revolver—and sits on the steps unsure of what to do next.

He enters the hallway heading in the direction of Ryan's suite. He hopes that by searching his dwelling he'll discover more about this murderer-rapist who has such expensive taste in housing and clothes, wishing to uncover things that make Ryan such a violent criminal. It takes him several minutes to pick the more expensive lock but he succeeds and enters Ryan's place slowly. Once inside Ryan's ultramodern condo, he searches for anything related to his suspicions.

Ryan walks rapidly past the front desk talking to himself preoccupied with the thought that someone knows about his actions. He is not concerned about it being the police but something worse—a victim's relative seeking vengeance. The desk clerk notices Ryan's departure and immediately remembers to page Jason. He searches under the logbook, papers and other items at the counter for the small piece of paper Jason's pager number is inscribed on but doesn't find it. Remembering that he has been in the back office once since the number has been in his possession, he proceeds there to continue his search. Ryan's anxiety frightens him more and causes him to stop at the door—although armed for his protection—and turn around heading back to his place for a bit of security of his own, the solitude and safety of his dwelling. The elevator doors shut before the security person returns to the front desk.

Jason searches Ryan's living room under pillows and through the drawers in Ryan's desk, making sure he places everything back in its original location. He takes his search to the bedroom as Ryan exits the elevator. Ryan enters the living room and throws his keys on the sofa while heading for his bedroom. Jason doesn't hear Ryan's entry, but he does acknowledge the noise of the keys bouncing across the pillows and conceals himself in the closet, leaving a small crack for his view. Ryan enters the bedroom heading directly for the closet where Jason is seeking asylum. Jason quietly pulls his pistol in anticipation for what is sure to be a conflict. As Ryan reaches for the knob on the huge walk-in closet, Jason's beeper sounds. Knowing that his sanctuary has been compromised, Ryan instinctively doesn't ask any questions upon hearing the high-pitched beeping tone and makes a mad run toward the door, knocking over a lamp and a chair to clutter Jason's path. Jason bursts out of the closet and follows Ryan's trail yelling, "Stop, Police. Stop or I'll shoot!"

The chase begins down the hall, down eleven flights of stairs where

Ryan bursts out of the stairway door through the lobby into the streets, running for his life with Jason following a few strides behind. The chase resembles something out of a movie as they weave down the sidewalk, then carelessly take their troubles to the busy street and simultaneously experience life-threatening situations.

Ryan's near appointment with death comes when a speeding car descends on him. Fortunately, and at the very last second, the driver is alert enough to veer out of the way with no harm to him. But, the tailgating car directly behind it contains a driver who's arguing with his female companion. Ryan becomes frozen in his tracks by the second car like a deer hypnotized by headlights at night. The car's screeching wheels release him from his trance, allowing him to use his athleticism by performing a sideways roll while jumping into the air onto the car's hood. The momentum of the car sends Ryan up the front windshield, across the roof, down the back window and off the trunk onto the solid street. Ryan suffers a bruised knee and sore ribs but his adrenaline-aided will helps him continue his escape.

Jason's happenstance is partially a direct result of Ryan's misfortune. The first car that swerved to elude Ryan found itself facing oncoming traffic with him dead center. Jason quickly computes his dilemma—one car approaching from the left, another attacking from the right and nowhere to run ahead.

The squealing wheels coupled with the blaring horns quickly formulate Jason's only rational option.

Closer...closer, Jason thinks intensely. "Now," Jason recites out loud with a grunt.

He bends his knees, lowers his arms in a downward motion with fists tight, and then thrusts his arms above his head, simultaneously straightening his knees to a vertical leap that propels him above the hoods of the colliding cars. Legs spread like a "V." A foot lands on each hood. As Jason leaps from the cars to continue his pursuit, he wonders if a dollar bill could fit between the vehicles that nearly destroyed each other, and him, he adds as a second thought.

Both men tire by the minute but continue running as if their lives depend on winning the foot race, taking them out of the pleasant surroundings of the inner-city, middle-class neighborhood to a lower-class section of town a few blocks away from the Regency. Jason finds himself running in the middle of several sets of train tracks, heading in the direction of the city's train yard. The full moon shining brightly provides adequate lighting for their unsteady footsteps between the train tracks. With a minimal lead on Jason, Ryan climbs to the top level of a stationary train car and jumps over to the top level of the next car. He jumps from train car to train car several times with Jason duplicating his actions closely behind. Ryan jumps off the top level of the last train car into an empty boxcar used for transporting sand or gravel. These rectangular boxcars have four sides about six feet in height. He tumbles as his feet slide upon landing on the leftover particles inside. After gathering himself, he runs to the end of the boxcar, starts his climb over the back wall, then suddenly stops extremely winded.

"What the hell do you want with me?" Ryan yells at Jason.

He leans against the back wall with his hands on his knees as he catches his breath. Jason, who shares the same exhaustion, stops a few feet away.

"I want you," Jason replies in a winded manner. "Is that simple enough for you?"

"Why didn't you shoot me when you had the chance? You are a cop and I'm unarmed."

"I'm worse than that. I'm a cop with vengeance on the mind. Besides, shooting you gives you an easy way out."

"Arrest me. I'm tired of running."

"I'm not here in a cop's capacity. This is personal."

"Personal. What have I done to you?"

"You attacked one woman too many. The woman whose car you stole. She was the first person I've been able to love in many years."

"Sasha?"

"How nice. You remember the names of your victims."

"Look, man, what do you want from me? Obviously arresting me isn't your intention. Money, anything?"

"I want justice. A prison sentence isn't justice enough for what you did to Sasha," Jason says in anger. "You know, she was pregnant—I'll guess that you used your talent as an actor to woo some of your victims. Aided by your many disguises you were able to rape and kill them."

"I see that you've done your homework."

"You probably picked out another victim last evening at Rosalina's."

"You were there?" Ryan asks surprised.

"You think you ended up in the hospital by mere happenstance?"

"All right. Make your next move," Ryan demands.

"Aren't you the least bit curious of who I am?"

"I don't need to know. When I escape, you'll be of no consequence."

"How do you plan to do that? I have the pistol."

"That doesn't scare me," Ryan says arrogantly. "All of this conversation shows me that you have too much pride to shoot me. Your vengeance makes you want to feel the pleasure of your fist crashing into my body."

"You're right," Jason says while putting his pistol away and changing his tone. "I wan to make jew feel pain."

"It's you!"

"Or should I recite your words," he replies in his normal tone. "This bod's for you, Jerrard."

"Detective Jerrard," he replies astoundedly. "How fortunate."

Jason approaches Ryan with his fist ready for battle. Ryan prepares for what's sure to be the fight of his life even though the physical advantage belongs to Ryan. He boasts a two-inch height difference and a two-inch arm's reach over Jason.

They clash like lions fighting for territorial domain—both initially forgoing any boxing strategies they know, causing them to receive several blows to the face and body. Jason's jaw shows the sign of swelling while Ryan's right eye bleeds just under the eyebrow. Ryan backs away from the swinging fist and tries a useful boxing technique of clutching the opponent when a fighter begins to tire. Transforming the unorthodox boxing contest into a wrestling match, they fall to the boxcar's floor with Ryan having a tight headlock on Jason. He squeezes tighter around Jason's neck to control his squirming body.

"I told you, you can't beat me, little man," Ryan confides. "I'm bigger and stronger. I have a greater advantage over your smaller frame."

"Don't be so sure," Jason brags, unsure if conviction carried with his words. "There's one thing that you overlooked."

"Enlighten me," Ryan says overconfidently.

"I won't allow," Jason says grunting, "myself to," he says fighting for a better position, "lose to you!" he says, grinding his teeth.

The macho talk ends. They roll and tumble, fighting for dominance. Jason repeatedly elbows Ryan near his sore ribs. The excruciating pain causes Ryan to free Jason from the almighty headlock. They both stand and Jason charges again. Unexpectedly Ryan delivers a swift kick to Jason's stomach, sending him flying backwards. Ryan flees over the box-car wall and descends down the ladder. Jason follows behind and the foot race is once again in progress.

They run in a small alley of the loose dirt and gravel between two sets of train tracks. A moving train gains on them from behind, sounding its horn, and they wisely step outside the train's deadly path but remain close enough for it to be a threat. Moments later, the train emerges as the new leader in the race.

Running alongside the train Ryan takes hold of the ladder at the front of the last boxcar. His grip on the moving train forces his legs to run faster, forcing him to adjust his stride to accommodate the hop necessary to land one of his feet on the bottom step of the ladder. His insufficient leap delivers his foot well short of the bottom step, leaving him struggling to regain his footing, but that struggle ultimately concedes to the speed of the moving train. Ryan retains his grasp on the ladder, choosing to let the train drag his body alongside the track. His upper torso clears the ground but his legs drag just above the ankles. Out of sheer desperation and fearing Ryan's escape, Jason leaps onto the ladder at the end of the boxcar, willingly letting it drag him much like Ryan's dilemma. The train drags them hundreds of yards before either notices the parked train ahead of them on the left.

Jason uses his remaining arm strength to pull himself up to the next higher step and holds it tightly with both hands. He bends at the waist to lift his feet from the gravel and forces his legs in front of him against the reverse force of the moving train. Then he places the heel of one foot down into the loose gravel and holds the other foot in the air bent at the knee, seemingly surfing on one foot between the dangerous parked train. His body barely clears danger. Full concentration is required to maintain his balance while he glides through the threat of the parked train. As fate would have it, his heel connects with a rock embedded in the gravel forcing his foot backward, causing him to fall from his self-made ski right after he passes the stationary train. Once again, he resembles a tied-on ornament of the moving train with his legs bouncing wildly like cans tied onto a car marked "Just Married."

Ryan's effort to avoid a collision with the parked train is different. He drops his grip to the bottom step of the ladder allowing his body to be dragged low enough to clear the bottom step of the parked train. After they escape the immediate danger, Ryan starts to yell and laugh at Jason, boasting how careless Jason was by not arresting him when he had the chance. The bright moon reflects off the outside of the shiny steel revolving wheel as well as the track on which the train rides.

Jason cries out, "The joke is on you," as he notices the train track to his left make a turn to the right, creating a cross track. Jason realizes that the cross track—which allows trains to cross from one track to another— is a greater danger than the stationary train ever was. He yells for Ryan to let go of the train but Ryan continues to laugh ridiculously. Jason forces his body one hundred-eighty degrees over to his back and releases the train seconds before Ryan meets the cross track. His momentum keeps him moving several more feet before his body stops its bumpy slide. But it is not before collecting loose dirt and gravel underneath his jacket, shirt and in the back of his pants as well as foreign particles in his shoes.

Ryan yells, "So long, sucker," when he notices Jason's release of the train.

Seconds later, Ryan's upper body clears the cross track. However, the rest of his body is not so fortunate because one of his ankles attaches itself into the "V" shape of the crossing tracks. He yells out in excruciating pain and releases the train...late, too late to prevent his ankle from being torn away from his leg. His agonizing scream echoes in the night as it is carried along with the train's back wind. The tear is jagged and bleeds profusely. Ripped muscles hang all around the mutilated leg with the shinbone break exposed lower than the skin and muscle tear. He calls out for help, Jason's help. Jason gets nearer and immediately feels queasy after seeing Ryan's foot wedged in the cross track.

Jason picks up the severed ankle only to discover a revolver fastened in a holster that remained securely tightened to the ankle. He walks toward Ryan in disbelief, noting too that Ryan let an opportunity pass.

"Help me. I'm going to die," Ryan cries.

"Help you," Jason professes. "Okay, I'll delay your death for a few more minutes—what is the first thing you should do with a severe laceration? Well, in your case," Jason comments while displaying the ankle to Ryan.

"I don't have a cut. My fucking ankle is gone," Ryan states obviously.

"Same rules still apply. You should stop the bleeding."

"Please help me. I beg you. Go..."

"Did you stop attacking Sasha when she begged?" Jason interjects. "Did you stop when your other victims begged and pleaded?"

"Get help. Please! I'm beginning to feel dizzy."

"I'll help your ass, literally. Do you know what they do to a rapist in prison? I won't subject you to that."

"I'll confess. I'll confess to everything. Just get me to a hospital. Help me, damn you!"

"You showed no mercy to your victims. Why should I show you any?"

"But you are a fucking cop!" Ryan reasons with anger.

"At this very moment, I'm a revengeful cop. That changes all of the rules, but if I were you," Jason suggests, "I'd use my belt to control the bleeding before you lose consciousness."

Ryan stares at Jason with an empty expression but heeds the good advice and removes his belt, securing it as tight as his remaining strength allows around the bottom of his torn leg.

"Now," Ryan pleads, "I need to get to a hospital."

"I admire your confidence," Jason boasts while tossing the ankle over Ryan's head, landing just a few inches out of his arm's reach. "As you said to me, you should have used your gun when you had the opportunity. The outcome could possibly be different, but it seems that your confidence has cashed in a ticket that your ass can't pay."

"You are not so tough," Ryan interrupts. "I beat you."

"Nonsense!" Jason snaps. "However, I will grant you one last chance to live. The next few seconds will determine your fate. You get five seconds to live."

"Get fucking serious. I need to get to a hospital."

"Five," Jason starts the countdown.

"Wait, you can't do this!" Ryan cries.

"Four."

"You're a cop, you can't..."

"Three," Jason breaks in.

Ryan, wracked with fear and a strong determination to live, musters enough energy to flip to his stomach and desperately drags himself to his pistol.

"Two," echoes between his ears.

The last second seemingly continues forever while he retrieves the gun from its holster and swings his body over, firing aimlessly in the direction he heard the last count.

"Die with me," Ryan rages as his fueled adrenaline rapidly fires the gun.

Several trigger pulls later, Ryan's mind recognizes the clicking sound of an empty gun. He is left in a sitting position with his legs spread, arms extended but resting on the ground coupling the smoking gun. With his adrenaline now drained, he breathes heavily while seeking signs of Jason.

"I don't think so," Jason responds as he rises from his prone position between the second set of tracks. No mercy struggles in his thoughts as he approaches Ryan. "How does it feel to know that you are about to die? Does your heart race, beating profusely, fearing the end?"

Ryan lifts his head slowly to meet Jason's gaze but is unable to respond. His body is just a few moments away from going into shock.

"Look at you," Jason teases, "at wits' end."

"Don't, please don't," he intrudes on Jason's thoughts.

"All is lost for you," Jason acknowledges.

But not for you, his subconscious recites.

"You have to pay," Jason continues, attempting to force his inner thoughts away.

But, you will pay too, with all that you believe in. Is the price of your soul worth it? his inner being speaks.

Jason raises his pistol, aiming it directly for Ryan's head. He closes his eyes and imagines an internal struggle between good and evil taking place between his mind and heart. Pressure begins to form on his pistol's trigger. Ever so slowly, the pressure increases to where he did not realize the pistol fired.

"Damned" rings through his mind, bringing him back to reality.

Ryan grunts. Jason approaches Ryan's body lying on its back. He notices Ryan's eyes staring into the night as he observes his body directly from above. Things appear not as perceived. There is no bullet wound, no blood splattered all over the ground to coincide with Ryan's lack of breathing. Jason closes Ryan's eyes feeling somewhat dissatisfied that Ryan beat him by simply dying of shock and not at the expense of his hand.

Afterwards, Jason sits on the train track next to Ryan. Thoughts of Sasha invade his mind, simply attempting to bring a sense of justice to this event. He gathers his composure and starts to walk away. Suddenly, he picks up a stick and writes in the dirt, "This bod's for you, Sasha."

He leaves saddened by the whole ordeal but surprisingly finds no joy in knowing that his toughest case to date has ended. Jason stops at the nearest pay telephone and reports the incident to his precinct. He walks down the street, headed for his car at the Regency while attempting to make sense of what he is feeling.

CHAPTER 33

Jason leaves his home around the lunch hour dressed in one of his finest suits with hopes that today will be a turning point for him, for Sasha. He rides down the street rather cheerful, considering the ordeal of the previous night enabled him only a few minutes of sound sleep. However, his tired and weary body endeavors to be at his beloved Sasha's side. An overwhelming delightful thought enters his mind, forcing him to pull on the side of the road to ponder the idea. Therefore, upon entering Virginia City, he stops once before reaching the hospital.

He walks down the corridor leading the intensive care unit, hoping that the almighty God will answer his prayers of last night and restore her vitality, her spirit, her back into his existence. Entering Sasha's room, everything is as he remembers it except for the fact that her IV rests in the opposite arm. The heart monitor continues to add rhythm to the silent room with her every pump of blood. He holds her soft hand between his and joins her at bedside before exercising his guilt, sadly expressing the things that plague his mind. With his head resting comfortably on her bed, Jason begins.

"Sasha, my beloved," Jason says somberly. "I know that you can hear me. I just know you can. You can rest easy. Last night I confronted Ryan and he paid heavily for what he did to you. I defied everything I believe in to take revenge for you...to remove the rage from my heart," Jason shamefully admits. "I broke laws that I swore to uphold and I sit here content knowing that you've been served justice. The kind of justice that is present on the streets every minute of the day. I watched him die, knowing I could have saved him. Part of my soul burns because of this and come judgment day, I will have to answer for my crime."

Jason stands and paces at the foot of Sasha's bed—truly emotional.

"You know when I met you it was heavenly. You surfaced many feelings that I've kept safe and suppressed for a long time. You added a new meaning to my life and I thank you for freeing my emotions. Many times I pinched myself to wake up from our constant dream but nothing changed. The rocket that soared our new relationship to the outer limits and beyond didn't dwindle and tumble back to the Earth. Instead, it found orbit and hovered in the heavens for our sake. Things were so perfect. Many doubts tried to infiltrate my mind. I doubted...I found myself asking, are you right for me? Since our meeting, things have been wonderful. You have been good to me but the negative powers of the universe attempted to make me believe that sometimes good may not be right. Respectfully and honestly, I won that battle by forcing those kind of negative thoughts out of my mind, taking control of my own destiny.

"We had an advantage with our start; unlike my beginning with Julie. I didn't have to establish myself financially and that was a great help, but the similar problem that plagued both relationships was my work schedule. I worked long hours with her and found myself in the same rut with you but amazingly, you grew to love me despite of it. You loved me greatly and I started feeling guilty about the amount of time I was devoting to our new relationship. You were so understanding—you even supported me and helped me keep my spirits up when there was nowhere to turn with my case. I kept wondering when you'd reach your breaking point and demand as much from me as you were giving to me. I wondered would the tables turn and would I reach my breaking point. Meaning, some part of me wanted to let you go because if I couldn't give you what you truly deserved, I would set you free so you could find someone who could treat and love you equally. That thought didn't make me happy but in some cases you have to sacrifice your own happiness for someone else's.

"It wasn't until your accident when I realized that I was creating problems that shouldn't exist. I knew you loved me. I realized that your actions at Rosalina's that night happened out of love for me. How stupid of me not to see it sooner. I remember one night on the phone, you wanted me to tell you that I loved you and for reasons I still don't understand, I made up some lame excuse for not telling you my true feelings. You see," he says standing along the bedside. "I do love you. I love you very much and when you get well I'm going to do everything in my power to prove it to you. This confession comes from the heart, somewhere deep down within its tiny tunnels. Every fiber of my being knows this to be true. I cry out, knowing you hear me...if not consciously, subconsciously. I love you, Sasha."

Jason's tone softens more with his words now being spoken shakily. He sits to help calm the turbulent wave of emotions stirring inside of him while viewing his greatest joy lying motionless, nearly lifeless. He caresses her face and stares directly into her closed eyes, praying that she feels his presence, knowing that somehow she does.

Jason reaches into his jacket pocket and produces a small case, opens it and places the huge diamond solitaire on the ring finger on her left hand.

"I stopped and bought this on the way here. I feel that the time is right. When you wake, I want it to bring you joy. I need you, I love you—marry me, please be my wife?" he asks with his heart crying out.

As in a movie when the boy gets the girl, Jason's prayers are answered. Powers beyond his comprehension grant Sasha movement. Her eyes ascend to a half-opened state while her free hand slowly crawls to the other hand boasting the ring. She caresses the ring, being too weak physically to lift her arm to enjoy its beauty. Jason jumps for joy. Having his prayers answered he falls to his knees and delivers a thank-you prayer to the same powers that seemingly granted Sasha new life. He celebrates with a huge smile. Extreme happiness runs through his heart as he bends and kisses her softly on the lips while gazing into her now open eyes.

"I love you," he confesses proudly.

Sasha's lips quiver as she smiles while looking intently into Jason's gaze. The rhythm of the room changes into a sour, constant long-held note, out of sync with Jason's joy, destroying his celebration.

"No!" Jason yells with his heart racing, pounding heavily inside its shell.

"Jason," a voice echoes softly in the room.

Jason lifts his head from Sasha's bed somewhat startled as his senses gradually return to him. He stands, shakes his head from side to side as if trying to lose the last thoughts of his unawareness. As if it were hypnotic, the rhythm of the room soothes his ears while bringing his racing heart to a calm idle.

"Jason," the voice calls again. Jason's head darts toward Sasha. A wide smile forms within him and lands pleasantly across his face upon noticing Sasha's open eyes. "You were sleeping. I didn't want to disturb you. Then, I guess you had a nightmare. Your scream was very startling."

"Sasha!" Jason bellows. "You're awake. I'm so very happy."

"I've been awake a while."

"But..." Jason pats his pocket where the ring resides and feels his face suddenly becomes flush with embarrassment. "Sasha, sweetheart, honey, I love you. I love you. I..." Jason halts in mid-sentence digging deep within himself, searching desperately for the strength to hold back tears. *Hold on. Hold on. No.*

"Love you," Jason says, letting the joy of those words fill the air. Out of place, out of time, "sorry," hastily follows.

"Don't be sorry that you love me. I love you more than you'll ever know."

"No, not for that. I'm sorry for the tears that fell onto your face. I couldn't contain them."

"No apology needed. Tears of joy have to be a good thing and you reciting that you love me is sweet music to my ears. Although," Sasha confesses, "I've known for quite some time."

"Did you now?"

"Just like I know that your personality wouldn't let you express it to me, so I didn't worry about it." Sasha pauses, letting her words trail off before continuing. "Much."

Jason smiles, kisses her directly between the eyes causing them to close. He reaches into his pocket, unfolds a single sheet of paper before sitting next to her on the bed.

"I wrote this the other day. I hope you like it."

"Poetry?"

"Listen, please." Jason clears his throat and continues.

My quest is to glimpse you in an unforgettable stare,
locking our visions, reminiscent of a waterfall,
constant,
never-ending.
My arms desire the sanctuary of your embrace,
holding tightly until the separateness becomes
one.
My lips yearn to taste the essence of your kiss.
To be enveloped by the passion secreting from the act itself.
My heart begs to hold you near,
until the timed vibrations that penetrate our souls synchronize themselves
with destiny.
Bringing peace to our being,
happiness to our existence,
and a Love,
driven by the passion of the universe.

"Honey," Sasha says, clearly moved. "That is so sweet and thoughtful. No one has ever done this before. What's it called? Something as romantic and touching as this has to have a title."

"If I must title it, we'll call it 'From the Heart.' After all, it is exactly how you make me feel inside."

"You're unbelievable."

"Then you like it?"

"I not only like it—I love it."

"Then, will you marry me?"

Silence.

Sasha's eyes widen with excitement. Her faster heartbeat being reflected by the monitor is the one thing that lets her know that she is not sleeping. Her mouth opens trying to utter the proper response. Jason plays magician by using a little misdirection as he points to the state-of-the-art monitor and uses his other hand to retrieve the tiny case concealed in his pocket. He opens the case with the same hand so when Sasha's attention leaves the monitor, a huge diamond solitaire regards her.

"Wouldn't you like to be a Jerrard, too?"

"Yes! Yes! I will," Sasha replies as exuberantly as her battered body would allow.

Without a word, Jason kisses her deeply, passionately and with more emotion than he can remember doing before. Their embrace ends. Jason lifts from her bed with their eyes locked in a gaze.

"Morning breath, huh?" Sasha jokes. There is momentary laughter followed by Sasha's next words that prove to be startling to Jason, considering the conversation they were just engaged in. "What happened last night?" Sasha inquires.

"Well," Jason pauses, raising a brow.

Immediately, Sasha knows that his comments are not going to be pleasant.

CHAPTER 34

Slam! Jason's and Sasha's heads turn toward the door in time to see that it virtually bounced off the wall, leaving a perfect circle from the impact of the doorknob. Julie enters the room wearing her customary full-length mink coat. This time its arrogance is being overshadowed by the fury in her eyes. Smeared mascara blackens her drowning raged eyes, and streams of tears flowing down her face leave a troublesome trail before falling from her chin. With her body trembling with rage, she studies Sasha, the foe, the competition with all the intensity that her piercing eyes will allow.

"You can't get away with it," Julie cries uncontrollably.

"Jason, who is she and what is she talking about?" Sasha questions, concerned with the appearance of the distraught woman.

"I'll tell you," Julie jumps in, abruptly dismissing Jason's chance to reply. "Your beloved Jason made love to me, fucked me, used me, all in one single night. I'm Julie Jerrard. I'll be his wife forever. I will not be replaced by some slanted-eye bitch he's using to get over me!"

Julie reaches into her coat pocket, pulls out a small-caliber handgun that ironically, Jason taught her to use. In a small lapse of time, she empties the six-shooter. Three rounds enter Sasha before Jason can respond or cry out. He watches terrified as Sasha's life-force seems to leak out of her, dissipating into nothingness with a failing attempt to wrap itself around him, accelerating the tension inside of him. Jason feels as though his ears are escape valves for the unwanted pressure that rapidly sweeps his being, but that won't suffice. It can't. His pain needs to be released from its main source before he explodes from within.

"Sasha!"

His cry echoes vibrantly throughout the room and halls, sending shock waves reminiscent of an atomic blast raging throughout the corridors, disintegrating all in its violent path. Jason panics as his happiness is ripped from his insides, boiling over like an overcooked pot, contaminating the very happiness he just recently rediscovered. Looking above him, Sasha's heart monitor display screen has flatlined, coinciding with the sour tone echoing between his ears.

"Please don't die. Don't leave me," he begs.

Jason's eyes widen with fear. He shuts off the alarm on Sasha's monitor and performs every form of CPR his knowledge allows, but the desperate attempts to save her fail to bring her rhythm back to the room. He flops down in his chair, grabs her hand and cries heavily, tormented with grief. Sitting, weeping for what feels like hours but in reality is only a small moment in time, he feels his heart harden with each breath of air he exhales.

"I just wanted you to feel the pain you've caused me," Julie utters. "The humiliation of what I feel for you seems like an all-too-familiar game. You of all people, you toyed with me!" Julie yells with the gun pointed at Jason.

Jason looks at her blankly, with evidence of pain showing on his face. Julie has succeeded.

Julie fires two shots toward Jason. The rounds enter his upper body, sending him flying back out of his chair and causing him to bump his head against the wall. His body lies motionless on the floor, mimicking Sasha's lifeless movement.

"I loved you," Julie cries.

The sixth and final round enters Julie's head. Her hand with the gun falls limp by her side instantly as the bullet punctures her skull. She takes one step toward Jason before her bodily functions quit and her lifeless form collapses to the floor. Seconds later, Dr. Bodou stands in the doorway awed by the murder-suicide.

Days later, Jason opens his eyes for the first time to the sight of Captain North. Jason's shoulder has a huge bandage taped to it. He's sore and half-dazed but conscious enough to record most of Captain North's words before the medication being pumped into him via IV sends him back into slumber.

Jason finds himself relieved to know that the sleepiness is coming on. This way he will not be coherent enough to absorb Captain North's reprimanding about his inability to follow direct orders, him not following proper procedures by staying at the crime scene until other officers and a medical unit arrived. He vaguely recalls some comment about a letter being placed in his personal file.

Captain North recites that it wasn't until the search of Ryan's home that they discovered his collective newspaper clippings of each of his crimes glued neatly in a binder. Each clipping has red felt-tip pen marked over the typed headlines explaining how he felt when he committed his vicious acts. Captain North continues explaining to an unconscious Jason that the DA is holding off judgment of him until a full report on the bizarre incident has been thoroughly reviewed, followed by a minor praise for ending Virginia City's toughest case.

ABOUT THE AUTHOR

Rique Johnson is a native Virginian, born and raised in Portsmouth, Virginia. After a quick stint in the U.S. Army, he planted his roots in Springfield, Virginia—located twenty miles south of Washington, D.C. His passion for writing started before his teenage years with little love notes to the girls that he liked. From there, he began writing songs and poetry. He's written many things, things that he simply calls thoughts. These sometimes expressed the mood that he was in or they were derived from things that were happening in the world at the time. He tries to develop his characters so that the readers can identify with parts of their personality or a situation that they are going through. He can be reached at rique@riquejohnson.com or you can visit him on the web at http://www.riquejohnson.com.

Excerpt from

Whispers from a Troubled Heart

by Rique Johnson

Coming Summer 2004

Craig Jones arguably holds the world record for coming out of a coma. He doesn't know how long he's been under, but he knows that he has been left for dead. Somehow, he believes that it is to his benefit. He is lucky to be alive, sprawled on the cold pavement, barely conscious, and bleeding from the mouth is better than not breathing at all. He feels that if he can get to his feet he'll be okay. This way he will be able to flag down someone who'd assist him and get him medical treatment. As far as he can tell, his legs aren't broken. He can feel his toes and has movement in his arms, but he suddenly discovers that any motion, even breathing, causes him pain. He quickly realizes that a rib bone infiltrating one of his lungs is the cause of his discomfort, limiting his movements.

The irony of the situation is that only a few moments ago, his movements were limited in a different manner. The sensitivity of his post-orgasmic ejaculated penis made him plead with his lady for hire to cease her movements while it was lingering in her hot box.

He has ignored these types of messages for years, but the notation of a two hundred mile-an-hour club inscribed on the bathroom stall intrigued him. It was his fortieth birthday present to himself; it had been perfect. Speeding around the track at an excessive speed had added a special exhilaration to the explosion when he came. He even felt a little special when his partner washed him after the session, but his excellent start to his birthday celebration turned sour.

He remembers standing outside the vehicle paying for the rendered services, then being blind-sided by a punch in the jaw that rocked his equilibrium. Before his weakened knees afforded him the pavement, the next thing he knew he was being lifted into the air at his rib cage in a tremendous bear hug. He recalls how quickly his breath escaped him, followed by the crackling sound of his ribs being crushed within. His own agonizing scream still rings between his ears.

As if that is not enough, he can feel the wetness of fresh blood flowing over the dried gash caused by the collision of his head on the pavement after literally being tossed away.

Still, he feels that if he can get to his feet or even roll over to his back, he stands a chance of living through the pain and suffering.

"And this, too, shall pass," he states weakly. "And this, too," he grunts while turning his body over to his back, "shall pass."

He repeats the statement quickly several times in succession. Upon completing the maneuver, he lies on his back feeling that it is a form of success, short-lived nevertheless. Suddenly, a different kind of pressure begins building within, making him feel as though he is being pumped with air like a balloon. It is virtually impossible to breathe. His chest tightens, expanding to near explosion. Desperately, he tries to exhale but only partially succeeds. He stops feeling his chest decreasing in size. Instead, he finds himself struggling to regain the precious air he has let out. The pressure grows unbearable inside of him. His breathing transforms into quick short jerky breaths which barely provide him oxygen.

"This too shall pass, this too shall, this too…"

His eyes are half-closed, staring into the early night, not really focused on anything, just searching for something to relieve his pain. He catches what he believes to be the tail end of a falling star. Coincidentally, as the tail dances across the sky, disappearing across the horizon and slowly fading in the night, the pressure within him releases with one gigantic exhale that follows the heavenly phenomenon's course, taking his life force with it.